THE LAST GOOD DAY

THE LAST GOOD DAY

A NOVEL BY

PETER BLAUNER

LITTLE, BROWN AND COMPANY

Boston   New York   London

First Edition

The characters and events in this book are fictitious. Any similarity to real persons, living or dead, is coincidental and not intended by the author.

Library of Congress Cataloging-in-Publication Data

Blauner, Peter.
     The last good day : a novel / by Peter Blauner. — 1st ed.
       p. cm.
     ISBN 0-316-09873-6
       1. Rockland County (N.Y.) — Fiction.   2. Stalking victims — Fiction.   3. Married
people — Fiction.   4. Suburban life — Fiction.   I. Title.

PS3552.L3936L37 2003
813'.54 — dc21

2003040029

10   9   8   7   6   5   4   3   2   1

Q-MART

Book design by NK Graphics

Printed in the United States of America

*To Peggy
and to Mac and Mose*

THE LAST GOOD DAY

1

IT WAS EARLY on one of those powder-blue late-September mornings when middle-aged commuters stand on platforms, watching airplanes pass before the sun and hoping the apex of some great arc in their lives hasn't already been reached.

On the far side of the Hudson from the train station, the Rockland County palisades glinted as if they'd been freshly chopped by God's own cleaver. From the rustling trees along the shoreline came the same sound of money in the wind that the old Dutch traders must have heard when they first rounded this little bend in the river.

The water was brownish and turbulent, as if a low flame were on underneath it. Out by the narrowing of the channel, a forty-five-foot cabin cruiser skimmed across the surface, leaving a broad foamy cape. The ripples spread, pushing the cattails and the submerged bluish-gray mass closer to the crooked-in elbow of land beside Riverside Station.

"Hey, what is that thing?" said Barry Schulman, standing at the platform railing.

He was a tall vigorous man of forty-eight, with curly brown hair, a rugged Roman profile, and the same generally rangy physique he'd had while playing point guard at Rutgers. In another era, he would've been referred to without self-consciousness as a man's man, since he wore his gray Italian suit with a certain casual grace but had never considered using gel, mousse, or Kiehl's skin-care products. His nose, broken years ago in a wild scramble under the backboard, was still slightly crooked, but his smile conveyed a kind of relaxed assurance that seemed to say, *If you guys just give me the ball, everything will be okay.*

"I dunno," said his friend Marty Pollack, who was squat and short, with hair singed on the top and whitened on the sides by the dragon breaths of stress and heredity. "Weren't they supposed to start dredging the river for PCBs? Maybe they're already churning shit up."

The shape moved with the pitch and roll of the tide, washing closer to the shore and then draining away while a half-dozen black ducks with iridescent green necks floated nearby, watching curiously.

"So how you doing?" asked Barry as more people descended from the overpass above the tracks and joined them on the platform, waiting for the 7:46.

"I'm dying, Barry. I'm dying." Marty Pollack sagged against a Club Med poster. "You see the story in the business section last week? Ad pages are down sixty percent this year."

"Is that right?"

"We've already laid off half of the staff, and the head of the magazine division's talking about closing down *Extreme Golf* before the end of the year. And we just refinanced our mortgage so we could pay for the pool and the new kitchen."

"Jesus." Barry touched Marty's shoulder. "Like Dylan says, 'High water everywhere.'"

"'He not busy being born is busy dying.'"

"Hey, he once wrote a song about Catfish Hunter too, so we all have peaks and valleys. . . . Listen, we're still alive, right? At least we're not buried under a couple million tons of rubble."

"I know." Marty grimaced. "But I still wake up in the middle of the night in a cold sweat with my heart pounding. It's awful. I'm turning into a NyQuil junkie, trying to get back to sleep. I just keep waiting for the other shoe to drop."

Barry turned and looked across the tracks at a parking lot full of imports with American-flag decals in the windows. Was it just his imagination, or were there actually fewer cars here than there were two weeks ago? It didn't seem possible. This town lost only four men. He remembered getting into the station late that night and seeing Carl Fitzsimmons's Honda Civic still sitting by itself in the lot as one by one everyone else got in their cars and drove home, leaving its solitary white frame glowing desolately under the vapor lights.

"Look, you can't live your life like that," said Barry. "It'll paralyze you. You can't give the bastards the satisfaction."

"What're you talking?" Marty drew back. "Did you think I meant the towelheads? I meant the economy, ya moron. Who's gonna pay my fucking AmEx bill?"

They both laughed uneasily as the platform filled up. Men and women trudged down the concrete steps in somber shades of charcoal and navy, turning on cell phones and PalmPilots like grim comic characters shedding their family identities and assuming their alter egos: Wall Street Man, Middle Management Woman. No one dressed down for work anymore. The boom was over. People arrived in year-old 4×4s from high up in the hills, from the sprawling McMansions, expanded splits, Contemporary Colonials, and Instant Estates that some of them could no longer really afford.

This was one of those places where the working people traditionally lived closer to the water while the striving classes ascended into the hills. But the New Economy had torn through town and scrambled the landscape as dramatically as the infamous 1899 tornado that left cows and bowler hats dangling from the oak branches on River Road. Through most of the nineties, real estate prices had skyrocketed; scrappy little linoleum-encrusted ranch houses with tiny unrenovated kitchens were selling for close to half a million. Precious little antique stores and galleries started popping up on streets that decent middle-class people used to be afraid to walk down. A French restaurant that managed to get a qualified rave in the *Times* replaced a hardware store that always smelled like turpentine and potting soil. But then the prosperity had suddenly receded, leaving everyone stranded. So now you had converted warehouse condos and supersize chain stores sitting vacant along the waterfront, while stockbrokers' wives up in the hills brutally nickel-and-dimed their Mexican gardeners.

"You know what I'm thinking?" said Marty, turning and looking down at the water again, fifteen feet below. "I'm thinking that's not driftwood or a newspaper. I'm thinking that's something else. Like maybe a dead seal."

"A dead seal?"

"I'm telling you, I've been coming to this station longer than you have. I've seen all kinds of things here. I've seen a bald eagle on the trestle. I've seen marriages break up while people were waiting for the 8:09. A couple of years ago, everybody got scared because there was a guy in an orange inmate's uniform on the platform, and we all thought he'd just escaped from the prison up the river. Turned out he'd just been released and couldn't wait to change his clothes before he caught the train back to the Bronx."

Barry watched the play of fragmented light on the water as other commuters joined them at the rail. The shape below was starting to take on more definition among the shadows and grains of river grit. A rounded white corner broke the surface briefly, and a gull swooped down to take a closer look.

"So how *you* doing?" asked Marty. "I guess biotech's been hit pretty hard like everything else the last few months."

"Yeah, well, I always said we weren't in it for the quick score." Barry cast a glance up the tracks, checking to see if the train was coming. "If I wanted absolute security, I would've kept litigating."

"So where's the stock at?" Marty glanced at the *Journal* folded under Barry's arm.

"Tell you the truth, I don't even look anymore." Barry put on a half-smile. "You get hung up on every little dip and rise in the market, you'd have three coronaries a day."

"Well, so long as you're not living and dying on your options."

"Oh, yeah, right. Hahahhahahahhaha . . ."

Barry felt a candle dribbling at the bottom of his stomach.

"We're doing fine," he said. "I'm a lot more worried about other people we know."

"Excuse me." A lady with birdlike features and corkscrew hair, wearing a chocolate-brown Donna Karan business suit, stopped baby-talking into her cell phone. "But what is *that* down there?"

"That's what we were just trying to figure out," said Marty, stepping up on the first rung of the railing to get a better look.

"Could be an old buoy," said a stocky man with a fifty-dollar haircut and a complexion like a cinder block, beside them.

"No, that's not an old buoy," said Barry, just as the lapping of the water revealed and then covered what he saw clearly as a shoulder blade. *No.* He looked again, trying to see a buoy.

The 7:46 sounded its horn in the distance, and the gull lifted off from the endlessly undulating surface of the water.

"Hey, is that a leg?" A ruddy white-haired man in a Burberry coat came over, looking as if he'd missed a few too many trains whiling away vodka-gimlet afternoons at the Oyster Bar.

"Maybe one of us should call nine-one-one," said the man with the cinder-block face, whipping out his Motorola.

"Hey, what is that thing?" said another man in rimless granny glasses. "That looks like somebody's back."

Barry glanced up and saw the doughy young cop who'd been directing parking lot traffic come hurrying through the overpass above the tracks to see what the fuss was about.

"Maybe it's just a mannequin," said Marty, leaning out over the railing. "Where's the head?"

"It's not a mannequin," said Barry, becoming very still.

"How do you know?"

The dribbling in the pit of his stomach turned into a milky curdle. Twenty or thirty people stood at the railing, watching the morning change shape. The train kept hammering toward the station, beating the air ahead of it like distant timpani.

"I was an assistant DA in the Bronx for four years," said Barry. "I know what a dead body looks like. Look at the wrinkling on the soles of the feet. They call that Washerwoman's Skin."

The swaying of the water brought the bluish mass halfway up onto the little spit of sand just beyond the mossy rocks below. For a few seconds, the gray puffy bottom of a foot, a well-toned leg, and the back of a thigh were visible.

"Oh my God," said the woman in the Donna Karan. The gulls' screech-song echoed over the water as the cop ran down the platform, trying to secure the gun bouncing at his side.

"But where's the head?" Marty said again, as if he was arguing with a store manager. "It's gotta have a head."

The water lifted her one more time and finally deposited her on the shore.

Barry first noticed a blue mark on the ankle, a tattoo with wings. Then a violin curve to the buttocks, ample womanly hips. A long marble-smooth back had retained its subtle hillocks and soft girlish indentations. The shoulders were slender, and the arms were spread as if she were graciously welcoming guests into her home. Veins and viscera sprouted from the place where her head would have been.

A smell like a seafood restaurant Dumpster, methane gas, and buffalo meat rotting in the sun rose up. Every other mouth on the platform had a hand over it, as if people were having nightmares with their eyes open. For a fraction of a second, Barry thought one of the bodies from the catastrophe in the city had somehow floated thirty miles north to their small river town.

The train streamed noisily into the station, dull silver grooves and gasping brakes rushing by mindlessly. Just as it came to a halt, a burly reddish rock crab, almost like an organ with legs, crawled over the gash where the middle of a neck had been.

The woman in the Donna Karan instantly erupted with vomit: beige and pink chunks of bagel and lox geysering out over the edge of the platform and splashing onto the rocks and body below.

The train's doors popped open. Barry stood immobilized, not sure whether to get on. The police would need witnesses. The young cop from the parking lot had just arrived, out of breath, trying to figure out how to proceed.

"All aboard!" the conductor called, his withered turtle face poking from the lowered window.

Barry looked down the platform and saw everyone else hesitating as well, not wanting to be the first to get on. *Whaddaya supposed to do here? What's the protocol?* No one wanted to pull a Kitty Genovese, but the train was huffing.

The man with the cinder-block face decided to break the embargo and end the standoff, turning off his Motorola and swinging his briefcase as he stepped smartly through the doors. *TCB, babe.* The ruddy guy in the Burberry followed, not looking anyone in the eye, obviously *damn* uncomfortable about this. But with the barrier breached, people flooded on after them.

Marty tugged at Barry's sleeve. "Hey, Bar, come on," he said. "We gotta get to work. It's not our problem."

His conscience would be bothering him the rest of the day, like a sliver of glass under the skin. But Marty was right; work was where they needed him this morning. Somebody else would stay. He took one more look over the railing and then reluctantly joined the boarding crowd.

2

"P.O. MUNCHAUSER never heard of letting a ball roll foul, did he? He couldn't just let her keep floating by."

The Riverside police chief, Harold Baltimore, stood at the platform railing twenty minutes later, watching his first deputy and former best friend, Detective Lieutenant Michael Fallon, try to secure the crime scene on the muddy bank.

"I had Munchie playing third base a few years ago in Little League, and he was exactly the same," said Mike, driving little wooden stakes into the ground to demarcate a clear path to the body. "Aggression was never the issue with that kid. You hit a grounder at him, he ran right at it every time. Only problem was, half the time he'd overrun it. One game, he made three errors and said he was gonna throw himself in front of a bus. I told him, 'Don't bother. It'll probably roll between your legs.'"

The chief allowed himself a small down-and-dirty chuckle. He was a heavyset walnut-brown man with basset-hound eyes, a trim debonair mustache, and large tenderized-looking hands. He wore a gray tweed jacket with a white Macy's shirt, an oxblood tie, dark pressed slacks, and cordovan loafers. And he carried himself with somber gravity, befitting his other job as a part-time funeral director.

A bicycle officer in a blue helmet and spandex shorts had herded commuters down to the far end of the platform, away from the crime scene. Yellow tape blocked the steps down to the muddy shore. The department's newest detective, Paco Ortiz, stood over the sheet-covered body at the water's edge, two shiny dabs of Vicks VapoRub under his nose, taking pictures of the surrounding area with a Polaroid while two patrolmen collected evidence in Ziploc bags.

"So, what are you hearing from the state police?" asked Mike.

He was a broad-beamed white guy in a yellow Polo shirt and Levi's with a thirty-six waist. He had a weight lifter's coconut-shell shoulders and a strong neck, but at certain angles, the child within the man was very much visible and people who hadn't seen him in many years recognized him easily on the street. What still disconcerted them was his habit of holding a clear steady gaze just a second or two longer than necessary, as if there were something not altogether trustworthy about even the most innocuous human interactions.

"They're saying it's all ours." Harold Baltimore ducked under the crime scene tape and started down the steps, avoiding the vomit splatter. "The body washed up on our property, and our man was the first on the scene at the train station. It's a no-brainer. They don't want any part of it."

"Were they pricks about it?" Mike asked.

"No, not at all." Harold moved toward him, stepping over places where shoe impressions were yet to be taken. "The inspector was very nice. Said if we needed a hand with the crime lab or dental records, such as it is, they'd be happy to help out. The county medical examiner's van ought to be here any minute. But it's our case."

"You had to figure as much."

Mike came halfway up the slope to talk to Harold, while Paco and the two other guys continued their work around the body.

"You being careful where you're stepping?" The chief watched Mike stumble a little in his thick-soled Timberlands.

"What do you think, Harold? Am I a fucking idiot?"

"Okay, okay." The chief massaged his eyelids with thick wrinkled fingertips. "So, what do we have?"

"Well, I just got here, so I haven't had a chance to look at the goods myself." Mike dropped his voice. "But Paco says we've got your basic traumatic disarticulation, with the head severed just below the cervical spine."

"Cutting's a little asymmetrical, like it was done with a hacksaw or something," the new guy volunteered, somehow hearing him from ten feet down the slope. "Not that professional, but not bad either."

"Any other bruising?" The chief looked past Fallon, getting it right from the source.

"Nothing obvious" — Paco took a Polaroid — "except maybe he tried to chain something around her waist to sink her, but it slipped off. We probably won't be able to tell about lividity because she's been in the water awhile. We're estimating six to eight hours, but that's the ME's call."

"Rigor?" asked Harold, ignoring the way Fallon was licking his lips and looking down at his feet.

"Still pretty strong in the limbs, so she was killed in the last forty-eight hours." Paco took the photo out of his camera and flapped it.

"So, what's your take on it?" Harold turned back to Mike as if he just remembered he was standing there.

"My take is maybe we cross suicide off the list."

The chief sighed and watched a tugboat churn its way down the sun-dappled river, a vision of tranquillity receding.

He'd never felt the need for all this nervous joking about death. His father had brought him into the family business early on. By the time he was fifteen, he knew how to suture a mouth shut, how to fashion a nose out of wax, how to avoid blowing the features with too many chemicals. Over the years, he'd come to feel not just a reverence but a kind of affection toward the little ventilated basement room where "Midnight Train to Georgia" was always playing on the tape deck. Because in those quiet moments — working side by side, draining fluids and prelubing veins — he'd been able to hold on to that closeness with the old man that other boys lost when their voices dropped. The only time he ever remembered Dad cracking wise on the job was when they laid Godfrey Chamberlain on the slab, dead in a car wreck six months after he'd broken a bottle of Brass Monkey over Uncle James Booker's head. And even then he'd had to strain to hear his father mumble as he injected the embalming fluid into the carotid artery: *So who's the big man now?*

The 8:09 to the city whipped by behind Harold, and he was aware of people on the train craning their necks, trying to look down onto the crime scene as they passed.

"Shit." He felt the vibration of the platform's pilings in the riverbank. "All my life, I lived in this town and there've been — what? — eight, nine homicides? I make chief, I get two in less than a year."

"You want to say eight or nine?" Mike looked at him sideways.

"Why, what do you say?"

"I wanna say like ten or eleven. You don't always think of the ones that don't bother the people up the hill. Not right away. But I remember cradling Tony Foster's head when he was bleeding to death outside the Front Street Tavern my first year on patrol. He kept saying, 'Tell Don I'll give him the money Tuesday,' like he didn't know he was going out of the picture."

"Loco Tony" — Harold knit his brow — "the Reefer Prince of Riverside. He was the first drug dealer I ever knew that had his own power lawn mower. Four-hundred-dollar Craftsman with six-and-a-half-horsepower engine. Man, he was an asshole, but he had a beautiful lawn."

"You saw I locked up his son the other week with three ounces. Loco Junior."

"The gift that keeps on giving."

"So how do you wanna play this?" Mike ran his hand over the sandy buzz cut that emphasized the shape of his skull. "Should we call Metro-North about holding the rest of the trains this morning?"

"*Hell no.* You know what kind of crap I'm getting? Do you know how many times the mayor's called already? Do you know how many of the town trustees have called?"

Harold wagged his chin, thinking about the other little cliques in town he hadn't even heard from yet, all the people who liked to pretend there was never any crime in Riverside: the cocktail-shaker-and-plaid-pants contingent from the Stone Ridge Country Club, the Saint Stephen's crew from halfway up the hill, the B'nai Israel crowd, the Rotary Club Mullahs, the Welcome Wagon Fanatics, the School Board Ayatollahs. The whole social strata of the town getting ready to tumble down on him if he didn't wrap this baby up fast.

"Word does get around," said Mike.

"Forget about it." Harold snorted. "The people on the hill don't wanna see this shit. Next we'll hear from the TV and newspapers. 'Paradise Spoiled,' 'Murder in Quiet Suburbia.' Emmie got me on the cell phone while I was running over here, half about to lose her mind because she's showing two houses today and she's worried the customers are gonna back out because they'll think they're looking at the 'Little House in the Ghetto.'"

"Well, Chief, we can't mess around with people's property values, can we?"

Harold narrowed his eyes, trying to read his old friend's expression. This was the first white kid who'd ever invited him into his home. They'd stood together on the defensive line on Riverside High School's football team, worked as a pitcher-and-catcher battery for two seasons, shared a squad car in their first years on the job, been best men at each other's weddings, saved each other's lives once or twice, and had dozens of sleepovers looking after each other's kids. But there were still times that those blue eyes were as inaccessible and mysterious to him as the chrysalis within an ice cube.

"We need to start doing a complete canvass and see if anybody saw the body being dumped," said Harold. "I want to keep officers up on the platform, questioning people for the rest of the morning rush, and then I want somebody at the station tonight to talk to people as they're getting off to come home. And I want somebody to go around the corner and talk to the Mexican day laborers hanging out in front of Starbucks. A lot of those guys are out on the streets late in the evening, and one of them might've seen something. I think until we find out otherwise, we have to assume this poor young woman is from our area." He glanced down the slope. "How old do we figure her for anyway?"

"Dunno." Paco looked up from mixing the Plaster of Paris that would be used to take the shoe impressions. "She was in pretty good shape. Late thirties, early forties. Those might have been stretch marks I saw before."

"You can usually tell the age by looking at the neck," said Mike.

"That ain't an option this time." Paco ladled out a generous dollop of plaster.

"Goddamn." Harold watched the river breeze riffling the white sheet, making it look as if the woman underneath were about to sit up. "I hate it when they have kids."

He found himself picturing a quick cremation and a short dignified memorial service to comfort the surviving kin. This was not the season of open caskets. He thought of the Fitzsimmons family, not even having a body to bury.

"So how you want to handle the security presence?" asked Mike. "We've already got a lot of edgy people in this town."

"I'm thinking we're going to have to go with a twelve-man rotation for the day shift and ten officers for tonight, or at least until we

can positively ID this young lady as coming from somewhere else."
Harold exhaled unhappily. "I'll talk to the mayor about overtime."

"One- or two-man cars?"

"Six one-man cars during the day and four at night. And let's put
another half-dozen officers out on bicycles. I don't want panic, but
we want the taxpayers to see they're getting their money's worth. I
want all our missing person reports compiled, and I want all our
available personnel calling around to the other departments up and
down the river to see who they have missing."

Harold took a quick mental inventory of the twenty-nine officers
in the department, unhappily sorting out the highly competent, the
functional, and the brain-dead. He wasn't cut out for this. In his
heart, he'd always known he was not a born leader or a follower, but
a loner. He'd always preferred solitary activities: sweeping up for his
father, washing out tubes, filling out arrest reports, and having the
quiet satisfaction of being a man alone in his own kitchen at midnight, paying every last one of his bills while the rest of his family
slumbered upstairs.

He saw Mike staring at him.

"What?" Harold glowered back. "Why're you giving me the
Look?"

"Just makes me feel glad I didn't get the job."

"Oh, we gonna start with that again?"

"I'm just saying it's a lot of pressure. I don't envy you."

"I didn't go begging for this job, Mikey, and you know it."

"I never said you did." Fallon blinked, his face suddenly as clear
and untroubled as a child's open hand. "I said, 'Let me be the first to
congratulate you.'"

"I know what you said. Let's not try to rewrite history."

They were both still smarting from that last awkward Christmas
dinner with the wives at the Olive Garden on Route 12 — Emmie
letting fly with that remark about the nerve of some people suggesting Harold got the job because he was black, Mike shrugging,
rheumy-eyed over his whiskey sour, and asking, *Well, why do you
think they gave it to him?*

It wasn't like Harold had been looking to step up. Come this January, he would have had his twenty years and been ready to turn in
his papers. He'd been thinking of selling his share in the funeral
home to one of the national chains. Pace University, just down the

road, was offering a couple of computer classes he wanted to take. He'd earned the right to coast awhile: with the money from his share and his savings with Emmie, they could afford to put the kids through college with a modest financial aid package and still have a little left over to buy one of those beachside condos in South Carolina his brother was telling him about.

But then, two days before Thanksgiving, that plan went bust. Yes, it did. He could still picture the Verizon Wireless bill he was about to pay when the phone rang. Mike saying there'd been a bad shooting in the Hollow. That damn fool child Replay Washington had taken a round in the back running from P.O. Woyzeck with a 3 Musketeers bar in his hand that looked just like a .22 at thirty paces. Shit happens. But this time it happened in the middle of Operation Ivory Snow, the hyperaggressive anticrack patrols Mike set up to make the waterfront safe for developers. After that, there was no way Mike would ever make chief. All the New York City liberals who'd moved up here for the boom a few years back went crazy, and the baggy old country-club Republicans who stacked the Town Board pronounced themselves shocked — *shocked!* — to discover there were only three black police officers in a town that was one quarter African American. And so Reverend Ezekiel P. Philips of the African Methodist Episcopal Zion Church down in the Hollow, whose great-great-grandfather Obediah had led a congregation of ex-slaves in horse-drawn wagons up from Elizabeth, North Carolina, after seeing a vision of a river running the wrong way, had taken Harold aside and said, "Son, it's time we give that big stick to one of our own."

So how was he supposed to say no? He would've been letting down not just his family, who'd been going to the church for three generations, but the whole community on Fenton, Shantytown, Bank, and all the other crooked little dogleg streets down by the river, all the people he'd sat next to in church and shared barbecue with since he was a boy. Still, on a day like this, he longed to be sitting quietly in an anonymous back room with a stack of pink invoices and an IBM calculator.

"Anyway," Mike said, "you want to have a couple of extra officers handling calls for dispatch?"

"That's a good idea. For the next few days, we're probably going to need all hands on deck."

"I promised all the moms I'd do soccer practice from four-thirty to five-thirty, but I'll shit-can it," said Mike, watching Paco smooth down the foot impressions.

"No, don't," said Harold. "At least put in an appearance. Make them feel like everything's normal and under control."

"All right. I'll stay just a few minutes and then come back here 'til midnight."

"What about Marie?" Harold knew they were at each other's throats about hours lately.

"I'll call and see if we can get the Mexican girl to stay late. It's all right. I'm a dead man at home anyway."

"Thanks, buddy." Harold touched him lightly on the shoulder. "You know, I'd have your back if things had broke the other way."

"Yeah, I know."

The wind had suddenly subsided, leaving a slightly unnatural calmness along the shore. The gulls that had been walking along the bank with pieces of yellow crime scene tape stuck to their beaks flew away, and the ducks that had been floating nearby like bystanders drifted off. Violent death in the outdoors always changed the ecosystems around it, Harold noticed. Blood seeped into soil, green bottle flies swarmed, gases expanded, putrefaction set in, eels wriggled in the shallows.

"You know what this is going to turn out to be, don't you?" Mike looked back at the body under the sheet. "This is going to be another dump job from upstate, like the one we had in May."

"What makes you say that?" asked Harold.

"It's obvious. Somebody goes to the trouble of cutting the head off a victim so she can't be identified, and right away you have to start thinking organized crime. This is probably another drug dealer's skanky girlfriend from Newburgh who pissed the old man off, got herself whacked, and then was driven down and tossed out in our parts. And it'll turn out that people around here will have gotten their bowels in an uproar over something that has nothing to do with them."

"Excuse me, but I don't think so," Paco, the new man, spoke up as he knelt beside the body, waiting for the plaster to dry.

He was a short pugnacious Hispanic guy from the Bronx, with a shaved head, a little earring, and a goatee that looked like a small dark hand over the bottom of his face. He'd been working his way up through the ranks of the NYPD when he discovered that there was a much faster route to promotion — not to mention a better chance of owning his own home — in these suburban towns with rapidly expanding Latino populations and no other Spanish-speakers on the job. Of course, some of the older guys in the Riverside Department resented getting leapfrogged and subtly insinuated that the ethnics were sticking together when Harold gave the newbie his shield this summer. But hey, Harold told them, they could always take night classes at Berlitz.

"So, what do you think it is?" Harold asked.

"Come over here and check it out."

Paco gingerly lifted the side of the sheet with his thumb and forefinger as Harold navigated down the incline in his loafers, with Mike close behind. Underneath the little tent was the mottled moonscape of a flank. Harold's eyes quickly found a light surgical scar on the underside of a breast. But Paco was pointing out another small white line in the flesh, this one low on the left buttock, a mark the size of half a matchstick.

"What is that?" asked Harold.

"Maybe she sat on a nail or something when she was a kid," Mike said in an unsteady voice as he crouched down to get a better look.

"No, man" — Paco dropped the sheet in disgust — "that's liposuction."

"What?" said Harold.

He was aware of Mike becoming very still, staring down so intently that the chief could almost hear the liquid dab of his blink.

"She had her fat sucked." Paco lifted the sheet again so they could see for themselves. "And that ain't cheap, bro. That operation costs about three thousand dollars. I'm thinking this lady wasn't broke, and I'm thinking maybe she *was* from around here."

3

THERE. SHE TOOK the shot and moved back into the doorway again like a sniper. You rarely saw grown men looking that scared in broad daylight.

She quickly changed her angle, worried that she was about to lose this moment. Something about the way the sun broke over the old warehouses and abandoned factories on Evergreen Avenue turned the clouds into light boxes and made the men down the street look dwarfed and vulnerable, like shadowy figures in a nineteenth-century daguerreotype. She ducked behind a Dumpster and changed to a shorter telephoto lens, reeling off a couple more quick shots from thirty yards away, making sure she was at least covered in case they didn't want their pictures taken today.

It had been such a struggle to get here in time for the morning shape-up, when eighty or ninety men from Mexico and Guatemala gathered in front of the Starbucks around the corner from the train station and waited for contractors to drive by and offer them work. She'd had to get up early, fix breakfast for the kids, make sure her equipment was ready, drive Barry to the station because the other car was still in the shop, drop Hannah and Clay off at school, sign up for the book drive and karate classes, make appointments for parent-teacher conferences, call the Dryer Man and Tree Guy again, and then race back here to find a place to park before the crowd dispersed.

A blue-and-white Chevy Suburban cruised by slowly, the contractor behind the wheel looking saturnine and jowly, a surly lump of a man with rolls of fat on his neck and a tiny stump of cigar tucked into the corner of his mouth. He could've been a corrupt Eastern bloc bureaucrat or the owner of a carnival with dangerous rides. Yet the laborers came rushing at him as if they were bobby-soxers and he was Frank Sinatra in the trim glory of youth. And for a few seconds, she was no longer Lynn Schulman, loving wife and mother of two children. She was all hand and eye. She shot and advanced, shot and advanced, as the men surrounded the van in their Gap T-shirts, Spackle-covered 501 jeans, and dusty Timberlands. She adjusted the f-stop, making sure she had the Starbucks sign and the flag in the window framed behind them. In their rising voices, she could hear that there was no longer enough work to go around. Friends and relatives — men who'd dragged one another barely alive across the Arizona border — were elbowing and shoving one another out of the way for the right to build a stone wall around some investment banker's McMansion up in the hills.

She found a milk crate to stand on as two muscular guys jumped in the back of the van, leaving their unemployed friends behind on the sidewalk. She clicked away, capturing the half-open mouths, the raised hands, and the hope getting extinguished in their eyes.

A powerfully built little guy with the face of an Aztec warrior and the haircut of a Beatle fan turned to a taller dejected friend, a frayed rope of a man in a straw cowboy hat and a ragged plaid shirt. The little guy grabbed the cowboy's stringy arm and patted his muscle, as if trying to assure him that they were both still robust and strong enough to somehow survive the long winter ahead. She took the picture and then slowly lowered the Canon, knowing that her morning had just been made.

An instructor at Pratt had once quoted Balzac to her: "Behind every great fortune there is a crime." In her heart, she knew that behind every good picture she'd taken there was an invasion. Certainly she should've asked their permission. Usually, she would have. In the rest of her life, she tried to be a decent, sensitive person. But *damn*, that was going to be a good shot. She could already see where it would hang in her show in the spring. Maybe a little Walker Evans in the composition, but it told its own story. It said, *This is what it's about*. It said, *You go until you can't take it anymore, and then you keep going*. It said, *You walk over mountains, hang over the sides of boats, crawl across the desert with your kidneys shriveling up like chestnuts, and have yourself sewn into the upholstery of vans smuggling you across the border because that's what a man does*. He endures. He persists. So here they were, still hustling, still squeezing one another's arms for encouragement and trying to scrape together a few crumpled dollars to send home.

All right, *fine*. She'd ask their permission so her conscience could take five and stop bothering her. She stepped down off the crate and hoisted the canvas camera bag up onto her shoulder. Two cameras dangled from straps around her neck, the old Leica M6 and the beloved Canon. She was a small woman with a lithe gamine body, delicate wrists, and slender ankles, but she'd gotten used to lugging heavy pieces of equipment long ago. Nowadays, she was traveling lighter, stuffing her black-and-white cartridges into the pockets of her red barn jacket.

She moved out from behind the Dumpster and started up the block, feeling the full warmth of the autumn sun on her face. *"Hola!"* she called out, flicking long straight raven-black hair over her shoulder.

The Aztec warrior with the Beatle mop stared down the block at her, moving his eyes from her face down to her camera and then back up again. It was always interesting to see what her subjects would react to first — the woman or the camera.

"Que pasa?" She drew closer, trying to look small and nonthreatening.

A few of the men regarded her curiously. Others slipped right to the back of the crowd, clearly not wanting the immigration authorities to see their photographs.

"You make a nice picture today?" The Aztec mop top smiled knowingly.

"Oh, you saw me?" She fiddled with the f-stop in embarrassment.

"I see you out here before. Why you want to take our picture?"

At close range, he had a young man's face with an older man's experience imprinted on it. A short brow, an Indian nose, Eskimo eyes with fine lines fanning out around them, windburned cheeks. A good photographic subject. Especially with the incongruous "Vassar" printed across the front of his sweatshirt.

"Perdón," she said. *"Mi español es muy patético."*

"Is okay. I know English very good."

"I'm a professional photographer." She glanced down at the Leica, making sure its lens cap was off as well. "My name's Lynn Schulman."

"Jorge." He stopped and corrected himself. "George."

He offered his hand with a polite little bow. She saw agitation

spreading among the men behind him as the sun cleared the roof-
tops and the possibility of finding work faded.

"Where you from?" she asked.

"Guatemala."

"Well, George from Guatemala, I'm doing sort of a special project," she said. "I'm just going around town, taking pictures of different scenes."

His chin drew back into the rest of his face as he struggled to understand her. It seemed so self-indulgent to explain that she was putting together a gallery retrospective, featuring pictures of her
hometown then and now.

"See, I'm from Riverside," she said. "This is my hometown. I was
born here."

"Ah." He seemed to be looking at her through a smudged bullet-
proof partition.

"The textile factory where my grandfather used to work was
right here. I used to ride past it on my bike all the time . . ."

Just keep talking. Find a way to connect. She'd long ago realized
that her greatest gift as a photographer was her own responsiveness,
the way people liked to see themselves in her eyes.

"See, I took all these photographs when I was a young girl growing up here," she said. "And now I've moved back, so I want to take
a whole new series. To show the passing of time . . ."

She sensed that she was losing him. A boy of about seventeen,
with almond eyes and ebony hair as long and straight as hers, came
over and started striking beefcake poses, showing off big brown
muscles in an American-flag T-shirt with the sleeves slashed off. She
left her cameras dangling around her neck.

"You know, if you don't catch these things, they're gone forever."
She stayed after him, riffing for all she was worth. "I mean, people
forget, or their memories play tricks on them. A picture is at least
something you can hold on to. *Comprende?*"

George turned his eyes into sideways dime slots, trying to find a
reason to go along with her.

"I mean, I took this picture a few years ago of my kids on the
World Trade Center observation deck, when they were about eleven
and seven. And now that's all I have left. Of them as little kids *and*
the towers."

"Oh." He rubbed the end of his nose and looked around shyly, gradually lowering the partition. "You know, I have a friend who works in this big building when it come down," he said quietly.

"Yeah?"

"He works in a restaurant at the top and . . ." He spread his hands, seeing no reason to explain.

"He was working in the kitchen at Windows on the World?"

She remembered going out to dinner there with Barry about twenty months ago when Ross Olson first offered him the job at Retrogenesis.

He moved a little closer to her. "He never have no papers."

"You're telling me he's buried under all that rubble, and no one knows he's there?"

"Jes."

"Oh, how awful." She pawed the air between them uselessly. It was like a cruel cosmic joke: let a man make it across thousands of miles of roiling seas and burning sand, let him struggle and make it to the pinnacle of one of the tallest buildings in the world, and then bring it all crashing down on top of him.

"Doesn't he have a family back home that wants to find him?" she asked.

He turned his palms up and stooped his shoulders. "*Qué más da!*"

What's the difference? She fingered the auto focus, not knowing how to respond. These were guys who probably went for years without seeing their families. They knew plenty about the nature of impermanence before the Towers came down.

"So, okay, maybe you make a nice picture of me." He suddenly straightened up.

The abrupt shift caught her off guard. She watched him smooth down his hair, fold his arms across his chest, and stare defiantly right into her camera. And then she understood. His friend was dead, but he wasn't. So now he was demanding to have the indisputable fact of his existence recorded, to make sure no one would ever forget.

"Maybe you make another picture so I can send it home to my family," he said.

"Good deal." She nodded, getting the camera ready and making sure she had enough film to shoot at least a full roll with him.

"And then maybe you take a picture of me working at your house." A sly grin appeared. "You have a lawn?"

"Oh, *I* see how this works."

She took out her Minolta light meter and tried to get a good reading, vaguely aware of a traffic cop blowing a whistle somewhere behind her.

"Okay. Please don't look right at the camera when I take your picture."

She started to change the lens on the Leica to a thirty-five, noticing that morning light was beginning to refract on the windows of Starbucks. She crouched down, wondering if it would be too corny to shoot from the exact same angle she used on the dilapidated exterior of her grandfather's factory twenty-five years ago so she could juxtapose the images on the gallery wall.

But then George was gone, and there was a whirlwind of movement outside the frame. She looked around to see several men scattering down the street like billiard balls, chased by a cop on a bicycle. A second cop followed, looking very much like an overgrown boy in a shiny plastic helmet, snug blue Lycra shorts, and a short-sleeved uniform shirt. He quickly rode ahead and cut off George and the other stragglers, using his bike as a roadblock. Lynn stayed in her crouch, clicking off shot after shot as if she was still working for the *Daily News*.

"Hey, hey," the cop called over to her. "What do you think you're doing?"

She kept shooting, finding it difficult to take orders seriously from a man in tight shorts and white socks.

"Excuse me, miss. Will you please put that camera down?" She got a shot of him dismounting, hairy white-guy legs against a background of gleaming silver spokes.

"What's going on?" she asked, finally lowering the camera.

"We need to talk to some of these gentlemen."

She saw George mutter something to the boy in the American-flag muscle shirt.

"Is this some kind of INS roundup?"

"No," said the cop, whom she recognized as the same guy who checked her ID at the Total Fitness Gym on South Warren Avenue three afternoons a week. "They may have some information that could be helpful to us in an investigation."

"Oh."

She saw a white van with tinted windows rush past the corner on its way to the train station, and her heart did a little stutter as she registered the fact that it said "Office of the Westchester County Medical Examiner" on the side.

"What happened?" she asked the cop. "Did somebody have a heart attack or something?"

"Uhhhh, ma'am, we're really not supposed to be giving out information like that."

She walked to the corner and looked down the block, seeing a couple of ME's assistants in navy windbreakers jump out of the van by the station's parking lot entrance.

"Well, it looks like *something* is going on."

She started jogging toward the station, drawn on by the sight of the men throwing open the back of the van and readying it for a body, feeling the ineluctable pull of an image forming down the street.

"Miss, they really don't want people getting in the way," the cop called after her. "Miss?"

"Okay. Thank you! Bye!"

She gave George a quick wave over her shoulder as she hurried on with her camera bag, knowing if she waited too long the picture would be gone. "*Que le vaya bien.*"

All right, so this is life. No matter how minutely you plan, the shadow always moves. The light always shifts. The face always changes expression a quarter-second before you click the shutter.

The cameras thumped against her chest as she ran across the street to the station. She used to be better at these little bursts of change. *Okay*, so she hadn't meant to get pregnant at twenty-five, when her career as a photographer was just taking off and she was about to make the long leap from splash-and-splatters in the *Daily News* to a contract with the *New York Times Magazine*. *Fine*, she'd scaled back to occasional catalog work and freelance quickies so she could be with Hannah and then Clay and not have to endure the painful separations that torture other working moms. *All right*, once they got older, she'd meant to start hustling jobs again, but then things got complicated. So you learn to improvise and compromise. You move to the suburbs because it's better to be close to Mom when she's sick and cheaper than paying for private schools in the city. You learn to go with the flow, budget ambition, work when you can, and stop on a dime when somebody needs a ride to the doctor or to piano lessons.

But just in the last two weeks, she'd lost some of that elasticity. As soon as she saw the buildings collapse, she froze, not daring to move from the phone until Barry called to say he was all right. Even now, she found herself tensing up for no good reason and wanting time to stand still. No, not just stand still. She wanted it to go *backward*. She wanted Mr. DiGamba's dry cleaning back on the corner of River and Prospect. She wanted the old bowling alley back around the corner, where the new police station had taken its place. She wanted the high school teachers she sometimes ran into at the mall to be the age they were when she was a sophomore.

She passed another young cop directing traffic in front of the train station, ignoring his calls for her to stop. When did they start hiring people who weren't even born when "My Sharona" was a hit?

Two burly ME's assistants were just coming down the steps from the platform, carrying a stretcher with a white sheet belted over the unmistakable shape of a body.

She froze just outside the parking lot entrance. The outline under the sheet was too short for a full-grown adult. Not Barry or any of their friends who take the train. But then her hand went up to her throat, and she found herself praying that it wasn't a dead child.

"Hey, lady, no pictures."

A brutish commanding voice snapped her to attention. She looked around, seeing rows of Explorers and Navigators with parking permits and flags in the windows, shiny expensive machines with no one to operate them.

"I said get the fuck outa here." A glowering man in a yellow sports shirt was coming down the steps after the body, a gold detective's shield twisting and untwisting on a chain around his neck. "There's no press allowed."

"I'm not press." She put a hand over her Canon. "And I wasn't taking any pictures."

"Oh, shit, what are *you* doing here?"

Something in Michael Fallon's face seemed to draw back, gather force, and then come out again. Lynn found herself stepping away a little, as if she were too close to a swinging door.

The last real conversation they'd had was probably twenty-five years ago. She was caught between relief at seeing him up close after months of ducking behind cars in the Stop & Shop parking lot and dread at hearing what he finally had to say.

Time had been more than fair to him. The short military buzz cut that looked so jarring and defiant in the seventies was actually fashionable these days. His face had lost some of the roundness that led boys to call him Baby Huey behind his back. Instead, there were more of the contours that made some girls privately admit that yes, the man certainly had his angles. But the wary blue eyes had receded even deeper under the ridge of his brow. Hobo eyes, she used to think. Like he was watching life from inside a boxcar.

"I was just taking pictures of the guys around the corner, and I came over when I saw all this commotion." She looked back down the block, wondering what had become of George and the other day laborers. "So, what's going on?"

"Ah, bunch of crap," he said, settling into a voice a half-octave deeper than she remembered. "We think somebody might have fallen off a boat and drowned around here. Just our luck she washed up onto the bank."

"Getting kind of late in the year to be boating, isn't it?"

"I don't know. It's been warm. I still haven't pulled my dinghy out of the water."

They both watched as the men carefully started to load the stretcher into the back of the van.

"So this is something, running into you like this."

"Isn't it?" he said lightly, as if it had only been two weeks.

"I'd heard you'd moved to Arizona a few years ago."

"Yeah, I tried highway patrol in Scottsdale, but I never really took to it. Hard to get used to the desert after you grow up next to the river. Big fish in a small pond, that's what I like."

"Sure." She started to fuss with her lens and then stopped herself.

"So how you been? When did you get back?"

"It's been — what? — about a year and a half." She hesitated, not quite believing that he didn't know already. "We'd been in San Francisco for a while with my husband's work. And then my mother's MS flared up again, so we started spending more and more time back here until finally we just decided to stay because we found a house we liked."

"Well, you know what they say about Riverside: 'Once you drink the water, you can never really leave.'"

He looked at her without speaking for a few seconds, just enough to remind her of their old staring contests.

"How is your mother anyway?"

"She died just after Christmas. Her heart." She nodded to Harold Baltimore, who was walking by, talking on his cell phone. "I'm surprised you didn't know. The chief handled all the funeral arrangements."

"No one tells me anything. I would've sent you a Mass card or something."

He raised his eyebrows, and two deep lines crossed the wide desert expanse of his forehead. Like Barry, he was a big man. That was what had first attracted her. Large hands, big chest, broad shoulders, strong legs. She used to joke with her friends that Michelangelo looked at a block of marble and saw David, but she looked at Michael Fallon and saw a block of marble. It was hard to believe she'd once felt so small, safe, and protected next to him.

"I was sorry to hear about your brother too," she said. "I should've tried to get in touch myself."

"I'm sure you had a lot going on."

That little extra bit of tension slid under the surface like a snake going under a rug. Was she supplying all the awkwardness here or was he helping? After all these years, it was hard to tell where one thing ended and another began.

"So, what's up with you?" he said. "I see you're still taking pictures."

He curled his lip slightly at the Leica and the Canon hanging between her breasts.

"Yeah, I'm just starting to take it up seriously again." She touched the cameras self-consciously. "I've been on the Mommy Track awhile."

"Hmmm." He grunted as men carefully guided the body into the back of the van.

They moved with accelerated somber efficiency, squatting and changing positions with pinched expressions, as though they were working in a snowstorm. They were doing things a little too quickly to be handling a mere drowning victim, Lynn noticed. She thought of raising the Canon to get a couple of quick shots, but realized that given her history with Michael, he would take it as an intolerable provocation.

"So how have *you* been?" she said, her eyes moving from the gold shield to the gold band on his left hand and then back again. "I see you made detective." She studied the lettering more closely. "Detective *Lieutenant*."

"Yeah, I'm working for Harold. How do you like them apples?"

"I always said you two would end up together," she said, trying out a little friendly banter to see how far she could go.

"Yeah. That might be the best relationship I was ever in."

She smelled something sour under his breath and saw a few tiny beads of sweat in the long groove between his nose and upper lip.

"You're married, though."

"Fourteen years, three kids." He studied the back of his hand for a moment and then shrugged. "I wake up some days, and I can't believe it."

"I know what you mean. You have pictures?"

He held up a finger to Harold, asking his indulgence, and then fished a wallet out of his back pants pocket. In short order, three small Sears studio portraits of kids under the age of fifteen were produced, two boys and one girl, all in identical white shirts buttoned up to the collar. Slicked-down hair and ready-made smiles. The children were lovely, but the pictures could've been taken back in the days of Ozzie and Harriet. Personally, she preferred to catch her own tribe unleashed and unaware, as if she was a *National Geographic* photographer. *But there you go*, as Barry would say. Things had worked out in the end. She could let herself off the hook. He'd finally found someone who could give him what he needed.

"They're gorgeous," she said with almost audible relief. "I have two of my own. So I guess we've both been very lucky."

"I guess," he said flatly.

The doors to the ME's van closed with a rude *thunk*. Harold Baltimore pocketed the phone and came over, his tie slightly askew, a little twitch already visible under one of his brown eyes.

"Hey, pretty lady." He kissed her lightly on the cheek. "How you doing?"

"Better than some, I guess."

She pointed toward the back of the white van and saw his eyelids droop even more than usual.

"How's Emmie?" she asked.

"Lots of deals, no closings. It's how it is." He turned to Mike. "I've gotta get back to the base. Phones are going crazy over there."

"Okay, boss man." Mike gave him a little two-fingered salute that stopped just short of outright mockery. "I'll be right behind you. *As usual.*"

Was this just the way men talked to each other? Even after all her years on the press barriers, she'd never quite understood this kind of brass-knuckled masculine affection. If one of her girlfriends teased her the way Barry razzed his buddies, she'd burst into tears.

The chief clapped her lightly on the arm. "Good to see you again," he said. "You still haven't aged a day."

"Well, there's a lie I can live with," she called after him.

The engine of the ME's van groaned and then kicked to life, a veil of gray-black smoke curling up into the blue sky.

"You know you're getting old when the people you went to school with start getting put in charge of things," she said. "Especially looking after the dead."

Mike studied her with a mild consternated frown, as if he was about to wipe a smudge of dirt off her chin.

"So I guess you'd better get a move on," she said as the white van pulled out of the lot. "Looks like you've got a lot of mopping up."

He shrugged and looked at his watch, and for a few awkward seconds she imagined she heard it ticking.

"You know, Lynn, I still feel kind of bad about the way we left things," he said finally.

"Oh?"

Her heart sank, knowing this had all been a little too painless and easy.

"I'd really like to clear the air one of these days."

"Uh, Michael, I don't know." She reached into her jacket pocket for a lens cap. "I mean, that was such a long time ago, and I'm sure you've got a lot on your plate at the moment."

He nodded. "Of course. But I was just thinking maybe we could catch a cup of coffee sometime at the Copperhead."

Her stomach made a sound like a boot squelching in mud.

"Oh my God, is that still there?" She smiled.

"And they still have the little jukeboxes at the tables. 'Year of the Cat.' That was your favorite song, right?"

"Was it?"

How humiliating, to be reminded of her half-formed mall-rat

tastes before she went off to the city and discovered the Velvet Underground and the Kronos Quartet. It was like seeing an old yellowing Polaroid of herself with stringy hair, braces, and thick ugly glasses.

"Give us a chance to catch up a little," he said. "I know *I*'ve had a lot of things on my chest."

"You have?"

She realized that they were about to pick up right where they left off.

"Oh, I don't know, Michael," she said, watching the other officers get into their squad cars. "I'm sure you're going to be really busy, and I've got a lot of things that I . . ."

"It's *a cup of coffee*." He gave her a baleful look. "Don't you think you at least owe me that much?"

His silence cornered her, reminding her of a dozen things she'd managed to delete from the hard drive of her memory until this moment.

"Well, look" — she swallowed — "maybe we could get together another time, with the families. I'd love you to meet my children and my husband. He's a great guy. I think you'd really like him."

She saw his small blue eyes dart back and forth, considering.

"Well, I guess that could be fun," he said after a few seconds, in a voice that made her think of a coin spinning on its side.

"We could do a barbecue or something," she offered brightly.

"Yeah, we're supposed to get one or two decent weekends before the weather really turns." He nodded, the knob of tension between his eyes shrinking slightly. "We're still down in the Hollow, on Regan Way, believe it or not."

"No kidding," she said.

"Yeah, just about the last white family on the block. You should see me coaching baseball in the summer with all the little Mexican and Guatemalan kids in the neighborhood."

"Is that right?"

The image warmed her unexpectedly.

"Oh, sure." His shoulders started to relax — a man talking about sports. "They call me Mark McGwire because he had the home run thing with Sosa a couple of years ago. And I'm coaching the kids from up the hill in soccer this fall. Either of yours play?"

"My son's just finally starting to get into sports. Strange it took so long because my husband was a big jock before he hurt his knee."

"Oh, yeah? Maybe we'll get him out there one of these days as an assistant coach."

She wondered if she'd been a little quick on the draw with him. People change. Maybe marriage and children had softened him. He wouldn't be the first. She'd once read that humans replace all their cells once every seven years. That meant each of them had been at least three and a half different people since they went out.

"Okay, so I'll call you," he said. "What's your number?"

She patted her pockets, not wanting things to lose this slender thread of civility. "Um, I don't know if I have a pen on me."

"I do." He tried to hand her a ballpoint and a small black notebook still warm from his back pocket.

She half-smiled. "Maybe it would be better if I called you. I should check with Barry about our schedule anyway."

"Oh, okay."

His face didn't fall. It slowly descended, the weight moving from his eyes down into his grinding jaw.

"I can get you down at the police station, right?"

"Fine." His eyes appeared to retract into his head a little.

"Good to see you again, Mike." She hoisted the camera bag back up onto her shoulder. "Take care of yourself."

"Yeah." He nodded as she turned away. "Don't be a stranger."

4

"I'M THINKING ONE of us should call in a bomb threat," said Steve Lyons, director of corporate communications, kicking off the morning meeting at Retrogenesis, the biotech company where Barry had become vice president in charge of legal affairs eighteen months ago. "About a half-hour before the shareholders arrive. They'll clear the whole Grand Hyatt, there'll be thousands of people out on the street milling around, news crews will show up, and that will be the story instead of our earnings report."

"Why not go for the big enchilada and report a full-scale nuclear attack?" Barry snapped. "That way, we'll all get locked up for causing a panic and never have to come back to the office."

Six other executives sat around a conference table the size of the famous Indian canoe at the Museum of Natural History, thumb-typing Instant Messages to one another on little BlackBerry interactive pages. A stream of natural light that hadn't reached this room until two weeks ago poured in through the windows overlooking Battery Park and New York Harbor. Barry stared at the wide blue gap in the skyline, thinking this, in fact, must be what Alzheimer's is like. The Twin Towers were here a minute ago, weren't they? He used to orient himself every morning coming up out of the subway by looking for them. Instead there was just a smoldering valley of rebar, concrete, and human remains down the block.

"I was serious," said Steve, a thin fretful guy with pale, almost translucent, eyebrows and the mannerisms of a lifelong chain-smoker condemned to live in a smoke-free world. "Well, I was half-serious. We're gonna get slaughtered at the meeting in January. We're looking at the third quarter in a row where we missed our numbers. The guys from Goldman Sachs and Merrill Lynch are gonna be like the villagers in *Frankenstein* with the torches and pitchforks, yelling for our blood."

"Bharat?" said Ross Olson, the company's CEO, seated at the head of the table like the tribal chief, with his silver-fox hair, craggy patrician face, and yoga-master posture in a dark Paul Stuart pinstripe. "What's our main line going to be?"

"I think we have to say that our business model was correct but that some of the basic drivers in the market have changed," said Bharat Singh, the earnest twenty-nine-year-old Princeton-educated chief financial officer. He was sitting halfway between Barry and Olson, a thick lock of black hair falling across his brow. "If you look at some of our early top-level assumptions from two years ago, the costs required to get our product to market seemed like a very attractive mountain. But when you bring in some of the current exogenous factors like the current economy, the anti-Alzheimer's drugs Merck and Pfizer are developing, and the lawsuit about the monkey, I think we have to model out a longer time frame for penetration."

"We're gonna be like the Dunk-a-Clowns at the county fair," Steve Lyons moaned. "They're gonna be throwing rotten oranges at us."

"Well, how are sales for Coridal?" asked Barry.

Even with development stalling on Chronex, the anti-Alzheimer's drug the company was working on, Coridal, a cheaper version of Prozac without the libido-killing side effects, was supposed to save the year for them. But Bharat was shaking his head.

"We just found out we lost the contracts in Pakistan and Indonesia," he said. "The generics are killing us. They're able to produce the pills for one dollar on every six we spend."

"And how are things going in the Monkey Suit?" Ross Olson, the CEO, turned to Barry.

"I was about to send everyone an e-mail. Judge Horgan turned down our motion to dismiss." Barry stretched and swiveled, his six-foot-three-inch frame feeling cramped in his small leather chair. "It looks like this baby is moving forward. We're going to start taking depositions next month."

Everyone in the room gave an audible groan; even Lisa Chang, aka Mrs. Spock, the company's petite bespectacled chief science of-

ficer, who usually communicated only on her thumb computer. The
$50 million Monkey Suit had been brought by two former Retrogen-
esis scientists who claimed to own the exclusive patent on the genetically altered breed of squirrel monkeys used in the company's
Alzheimer's experiments.

"That's going to do wonders for our stock," said Steve Lyons.

"Well, that's not even our most immediate concern." Ross Olson
raised his craggy eyebrows. "Did anybody see Mark Young on
CNBC this morning?"

"I was on the train; I missed it," said Barry.

He thought of mentioning the headless body he'd seen on the
riverbank and the vomiting woman in the Donna Karan. But what
did they care? They were already sitting a few blocks from a massive
graveyard. They didn't need to hear about another corpse.

"You're talking about the short seller?" he said, trying to stick to
the subject. "With the hedge fund uptown?"

"The one and only." Ross sighed. "He was using phrases like
'managerial brain cancer' and 'absurdly overvalued' about our modest little enterprise."

"Ah, fuck him, he's just trying to drive our stock price down."
Barry rolled back in his chair and crossed his long legs.

Lately, he'd come to think of short sellers the same way he
thought of the degenerate gamblers who sat behind the basket at
Rutgers, cheering every time he missed. The whole concept of betting on stock going down instead of up seemed like the ultimate
cheap shot. Especially since short sellers never actually owned the
stock they were trading but merely paid a nominal commission to
"borrow" it from brokers in the hope of buying it back later at an
even lower price. No wonder there were rumors the terrorists had
shorted airline stocks right before launching the attacks.

"Well, he's doing a helluva job." Ross's eyes roamed past him.
"We opened at nineteen this morning. We're trading at sixteen
now."

OH, THE PAIN! THE PAIN! SOMEBODY SAVE MY BABY! An Instant
Message from Lisa Chang flashed on the BlackBerry in Barry's lap,
even as Lisa herself remained calm and impassive behind her black-
rimmed glasses at the far end of the table.

"And how many shares of ours is he holding?" Barry asked.

"About ten thousand." Bharat dipped his head shyly.

Barry gave a dry whistle and felt his blood pressure slowly rise.

"The thing is," said Bharat, "some of his information is accurate and some of it isn't. We *have* been stuck in Phase Two trials for our Alzheimer's drugs for a long time. We *didn't* nail that contract with Pfizer. The Monkey Suit *is* a problem. Our stock *did* go from fifty-one to nineteen in less than a year. But then a lot of what he's putting out is just scurrilous rumors."

"Like what?" asked Barry.

"Oh, all kinds of crap on the message boards, like we had a couple of our monkeys die during the clinical trials and that some of the volunteers are getting sick. And then he says we're hiding recurring expenses as one-time capital spending and our management is unstable and about to get the boot."

"And is it?" asked Barry, whipping the question down to Ross Olson at the other end of the table like a bounce pass.

"Not as far as I know." Ross blinked with clear Nordic-blue eyes. "I met with the board in Aspen last week, and they told me I had a total vote of confidence to keep sailing, head winds or not."

The words DEAD MAN!! lit up on the pager in Barry's lap, an Instant Message sent from Bharat three seats to his left.

"We're gonna get totally shit-bombed at the shareholders meeting." Steve Lyons drummed his fingers on the conference table. "I've seen how Mark Young and his guys operate at these open-mike forums. They do these sneak attacks to undermine confidence in the company. They just humiliate you in public to keep driving the price down. It's like better investing through intimidation. I've seen some of the top CEOs in the country walk out literally red and shaking with rage."

THESE ARE TIMES THAT TRY MEN'S SOULS — AND MINE TOO! said an Instant Message from Lisa Chang, who was adjusting her frames without looking at Barry.

"So, what do you suggest?" asked Ross Olson, with the kind of cool equanimity that only the most experienced senior managers can muster when bereft of any ideas of their own.

"I think we cut and run," said Steve Lyons, mouth pulling down at the corners. "I'm thinking we put out an announcement that we're reorganizing and looking at layoffs, and then we quietly change the location of our shareholders meeting to someplace like Missoula so people will have to work to get at us. Look at Disney.

Didn't they do it in Kansas City a couple of years ago because it's the birthplace of old Walt or something? *Yeah, right.* They just didn't want to talk about that little European theme park adventure."

"I don't think layoffs are the answer." Barry shook his head. "We've only got thirty people to begin with. I don't think you make a company grow by having the senior vice presidents act as your bike messengers."

"Bharat, what do you think?" asked Ross Olson.

"I think we have to back-channel this as much as possible." Bharat slumped down in his seat. "Set up private meetings or conference calls with Mark Young as quickly as we can and try to quietly make our case that the stock price is stabilizing and that he should cut us a little slack. Because I have to tell you guys, my father came over here from New Delhi and drove a cab in Queens for twenty years, and he got held up at gunpoint about once every other week. So my top priority is not going out in a blaze of glory. My top priority is survival."

"I'm thinking we could have Mark barred from the meeting," Steve Lyons said. "He doesn't actually own the stock he's trading, so technically we're on solid ground."

"I think that would be a *serious* mistake," Barry spoke up, flexing his right hand impatiently.

Everyone stopped thumbing their BlackBerrys and looked over at him. Lisa Chang took off her glasses, revealing the bright unspoiled plain of her face.

"I think if we have him barred from the meeting, it just gives him more credibility," Barry said, raising his voice. "He can still go after us in the newspapers and on the Internet. And trying to keep him out just makes it look like we have something to hide."

He let that thought simmer on the table for a moment. I STILL VOTE FOR DIPLOMACY, said an Instant Message from Bharat. ANYBODY GOT A PROZAC? asked one from Lisa a moment later. SECOND THOUGHT, MAKE THAT A CORIDAL.

"Well, I for one am not relishing the idea of a showdown in front of our shareholders," said Ross Olson with a mild Virginia twang that made him sound more like a gentleman farmer than the research scientist he once was. "Clearly there are things we could've done differently in the last year, especially in the Alzheimer's market, and we're going to get called on them."

"I don't have any problem with confrontation," said Barry, arm flung over the side of his chair. "Listen, if he's going to make accusations about our mismanagement, we ought to be ready with the rapid response. When I was a prosecutor in the Bronx, I learned that if you've got a witness with a problem, you damn well better tell the jury about it before opposing counsel does."

BUT I WENT INTO GENETICS TO *AVOID* ALL THIS, Lisa Instant Messaged him.

"Look, I didn't want to say anything about this" — Steve Lyons leaned forward, cracking his knuckles anxiously — "but I had a conversation the other day with a friend of mine who's at one of the major pharmas — I don't want to say which one — but he fairly intimated to me that they might be willing to enter into a package deal to buy up some of our patents and research so we could get out of this with maybe some of our skin intact . . ."

"You're talking about everyone selling their stock?" Barry stared at him incredulously, noticing for the first time that Steve's head was shaped vaguely like a bent knee.

"At least we could end up with something," Steve said. "No one wants to be sitting at their desk when the roof falls in."

"Well, the hell with that." Barry sat up, still waiting for everyone else in the room to start yelling.

"No disrespect, Barry" — Steve cleared his throat — "but you really haven't been a businessman long enough to see what happens in a serious downturn."

"But is this what everybody else wants?"

Barry looked from face to face at the conference table, forcing each person to meet his eye, noting the uncertainty in everyone under thirty and the exhaustion in everyone over forty.

He didn't have to do this, he told himself. He didn't have to give up the corner office he'd had at Bowman, Wallace, Fisher in San Francisco. He didn't have to give up flying around in private corporate jets or meeting clients in Aruba. He didn't have to give up the chance to make seven figures annually and maybe buy a villa in the South of France someday.

Except, of course, he did. He did because he'd given five years of his life to defending Brenner Home Care from charges that its products caused everything from migraines to serious birth defects. He did because that case had been a dog from the moment he opened the first file. He did because a mother in Marin County had a baby born without eyes after she'd used Brenner's "environmentally tested and safe" Virulant pesticide. He did because he'd spent those five years filing motions, asking to get subpoenas quashed and evidence suppressed, trying to wear down the plaintiffs, muddy the issues, and turn clear-cut liability into murky ambiguity. He did because no matter how much he insisted to Lynn he was just an officer of the court giving the client the representation he was constitutionally entitled to, he found himself gradually starting to suffer from some of the symptoms he was denying the existence of in his papers. He did because just two weeks before opening arguments were finally scheduled to begin in the long-awaited trial, he found himself almost driving off the road in his leased Lexus with a blinding migraine.

It was a minor miracle that he'd managed to pull off a last-minute settlement for under $1.5 million. But for a month afterward, he felt oddly chastened and depressed, as if he'd lost the case. But then he'd brought Lynn on a trip back to the city, and Ross, a straight shooter who'd been a senior vice president at Brenner, took them out to Windows on the World to talk about this new drug company he was starting. Of course, Barry jumped at the chance to be part of it. Not just because he wanted to stay back in the east, where his kids were born and his mother-in-law was sick. Not just because Bill Brenner was a horse's ass. Not just because of the headaches and the photos of the little boy with fleshy protuberances where his eyelids should have been. But because he wanted to have someone to throw the ball to. To play on a team again, even a losing team. Just to be in a room with young people throwing up ideas instead of shooting them down. And he could still see a half-dozen bridges stretching across the two rivers below like pearl strings as he clinked glasses with Ross and toasted the bright promise of their future.

"Look, I was doing okay as a lawyer in the old slip-and-fall trade." Barry shot his cuffs with a touch of self-mockery. "But do you remember what you said to me that night at Windows, Ross? You said, 'Let's cut the crap.'"

"You had to remind me." Ross stared out the window, toward the blue gap where the restaurant had been.

"You said, 'Why are you wasting your life defending somebody else's stand for selling bad hot dogs? Let's go out and make something. Let's be entrepreneurs. I know these demented kids from MIT who are doing these crazy experiments with monkeys and Alzheimer's. I can get my hands on some serious venture capital. All I need are some equity partners who are willing to take a chance. Come on. Do you want to miss another revolution?'"

He saw everyone at the table cast their eyes down, contemplating how they'd gotten to this spot themselves. "I convinced my wife to let me put two thirds of our savings into this company," said Barry. "If I'd done that for some flimsy little dot-com that opened on a Wednesday and closed on a Friday without ever making anything except an IPO, then that would be fine. I'd deserve to go fuck myself, if you'll pardon the tautology. But I thought that we were putting together something real."

"They're gonna turn the lights out on us." Steve Lyons shook his head, sun reflecting dully off his oddly flat scalp. "I've got half my savings tied up in this company. I'd like to see at least some of it again."

"I'd hate to tell you how much I had to borrow." Bharat sank down another inch or two in his seat so he was almost looking straight up at the ceiling. "My father's going to kill me."

"Yeah, but you're not even married, Bharat," said Steve, sniping across the generational lines from a distance of twenty years. "I've got two kids going to college."

I'M MAXED OUT ON ALL MY CREDIT CARDS, said an Instant Message from Lisa. ANYBODY WANT TO BUY A POOR DESTITUTE MIT GRADUATE DINNER AT ODEON?

"Well, I have no interest in just folding my tent and slipping away in the night," said Barry, ignoring the flare of acid indigestion in his stomach at what he hadn't told Lynn. "Do we have a drug that works or not?"

"I believe we do," said Ross.

"Then let's tell them to go to hell and make our case. I say I get in touch with Mark Young and tell him to back down or he's looking at a major lawsuit."

THIS IS TOO MUCH TESTOSTERONE, said the Instant Message from Lisa. HELP ME. I'M DROWNING.

But Ross Olson, who'd led an artillery company in Vietnam, was already nodding as if hearing the call to battle again. Bharat sucked his lower lip and stared at a fixed point between the ceiling tiles, be-

ginning the long march from reluctant engagement to steely determination. Chris, Amy, and Joel — from Operations, Marketing, and
Sales, respectively — who'd been sitting there quietly like an audience at a play, began to message one another with growing animation on their BlackBerrys.

"So, what do you all say?" asked Ross Olson, turning to the table
at large. "Do we stay the course or bar the door?"

"Stay the course." Barry raised his hand.

"I guess, stay the course," Bharat said reluctantly, closing his eyes
as if bracing for impact. "We've gone this far; I'm not even sure I can
still find my way home."

Chris, Amy, and Joel, all under thirty and Ivy League graduates,
looked up from their BlackBerrys and nodded in a daze, as if the ver-
bal mode was archaic and unfamiliar to them.

"All right, all right." Steve Lyons threw up his hands. "I guess I
wasn't really serious anyway."

IS THERE ANYTHING MORE SHAMEFUL THAN THE MAN WHO LACKS
THE COURAGE TO BE A COWARD? Instant Messaged Lisa.

Yes, thought Barry, without touching his own device. A MAN WHO
GAMBLES WITH HIS FAMILY'S FUTURE AND LOSES.

5

"ANYWAY," SAID LYNN'S friend Jeanine Pollack, "the *pool*."

"I didn't realize it was such an ordeal."

"It shouldn't've been. But they were out there for *days* with the backhoe, and then all of a sudden, they're in my kitchen, tracking dirt on the floor, saying, 'We hit bedrock; we're gonna have to blast.'"

The two of them were having lunch at Charlie's Blue Skylight Café, one of the half-dozen small upscale restaurants that opened on Fairview during the boom a couple of years ago. Charlie Borrelli, an old high school friend of Lynn's, had installed an espresso machine, painted the walls butterscotch, and put 1950s jazz on the sound system and goat cheese salad on the menu, making it a kind of refuge for the Volvo-driving dissidents rejecting the tyranny of the Starbucks around the corner. To add a little local atmosphere, Lynn had loaned Charlie six of her early black-and-white town scenes to put up on the walls. But nowadays, the restaurant was mostly half-empty, with Stay-at-Home Moms sneaking conversation over sleeping babies like prisoners in adjoining cells and Downsized Dads perusing the *Wall Street Journal* at the back as if every unemployed minute wasn't weighing on them.

"So, what did Marty say?" asked Lynn, moving her camera bag onto a chair beside her.

"*Martin* is working late every night, trying to put out the magazine. *Naturally*. So, what am I going to do? They say meet this guy at the foot of your driveway at six-twenty tomorrow morning with thirty-six hundred dollars in cash. 'Don't tell anyone.' Lynn, I swear he looked like one of the terrorists."

"Oh, come on . . ."

"I'm *serious*," said Jeanine in her raspy throaty voice, Peppermint Patty with a Marlboro habit. "This is like a month and a half before the eleventh, but who knows? Maybe it was a practice run. He's this swarthy little guy with beady eyes and snaggly teeth. 'Don't worry, lady. I take care of everything.'"

"He's the dynamite guy?"

Jeanine, normally preternaturally blond and cheery with bright blue eyes and a snub nose, got a hooded hunted expression as she nibbled on her cheddar-and-prosciutto omelet. "I have to be careful" — she lowered her voice — "because we didn't get all the permits. So he's out there blasting away. Mr. FBI-Watchlist Pool Man. And every time he sets off a charge, the whole house shakes a little. I hear the Williams-Sonoma china rattling in the cabinet, and I'm thinking, *Great, I'm going to lose every plate in the house.*"

"I thought they weren't supposed to blast that close."

"They *aren't*. The dishes were fine. But you know what I found after they were gone? My lawn: covered with dead animals."

"What?"

"On my honor." Jeanine raised her right hand, as earnest and wide-eyed as a Girl Scout again. "Woodchucks, gophers, hedgehogs. It was like Jonestown for rodents. They didn't even look hurt that badly. I think half of them may have just had heart attacks."

"Midlife Crisis in the Wild Kingdom." Lynn nodded solemnly.

"Tell me about it. You know how I can tell I'm getting old? Every week I'm carrying bigger and bigger corpses off my property. First, it was the kids' goldfish. Then it was the hamster. Then I had to get rid of all these dead hedgehogs without the town finding out about it. You know what I think? I think it was an omen. I should've paid more attention to it. Death is coming closer and closer all the time."

"Oh, Jeanine, will you stop that. You're really starting to get paranoid."

Lynn tried to take the long view with her friends. Other people looked at Jeanine and saw a hard-eyed former bond trader channeling her restless energy into maintaining a perfect house and keeping her twin twelve-year-olds well groomed and occupied with afterschool programs five days a week. But Lynn still saw the debauched former cheerleader who lost her virginity in the back of a blue

Chevy on prom night and still grew hydroponic marijuana occasionally in her backyard greenhouse.

"So did you hear what happened at the train station this morning?"

"Somebody fell off a boat." Lynn swiped her hair back from her face. "Who knows what they were doing out there this time of year anyway."

"What are you, crazy? She didn't fall off a boat." Jeanine gave her a withering look. "She had her head cut off. Marty saw the whole thing."

"What?"

"And Barry was standing right there with him when the body washed ashore. He didn't tell you?"

"No way." Lynn blinked as if she'd stepped out of a darkroom and straight into blinding daylight. "Are you serious? How do you know?"

"Marty called me from the train and told me," Jeanine said.

"That's so bizarre." Lynn patted her barn jacket pockets, cursing herself again for leaving the cell phone at home. What if Barry had been trying to call her? What if the kids were worried? She looked around Charlie's, noticing a couple of young mothers prematurely breaking up their children's fights over Lego blocks at the back. All at once, she had an overwhelming, almost vertiginous, need to have everything in its proper place. She should've checked home for messages. She should've driven by school to make sure the kids were all right. She remembered having this same surge of anxiety two weeks ago when Sandi Lanier called a few minutes after nine and said, *Turn on CNN; you're not gonna believe this.*

Hadn't they moved here to get away from all this? Why didn't anybody tell her what was going on?

"Everybody's fine." Jeanine touched her hand.

"You sure?"

"Yes, I'm sure. It's probably like that other one who wasn't from around here. But don't tell me I'm being paranoid. You want to know about paranoid, talk to Sandi."

"Why?" Lynn blew on her latte, trying to settle herself down again. "What's up with her?"

"Oh, she's gone hog-wild with the whole terrorism thing. I saw her over the weekend, and she was going on about trying to buy all these antibiotics in case there's a biological attack. I told her, 'Honey, what's the good of that? Number one, they're probably not coming *here*. And number two, you've been giving the kids that crap for every ear infection since they were babies. Haven't you heard about building up resistance?'"

"I don't know what's going on with her." Lynn watched the foam in her cup recede. "She stood me up for dinner last night and never called to apologize. And she still hasn't invited me in to the new house."

"Yeah, she's getting to be a real flake." Jeanine coughed into her napkin. "I was thinking of giving our friendship a rest for a while. I've got enough drama going on already."

"I wouldn't go that far." Lynn softened. "I've still got a lot of time for Sandi."

"Well, you're a better woman than I am."

"Remember her mom? She was such a cool lady."

"God," said Jeanine, "she must've been our age when she died. Breast cancer, right?"

"Just like Sandi. Except people didn't beat it that often then."

"Shit, Lynn" — Jeanine sagged — "now you're really making me feel old."

Lynn stared off into the mid-distance. "You know, I remember playing in their backyard when I was six. Her mom helped me climb their big old oak tree. I used to feel so guilty about that for years 'cause she died like six weeks later. I always thought she should've been saving her strength for Sandi."

Jeanine speared a new potato and lifted it to her lightly rouged mouth. "Jesus, how do you remember these things? I can barely remember most of high school."

Lynn decided not to suggest that that might be because Jeanine had spent too many days and nights engulfed in mighty clouds of cannabis, huffing and puffing over her bong like a Juilliard bassoonist.

"So, speaking of old friends," said Lynn, finishing her latte, "you know who I ran into this morning?"

"Who?"

"Michael Fallon."

"Really?" A forkful of omelet stopped halfway to Jeanine's mouth, dripping melted cheddar off the tines. "How's he doing?"

"He looked good. He was over at the train station while I was taking pictures across the street for my show. He was the one who told me somebody drowned."

"Well, maybe he was just trying not to panic you," said Jeanine.

"Hmm, wouldn't that be ironic? Considering."

"I guess so." Jeanine chewed on one side, regarding her carefully. "So how was it, seeing him again?"

"It was a little odd, though mostly he couldn't have been nicer. A couple of strained moments. It helped that Harold was around."

There was a pause, and she watched the locomotion of Jeanine's jaw, the long bone rising and falling under the taut skin as she worked her way from one end of a thought to the other.

"Well, for whatever it's worth," she said finally, "I think he's finally got his act together."

"What makes you say that?"

"I see him from time to time." Jeanine crossed her legs, a thick tan ankle showing between the cuff of her jeans and white tennis shoes. "He was the kids' soccer coach in the AYSO league a few years ago."

"Was he?"

"And I have to tell you, he was wonderful. Patient. Considerate. Never raised his voice. The first three games, Zak wouldn't leave the sidelines. He'd just lie there, sucking down juice boxes and staring up at the clouds. It was Mike who got him in the game, and now he's a little tiger on the field. He just needed a male role model to show him how to be aggressive without losing his temper, and Marty's in the office so many Saturdays . . ."

Lynn thought of Barry trying to set up basketball drills with Clay in the driveway this summer, the boy's halfhearted enthusiasm quickly fading into indifference and a long afternoon in front of the Sega Dreamcast. She pictured Barry going back to shooting baskets by himself, trying not to be disappointed that his son didn't share his love of the game.

"And you know he was up for the chief's job last year, didn't you?"

"No, I didn't."

"Oh, yeah. Supposedly, *he* was the one who really cleaned things up downtown. Remember how sleazy it used to be along the waterfront?"

"So why didn't he get the job?"

"A black kid got shot, and they decided to go with Harold instead." Jeanine wrinkled her nose, not needing to spell out the implications.

"That must've been quite a blow, with them being such good friends and all."

Lynn thought of the way they slid past each other like sandpaper blocks this morning.

"I think Mike was okay about it," said Jeanine. "He's just a real true-blue straight arrow. Did you know he was one of the rescue-and-recovery guys at Ground Zero?"

"Really?"

"Just jumped in his car and drove down there because he wanted to do something to help. They showed him on Fox news lifting a girder with a couple of guys." She leaned across the table, confiding. "I have to tell you, I looked over at Marty in his Jockey shorts with his stomach hanging out and his little bottle of Evian, and I thought, *And what are* you *doing, ya big slug?*"

"I'm glad Michael finally seems to have straightened out," Lynn said, bending a little red coffee straw around her fingers.

"Well, you two were always kind of an odd combination."

"What do you mean?"

"I mean, you were kind of this arty chick, and he was this bottom-dog guy whose dad worked at the prison."

Lynn sat back, experiencing the uncomfortable sensation of being in front of the camera for once.

"Hold on a minute," she said. "Don't you think that's kind of oversimplifying it?"

"No, why?" Jeanine dabbed at the sides of her mouth. "It's true. He's from that shantytown crowd that's always worked down by the river. And you're from halfway up the hill, where people can come and go anytime. Your dad was in *advertising*. It's just an accident of geography that we all went to the same high school."

"But I never looked down on anyone." Lynn crossed her arms defensively. "I never put anyone down because of where they came from."

"You don't have to. *It's in your pictures.*"

"How can you say that?"

"Well, come on. Look at them."

Lynn turned, elbow on the back of her chair. Each of the prints on the wall had been matted and framed. The Michelangelo clouds and the guard tower overlooking the Hudson at dawn; the Great White Commuters with their trench coats and briefcases on the platform; the Town Fathers with their rictus grins and nine irons on the Stone Ridge Country Club golf course; twilight in the windows of the old map factory by the river; the middle-class homes up in the hills with their roofs spreading out like the skirts of girls on summer lawns; the empty cracked swimming pool full of leaves on the grounds of the old Van Der Hayden estate.

"What's the matter with them?" She turned back to Jeanine.

"Nothing. Unless you mind your hometown looking like a cross between a war-torn Bosnia and a Coney Island sideshow."

"I thought you liked my work."

"I do. It's very *accomplished*," Jeanine said crisply, pushing her plate away. "But it's like you're looking at us through a microscope."

"That's not true. I love this town. That's why I came back."

"Oh, yeah, right." Jeanine smirked. "And you're really doing a lot for our property values with those kinds of pictures."

Lynn looked down at the little round table between them. In the last few seconds, it seemed to have widened into a small icy pond.

"Well, I think there's also a lot of affection in these photos," she said.

"Sure, like the ones you won that award for. What was it called?"

"The Thomas Cole Prize." Lynn lowered her voice. "You say that like it's something I should be ashamed of."

"Well, it got you into Pratt Institute, so I guess they must have done somebody some good."

"Are you saying I used him to get ahead?"

Jeanine raised her eyes to flag down a passing waitress, as if she had no interest in continuing the argument now that she'd gotten her digs in.

"*Jeanine* . . ."

"Honey, we don't need to talk about it anymore. That's all ancient history."

"I *know*, but what are you saying? You can't just leave it like that."

"I'm just saying that things are more complicated than they look sometimes . . ."

"So you think that what happened with Michael and me in the end was only *my* fault?"

She saw Jeanine hesitate, as if she were standing at the edge of a cliff. This is the place where a friendship drops off, Lynn realized. This is a place where you stop calling each other and just give each other chilly smiles across the Stew Leonard's parking lot. This is where you start looking for another doubles partner and rolling your eyes when your husband asks why you guys haven't seen the Pollacks for a while.

"Listen, it was a long time ago." Jeanine gave her a quick reassuring smile, deciding to pull back from the edge. "We're all different people now. Right?"

"Riiight," said Lynn, trying to let the moment go.

"Seriously, if you told me I was going to spend my evenings making cupcakes and reading *The Berenstain Bears* over and over when I was on the trading desk at Merrill Lynch, I would've had to slit my wrists."

"I guess that's true for me too." Lynn cleared her throat uncomfortably. "I never counted on carpooling and sewing sequins on little tutus when I was shooting for the *News*."

"And now look at us, a couple of middle-aged broads eating lunch . . ."

"Thank God we get to be seventeen and do it all over again," said Lynn.

"Oh, yeah, right . . . hahahhahhaha . . ."

But having gone around this treacherous bend in the conversation, Lynn found herself restless and not quite able to sit still. She kept looking over Jeanine's shoulder at her old pictures on the walls, finding the light a bit harsh in some, the focus too tight in others. If she were to go back to some of these subjects, she'd want to use softer lighting, more shades, maybe a wider-angle lens.

"Anyway, let's talk about something else." Jeanine reached over to touch her arm. "How are the kids?"

6

"COME ON, DANIEL. Move up a little."

The kid looked petrified as he hung back in the goalmouth. Not a natural athlete at the best of times, thought Mike, watching the other seven-year-olds hurl themselves around the practice field. A beanpole with a head too big for his body who cowered every time the ball came his way.

"Come on, Dan the Man, get your head in the game." Mike clapped his hands, aware of the kid's mother watching from the sidelines, where she had just given him an earful about how badly this child needed a father figure at the moment. "We're down a player. We need you on offense."

He came over to give the boy a nudge. *I don't have enough to worry about?* He pictured the warped blue butterfly on the cold white ankle again. But then Carl Fitzsimmons's son looked up at him with those crooked Chiclet-size teeth and those old-man eyes. He patted the kid on the shoulder, and Danny started to edge out toward the middle of the field.

Maybe it was good to get away from the station for a few minutes, clear his head. Sometimes, you could see things more plainly on a field than you could sitting behind a desk. All the little holes in the chaos, all the little patterns and openings in three dimensions that might never occur to you otherwise. *She was from around here.* Even the New Guy could tell.

Come on. Get *your* head in the game. Harold asked him to show up and try to maintain appearances. So here I am. See? Everything's under control. He looked around, wondering how long it would be until the other moms on the sidelines realized that Carl wasn't the only one of their friends missing now.

Meanwhile, Danny Fitzsimmons glanced back at him, making sure he was doing the right thing, and then disappeared into the scrum of boys surrounding the ball.

"Stay on it, Danny!" he shouted, wondering how the hell he was going to make a graceful exit. "Go for the ball!"

Once you put a foot in these things with kids who'd lost a parent, you had to chew your own leg off to get out of them. A week after his dad disappeared, Danny got a bloody nose at practice and said he didn't want to play anymore. So Mike had to start calling the kid's house every day, telling him that the other guys really needed him. Because what the fuck else were you supposed to do when the roof was falling in? Stand there, waiting to get crushed?

He started to trot toward the scrum with the whistle in his mouth, ready to break things up before the tears began. All right, you're stuck for the moment — play the part until the ball goes out of bounds. Keep up the game face. Act like everything's perfectly normal. But then he saw a skinny white leg kick out stiffly and the ball squirt out of the jam. Javier, the little ringer from Ecuador, tripped and fell going after it, and then all of a sudden Danny was breaking from the pack, running past him, chasing it toward the goal at the other end of the field. The kid ran like a crippled sand-piper, matchstick legs staggering and arms flapping uselessly at his sides, but he was getting there. He hesitated for just a second, still not sure if he should really cut loose, and then reared back and kicked the ball with the side of his foot. It hit a rock, bounced, and then rolled into the far corner of the net.

"Yeah, baby. That's what I'm talking about."

And hearing a grown man's voice celebrating his little victory, Danny threw his arms up, let out a war whoop, and came flying over to give his coach a hug.

The odd thing was, up until two weeks ago, Barry had hardly no-ticed the other people on the train ride home. Usually he was so deep into reading or looking out the window that everything else just seemed like background noise. But tonight the Metro-North car seemed emptier than usual. He realized that most times he caught the 8:07, the same guy would be sitting across the aisle. Always wearing the same kind of navy Men's Wearhouse suit, white shirt, and red tie. Always breathing hard and sweating like a horse when he first got on, as if he'd been running for the train. It usually wasn't until they were well out of the groaning bowels of Grand Central and clearing the clotheslines of Harlem that he'd seem to relax a little. And then he'd slump against the window, an automaton turned off, oblivious to the expanding glory of the Hudson, the blue bridge at Spuyten Duyvil, the little sailboats rocking gently on the current. Once or twice, Barry had found himself imagining the guy's life. Probably just another poor shlub trying to hold on to a cubicle at Citicorp and a saltbox in Hawthorne, working the phones all day and then being too tense and tired to deal with the wife and kids when he got home. He remembered smugly thinking that he'd never allow himself to live like that again, always running late for the train. But something about seeing that body this morning had made him just a little more attentive to his daily routines. It occurred to him that he hadn't seen the guy since the Eleventh. And as the train rolled by the old Jack Frost sugar refinery in Yonkers, he saw the sun melt into a red puddle on the river and turned to the *Times* "Portraits in Grief" section to see if he recognized any of the pictures.

"Sandi, this is the third message I've left." Lynn sat in the Saab, making a call while she waited for Barry's train. "I just want to say it really sucks that you stood me up like that last night. Friends don't treat each other that way."

She saw a line of cars slowing down before they left the lot and a big man with a clipboard and a flashlight leaning in to talk to each driver. Something about the way the brake lights glowed in the gathering dusk sharpened the sense she'd had all day that a connection in the town's underlying mechanisms was not functioning properly.

"Look, just call me and let me know everything's all right," she said. "You're so fucking irresponsible sometimes it drives me nuts. Call me, you old whore. I miss you."

———

A fine haze was coming off the river as the 8:07 pulled into the station with a gust of relief. Doors popped open, and commuters stumbled out onto the stark fluorescent-lit platform like big-headed aliens disgorged from a flying saucer in a Spielberg movie.

Mike stood by the parking lot exit with his clipboard and flashlight, watching the elongated silhouettes descend the stairs, remembering how he used to love to come to this station as a kid for its hypnotic rhythms, the tide of commuters coming and going, the unholy racket of the old diesel engines pulling in. The hours he wasted on the bedroom floor with cruddy old toy trains he'd inherited from his brother, Johnny. There was a shiny Tonka model he wanted his mother to get him from Angelo's Candy Store and Deli around the corner. A midnight-blue die-cast model of an Old 58 Union Pacific steam engine. It killed him not to have it. Every day he'd beg for it, his need churning like wheels in his head. But she squeezed every nickel so tight she made Jefferson look like a forceps baby. And so one day he just *took it*. Put it right in his pocket when no one was looking, where it became another part of the secret world he always kept hidden from her.

He watched the commuters getting into their shiny Outlanders, Caravans, Escapes, Expeditions, Land Cruisers, Sequoias, and Tahoes. Rich people's toys. Two by two, headlights came alive in different sectors and gradually formed a line moving toward him, their beams piercing the dark and revealing little misty swarms of circling gnats.

"Excuse me, sir?" He stopped a fiftyish guy in a white '99 Lexus and came around to the driver's window. "We're doing a routine canvass because of the incident at the train station this morning."

"Oh, look, I really need to get home."

The guy's breath smelled like Cutty Sark, and his eyes were lightbulbs with the filaments burned out. *What the hell's he doing getting behind the wheel of a fifty-thousand-dollar car stewed to the gills?* On almost any other night, Mike would've pulled him out and made him walk a straight line.

"We're just trying to see if anybody might have any relevant information about how this body turned up here . . ."

"No, no, and no . . . I took the later train."

"How about last night? Were you at the station?"

"No, I drove yesterday. Can I go now?"

A lone Volvo horn beeped behind him, remote and cautious. "Thanks for your help, sir."

"Yeah, you too, buddy."

Four more cars passed with nothing to say. No one saw anything. No one knows anything. City people. He remembered the way his father would shake his head and hiss through his teeth when they cut him off at the River Road intersection in their snazzy European gas-guzzlers. Middle-aged men with cue-ball scalps and long sideburns. Mike looked at his watch, seeing he'd been at this for almost two hours. His calves ached, and his knees were still killing him from soccer practice. More than two weeks since his last real full day off. He noticed that his lungs were still bothering him, and again he wondered about the toxins he'd breathed in at Ground Zero.

Some things kill you quickly, and some kill you so slowly that you hardly know you're sick.

A polished black Saab with a light scuff on the hood pulled up, and Mike pointed the flashlight beam at the driver's eyes, taking some satisfaction in the dazzled grimace.

"Yo, roll your window down." He spooled a finger in midair.

The driver looked like a wiseass, with beady eyes and a slightly crooked nose. Banker or a lawyer, Mike guessed. The profile of a pretty wife was half-shadowed in the passenger seat.

"Excuse me, sir, we're following up on the incident at the train station this morning . . ."

"Hey, Fallon . . ." The lady in the passenger seat leaned across her husband's legs.

It took him a split second to bring Lynn Stockdale's face into focus.

"Hey, you," he said. "Twice in one day. We've gotta stop meeting like this."

The husband half-closed one eye as he glanced over suspiciously.

"So why'd you tell me you had a drowner before?" she asked.

"We were going on what we had at that point."

Mike took her gaze and held it for as long as he could, remembering just what it was like to stare at that Union Pacific engine.

"Can't have all the soccer moms making another run on the Prozac without a good reason." He gave her a small wink.

"She didn't look like any drowner to me," mumbled the husband.

Mike slowly turned his glare on him, making it clear that nothing this man could say would ever impress him.

"Michael, this is my husband, Barry Schulman." Lynn tugged lightly on the driver's tie.

"Detective Lieutenant Michael Fallon, Barry. Glad to finally meet you."

He waited until the husband turned and mouthed, *"Finally?"* to Lynn before he reached through the window and gave him the old inmate's Iron Man handshake, crushing the joints and giving the hand a slight turn to the left and a pull forward. His father used to tell him that if you could get a man a little off-balance, you could probably get him to do anything else you wanted. But instead, Schulman gripped him back hard and kept his wrist rock-steady.

"Hey, easy there, partner." Mike took his hand back. "These is delicate instruments."

"You got a pretty good grip there yourself."

"So, Barry" — Mike stretched his fingers — "you look like you might be part of the commuter class. You see anything this morning?"

"Yeah, I was on that train," the husband said a bit too quickly. "But I don't think I saw anything that everybody else didn't see. Sickening goddamn thing. Didn't look like she'd been in the water long."

"Yeah, and what makes you say that?" A small muscle tightened above Mike's eyes.

"The skin hadn't started to separate."

"Is that right?" Mike put his hands on the door frame, not giving the car too much respect. "You just happened to notice that?"

"Barry was an assistant district attorney in the Bronx for four years before he went into corporate work." Lynn touched the side of her husband's face. "We met outside a courtroom. I still tease him sometimes that he never really lost the bug."

"Ah, you know how it is." Schulman raised his palms. "It's more interesting debriefing a witness in a mob case than filing papers with the FDA. Work is work, though."

"So, you used to be a prosecutor, huh?" Mike's eyes cut sideways, as if he was trying to see around a corner.

"Yeah, I work in the city. But up here I'm just a citizen like anybody else."

Got that right, asshole. Mike stared at him without speaking for a few seconds. A talent he'd had since he was a kid. The Ice Man stare. Glare at someone long enough, and eventually they either back down or start babbling.

"Interesting you'd notice that," he said, deciding to spare him the full treatment. "Most people wouldn't."

He saw Lynn fidgeting, trying to find the right attitude to take in front of her husband. Mike wondered how much she'd told the old man, whether it was enough to put a wild hair up his ass. Over the course of the day, he'd changed his mind a couple of times about their conversation this morning. At first, he'd thought she was just putting him off with that crapology about the phone number. But here it was obvious she was simply afraid that old embers would start smoldering again.

"So how's it going?" said the husband. "You have any idea who she is yet?"

"No, but we will soon. They've got all kinds of DNA crap for identifying victims at the State Crime Lab. You can't spit on the sidewalk anymore without us finding out who did it."

"Yeah." Schulman nodded. "Once you find a match."

"Of course," Mike said slowly, acknowledging the obvious. "But that takes time, which I'm sure you can appreciate as a *former* law enforcement professional."

Mike looked from the husband to Lynn, rolling his tongue under his lip.

"Oh, yeah, of course," said the husband, taking the hint. "Look, I didn't mean to step on anybody's toes here."

"No problem, amigo." Mike took his hands off the door and hitched up his gun belt. "Anybody who ended up with Lynn is okay in my book."

"Oh, I see." Schulman looked over at his wife. "You guys are old friends?"

Mike saw Lynn scrunch down in her seat a little, as if she meant for both of them to forget she was here.

"Oh, yeah." Mike grinned. "You trying to tell me she's never mentioned me?"

"Michael and I went to high school together," she said quietly. "I think I've told you."

"You did?"

Mike felt his smile strain as if it were held up at the corners by thumbtacks.

"You know I'm terrible with names," the husband said, almost apologetically. "They go in one ear and out the other. That's what happens when you move back to your wife's hometown. You're always playing catch-up."

"Well, I wouldn't know about that." Mike pointed the light into Lynn's eyes, feeling something shrivel and harden inside him.

"Mike's family's been in this town for generations," she said, almost shyly.

"Oh, yeah?" The husband's fingers began to tap the steering wheel.

"And now Mike's a big man in the department here. Somebody was telling me this morning that he was the one who drove all the crack dealers out of the Hollow."

"That right?" The husband looked up, only half-interested.

"Yeah, we did such a great job cleaning the town up that most of us can barely afford to live here anymore." Mike's cheeks bunched up as though there were two little fists inside his face. "Isn't that terrific?"

The husband stopped tapping the wheel and looked back at Lynn.

"Well" — he sighed — "I guess we better be getting home. I'm sorry I don't have anything more intelligent to add. I'll give you a call at the station if I think of something."

"That would be great." Mike clicked the flashlight off and then on again. "Lynn and me were talking about us getting together one of these days anyway."

"Were you?" The husband's mouth puckered slightly. "I'm always the last to hear about these things."

"Yes," Lynn said, raising her chin and deciding to defy him for a moment. "I thought it might be fun sometime. Mike's big into sports with the neighborhood kids. He coached one of the AYSO soccer teams. Barry, you remember how we used to try to get Clay to play?"

Aha. So she really had been checking up on him.

"We'll get him out there again." Schulman rubbed his eyes.

"Hey, Barry, your wife tells me you were quite the athlete in your time."

"Does she?" Schulman took a moment to size him up, one old player to another. "You two must've covered a lot of ground today."

"Maybe one of these days we'll get you out on the field and see what you've got left."

"Actually, basketball's my game, but what the hell. Nice meeting you, Lieutenant."

Schulman eased the car past him, the idling motor revving suddenly to life and then settling back into a steady *pocketa-pocketa-pocketa*. From behind, Mike saw the brake lights flaring and the two heads leaning together to begin a serious discussion as they came to a halt at the stop sign. *No one saw anything. No one knows anything.* And just before they made the right past the chain-link fence and out of the lot, he put the flashlight under his arm and copied down their license plate number on his clipboard.

7

"HEY, WHAT'S UP with Barney Fife?" asked Barry, flexing his hand after he made the turn. "I thought he was trying to twist my arm off."

"It's a guy thing," yawned Lynn. "I guess he wanted to show you they build 'em rugged here in Riverside."

"Yeah, I got that. Macho man. It looked like he was making a muscle with his ears."

They made the left off River Road, passing the immigrant day laborers playing dominoes by the light of the Barnes & Noble superstore, and headed straight up Prospect Avenue toward the West Hills. They didn't have the type of relationship in which the husband always had to drive, but tonight she'd found herself feeling a little out of sorts at the station and she'd asked him to take the wheel.

"So, what, is he an old flame of yours or something?" Barry asked.

She started to roll up her window. "Sort of."

They drove on through the sloping darkened streets of the Hollow, where black kids in head scarves popped wheelies on ten-speed bikes and a badass in a do-rag and a yellow Lakers jersey blew autumn leaves off his lawn with a three-foot-long blower.

"I got the impression he's maybe still a little sweet on you," said Barry. "How come you never told me about him?"

"We did not end on a graceful note."

"Oh?"

"Can we not talk about this right now?"

The incline steepened as they drove up through the more middle-class neighborhood of Indian Ridge, where the houses fattened into chubby little Cape Cods and split-level ranches with flags draped over the front porch railings.

"So how come you didn't tell me you saw a woman's body without a head this morning?" she asked.

He watched telephone wires stretch out through the glow of streetlights, like lines of radioactive sheet music.

"I don't know. I guess I didn't want to scare you. Everybody's so jumpy already. How are the kids doing? They hear about it?"

"Yeah, but you know, they're still city kids." She hunched forward, warming her hands between her knees. "They don't let much faze them. They don't talk about these things too much in school anyway. Everybody's too focused on testing and getting into the right college."

"I'm not sure if that's a good thing or a bad thing." Barry shrugged. "I remember my freshman year in Newark after the riots; we had police on motor scooters in the hallways. I used to walk right past them on my way to practice."

"So was that good or bad?"

"Hey, I ended up here, didn't I?"

He reached over and cupped his hand over her knee as they passed her parents' old house, the rambling Victorian on Birch Lane where a Japanese architect and his family had planted a bonsai tree on the front lawn.

"What does that mean anyway? You didn't end on a 'graceful note'?"

She sighed heavily. "If I say that neither of us was at our very best at that particular point in our lives, can we just leave it at that?"

"Sure. Fine. You're the boss."

He drove on in silence for the next two minutes as they passed the bulldozers resting by the new golf course, the old Van Der Hayden estate with its new stone wall, and the great open pasture that Barry had only recently learned was populated with cows leased by the telecommunications mogul across the road to make it look more picturesque.

Just past the old millpond, Barry made the right onto Grace Hill Road and saw the empty lot where that grand Tudor used to be. Some investment analyst bought the place last year and knocked it down, presumably to throw up a Steroid Colonial with a Garage Mahal. But he must've run out of money, because no work had been done since then. So now a small deer family stood over the hole in the ground where the house once was, trying to figure out if their trail used to run by here.

Barry cruised by them slowly, reminded that even after eighteen years of marriage, his wife was still sometimes as much a mystery to him as the suburbs.

"So how was work?" she asked.

"You know. The struggle continues. What does not kill us makes us stronger."

"Does that mean we're still going to be able to go to Paris for Christmas?"

"Of course," he said, having forgotten about the plan until this very moment. "I've got it covered."

Even with fares to Europe down to encourage flying, tickets and a decent hotel for a week were going to be at least six grand. He hoped he wasn't going to have to sell a treasury bill to pay for the trip. He'd already promised Lynn he wouldn't touch the Keogh accounts or the kids' college savings funds.

"Good," she said. "Because this may be the last trip we get to take as a family. I can barely get Hannah to go to the store with me anymore."

"What goes around comes around. I bet you felt the same way about your mother when you were that age."

"That's not true. By the time I was her age, I was *taking care of* my mother."

"And resenting every other minute of it, probably."

"Didn't stop me from doing what I was supposed to, though."

They made the abrupt right into the hidden driveway a quarter mile past the horse farm.

"Have I told you lately how much I love our house?" she said.

"Don't hold back."

"It's just such a relief when I make that little turn and see it standing there."

"I hear *that*," he said, feeling the cool touch of her fingertips on the back of his neck.

He remembered the first time they came up this long gravel road with the grass centerline and the canopy of oak branches, a year and a half ago. As Lynn put it, it was like stepping from black-and-white into supersaturated Kodachrome amber and green. He hadn't realized how accustomed to washed-out grays he'd got while growing up in Newark and living in Manhattan. Everything stood out here so vividly. The red feathers of a cardinal in its nest. The yellow leaves rustling in a light breeze, and the Canada geese honking overhead. The distant whinny of horses from down the road, the vapory shimmer of the river at the bottom of the hill. And at the summit of their little rise, the old brown farmhouse — stolid and impervious, a Winslow Homer painting brought to life.

"Everything's going to be all right, isn't it?" She gripped his arm as he pulled up in front of the basketball hoop at the top of the driveway.

"Yeah, sure," he said quickly. "We're fine."

But as he opened the door and the dome light came on, he saw his own uncertainty reflected in her eyes.

"Really," he said. "We're the lucky ones."

He got out and checked the bumper sticker on the car blocking the garage entrance — a lime-green '86 Datsun belonging to their daughter's boyfriend, Dennis Paultz. "If You're Not Outraged, You're Not Thinking."

"I can't believe she's still going out with this kid." He wagged his head. "When is she going to outgrow him?"

"Maybe she won't. Maybe this is true love."

"Please, God, have mercy on my little black heart."

They crossed the lawn, passing Slam, the garden gnome with the basketball and sunglasses that Lynn got Barry for his last birthday. The figure was in the shade of the apple tree that Barry fell in love with when they first visited. A hell of an idea, being able to grow food in your own front yard instead of stumbling out to Gristedes with an ATM card on a Saturday morning. *His* tree. Just like the one his father always wanted to grow in their scrappy little front yard on Clifton Avenue. He would've loved to have seen Dad sitting under this one, but getting 50 percent of a dream to come true wasn't too shabby, was it? With the temperature dropping quickly tonight, though, he wondered if the small green nutlike apples would have a chance to fully ripen.

"Anybody home?" Lynn called out, pushing open the heavy mahogany front door that she'd found in Pennsylvania farm country and bought because it reminded the kids of a medieval castle entrance.

He stood on the threshold behind her, granting himself a small ephemeral moment of satisfaction, the lion setting a heavy contented paw down in his lair.

This is our home. This is where we belong. It almost broke them financially to get it just so. Another quarter-million and counting beyond the $650,000 they spent in the first place. But what choice was there? The kitchen was from General Eisenhower's era, and Donna Reed would have found the living room way too squaresville. All the linoleum and wood paneling had to be stripped away. The ceiling beams had to be exposed. The place needed to be taken down to its bare bones so they could make it their own. He remembered how Lynn went at the design with the architect as if she was telling a story, embedding little details that only the two of them would understand. A marble mantel over the fireplace like the kind they had in their first apartment on East 10th Street; an oak bed glimpsed in a sexy Rohmer movie; the acorn newel post from her parents' house; a small bar counter she'd rescued from an old bootlegger's yacht and stripped and stained herself; French windows in the living room like the ones Oliver Twist threw open on that first morning at his benefactor's home; a series of Lynn's black-and-white prints of Vermont barns and Cape Cod sand dunes on white matte backgrounds. At one point, he'd started to fret about all the dollars flying away in a jet stream, but then he saw the green studded-leather door she'd gotten for his study, just like the kind M had for his office in the James Bond movies. After that, he was on board for anything. The hardwood floors in the main hallway like Alan Bates had in his artist's loft in *An Unmarried Woman*. The little secret passageway from Hannah's bedroom to the hall bathroom so she could feel like Alice with her own rabbit hole. The special window seat in Clay's room, where he could squirrel himself away. A crazy quilt of memories and impressions, but somehow Lynn balanced them and made them all feel like parts of an organic whole, a place to lay your weary burden down.

From upstairs, Barry heard the thump of feet coming off a bed and the sealed-off hysteria of a crowd on television.

"Does that sound like homework getting done?" He stepped into the foyer.

"I'm going to have to talk to her again." Lynn rolled her eyes.

"Yo, word up."

Hannah had appeared at the top of the stairs. A brand-new white Susan Sontag / Pepe Le Pew streak heightened the Gothic drama of her dyed black hair. A creamy white crescent strip of belly showed between her skimpy black top and baggy green fatigues, neatly drawing the line between slim hiplessness below and blossoming womanhood above. At her side was her inamorato, Dennis from Mopus Bridge Road. Something about this boy made the plaque in Barry's arteries harden. It wasn't the tongue stud or the Caesar haircut with the bleached strands, the mild body odor, or even the "Nature Bites Back" T-shirt with the peace symbol button on the collar. It wasn't the "Pass" and "Fail" written on the knuckles of each hand. It wasn't even the fact that he still suspected Dennis of egging the windshield and leaving that crank note accusing him of being an "ecocriminal operating a mobile pollutant" under the wiper blade of their Explorer. It was the way his daughter melted into him a little as they were standing there barefoot and giggly, not quite keeping herself distinct.

"So, what's going on?" Barry asked.

"I dunno."

She held Dennis's arm as they descended the steps. Barry remembered how she walked around with a nervous smile when she first got breasts a couple of years ago, as if she were carrying a loaded gun that she didn't know how to handle. Now she swaggered and smirked like Jesse James.

"You guys working on your college essays?" Barry asked.

He saw the flicker of conspiracy between them.

"We were just getting started," Dennis mumbled.

"Were you?"

He saw the boy eyeing him with the kind of jaunty insouciance that can only be born of believing one is about to bed the Lord of the Manor's daughter. Well, we'll see about *that*, won't we, Young Bunny Hugger?

"Dennis, where are you applying?" asked Lynn, ever the gracious mom.

"Ah, my old man's after me to apply to Penn State 'cause he went there, but I heard about a school in Vermont that lets you work on a farm for a year." Dennis rolled the question off his scrawny shoulders.

"Hannah's applying to Amherst, Yale, and Princeton," Barry cut in, and then he immediately regretted shooting his mouth off.

Who cared if she went to a snooty Ivy League school? On the other hand, this was a girl who breezed through twelfth-grade Latin in ninth grade at one of the best private schools in San Francisco. This was a girl who read all of Edgar Allan Poe and half of Shakespeare while her classmates were watching *Buffy the Vampire Slayer.* He wasn't scrounging around for forty thousand dollars a year for her to learn to milk a cow.

"I just have a hard time writing about myself." Hannah cocked a hip and wrapped a black curl around her finger, all hippie girlish modesty nowadays in front of her less-accomplished boyfriend. "It feels like bragging."

"Blow your own horn or else there is no music," said her father.

He wondered if it was his fault that she'd tried on so many different identities in so few years. She was a hyperfastidious little apple-polisher when they were living in Manhattan; but on the West Coast she'd started running with a crowd of status-mongering little fashionistas who hassled their parents to buy them Lexuses and encouraged one another to starve themselves. Now that she was in the burbs, she'd thrown in her lot with the Junior Environmentalists, the Goths, the punks, and all the other misfits who'd banded together because there were too few of them in each group to have a market share of their own. Maybe if he hadn't moved the family around so much for work, she'd have a more stable crew to hang out with.

"Yeah, well, so that's cool," said Dennis with a kind of hangdog acceptance. "So, Mr. S, I heard you saw that body at the train station this morning."

"Well, I guess I was one of the people."

Barry looked uneasily from his wife to his daughter, trying to figure out who would have said anything.

"So, what did it look like?" asked Dennis.

"You know." He looked over the boy's head, trying to keep it casual. "It was a crime scene."

"Is it true a crab crawled out of her neck?"

"Eeeww." Hannah's face stitched up.

"It was upsetting," Barry said evenly, trying to keep the image out of his head. "But I'm sure they'll find out who did it soon enough. In most homicides it turns out the victim and the suspect knew each other. So there's not that much for the rest of us to worry about."

Why they should have felt reassured by him, he didn't know. By the time he was their age, he'd stopped believing three quarters of what his parents said.

He looked at his Rolex and then back at Dennis pointedly. "I'm sure you still got some more work to do tonight, don't you?"

"No, I'm cool," said Dennis, poker-faced and pretending to be oblivious to the hint.

"Hi, Daddy."

Clay came trudging down the stairs in his big potato-sack jeans and black Stone Cold Steve Austin T-shirt, with Stieglitz, their horny old springer spaniel, following close behind.

"What's the report, commander?" said Barry, trying not to let any of his concern show.

Once again, the kid's weight had shot up alarmingly. He was look-ing a bit like one of the carnival cutouts of a little boy's face on top of a huge bulging man's body. Lynn had asked him not to say any-thing about the boy's erratic eating habits. *He's getting self-conscious about his body,* she'd said. *It's different for boys these days. Everybody's sup-posed to be so fit and buff.*

Well, he could come out and throw a ball around with me sometime, Barry argued. *It wouldn't kill him.*

"How's the Torah going?" asked Barry as the dog tried to jump up and lick his face.

"It's okay," said Clay, who was less than two months from his Bar Mitzvah. "You know, scrolling along."

"I love the Old Testament," Hannah interrupted, her voice drip-ping with sarcasm. "It's so full of blood and human sacrifice. Dig it, man. It's like Ozzfest."

"So, what are you up to?" Barry ignored her as Stieglitz started to hump his leg.

"Um" — Clay's eyes wandered up toward the exposed wood beams — "I think 3:16."

"Oh, you are *so* busted." Barry pushed the dog down. "You think I don't know what 3:16 is? '"That's the bottom line," saith Stone Cold.' You're really going to make me and your mother proud if you get up and do that at B'nai Israel in front of two hundred people. I thought you were doing Abraham and Isaac."

"I practiced for an hour and did homework for an hour. What do you want from me?"

"Hey, listen, it's no skin off my nose. We can cancel the whole party if that's what you want. I'm not looking to spend another seven thousand dollars this year."

He saw the boy's face fall and immediately admonished himself for wounding him. Very nice. The kid looks up to you and you embarrass him in front of his sister and her boyfriend because *you're* feeling insecure about money.

"It's all right." He put an arm around Clay, noticing brownie crumbs by the corner of his mouth. "I'll work with you on it later. I could use a little brushup myself."

"Then can we play a little *House of the Dead*?"

"Only after we get through the sacrifice. I don't want you turning into a total mook."

He loved his children with an intensity that scared him sometimes. He agonized through their minor illnesses and exulted in the tiny triumphs of their daily lives. He praised their finger paintings as if they were Rothkos, negotiated their endless demands for Barbie and *Mortal Kombat*, let them stick their grubby little fingers in his ears while he carried them on his shoulders, and bare-handed their vomit on long car rides to Maine. Occasionally, he missed his bachelor days, when he could afford to be a little more reckless about himself. Because over the years, he had learned that love did not, in fact, make you whole. Love broke you up. Love smashed you into a million different pieces. Love left you distracted and worried. Love put your business in the street.

"Well, I think it's time for my boot heels to be wandering," said Dennis, going for a pair of steel-toed Dr. Martens by the front door. "I actually haven't cracked the books for that trig test yet."

Clearly, the party was over now that the old Chastity Brigade had arrived in the '97 Saab.

Barry wondered if his daughter was actually *doing it* with this malodorous milky-looking boy and, if so, whether Lynn had already taken her on a long car ride to discuss the appropriate measures to protect her personal environment.

"I'll walk you to your car," said Hannah, opening the door.

Stieglitz jumped up and down in front of the two of them, sticking his nose in their crotches as if he smelled some special heat there.

Barry watched them swat the dog away and go out, wishing for a moment that the house had a screened-in porch with an old rocking chair so he could sit with a twelve-gauge shotgun across his knees, creaking back and forth and reminding skeezy little Dennis to mind his manners with his daughter. For all her butt-twitching and occasional bratty sarcasm, she still seemed fragile to Barry at times, and as the door closed behind them, he thought he understood for a moment what it was like for air traffic controllers watching little turbo-prop planes disappear off their radar screens.

"Hey, somebody from your work called while Mom was out." Clay started up the stairs.

"Who?" Barry called after him.

"Some lady." Clay slouched over the railing. "Mrs. Spock."

"That's Lisa, our chief science officer," said Barry out the side of his mouth. "She leave a message?"

"She said she has the tricorder readings and needs to be beamed up right away."

Lynn probed him with her eyes. "What does that mean?"

"It's just corporate hyperbole. Hey, Clay, do me a favor. Don't press against that thing so hard. You're gonna break the spindle, and then we won't be able to find one that looks the same to replace it."

The boy straightened up, looking slightly hurt, as if his father had criticized his weight directly. Barry reached over to muss his hair, but Clay raced the rest of the way up the steps, tramped across the landing overhead, and slammed his bedroom door.

"Is something going on?" asked Lynn.

"No, everything's fine. I'm just working with a bunch of thirty-year-olds who've never been through a downturn. Every little dip feels like Armageddon to them."

"I saw the stock took another pounding today."

"Well, I told you not to look at it every day, didn't I? That's how you drive yourself crazy. It's a long ball game."

"You'd tell me if we were in serious trouble, wouldn't you?"

"Of course."

He kissed her on the forehead, picturing himself as a suspicious package on an airport security conveyor belt, encased in lead and impervious to X rays.

"Listen, we have our health, we have our children, and we have a home in a relatively safe place," he said.

"Don't fuck with me, Barry Schulman. I know you too well."

"Hey, you're the one with all the deep dark secrets about your old boyfriends." Her lips parted slightly, just short of a knowing smile.

"How bad was that breakup anyway?" he asked.

"He messed up some of my pictures at a high school show."

"Really?" He felt like someone had just popped him on the shoulders with two open palms. "And that guy's a police lieutenant and he knows where we live?"

Instinctively, he found himself sticking his chest out.

"Relax." Lynn patted him. "It was a long time ago, and he has a wife and three kids now. I'm sure he doesn't still feel the same way. And to tell you the truth, I wasn't a totally innocent party either."

"Whatever that means," he said.

He studied her, discerning the things that would turn a sensible man into a disgrace. Not just the cheekbones, the slender responsive body, the dark hair, or the way her skin glowed as if she were lit from within. It was her eyes. Her way of looking at you and seeing things you didn't know yourself. Over the years, he'd seen other men — sometimes even close friends — quietly get hooked on her, but never to the point where he actually had to tell one to back off.

"I'm going to take a shower," she said, starting up the stairs. "But can we have a serious talk about money one of these days?"

"We're always talking about money, even when we're not talking about it."

"Ugh. What a terrible thought."

He studied the arch of her back as she climbed the steps, leaving him to his own devices in the living room.

Outside the front bay window, the stars in the night sky were fragments of bone china smashed on a black floor. He listened to Stieglitz barking and Dennis's phlegmy old V-6 engine fading down the driveway as his daughter started that long lonely walk back up the gravel path. He remembered that she didn't have any shoes on when she left the house, and the image of her walking over sharp little stones for this boy filled him with tender foreboding and wonder.

Light fog filled in the corners of the windows. A stiff wind rattled the shutters and made the pool cover in the backyard flap like a great fallen wing. This summer had lasted longer than any he could remember. It was even warm and clear that morning when he first saw that American Airlines plane flying so low between the buildings that he could almost read the lettering on its side. But now he felt the chill in the air and sensed that the long arrogant season was finally ending.

8

BY AROUND MIDNIGHT, Mike had reached the point in the evening when he was too exhausted to keep working but way too wired to go straight home. He'd been up since six, and his mind was full of flying dust and seeping gases. In the old days, he could've rallied the guys from his shift for choir practice in the parking lot behind the old station on Bank Street, drinking like lords and bellowing into the night until somebody fell face first into a puddle of his own piss. But these days, everyone was so temperate and married, a bunch of Baby Bores rushing home to change diapers and sing lullabies. Bit by bit, he'd become one himself, though there was still that side of him that *needed* to bay at the moon once in a while.

Shit. *What was he going to do?* He knew he should just drive home, tuck the kids in, have the usual tense few words with Marie in the kitchen, and then go downstairs and start working on a game plan. But the thought of sitting still at this point made him gnaw the inside of his mouth.

Where else could he go, though? It wasn't like he could just pick up the phone and hash things out with Harold anymore. The man was chief. You had to watch your step around him. All the same, he found himself wanting to be around familiar things.

He thought of cruising past Lynn Stockdale's house again. Just for the hell of it, he'd run the license plate number on the Motor Display Terminal in the car to see if the husband had any outstanding DUIs or moving violations. Not that he was looking to make trouble or get his balls in a jam. He'd only gone by the house — what? — maybe three or four times since he spotted her crossing the supermarket parking lot in March and looked up her address on the computer. You couldn't call that a habit, could you? He was satisfying his curiosity, that's all. Seeing how she'd made out for herself, coming a little farther up the driveway each time, to get a better look.

It was only five minutes from his house anyway, so what the fuck. It wasn't doing any more harm. He made the abrupt turn off Grace Hill Road and cut the lights on his unmarked Caprice halfway up the long gravel path. The old farmhouse with the leaky roof and the sloping property lines. Local legend was, Farmer Grace, who used to live here, got captured and tortured by British loyalists in the Revolution. Supposedly, they hung him by his thumbs trying to get him to tell where he'd hidden all his money. Must have been a tough bastard, because he never cracked; his wife, on the other hand, gave up the booty in a New York minute, wailing about how she couldn't stand to see the man suffer. *Women.*

He pulled off to the side and got out with the binoculars he used for his occasional on-duty birding expeditions. Shafts of light streamed out of the house, stark white diagonals stabbing through the trees. He raised the binoculars, adjusting the focus knob with his index finger. Lynn blurred and then came into focus. She was downstairs in the kitchen, rubbing lotion on her chin and hands and fixing herself a drink. The usual routine. She'd taken a shower, and her hair was still damp and sleek, as if she'd just emerged from the river. A white terry-cloth bathrobe parted at her collarbone, revealing a fair glistening delta. *This was insane.* He knew he shouldn't be doing this again, especially not today of all days. But certain women were viruses. You couldn't get rid of them. They got into your bloodstream and seared your veins.

He turned the knob another three or four degrees until the view was sharp enough to read the label off the Chardonnay bottle and see the little hairs clinging to her temples. When he tried to fine-tune the focus a little more, she turned into a cloud of white cloth and floating dark hair.

He raised the glasses and saw the husband upstairs in the bedroom, taking off his tie and sneaking in a quick furtive phone call. Kiss my ass. He'd never liked these city guys anyway. Always jabbering at you when they came to renew their parking permits for the station, always making speeches at the School Board meetings — *Let me tell you something, I pay taxes here too* — as if they were volunteering at the firehouse every Saturday washing the hook-and-ladder truck. All right, you bought your wife a big house with a swimming pool and a rolling lawn that you pay somebody else to mow once a week. *The skin hadn't started to separate.* Okay, jerk-off. Let's trade places. I'll give you the shield and you give me the big house and the wife and we'll call it even.

He panned around the grounds with the binoculars, taking in the vinyl-mesh deer fence, the covered pool, the gnome with the basketball, and the small blue ADT security system sign on the window near the door. *Incredible.* A man pays more than a half-million dollars for a house with less than four acres, jacking up the prices on all the working people, and then pays less than two grand to have the property protected? Any moron crackhead burglar knew where to cut the line so he could have the run of the place. A man that careless didn't deserve what he had.

He took a few more cautious steps up the driveway, raising the glasses to see if he could find the kids' bedroom windows. There was a dim pale glow from behind one of the curtains. One of the children was still up. The girl was about the same age Lynn was when he'd gone out with her. Was it possible that that much time had passed? He remembered how she used to buck and try to roll him off when he got on top of her, especially when he got a little rough. One time, he found his hands around her neck, squeezing. She said she didn't like it, but he knew she did. She liked to feel his power over her. The fact that she wasn't easy to push around only made it better. He hated the ones who just rolled over and played dead.

He lowered the binoculars and turned the focus knob back a few degrees, and there she was again, still gleaming and damp from the shower. He remembered that day they went swimming in the river. The cocky way she hooked her thumbs under the bra straps and gave him that look over her shoulder, daring him to follow. A sense of yearning rose in him like a compass needle finding magnetic north. She always managed to stay a little bit ahead of him, no matter how hard he fought the current. She was absolutely fearless back then. He could still see her pitching her white body against the black tide, riding the swells, always receding, never looking back. That was the thing he should've noticed then: *she never looked back.*

He fine-tuned the focus again, wondering why any woman with two children had the right to look this way after twenty-five years.

It was as if several other ladies had given more than their share of ugliness to make her. His own wife was getting a little thick and knobby these days. Shouldn't Lynn be marked, wrinkled, or tainted somehow, especially after what she'd done to his family?

But now she was back. He thought about the way she stared up at him from her husband's lap tonight. *Mike's a big man in the department. . . . Mike's family's been in this town for generations.* Maybe she finally realized what she'd done. He wondered if he could forgive her. One thing was for sure — it was going to take a helluva lot more than a family barbecue to make up for all the damage.

The Nextel cell phone suddenly rang out in his jeans pocket, a tinny minuet that jump-started his heart. He grabbed it quickly and stepped back behind the tree line as bats circled the chimney and crickets made a sound like a thousand tiny watches being wound.

"Yo," he muttered, knowing it was either his wife or somebody from the station house with info they didn't want to put out over the radio.

The husband pulled back the curtain upstairs and looked out into the driveway to see what the noise was about. The new trapezoid of light from the window ended less than a yard from Mike's feet.

"Hey," said Harold. "What's your location? I just called the house, and Marie said you weren't there yet."

"I'm over on the Post Road." He lowered his voice, hoping one of the bicycle guys wouldn't be riding by that location at this very moment to blow him in. "I was just heading back, and I saw a bunch of kids looking in cars at the Pizza Hut parking lot."

He heard a rustling in the bushes behind him and turned just in time to see an animal go leaping off into the woods. Too big for a raccoon.

"We need you back at the base forthwith," said Harold. "I think we may have just caught a break."

"Oh, yeah? What's going on?"

"A gentleman just came in to give us a missing person report about someone we both know."

"Who?"

Mike sensed that whatever had jumped off into the bushes was still lingering nearby, watching him.

"Just get your ass back down here," he heard Harold snap as he covered the mouthpiece. "Things are starting to move."

He pushed the Off button as the husband opened the bedroom window and stuck his head out.

Mike drew back, hearing an owl screeching in the woods behind him and a bullfrog croaking like an untuned banjo. His heart was beating so hard that it felt as if a second heart on the other side of his chest was answering it. *You have really lost it this time.* You are going to turn your life into a federal disaster site.

He raised the binoculars for one last look at Lynn tightening her belt and turning off the kitchen light. For a few seconds, the brightness of her robe lingered, gradually darkening and leaving just nine black panes in the window frame. He thought of something he'd read in the paper the other day, about how certain powerful telescopes could see light from stars that died millions of years ago.

But what did it matter when they died as long as you could still see their glow? And how could you be sure they were really dead anyway? Maybe their energy was still pulsing out there somewhere in the great dark void. He lowered the glasses with quiet satisfaction, knowing there were still parts of her that no one else could see. That not even her husband or children would ever know her as long or as well as he had. And nothing could change that because nothing could change the past.

He walked to the end of the driveway and got back in his car. As he turned it around, two deer sauntered out from the bushes, where they'd been watching him the whole time. Taking a leisurely stroll through his high beams, their coats the color of whipped cream and stained wood, their eyes turning android green in the lights. Stupid beasts, he thought, cruising around them. They used to know enough to be afraid of us.

9

AS LYNN PADDED past Clay's bedroom, she saw a dim light still on and pushed the door open. Her son was kneeling on the window seat, peering out at the driveway from behind his white-on-black World Wrestling Federation "Raw is War" curtains.

"What are you doing?" she said.

"Nothing."

"It doesn't look like nothing. Aren't you supposed to be getting ready for bed?"

"I thought I heard something." His stubby fingers let go of the curtain. "There was a car in our driveway."

"Probably just somebody who got lost and needed to turn themselves around."

He got up from the window seat. This room seemed smaller every time she walked in it, as if she was deliberately being crowded out. Clothes on the floor multiplied. The bookshelves groaned with the wrestlers' biographies — *I Ain't Got Time to Bleed; The Rock Says . . .*; and Mick Foley's immortal *Foley Is Good: And the Real World Is Faker Than Wrestling* — sharing space with *Jewish Literacy* by Joseph Telushkin and the *Great Jews in Sports* that Barry had given Clay for his twelfth birthday. She used to feel mildly put out that a child of hers didn't take more interest in the Protestant side of the family, but then his sister started wearing crosses the size of staple guns and Lynn decided to keep her own counsel.

The huge neo-Federalist desk she'd carefully picked out for Clay in Fairfield last year was disappearing in a deluge of half-finished math homework, mammoth American history textbooks that looked as if they'd never been opened, and well-thumbed stacks of *Magic* cards — the latest of the arcane, vaguely medieval-sounding boy games he was obsessed with. She took some small comfort in the fact that as transplanted city kids, both her children still confined anarchy to their own rooms, instead of suburban-sprawling down the stairs and into the living room.

"I don't like it here," he said.

"Since when?" She sat down on his bed and carefully arranged the folds of her bathrobe to cover her bare knees.

"It's creepy. I hear noises at night."

"It's called *nature*. Some people even love it."

"I miss the city," he said.

"You're kidding me."

"There's nothing to do here." He fiddled with an old gyroscope that he'd had since he was seven. "I never get to see my friends, you can't walk anywhere, and I always have to wait for a ride."

She hesitated, not wanting to remind him that he always depended on her for transport when they lived in a city.

"You're safe here," she said.

"I could be safe in the city too. And I wouldn't be *soo* bored."

She smoothed out the bedspread, quietly regretting the little eccentricities he'd been dropping one by one to fit in with the other kids in the suburbs. The bagpipe lessons he'd been taking in the city. The Russian-English dictionary he used to study in bed. The little Crusty Man comic book he'd been drawing and keeping under his mattress, trying to make it good enough to show her someday.

"You don't remember what it's like," he said.

"Believe me. I do."

She remembered those lonely nights, that desperate yearning for something beyond the end of Birch Lane and her well-worn copy of *Goodbye Yellow Brick Road*. She saw herself again in a darkened bedroom, lighting incense candles and trying to tune in Allison Steele the Night Bird on WNEW FM. Oh, the crackling in the ether. Oh, the solemn tribal flute music and the opening thrum of "Nights in White Satin." Oh, the Kahlil Gibran poetry and the visions of long-haired sloe-eyed hippie boys in leather vests offering to induct her into the mysteries of foot massage and rolling a joint with one hand. Even the names of the bands seemed to conjure a lurid sensual carnival going on down the river. *Tangerine Dream. Tonto's Expanding Head Band. Renaissance. Caravan. Lothar and the Hand People.*

"Then why'd you make us come back here?" Clay asked.

"Because when you get older, you learn to appreciate other things about a place," she said, sounding a little more pat than she'd meant to.

"Like what?"

She thought of the children near the Trade Center who'd thought the people falling were birds on fire. "Good schools," she said.

"Ha!"

"Oh, so now you don't like Green Hill?"

"It's all about sports," he said. "And I suck at sports. I'm too fat."

"What do you mean, you're too fat?"

"I mean, look at me! I'm a blimp!" He squeezed a flab roll the size of a Wonder Bread loaf at his waistline. "I've been dieting for weeks, and I can't make this go away. I'm *disgusting*."

"You're not. You're beautiful to me."

"I wanna go on Nutri/System, where you just have one milk-shake a day," he said. "I'm ashamed to take my shirt off in front of other guys in the locker room."

She went over to put a hand on his shoulder, remembering the can of Lysol she'd found under his bed last week. At the time, she'd thought he might be smoking pot, and she gave him a righteous lit-tle antidrug lecture. But since then, she'd pulled up all these articles on the Web about boys his age developing anorexia and, in a few ex-treme cases, bulimia. She wondered if he could be making himself throw up and then using Lysol to get rid of the smell. She'd noticed him skipping dessert and dissecting his food obsessively lately. *Try-ing to cut down on carbs, Mom.* She cringed inwardly, thinking about her precious child secretly making himself vomit in the bathroom so he could have washboard abs.

"So, what else is so good about this place?" he asked, sitting down.

A vulnerable nasality told her that he was opening a door a crack. "Well," she said, "it's true, there's not a lot of big buildings or movie theaters you can walk to. But what you do have is a lot of freedom."

"Yeah. How do you figure that? Freedom to go where?"

"Oh, come on. One of the greatest rivers in the world is just down the hill from us. I used to ride down there on my bike all the time when I was your age so I could hang out along the banks and let my imagination run wild."

"So what?" His chair squeaked as he turned to face her.

"It was just like this magical place where I could go and make up stories with my friends." She pushed on, trying to unhook the latch in his mind. "You couldn't really swim in it before the Clean Water Act because it was so polluted. So we used to just sit on the rocks and talk about all the cool things we could find at the bottom if we ever got scuba gear. Indian arrowheads. War axes. Sunken treasures. I had this friend whose father worked at the prison up the river, and I used to have this whole fantasy of helping these two innocent boys escape. I'd have a rowboat waiting at the shore when they came out of this tunnel they'd dug with spoons. And then they'd shoot at us from the guard tower as we rowed away . . ."

She could see he was starting to get interested. That little telltale jiggling of his knee reminded her of how he used to squiggle around in bed when she was telling him a particularly exciting good-night story.

"One time," she said, "my friend's brother dove into the water looking for a gun."

"Why?"

"He was a cop and a diver." She paused, trying to remember exactly how Mike's older brother, Johnny, told this story. He always managed to wring a loud laugh out of it. But she didn't have his bravura, his way of tossing a good line up in the air, letting it hang there until everyone was leaning forward, and then banging it home.

"But, you know, the Hudson was like pea soup in those days because of all the sludge they'd dumped in it," she said. "You couldn't see your hand in front of your face. So he's swimming around in his wet suit, feeling around at the bottom, and all of a sudden he reaches up and realizes he's surrounded by steel bars."

"What happened?"

"He'd swum right into a huge animal cage. Like something you'd keep a lion or a tiger in."

"Really?" His eyes widened. "And where did the animal go?"

"I don't know. Maybe the tiger got out. Or maybe it was just an empty cage that fell off the back of a boat. The point is, he swam right into it and couldn't see enough to find the way out. And his oxygen tank only had about five minutes in it."

You could see how Johnny would get himself jammed up. He was all sinew and nerve. Always looking to dive right in and mix it up. *A live round,* his father called him. *You never know where he's going to end up.* As for Mr. Johnny, he said the only time he ever truly felt free was five fathoms down. But he had a good heart. That was his saving grace. And in the end, probably the thing that killed him.

"So, what'd he do?" Clay's knee jiggled more frantically.

"I guess he just had to feel his way along, bar by bar, until he found the opening," she said. "And pray that his air would hold out."

"And did it?"

She felt a diving bell of sadness descend within her chest. "Well, I guess it did," she said. "Otherwise, I wouldn't be telling you this, would I?"

He exhaled with relief, as if she'd just regaled him with the plot of a great horror movie, and she felt a small sunbeam expand in her chest, a quiet delight in knowing that she could still hold his attention sometimes.

She was beginning to wonder. These days she often found herself skulking after the children like a spurned lover, mooning over happy times they'd had at the sandbox and the dinosaur museum, conveniently forgetting the hours of stupefying tedium watching *Barney* and the mortifying tantrums in overpriced theme restaurants. She missed being the center of their universe — the Golden Idol on an island where no one could swim. But she tried to tell herself it was a good thing, all this growing independence. Who wanted to be worshiped all the time anyway? Still, a part of her could not quite accept that time was passing, that something forged so deep in the wellspring of her body could just paddle away without a backward glance.

Clay's brow began to furrow. "Mom?"

"What?"

"Why're all your stories about people trying to get away?"

The question brought her up short. His voice was finally starting to change, she noticed, dropping into a wobbly alto.

"I hadn't really thought of that," she said. "They were just stories I wanted to tell you about the river and the kind of things that used to happen to me . . ."

"But that's where they found that lady dead this morning. Are you saying you want me to go down there by myself?"

"Um, not exactly . . ." The spell was breaking. "I was thinking you could find other places here you could make your own."

"*Yeah*, right. As soon as I get my own car. In *three* years."

He turned away and glanced toward the door. She wondered if he was going to sneak down the hall to the computer room and start downloading porn off the Internet as soon as she left.

"Well, I guess I better get back to work," he said. "I still have to work on my history outline."

"You need any help with it?"

"Mom, come on. When have you ever helped me?"

So this is how it's going to be, she realized. Bit by bit, the child goes away. The bedtime stories no longer enchant. The cuddles embarrass. The voice changes. The world scratches at the windows. And nothing that a mother says makes any difference.

"'Kay, good night." She went to kiss him on top of the head, trying not to notice the way he flinched slightly. "Don't stay up too late."

10

WITH GRAVEL AND grit from Lynn's driveway still wedged in the soles of his work boots, Mike came crunching back into the police station at twelve-thirty and found Harold Baltimore in a small gray room at the back, watching the interrogation next door through one-way glass.

"How's the show?" he asked quietly.

"Pull up a chair and see for yourself. The reviews aren't in yet."

In the next room, Detective Paco Ortiz was moving around the hunched-over man seated at the black table, his shaved head shining like a honeydew melon under the fluorescent light.

"So when you got home from the airport this evening, your wife wasn't home and you started to get worried," said Paco, his blue Riverside P.D. T-shirt snug across his oil-barrel chest and his goatee narrowing like a trowel. "Is that right?"

"At first, I was just a little concerned that she hadn't left a note," said Jeffrey Lanier in a high nasal voice. "But then after the kids got home and I talked to the baby-sitter, I started getting really nervous. She hadn't heard from Sandi since last night."

Lanier was a tan youngish-looking man in his early forties with the kind of V-shaped all-American face some women liked, hazel eyes behind Clark Kent glasses, wide thin lips, and a cleft in his chin. From the front, he had an impressive mound of chestnut-brown hair, but when he turned, he revealed a bald patch growing like a spotlight on the back of his head. He was dressed as if he'd just been tossed out of bed, in a maroon Harvard sweatshirt, rumpled khaki shorts, and Teva sandals. So this was what a so-called Internet millionaire looked like these days, Mike thought dourly.

"Is it unusual for your wife to be out for so long without letting you know where she is?" asked Paco, hitching up his gun belt.

"She doesn't give me a daily schedule. All I know is it's almost eight o'clock, she hasn't been home since last night, the kids need dinner, the baby-sitter needs a ride to the train station, and her friend Lynn Schulman is on the answering machine from a restaurant last night saying, 'Where the hell are you?' And I hear that, and I start to freak out."

Mike felt Harold nudge him with his elbow but willed himself not to look over. Life in a small town; eventually everything connects.

"Uh-huh." Paco sat down on the opposite side of the table and balanced a legal pad on his knees. "So your wife was supposed to be meeting somebody for dinner?"

"Girls'-night-out kind of thing," said Jeffrey. "You know, everybody's gotta let off steam once in a while. But then I hear *this*, and I know that Lynn's one of her best friends forever and I start to think . . ."

He sniffed, touched the centerpiece of his glasses, and his nostrils turned red at the rims. This was the type of slightly callow boy-man who'd gotten so used to people cutting him slack that some essential muscle in him had started to atrophy.

"So when was the last time you spoke to your wife?"

"Yesterday around lunchtime. She called me on the cell. She wanted to remind me we had a parent-teacher meeting coming up later this week, and she didn't want me to miss this one. We've had some scheduling conflicts in the past."

"I hear that," said Paco with an encouraging half-smile. "There ain't enough hours in the day for me to be with my kids."

"Since when is he married?" asked Mike behind the glass.

"He isn't." Harold shrugged. "But he's got two kids living in Florida."

"So were you guys knocking heads a little about your schedule?" asked Paco.

"Just the usual stress of me being on the road all the time and her having to stay home with the kids." Jeffrey Lanier crossed his legs, a big toe flexing under a Velcro strap. "It's hard for her, me being away so much. Look, it's hard for me too. I miss them like crazy when I'm away all week."

Yeah, right, thought Mike. And then try to make up for it by screaming at them on the soccer field Saturday morning and falling asleep on your wife before the opening skit on *Saturday Night Live*.

"So how long were you away on this trip anyway?" asked Paco, staying focused. "Five days, did you say?"

"I took the shuttle to Boston early Thursday morning so I could get in all my meetings, see some friends, and be home tonight." Jeff hunched forward earnestly, like a seventh-grader trying to read a blackboard. "That's part of our new deal. I'm supposed to get home to watch the kids so she can go out one or two nights a week."

"I hear you." Paco made a quick note on his pad. "And so you've got phone numbers for people in Boston we can double-check everything with."

"Yeah, sure, but look . . . what's going on?" Jeff put a hand over his bald spot, protecting his tender vulnerability. "*I* came down here to give a missing person report. Is there something you guys aren't telling me?"

"Sir, I'm just trying to get all the facts together so we can proceed to look for your wife," Paco said patiently. "Now, what time did your flight get into LaGuardia today?"

"About five o'clock, but . . ." Jeff was distracted, noticing the window in the wall for the first time and realizing somebody might be behind it listening. "Look, I'm really starting to get scared here. These children need their mother . . ."

"Sir, we're gonna try to find her as fast as we can," said Paco, swiveling his chair around the side of the table to get close to him. "Do you have a picture of your wife that we can work off of?"

Mike watched the husband fish around in his pocket for a wallet photo, his nostrils expanding and contracting more quickly, his agitation filling the interrogation room like helium.

"What do you think?" Harold murmured.

"He's making the right noises, but it's too early in the song." Mike moved back from the glass. "Why's he so hinky already?"

"This is a head shot." Paco thumbed his lip as he studied the wallet photo. "You have anything that shows, um, a fuller view?"

"What do you mean?" said Jeff, pushing back in his chair and holding on to the armrests, his bare knees starting to double up like knuckles. "Why would you need that?"

"It's standard." Paco shrugged. "Just to see if there are any distinguishing marks and characteristics. People can change their hair or even their eye color nowadays if they decide to run away. Body type can be harder."

"She was tall, about five foot eight, and . . . well, you know, she'd had two children." He touched his glasses and looked up at the ceiling, trying to concentrate. "And she'd had a lumpectomy. And then, um, a little liposuction."

"She got her fat sucked?"

"It was for her, you know, not for me." Jeff started breathing harder. "And, ah, I guess she'd just gotten some kind of a tattoo on her ankle."

"A tattoo?" Paco's eyes batted up at the window and then landed back on Lanier. "What kind of tattoo?"

"A blue butterfly." Jeff's chest began to heave, and he coughed. "She got it in the city this summer, on Saint Marks Place. Midlife crisis kind of thing. She started doing a lot of crap like that after she got past the cancer."

"Shit, it's her," said Harold, a radiator hiss leaking through his front teeth. "I *knew* it."

Mike pressed his lips together, carefully containing himself.

In the other room, Jeffrey Lanier removed his glasses and put his hands up to the sides of his head as if he'd just realized he had a splitting headache.

"Hey, you're not asking me this because that's what they found on the body at the train station?"

"Sir, we honestly don't know who that was, but we just have to follow through on every possibility . . ."

"Oh my God . . ."

Jeff started to rise, and his face turned a deep arterial shade of red.

"Oh, here we go," said Mike.

"Shit." Harold grimaced. "Is this guy gonna stroke out on us?"

It was like watching a controlled demolition. Jeff's left knee went first, bending and buckling, his shoulders sagged, and then the rest of him fell sideways against the table, scraping the legs on the linoleum floor. He grabbed the edge to try to keep his balance, and a high rasping honk choked his chest.

Paco half-rose and slid a box of Kleenex across the table. "Mr. Lanier, you gonna be all right?"

"Yeah, I'm all right. I'm all right." Jeff gasped and waved him off.

"I only have a few more questions. I know you're anxious to get back to your kids."

"What am I going to tell them?" Jeff sat down again, the rhythm of his breathing becoming more spasmodic, as if he were turning inside out. "How am I going to do this?"

"Well, hopefully, you won't have to. It'll turn out to be somebody else."

Mike heard himself snort. Harold looked over at him impassively, as if they were strangers on a park bench trying to read the same newspaper.

"Mr. Lanier?" said Paco, waiting patiently for the subject to get himself under control. "I'm sorry to have to ask this, but are you and your wife having any emotional or financial difficulties?"

"I don't understand."

Jeff Lanier blew his nose and wiped his brimming eyes.

"Do you have any money problems?" said Paco. "What kind of business are you in?"

"I've got an Internet outfit, selling sports memorabilia, sports-memories.com." He put his glasses back on, trying to keep it together for just a little bit longer. "We're doing fine. It's not like we've had to borrow money from the mob to pay our mortgage, if that's what you're thinking."

"Wall Street hype," Mike muttered, earning himself another lingering glare from the boss.

"And how are things in the marriage?" Paco was asking. "You said something before about 'conflicts.' Are you guys getting along okay?"

"Far as I know." Jeff glanced around, genuinely bewildered. "I gave my wife everything she asked for."

Mike made a conscious effort not to say any more, knowing that Harold was watching him almost as closely as he was watching the husband.

"So were either of you seeing other people?" Paco tossed the legal pad on the table, as if this part of the discussion was just going to be regular guys talking.

"You mean, did she have a boyfriend?"

The prospect caused Jeff to sink down in his seat and lose whatever meager composure he'd gathered. "No . . . I don't think so."

"I'm sorry to have to ask you that, but again, it's standard in a missing person case . . ."

Jeff began to shake violently, an uncontrollable tremor that started in the chin and vibrated down to the shoulders. Paco averted his eyes for a moment, not enjoying the spectacle of a grown man going to pieces.

"He did her, that son of a bitch," Mike said in a low voice. "I fucking knew it."

Harold turned to him. "Come on," he said, like a man who'd got tired of waiting for a bus. "Let's get out of here a second. There's something we need to talk about."

The chief's office was a long rectangular room on the second floor, where the manager of this converted bowling alley used to sit. It had a sky-blue carpet, forest-green file cabinets, and pictures of Harold's wife, Emily, and their kids, Keith and Crystal, in their soccer league uniforms on the credenza behind his desk chair. The shelves were full of law books, Nelson DeMille paperbacks, and three-ring binders full of up-to-date administrative codes and law changes. There were degrees on the walls from the FBI Academy in Quantico, where Harold had taken a special six-week training course years ago, and from LaGuardia Community College, where he'd majored in mortuary science. A tiny brass coffin engraved with the name of his parlor — the Baltimore-Langston Funeral Home — sat at the edge of his mahogany desk.

"Sounds like you were getting a little worked up in there, Lieutenant." Harold's old leather seat puffed out as he sat on it.

"You can just tell the guy's lying, that's all. Pisses me off."

"Didn't you used to go out with Sandi?" Harold closed one eye, trying to remember. "In high school?"

"Nah, you're getting things mixed up again." Mike turned sideways in the guest chair with the copper studs along the armrest. "She was a hag back then. I felt sorry for her. Or maybe she felt sorry for me because of what happened with Lynn. Whatever. We were friendly."

"So have you seen her lately?"

"Just the little bit earlier this summer. I put up a deer fence in her backyard. I told you about that."

Harold tilted back, pulling that long church deacon face on him. The one that was supposed to make you think he'd never taken a drink on duty or considered nailing a pelt that wasn't his wife's.

"That all there was to it?" he said.

"What are you asking me?"

"You seem very . . . emotional."

"You're damn right I'm emotional, Harold. This is a girl we both knew since we were fourteen, got her head cut off. On our watch. What the fuck's the matter with *you?*"

"I'm trying to be . . ." — Harold waited, choosing his words judiciously — "professional."

"Well, so am I. What do you think I'm doing?"

Small bright-purple patches appeared high on Mike's cheeks.

"Look, we've known each other a long time," Harold said. "You're the godfather of my children, and whatever bullshit problems we've been having lately, I'd still trust you with my life, man. But I also know how you get around with the ladies sometimes."

"I've made my mistakes, and believe me I pay for them on the fifteenth of every month with an alimony check." Mike rubbed his ring finger with his thumb as if it was sore. "But I'm back with Marie and the kids now, and we're solid. I'm through wandering off the reservation."

"You're sure about that?"

"I did a fucking twenty-five-hundred-dollar fence job for them. You gonna make that into a major conflict, Harold?"

"Not if that's all it was."

Harold hunched forward heavily on his elbows, once again the high-school catcher waiting to see if his signal was going to be shaken off.

Mike blinked, letting himself go far away and then come back again, knowing that whatever words he spoke here would be a house of his own construction that he'd have to live in from now on. He looked past Harold for a moment, trying to buy himself a little more time.

"So is this what happens when you get the big office?" A half-moon smirk carved its way into his face. "You make all your old friends jump through hoops."

"I have a department with twenty-nine officers covering twenty square miles," said Harold. "I don't have anyplace to hide a man who's going to make life difficult, particularly my number two. I already have a youth officer who's afraid to go out on patrol and a K-9 officer who's too drunk to clean up after his dog half the time. And now it looks like we've got a major homicide of one of our citizens landing right smack in our front yard. So if you have some conflict here, I'd expect you to tell me about it *now* so I can ask you to take a step back and let Paco run the show."

"A step back?" Mike cocked his head to one side as if he hadn't heard properly. "I *trained* Paco for this job. He's supposed to answer to *me*."

"And if you've got a conflict, I'd expect you to remove yourself from the chain of command, just like you'd expect me to do the same for you. I don't need to read a story in the *New York Post* about how this department blew its first major investigation with a black man as its chief. So I am trusting you to tell me if there's something I need to know."

"Thirty-five years I've known you."

"Thirty-two," Harold corrected him. "They didn't integrate the schools until we were in fifth grade. So let me ask you one more time: Is there something I need to know here?"

Mike looked down, realizing he'd been tracing a circle around one of the armrest studs with his finger.

He made himself stop, understanding that if he took the detour here, there would be no getting back on the main road. Harold's chair creaked slightly as he rocked in it, awaiting an answer. Mike's eyes fell on the little coffin at the edge of the desk. Okay. You either hit the brakes now and risked the pileup, or kept plowing straight into darkness without headlights.

For a moment, he was seven years old again. Lying in bed, with his collection of trains and cars under his pillow, listening to Dad come in after the four-to-midnight shift. The prison seemed to follow him into the house. The smells of piss, cigarettes, ammonia, and WD-40 for the locks. You could hear the heavy sound of his keys hitting the table and the squeak of the refrigerator being yanked open, its chilled breath slowly escaping.

And then, after it shut, the sibilant incitement of his mother's voice and the muffled slap of her slippers on the linoleum floor, pursuing Dad around the kitchen, trotting out her children's sins one by one. *Stap, stap, stap. Johnny smart-mouthed me again. Stap, stap. That little one's a liar.* The way she talked about them made them seem so much worse than they were! He could still taste the blanket's binding in his mouth as he chewed on it, thinking about the hiding he stood to get off this windup. *Stap, stap.*

I caught Michael trying to steal a fire truck from Angelo's. He'll be the death of me, that one . . .

And what made it even more terrible was the way she kept comparing them to the children she took care of at other people's houses. With their exquisite manners. And their Bloomingdale's clothes. And their riding lessons. *Stap, stap.*

To the manner born, they are. You never have to ask them to do anything twice. . . . You should see the little one. The spitting image of John-John, he is . . .

Sometimes she'd even come in the house smelling from the sirloin and lamb chops she cooked for "her people" while her own kids ate Chef Boyardee and sucked the marrow from leftover chicken bones in the fridge. *Stap.*

He remembered the bedroom door opening and the slant of kitchen light falling across his pillow. The small plastic wheels making a cracking sound under his head. The groan of the floorboards as his father crossed the room with his work shoes still on. The long pause while Dad stood at the foot of the bed, just watching. His mother moving around just outside the door, impatiently tidying up in the kitchen, letting them both know she was listening. The burner on the stove making a dry *tsk-tsk* sound. And then the light on his nightstand going on. Christ, he loved the old man so much more than he loved her. In some little boy way, he understood his father's exhaustion, his white-knuckled grip on the throttle, the second-by-second struggle to keep the noises from the cell block from getting in the room with them.

So, what's the story? Dad said.

This was his father. His idol. The man who was going to give him his old uniform shirts when he was big enough and take him hunting up in the Adirondacks one of these days. The man who was going to teach him how to shoot a gun and put a tie on. If you couldn't trust your father to understand, who could you trust? The old man probably did the same thing when he was a kid. Wearily, Mike had sat up and rubbed his eyes.

Dad, I'm sorry . . . , he'd started to say.

But his father had already spotted one of the little trains sticking out from under the pillow.

The back of his hand caught Mike under the chin.

When he thought back on it, though, Mike didn't so much remember the taste of blood or even the embarrassment of not being able to stop crying. What still haunted him was the look on his father's face. Like seeing the wind go out of a sail, the realization dawning that after spending all day guarding scum, he was raising a little thief at home. After that, things were never the same. There was never any hunting trip to the Adirondacks or uniform shirt passed down. And so Mike took to hiding his trains under the mattress and never telling anybody anything.

"No," he said to Harold. "There's no conflict. You know everything you need to know."

11

AT A QUARTER after nine the next morning, Lynn headed out to her garden in the backyard in a ragged old T-shirt and gray sweatpants to pull up dahlia tubers and deadhead yarrow. A rare hour of having no particular place to go. Soon it would be time to start turning the soil over and putting the garden to bed for the winter.

She was forty-two now and old enough to know that the cycle of renewal didn't always follow decay. Some of the tomato plants had withered, leaving thin black stems like umbilical cords sticking out of the ground. Slugs had gotten to the squash this year, and the broccoli rabe never really took. Rabbits ate the radishes, and birds had pecked at the sunflowers and stolen the seeds, leaving the heads as blank as the faces of showroom dummies.

What most disturbed her, though, was the fact that deer had jumped over the eight-foot mesh fence and eaten some of her carrots, leaving stubs strewn around like small orange fingers.

She decided to ignore them for the moment and instead to dig deep into the dirt for the last of the heirloom potatoes, hoping the season hadn't been a total loss.

For a few seconds, she was back on Birch Lane, trying to rescue her mother's garden. The big stalky weeds sticking up amid those seventies Day-Glo flowers. She saw herself as a skinny hippie girl trying to step gingerly between the flower beds to break the weeds off. Not that Mom let it all go to hell at once. The multiple sclerosis crept up on all of them. That sudden tiredness at the A&P, then the numbness in the limbs and the lopsided staggering in the school parking lot that had all the other moms whispering that they always suspected Liz Stockdale was a bit of a lush. The embarrassment of defending her own mother in the girls' locker room (*She's not drinking, it's a disease!*) and the shame of resenting all the extra household tasks she had to take on. The folding of laundry, the hand-washing of dishes, going up and down the stairs with dinner on the tea tray, getting her sister ready for school, the clumsy raking of topsoil — all in a vain effort to somehow keep things together until Mom could maybe get back on her feet again. Instead of sinking deeper into her wheelchair by the garden, smoking a Newport, kicking her leg like a Rockette on disability and singing, *If they could see me now, that little gang of mine* . . .

Lynn remembered the crack in her father's voice as he shouted, *One of us has to have a life!* from the bedroom a few weeks before he moved out, unable to handle the strain. Well, okay then. At least one of them did end up having a life. One of them did end up having a husband, a career, two kids, and a house on the hill that Mom got to see before she died last year. Was it all absolute perfection? Of course not. But she was here on top of the hill, gathering the potatoes against her T-shirt, looking at her house, thinking about Barry's lips on the back of her neck, and hearing her mother's Newport crackle in the wind and her voice saying, *Didn't I tell you, baby?*

But then everything seemed to go quiet around her. A blue jay cut off its morning song midsquall, and a woodchuck scurried past. She listened for Eduardo and the other gardeners mowing the lawn in front, but for some reason the whine of their machines sounded like it was coming from miles away.

The house was surrounded by an acre of woods on three sides, with the fence marking the boundaries before the slopes. She saw a flicker of movement behind the tree line to her left and realized her wheelbarrow wasn't where she had left it.

"*Hello,*" she called out, dropping her potatoes and picking up a shovel.

A light breeze made maple leaves shiver like digitized pixels and swayed the clothes she'd put out on the line because the dryer was on the blink. A red-tailed hawk glided silently through the cloudless sky, its wings spread out against the sun.

"Hello!" She raised her voice, tightening her grip on the shovel and wondering where the gardeners could have gone.

Just a little bit down the slope to the right, the gate between the backyard and the gravel driveway was slightly ajar, though she distinctly remembered having closed it when she went to get the shovel from the garage. A chill crept up between her shoulder blades as she edged down the incline and saw an unfamiliar car in the driveway.

"Hey."

She whirled around with the shovel raised over her shoulder.

Mike Fallon put his hands up and laughed.

"You fucker," she said.

"Whoa. I didn't mean to scare you. I saw your Mexicans working out front, so I figured it was okay if I just came in."

He shielded his eyes, checking out her studio just a few yards past the garden.

"It's quite a spread you got. Your husband must be doing all right. He say he's a lawyer?"

"He provides." She lowered the shovel without putting it down.

It always made her uneasy, this suburban ritual of people coming over to your house and estimating the cost of everything. *Who did your garden? How much do they charge for that tile?* It was like having bitchy commandos descend on you.

"I see the deer got to your vegetables," he said, glancing over at the chewed-up carrot tops.

"Yeah, they're beautiful, but they're vermin."

"I noticed that's not much of a fence you got. I bet they jump right over it."

"Yeah." She brooded, thinking of the twelve hundred dollars they'd already spent. "Not as ugly as the stockade we used to have, but it's not getting the job done."

"I got a little side business, doing fences. Have you thought about solar panels? Give 'em a nasty little two hundred volts next time they try that high jump."

"What are you doing here, Mike?"

She noticed that he was dressed more neatly today, in pressed chinos and an ironed yellow Ralph Lauren shirt with a small red polo player over the left breast.

He wiped his brow with the back of his hand. "I've actually got some official business to take care of with you."

"Oh?" She rested the shovel against her leg.

"Have you seen Sandi Lanier lately?"

She crossed her arms. "Why do you want to know?"

"Were you supposed to have dinner with her the other night?"

She felt the tiny dorsal hairs on her neck stiffen slightly. "Who told you that?"

"She ever show up?"

"No. Look, what's this all about?"

She noticed the Doppler effect of the lawn mower in the front yard, fading and coming in again at the far edge of her hearing.

"I'm sorry to be the one to have to tell you this."

A small black circle throbbed inside her. "No way."

"The lady we found by the train station yesterday . . ."

"No fucking way."

The circle enlarged, and she raised her hands as if she was about to slap him.

"Jeff came in last night to file a missing person report . . ."

The circle became a heavy black ball, expanding, threatening to crush her lungs. She saw a flash of light among the trees, and her knees started to give way.

"We're pretty sure it's her," he was saying. "She's got the same scars and the tattoo on her ankle . . ."

She wondered if he'd actually just punched her in the stomach or if it only felt that way.

"This is not happening," she said.

The ground seemed to come rushing up and then fall away as if she had been dropped and then jerked back on a bungee cord.

"Hey, maybe you better sit down." He touched her arm. "You're starting to look a little pale."

The lawn mower faded back in, as fierce and noisy as an old air force bomber.

"Oh God . . ."

The bottom of her stomach squeezed, and a wave of nausea washed up through her chest.

"So you're telling me somebody killed her and threw her in the river like an old tire?" The ground came rushing up again.

"It appears that way." She touched his arm to steady herself and noticed how his wrists looked like they had small barbells inside them instead of bones.

I'm not going to faint. I'm not going to throw up. She willed herself to try to stand straight without his help.

"And her head was cut off?"

"We haven't located the head."

She stuck the shovel blade deep into the ground, balancing precariously and inhaling deeply.

"Who did this to her?"

"That's what we're trying to find out."

"I can't believe this." She felt herself start to wobble again, like a top losing centrifugal force. "She just beat cancer."

"I know."

She sucked air, trying to fight gravity. "I went with her for her last test in March. She'd just got the all-clear."

"These things never make sense."

"You know, I never even got to see her new house." A laugh and a sob tried to fit through her throat, like two fat people trying to get through a narrow doorway. "She kept putting me off, saying it wasn't ready yet. She wanted to have this grand unveiling . . ."

She remembered all those endless discussions about Thermador versus Miele built-in ovens, the questionable hegemony of Sub-Zero freezers and Viking ranges, and the pros and cons of mid-century furniture.

Then a light showed down the corridor of years, and she saw the two of them again as giggling gangly teenage girls, heaping bales of spaghetti into boiling water, jumping back from flames shooting up from the backyard grill, trying to make hamburgers for their ungrateful younger siblings in the little GE toaster oven. The two of them just looking at each other when that Eric Clapton riff came around on the radio and that husky voice intoned, *Motherless children have a hard time when mother is dead, Lord . . .* , and then Sandi rolling her eyes and saying, *Yeah, tell me about it, pal . . .*

The lawn mower rounded the side of the house, its mindless grind rising in pitch as she tried to wipe her eyes. She saw Mike looking past her, a great blue distance in his sunken eyes, as if he was waiting for her to get through this.

"Lynn," he said finally, "it's very important that we know if Sandi was having a problem with anybody lately."

"No. No. She never said anything like that."

She shut her eyes, trying to keep her thoughts in order even as the sound of the lawn mower scrambled them.

"Well, what'd you guys talk about last time you got together?"

"I don't know. It's hard for me to think straight. I feel like you just dropped a bomb on me. *What'd we talk about?*" She watched the clothes billowing on the line. "It'd been such a long time. She kept canceling on me because she said she had contractors coming over. That last time was, what? Maybe August, while the kids were in camp. What'd we say? God, I can't remember. The kids. Our lives. Baby-sitters. Pilates classes. Imus. This new restaurant on the Upper East Side that was thinking of hiring her to do some PR. How we went to these really good liberal arts schools and wound up making Halloween cupcakes at midnight."

The clothes sagged, and her jerry-built composure began to fall apart again. Sandi. She had almost gotten it together this time. All her life she'd been off by just a few degrees. Her teeth were always too big, and her hair was always too frizzy. In high school, she was always coming on a little too strong for most boys. They never got to see her loyal soul or her priceless Raquel Welch–as-Latin-spitfire imitation: *Wh-hut coood mek a maan do a theeng like dees . . .* Even after she got married and had the kids, she still struggled. Always felt guilty about not seeing the kids when she was working and then guilty about not bringing in any money once she'd quit. And then there'd been that spasm of craziness right after the lumpectomy, when she got the tattoo and the liposuction, as if she was going to start being a teenager again. But the last couple of times, she seemed so much more settled. Bragging about the kids' soccer, talking about the new house, and saying she was back on speaking terms with her father after years of refusing to have anything to do with him. She'd even given up on the idea of a nose job, saying that she finally understood it was a compliment when people called her "striking."

"She ever talk to you about her marriage?" Mike asked.

"Yeah, sure," she heard herself muttering like a derelict. "We talked about our husbands all the time."

"She say anything about having some trouble?"

She stopped and tried to get her thoughts aligned again. "I know that she and Jeff have had their problems, but who hasn't that's been married this many years?"

He looked at her a beat too long, clearly reading more into the remark than she'd intended.

"Don't you think?" she said, wanting his eyes off her face.

He rubbed his chin with his knuckles, and she heard Stieglitz barking from behind the screen door, wanting to be let out.

"Can you think of anybody who would have wanted to hurt her? Any running disputes with neighbors or financial problems?"

"No. I think Jeff's business is surviving, and her dad's loaded. And now that they're talking again, he can't stay away from the grandchildren, and she's going to go on vacation with . . ."

Her voice trailed off as she realized she was talking about Sandi in the present tense. The shockwave washed over her again. *We haven't located the head.* It was more than she could take in at the moment. The ground yo-yoed once more. She felt herself start to go dim.

"You're telling me this is real." She looked at him.

"Sure as I'm standing here." He touched her shoulder lightly.

Eduardo the gardener came back around the side of the house with his lawn mower and a pair of orange headphones clapped over his ears. The smell of chopped chlorophyll sprayed the air and whirring blades filled her head. Once again, she needed to sit down and secure the essentials. Call Barry. Call school to make sure the kids were okay. E-mail her sister and all her other friends to make sure none of them had mysteriously disappeared.

"Oh, shit." She turned back to Mike, as if she'd forgotten about him for a few seconds. "I almost didn't remember you knew her nearly as long as I did."

12

A RAZOR-THIN lookdown fish slithered by like a strip of living aluminum foil.

At that moment, Barry stood before the saltwater tank in the waiting room of the Montgomery-Young hedge fund. It was one of those expensive eight-foot-long five-hundred-gallon numbers equipped to perfectly re-create the environment and ecosystems from the bottom of the ocean, complete with orange sun coral, giant carpet anemones, and precured Fiji live rock.

In the thick tinted glass, he saw the reflection of Mark Young as he came around the reception desk to talk to him.

"Nice tank," Barry said, turning to introduce himself.

"We like it." Mark Young offered a quick tepid handshake.

He was a tapered blade of a man in a gabardine suit with sharp lapels and a narrow waist that seemed to suggest he was too busy eviscerating struggling companies to be bothered by trivialities like eating.

"So is that a black-tip reef shark?" Barry turned back as a sleek Cadillac of a fish glided by with silver sides and dead eyes.

"Certainly is." Mark came to stand beside him. "Nasty-looking fucker, isn't he?"

"He has a kind of sullen charm."

"Have you heard this expression, Jumping the shark?" Mark grinned, a deep U shape in his long taut face.

"Might've come up at some point, but I can't remember where."

"It actually comes from television." Mark Young wiped a light smudge off the glass. "Did you ever watch the show *Happy Days*?"

"With the Fonz and all that?" Barry shrugged. "I tuned out after *The Many Loves of Dobie Gillis*."

"Well, it was a pretty good show for a few years, and then they had this episode where the Fonz goes waterskiing in his black leather jacket and tries to jump over a shark. After that it was never the same. They lost all credibility. So now whenever we talk about a company that's going down the tubes, we say it's jumped the shark."

"Oh, yeah?"

"And we think you guys jumped the shark a long time ago."

Barry didn't answer immediately. Instead he stooped a little, with his hands on his knees in order to study a sluggish mottled blue-gray fish dwelling near the bottom.

"You know, I used to work in a corporate office that had a tank just like this in the conference room," he said. "It had a lot of these same fish too. Your unicorn tangs, your clown fish, your lion-fish and moray eels, your bird wrasses and chocolate chip stars and all that. It must be the same aquarium that services all of them."

"I don't know that much about it." Mark Young looked at the Patek Philippe on his wrist. "Somebody else handles the maintenance."

"I've always been interested in this one." Barry tapped the glass in front of the somnolent blue-gray fish, which lay there munching gravel with a mouth like Edward G. Robinson's. "It's a diamond goby. He's a bottom-feeder. See what he does? He just takes mouthfuls of gravel or whatever else falls his way, sucks all the bacteria off it, and then squirts it out of his gill pouches. You know why? Because he's too much of a pussy to go and hunt for himself."

"So, what can I do for you?" said Mark, straightening a brash purple tie with small gold links on it.

"Well, I figured since I seemed to be having trouble getting through to you with my phone calls and e-mails the last day or so, I might as well just take a stroll on up here."

He stood up, shoulders back, emphasizing the six inches he had over the short seller.

"I hear you've been giving us hell on the Internet and CNBC."

"No more than you deserve." Mark bounced lightly on the balls of his feet, clearly not intimidated. "You guys way overstated your potential for growth. Twenty-seven million in your second year of operations? I don't know what drugs you're on, but they're stronger than whatever you're making."

"We missed some of our numbers, there's no question about that . . ."

"You did a helluva lot more than that. You went from fifty-one to sixteen in less than twelve months."

"It's been a volatile market." Barry shrugged. "Everybody knows that. But things were starting to pick up this quarter until you shit-bombed us."

"Excuse me," Mark cut him off, raising his voice slightly. "If you're a public company, it's all about debate and disclosures. You guys didn't get the overseas contracts you promised your investors. You've been hiding recurring expenses as capital spending. And worst of all, your drugs don't deliver. You've been stuck in Phase Two trials for Chronex since March."

"That's because we felt we needed to broaden the study group," said Barry.

He was aware of the receptionists watching them, two brightly attired dissatisfied middle-aged white women muttering into headsets before a late-period de Kooning abstract. The audience. He realized they'd seen Mark do this act before.

"Look," he said, "you're certainly entitled to your opinions. What you're not entitled to do is spread false rumors and allegations to drive our price down."

"We do the best research on the Street." Mark's Adam's apple went up and down like the pump action of a shotgun. "We know more about the companies we look into than most of the major institutional investors. Sometimes more than their own executives. So I'd suggest to you, Mr. Schulman, that a company that sends its general consul trudging around town to try and stifle legitimate criticism is wasting its investors' time and money and doesn't have much of a future."

"And I suggest to you that you work harder on getting your facts straight."

Barry reached into the brown Coach attaché case at his side and pulled out a small stack of court papers. "You have a report on your Web site saying our company stands to lose fifty million dollars in the lawsuit over the squirrel monkey patent," he said.

"They're not your monkeys," Mark Young replied stiffly. "Nieman and Tsyrlin developed them in their lab at MIT. They were the ones who figured out how to give the monkeys Alzheimer's for the experiments. By the time this suit's over, they're going to be taking over your office and picking out the new curtains."

"I am now giving you a half-dozen depositions and research papers from six of the top geneticists in the country, telling you that's not true." Barry thrust some of the documents at him that Lisa Chang had helped him gather. "I've got the best people from Yale, Berkeley, and Princeton on the record saying these claims are worthless. This case will probably never make it to trial. You now have this information in your possession. So if you continue to spread these false allegations about us on your Web site and on TV, I guarantee you that we will sue you for slander, and when we win, we will not only pick out the new curtains in this office but the new fish in your tank."

A half-smile flickered across Mark's bony face and then faded. Clearly, here was a man who was up for a little midmorning jousting. In a different part of his life, Barry would've enjoyed going one on one with him.

"Snake oil is still snake oil," Mark said. "You guys said you were going to get a product to market within four years that would reduce amyloid plaques and tangles in the human brain, and you're nowhere near that. And in the meantime, you're about to get lapped by half a dozen other drugs. Why don't you just admit the jig is up and shut the circus down?"

"Listen." Barry lowered his voice. "I've read some of your research, and I know you're a sharp guy. But this is not my first rodeo either. I've got my own money tied up in this company."

"I'm sorry to hear that." Mark laughed. "It's usually better to be the knave than the fool."

"I know we've had a few setbacks, but I believe in what we're doing. Let me tell you something. My old man was the strongest guy I ever knew. He was the only white store owner who didn't move off his block after the riots in Newark. He rebuilt the place with his own hands, and when they came to burn it down a second time, he stood outside and said, *Kiss my ass, motherfucker.*" He decided to omit the detail that Dad had ended up bagging groceries at a Pathmark in Nutley after the second store failed. "And I saw this man slip away right before my eyes because of Alzheimer's. So believe me, this isn't any scam."

"Then why did your CEO sell off four thousand shares of his own stock right before it fell to thirty this summer?" Mark asked.

"Bullshit."

"No, it's true," Mark said evenly. "Ross Olson dumped about a fifth of his holdings in August. He did it through a third-party sale, but our researchers picked up on it. Hey, it's not against the law. People need the cash sometimes. Or maybe they just want to spread the risk around . . ."

Barry's tongue stuck to the roof of his mouth. From the corner of his eye, he saw a blue triggerfish tear off a piece of coral and start chewing so loudly that its jaw could be heard snapping through the glass.

The cell phone rang in his breast pocket. He took it out long enough to see that it was Lynn calling and then put it back again.

"Look," he said, staying poker-faced, "we're in it for the long haul. We've got drugs in the pipeline that we haven't even started to tell people about. You want to keep betting against us and get yourself caught in a short squeeze, be my guest."

Just the mention of a squeeze, in which Mark would lose money because stock price suddenly shot up, made the cords in his neck bulge slightly. A tiny piece of coral fell out of the triggerfish's mouth and drifted down toward the goby at the bottom.

"I just don't know why a bright young guy like you spends all his time ripping other people's companies apart when they're trying to make something worthwhile," said Barry.

"Well, then, I'll tell you why." Mark stood back, planting his feet firmly. "It's because there's a lot of crappy companies out there, taking money away from legitimate investors. Or, in a case like yours, steering money away from other companies doing serious work. You were asking about the fish tank before. It's the same thing. There's an ecosystem. The wrong kind of bacteria gets in, it'll poison all your fish. You need a few bottom-feeders to eat the excess and keep the tank clean. It may not be pretty, but we get the job done. And if we keep a little something for ourselves in the meantime, what's it to you?"

Barry watched the goby swallow the coral, along with a few gravel stones, and then squirt the residue out through its gill pouches, oblivious to the kaleidoscope of Cuban hogs, yellow tangs, lion-fish, angel flames, and red-breasted mattress thrashers circling above it.

"Hey, that's all well and good," he said. "But don't you think that once you start paying more for your fish tank than you do for your secretaries, you maybe lose just a foot or two off the moral high ground?"

He turned and saw the receptionists giggling into their headsets.

"I guess you know your way out." Mark nodded toward the elevators.

13

STILL FEELING DIZZY and vaguely sick, as though she'd been inhaling paint thinner, Lynn went fifty in the Saab along the narrow little roads climbing higher into the West Hills, suspension rattling, springs squeaking on the turns. She made the quick right off Prospect and found the brawny new center hall colonial at the end of the cul-de-sac called Love Lane, a great gift-wrapped Macy's box of a house, a run-on sentence of a house, a house she'd really hoped to like, with huge black shutters, tall Greek revival windows, gables the size of small planes, and Georgian columns on the front porch.

She parked halfway into the long circular driveway, jumped out, and raced up the steps to the front door. Even though the family had been there since August, Sandi had never invited Lynn in, saying she didn't want her oldest friend to see the place until absolutely everything was ready. As if Lynn was going to bring a camera and a writer from *Architectural Digest*. She rang the bell, a stately remote chime barely audible under the bank alarm wailing in her mind.

After a few seconds, the door opened, and Isadora, Sandi's seven-year-old, in a black leotard top worn inside out, a white tutu, and a pair of black jeans and untied Keds, looked up at her. A silver lamé scarf was tied haphazardly over a long uncombed brown ponytail.

"Where's Mommy?" she said impatiently, as if Lynn had been hiding her.

"Um . . ."

Lynn's mind emptied out. What were you supposed to say to a child under these circumstances? Her eyes probed into the darkness of the foyer, hearing the echo of voices from deeper within the house.

"I don't know, sweetie." She touched Isadora's crusty white cheek and saw no one had washed the girl's face yet this morning. "Is your daddy around?"

"Yeeeahhhh . . ." She rolled her eyes with the same premature exasperation that Sandi had at that age, as if she already knew the best she'd get out of the men in her life.

"He's up in his office," she said, a slight lisp whistling through the gap in her front teeth. "Still on the phone. *Blah, blah, blah.*"

She rolled her eyes again to show she'd given up trying to get his attention. God, she really did look just like her mother. Lynn shuddered a little, thinking about the sorrows that awaited this child.

"Has anybody given you breakfast today?"

"I made myself a waffle in the toaster." Isadora smiled proudly. "I made one for Dylan too. *With* butter."

"Your little brother's lucky to have you."

"That's what I keep telling him."

Lynn stepped across the threshold and closed the door behind her. Dylan, the five-year-old, was more brittle than his sister, always had been. Kept his mother on bed rest for the last four months of her pregnancy and still slipped out six weeks early. Lynn remembered seeing him under the bilirubin lights in the Neonatal Intensive Care Unit, a scrawny little red chicken fighting for his life in the incubator. He'd been a little neurasthenic ever since, dragging one of his mom's old silk slips to nursery school as a security blanket. So how the hell was he supposed to make it through the next seventy-five years?

"Would you run upstairs and let Daddy know I'm here?" Lynn said, resisting the urge to scoop the little girl up in her arms and hug her, lest she get frightened by Mommy's friend starting to cry for no reason.

"Okay. And then will you play chase with me?"

"What? Oh, yeah. Sure."

All right, smile. Act normal. Don't let on that her world is about to disintegrate. Children need routine.

She watched Sandi's daughter run down the long dim hall, the plastic ends of her untied laces scatting on the onyx floor. She stopped at the foot of a stairway and did a little splay-armed, stiff-legged twirl before the newel post. Shafts of sun poured through a skylight above her, shining down on her upturned face and turning her skirt into a fine diaphanous mist. And for the only time this morning, Lynn wished she had her camera with her so she could somehow freeze this last careless moment and give it back to the girl years from now when she would surely need it again.

She listened for the scampering of feet up the stairs and then allowed herself to sink a little, relieved of having to prop up this cheerful facade. Why wasn't the girl in school today anyway? Hadn't Jeff thought of asking one of Sandi's friends to take her? God, the last thing she would want would be her kids hanging around the house waiting in vain for her for the rest of their lives.

She moved cautiously down the hall, drawn by the sound of a TV droning. The echo of her footsteps seemed to amplify her grief. She always thought of Sandi as being so busy and eclectic that she was sure there'd be some off-the-wall touches, like carved wooden duck decoys or her oil canvas of Mr. T in a ruffled Elizabethan collar or her acrylic portrait of six great American first ladies dressed as astronauts. Instead there was just cold austere space, bland beige wallpaper, and a twenty-foot-high domed ceiling above the stairs.

She pictured Sandi with a man's hand over her mouth. Someone had held her down and cut her throat.

Had she understood what was happening? Had she begged? Had she thought of the children just before her head was severed? It was an image that Lynn didn't want in her brain, but it kept coming back at her.

She rounded the corner and saw that the living room had scarcely more furniture. The women's morning talk show *The View* played on the four-foot-wide Sony flat screen against the wall, Barbara Walters holding forth with memories of Lady Di. A floor lamp stood uncovered in the corner, its bare bulb making a soft singing sound and revealing ghostly outlines of places where chairs and couches had been pushed against the walls. Dylan lay on the cream rug next to the long glass coffee table, playing with scuffed plastic Pokémon toys.

"*Peeeeek-aaaahh*," he screeched in a demented tinny voice, wagging a stumpy yellow mutant cat at an orange dragon-troll. "*Peeeekk-ahh-choo!!*"

"Charizard, SLASH!" he answered himself in the deepest baritone he could muster. "Fire spit! Get back, or I'll lock you in your room and never let you out."

"Whaddaya doing, Dyl?"

She knelt down beside him, a little catch in her throat as she remembered Clay at this age, playing on the floor with his Teenage Mutant Ninja Turtles. Donatello. Michelangelo. The names were so much more poetic then, weren't they? And weren't Pokémon sort of old hat anyway? She was surprised he didn't have newer toys.

"Dyl?"

A straight ash-blond curtain of hair refused to turn and acknowledge her.

"I'm going to put you in a cage and make you my slave," he nattered on in his heavy-breathing dragon voice. *"Peek-ahhhhh!"*

She noticed the higher voice edging toward hysteria.

"Dylan, are you okay, honey?"

"Shut up, you stupid bitch."

She lurched back, as if he'd just turned in on her with dripping yellow fangs.

"What'd you just say?"

He ignored her, off in his own world again. "Charizard, flamethrower! Hyyuhhhh!"

"Dylan, what'd you just say to me?"

A squished moppet face finally turned around with a ring of syrup around the mouth. "Will you play Chinese checkers with me, Lynn?"

"Um, sure. But, Dyl? Who did you hear talk like that?"

She remembered Sandi and Jeff prattling on like old fogies about using bad language in front of the children, even though they both swore like teamsters when the kids weren't around.

"Inspector Gadget, *goynk, goynk, goynk!* Inspector Gadget, *goynk, goynk . . .*"

He picked up a dismembered robot leg and waved it in her face, almost as if he was warning her off. A cheapo plastic made-in-Taiwan movie tie-in from a McDonald's Happy Meal a couple of years ago.

"Dylan, put that down for a second. I'm trying to talk to you . . ."

"Inspector Gadget . . ."

"Dylan, *please . . .*"

She shook her head in frustration, and for a second her eyes lingered on a light brown-red smear near the phone jack on the baseboard.

"Hey, Lynn, thanks for coming."

She whipped around and saw Jeff in a blue bathrobe, standing in the wide proscenium doorway behind her and looking like he'd been up all night giving blood. His jowls were heavy, and the middle of his face was dull and smeared-looking, as if someone had tried to rub it away. A lock of hair lapped over his brow like an exhausted dog's tongue.

"Jeff, oh my God . . ."

She got up to throw her arms around him as he stood there, stiff and wavering, smelling of sweat and Smirnoff.

The truth was, she'd always felt the same way about Jeff as she had about the house: that she'd really wanted to like him. Sandi had always had *such* terrible taste in boys, going all the way back to high school. There'd been Dougie Mason, the back-up quarterback, who always had two or three girls on the side. Then Larry the Mooch, who always made her pay for everything. And worst of all, that dunce Sir Jimbo of Piscataway, that horseback-riding idiot she'd met at the traveling Renaissance fair where she'd worked for six months after she flipped out at Sarah Lawrence. So Lynn had been thrilled back in '93 when Sandi called her and told her that she'd finally met her Barry, a handsome successful Harvard-educated "Love God" she called him. In fact, Jeff was kind of a stud then. His chin was a little firmer, the union of man and hair a little more certain. But even during the first dinner at Bouley, she'd thought there was something a little young and unformed about him. That he was not quite a full-grown man yet but still a boy collecting baseball cards in his father's garage.

Now she gave him an extra hug, silently urging him to bear up.

"I came as soon as I heard," she said, taking his hand and leading him into the hall, wondering if the police had already been here.

"Lynn, I'm such a mess."

"I know. All the way over here, I was telling myself, 'This is a dream. You're going to wake up any minute.'"

And this was only the first day's sadness. From Mom's death last year, she knew grief had its own inevitable arc. The shock and numbness, the faltering effort to carry on for everyone else's sake, and then the way your mind keeps circling back unexpectedly. A Post-it note on a refrigerator or an old phone number scribbled in familiar handwriting on the back of an envelope could plunge you into months of despair. All this and more awaited poor Jeff. At least she'd had a chance to prepare herself in her mother's last days.

"She was the love of my life," Jeff said. "What am I going to do without her?"

"You're going to lean on the rest of us. You're going to pull your friends around you."

She squeezed his hand tightly, trying to send a stronger pulse to his heart, and noticed how small and clammy his palm felt, almost like a little girl's.

"So, what have you told the kids?" She sniffed.

"Nothing. I haven't figured out what to say." His eyes were burned-out flashbulbs behind his glasses. "I'm still trying to get my mind around what happened. I talked to her Sunday afternoon on the cell phone. I told her I was taking the four-o'clock shuttle from Boston so I could see the kids before they went to sleep Monday night. And then I get home and there's no sign of her. No message. No nothing. Just your voice on the machine."

She felt a stirring at the base of her spine and realized she was starting to grow a little impatient with him. Unfair, she knew. The man was still reeling, just like she was. You couldn't hurry him through this. His wife had been slaughtered. Someone had slashed her throat and shredded her larynx. They'd left her children motherless. The impatience gave way to churning revulsion again.

There were children running around this house with unwashed faces. The baby-sitter clearly wasn't here yet, so someone had to start thinking about dinner for them.

"Look, you have to tell the kids *something*," she said, realizing that she had to think about dinner for her own brood as well. "Izzy still thinks her mother's coming home."

"What am I going to say to them, Lynn? God, *I* can't even deal with it."

His voice bounced down the empty hallway, and she looked around, making sure neither of the children was in earshot.

"First of all, you're going to keep your voice down." She took a deep breath. "Second of all, you're going to spare them all the horrible details. Because, frankly, they don't need to know and they won't want to know. But don't lie to them. They're tougher than you think, and they'll never believe you again if they see you've tried to fool them. Just answer their questions as honestly as you can without frightening them and let them know you're not going any-where."

She remembered hearing a kindly old detective from the 43rd Precinct give a grieving Dominican grandmother the same advice in the Bronx after her daughter had been found raped and stabbed to death on a rooftop, leaving five children for her to raise on her own. *Let them know you're not going anywhere.* She found herself struggling through the flood tide of grief to get to him and keep him from drowning.

"You do it," Jeff said suddenly.

"What?"

"You're stronger than me. They've known you all their lives. They trust you. You tell them."

"Jeff, you are their father. No one else can do this. It has to come from you."

He sagged against the wall, and his bathrobe fell open slightly, revealing a gut that had added a small front porch since the last time she saw it and a pair of red Jockey-style underwear. She averted her eyes, not quite ready for this much humanity.

"I know. You're right." He straightened up, trying to gird him-self. "But they're never going to get over this. *I'm* never going to get over this."

She felt a shimmer go through her body, her sadness shading inch by inch into anger. She told herself that it was a natural animal response against the viciousness done to her friend, a girl she shared a bed with when she was six and a suede skirt with when she was twenty-four.

"So have the police been here?" she said, trying to maintain her outward calm. "What have they told you?"

"I went in last night to give a missing person report, and then they called me this morning. The chief. I guess he knew Sandi from school or something. He was very . . . decent about it."

"Harold's a good man." Lynn nodded.

"He asked if they could send somebody by in a few minutes to collect some of her things and dust for fingerprints to make sure it's her, but he seemed pretty certain." He shriveled again, like a balloon losing all its air. "God, I can't believe anybody would do this . . ."

The brown-red smear on the baseboard appeared in Lynn's mind again. She wanted to go back and look at it, but she didn't dare. It couldn't be what she thought it was, could it? Other people's memories were triggered by words, hers by pictures. Where had she seen that exact shade before? A mashed-up yam Hannah had flung at the wall of their 10th Street apartment when she was a baby? Something awful in Clay's underpants? Evidence of forbidden M&M's before dinner?

"I haven't even started thinking about how to bury her," Jeff was saying. "And I think it's the Jewish tradition that you have to have the funeral right away . . ."

Another image flared in Lynn's mind. A tenement hallway. A crime scene photo taken on assignment. Dried blood on white cinder block. The *News* hadn't used it. No color presses back then.

"So now I'll have to call her father and stepmother in the city and all the relatives in Florida . . ."

"You want me to make some of those calls for you?"

"No, you're right." He banged the back of his head lightly against the wall, as if reminding himself of what he had to do. "I've got to try and get it together here. For the kids. That's what it's all about. Right? I've got to be strong for the kids."

"They need you, Jeff." She reached out and squeezed his elbow harder than she'd meant to. "But don't forget, the rest of us are here for *you*. Anything you need. Call me anytime. I'll help with the funeral, and I'll make travel arrangements for the family. I'm serious. Use me. *Lean on me.* I'll come and cook for the kids. Or they can come and stay with us. We've got plenty of room. Sandi would have done the same for me in a heartbeat."

She pushed the sepia image of the blood smear out of her mind and tried to think of something she could make and bring over later so the kids wouldn't starve. Lasagna. Pot roast. Lamb chops. Did these kids eat anything other than chicken fingers and French fries?

"Is there anything you need right away?" she asked, desperate to help, to do anything to alleviate this sense of suffocating helplessness.

"How about a new wife to help me raise Dyl and Izzy?"

Her jaw went slack. "Jeff . . ."

"I'm sorry. I'm sorry." He put up his hand. "I don't know what got into me. I'm still in shock."

"I understand."

She heard a car pull up outside and grind to a halt. The squeaky cry of a door opening and then a brisk aluminum slam. The stately bell rang once more.

"I think that's the police," he said.

"You want me to stick around while they're here?"

"No, I'll just put on a video for the kids. It'll be fine. I rented *Bambi*."

"Did you?" She looked stricken, remembering what happened to the mother in the movie.

"Oh, shit. You're right. Bad choice. Maybe I'll just put on *Yellow Submarine* instead. They always like that."

14

"SO WHO WAS the *mujer bonita?*"

Paco sat on the rim of a tub in an upstairs bathroom five minutes later, watching Mike Fallon dust the sink counter for fingerprints.

"Who? The one we just saw on the porch going out?"

Paco wrung his hand as if he'd just touched something hot. "I seen you talking to her before at the train station, right?"

"An old flame of mine." Mike shrugged, delicately brushing the dark powder across the white surface. "You know how that is."

"*Ai, pappi!* You put all my old ladies together in a room, they'd form a coalition. Women United Against Paco. They'd form sub-committees to talk about different things I did that pissed them off."

"Hey, you guys got everything you need in there?" Jeff Lanier called out from the bedroom just outside the door.

Mike's eyes fell on a red toothbrush, and his stomach dropped, realizing her DNA was in its bristles. He thought of tagging and bagging it, but then Paco would ask how the hell he knew it was hers. *Damage control.* That's what it was all about today.

"Ah, we'll just be another couple of minutes, sir," Paco answered in his hoarse Bronx accent. "Sorry for the inconvenience."

Mike shook his head and mouthed the word *asshole* as he went back to brushing and tapping powder out of his little vial, watching latent patterns beginning to emerge as whorls.

Say something. Don't say anything. He'd had a terrible night and a worse morning. For twelve hours, he'd been steadily replaying last night's conversation with Harold every fifteen minutes, second-guessing himself, seeing the obvious places where he could have given himself a little more breathing room. But, no. *You know every-*

thing you need to know. Why didn't he just find himself a nice tight iron maiden to climb into?

"See this, man?" Paco leaned over the edge of the tub and touched a little silver nozzle in the side. "They got a Jacuzzi right here in the bathroom. Think they got a sauna too?"

Mike ignored him, patiently sifting grains across the white surface, waiting for more of the dark patterns to appear next to the sink with the shiny brass basin.

He remembered how large the Castlemans' bathroom used to seem to him, when in truth it was probably half this size. He could still picture the white marble floor, the deep sunken bathtub, the greenish Jean Naté bottle with the black ball on top that looked like the dot over an *i*, the white Lancôme powder puff on the sink counter, the potpourri basket, the individual paper hand towels with flower designs draped elegantly over the brass rack, the little pink and purple seashell soaps, and the space-age toilet so clean and shiny that he felt guilty just squatting on it.

His mother used to clean the place twice a week when she'd come by to help take care of the house and the kids for Mrs. Castleman on High Plains Road. Years later, it would finally dawn on Michael that the occasional seashell nugget and flowered hand towel that he later saw in their bathroom at home were items she'd spirited away from her employer, at a rate of about one every two weeks.

Not that he blamed her for wanting things they had. The Castleman kids, Bobby and Erica, looked like Kennedys. They played chess and took riding lessons. They had an old-fashioned player piano in the living room, a refrigerator that made its own ice cubes, a clay tennis court in the backyard. Everything in the house had that fresh new-catalog smell. He remembered going over there when he was eight and noticing the dirt under his fingernails and realizing he'd never heard of this science show *Nova* that Bobby kept talking about. Erica, who was a year younger than him, killed him at Scrabble with words like *franchise* and *gullible.*

"I'll tell you what," said Paco, opening a Ziploc bag and blowing into it. "I get a little bit ahead on my support payments, I'm gonna put all that shit in my bathroom in Port Chester. My kids would love it, man. When we stayed with their grandparents in Florida, they'd spend all fuckin' day in that Jacuzzi. I worried their little *cojones* were gonna get boiled . . ."

"Hey, as long as you're sitting there, why don't you try and see if you can snag a pubic hair from around the drain so we have some fibers to work with?"

Paco curled his lip in distaste as he pulled on his latex gloves. "But then who's gonna get the sample of *his* pubes so we know what to compare it to?"

"Ask not what your supervisor can do for you; ask what you can do for your supervisor."

Mike put the brush down for a minute and went to look out the door, making sure Jeff Lanier had left the bedroom.

"So, what do you think?" Paco asked sotto voce.

Mike listened for a moment, making sure he heard the husband talking to his kids downstairs. "I think I'm gonna take a look around their bedroom."

He pissed in the Laniers' toilet, flushed, and then stepped across the threshold and sniffed deeply. A red incense candle sat unlit on an Early American cherrywood chest of drawers. The white linen canopy sagged slightly over the four-poster bed with green wall sconces and a red-and-green Persian rug underneath. The ceilings were high, and the closets were big enough for Volkswagens. He turned his attention to the bookcase across the room and saw that its shelves were equally divided between Oprah choices and the kind of meaty World War Two volumes Dad always fell asleep with on his chest. But at the very end of the top row he spotted a familiar slim blue spine. The diary. Just sitting there like an eyeball staring back at him from the shelf.

"You know, I really like what they did with this room, man." Paco moved into the doorway beside him. "It's got a lot of light and space. And the wall sconces and window treatments really warm it up."

"It's all her." Mike sniffed.

"Yeah, how do you know?"

He walked over to the cherry dresser and pretended to study the lacquered Japanese jewelry box on top.

"Hey, bro," Paco said quietly, "we gotta tread lightly here. We don't got a warrant. We're just supposed to be collecting hair and fingerprint samples. Anything else we pick up this time is gonna get thrown out of court."

"I know the law, Paco. You don't have to school me."

He turned and dropped down into a squat, as if what he really cared about was under the bed.

"Nice house, though," Paco sighed, going to check out the valance and detail around the windows.

"Big, that's for sure."

The diary. He'd completely forgotten about it. He remembered asking her why she had to write everything down in the first place. Wasn't she afraid her husband or somebody else would see it? *Who cares?* she'd said. *At least then I might get some attention.* At the time, he'd put it down to the usual bellyaching, never thinking she'd do any real damage with a pen. But now she had him spooked, and he realized that he might have to look for her laptop as well, just in case she didn't delete all her old e-mails.

"The lady I'm hooked up with now, she's after me to get a bigger place." Paco yawned. "She got three kids of her own, almost grown. And they wild, man. They need a lot of space. *I* need a lot of space. We livin' in two bedrooms, man, and I fuckin' hate it. I got J.Lo and Christina Aguilera screeching in my ears at two in the morning. Fuck that shit, man. I want a garden. I want to grow roses and, whaddayacallem, rhododendrons big as fuckin' water buffalo. I want an island in my kitchen the size of San Juan. Say, you gonna let me know if you see a head down there, won't you?"

"I'll try and mention it."

Mike stood up and smoothed the wrinkles from his trousers, trying to guide his thoughts through the heavy traffic in his mind.

"So how you liking my boy downstairs?" Paco dropped his voice into a whisper.

"I'm liking him okay."

"Gave his old lady the big house with the big kitchen, though."

"And hardly anything in it. You notice that?" Mike listened, making sure he heard Lanier downstairs on the kitchen phone. That was at least one obstacle out of the way. "Except for this room and the kids' rooms, the house is barely furnished. He's got a great big sunroom downstairs that's totally empty except for a card table. So, what does that tell you?"

"You think he got in over his head?"

"Wouldn't be the first one. Lotta people living beyond their means these days. Big house, big problems."

"He told me his company was doing okay down at the station."

"Yeah, how about that?" Mike grinned. "Maybe we ought to check out his cash flow. See what else that leads to."

Paco stayed by the window, a day's worth of stubble grown out on his head.

"See that Benz four-by-four in the garage?" he said. "Man, that's a sweet ride."

"If you don't mind emptying the kids' college savings."

Mike shook his head, trying to think of how to get his partner out of the room for a few minutes. A diary. Fuck. AND a laptop. Whatever happened to discretion? Whatever happened to just sucking it up and taking it? Why did everyone go around these days bursting to tell their secrets as if they were about to get booked on some talk show Freakfest.

"So let me ask you something, man." Paco looked back at him, fingering his earring. "You said you went out with that little fox we saw on the porch."

"Yeah, so?"

"And she's like a friend of the lady who lived here?"

"Yeah, what's your point, Paco?" Mike felt his back teeth come together, not liking where this was heading.

"So did you know our victim here too?"

"Yeah, sure." Crown and enamel began to grind and scrape. "Didn't Harold tell you that? We all knew one another in school."

"Fuck, man. I didn't know that. What's up with that?"

"Are we having a problem here?" he asked, pausing and letting the silence between them become a weapon.

"Well, that's fucked-up." Paco's goatee became a long V. "Your victim and your investigator knowing each other."

A cartoon sycophant's voice brayed, "*No, Your Blueness*," downstairs.

"We're in a small town," Mike said slowly. "Less than twenty thousand people live here."

"I understand, but *que le pasa?* Come on, how's it going to look when we go to state court and . . ."

Mike held the Ice Man stare, allowing the silence to freeze and harden, even as he imagined the laptop screen starting to pulse a bright blue aura from somewhere in the room.

"Look, I've been with this department almost twenty years," he said. "You've got a little over eighteen months. If you don't like the way we do things, why don't you just get the fuck out of here?"

"You guys almost done?" Jeff Lanier appeared in the doorway with a black mobile phone cradled to his ear.

The detectives shot each other recriminating looks, neither of them having heard him come back upstairs.

"Five minutes, sir." Paco held up a rubber-gloved hand.

"I thought you were only looking in the bathroom." Jeff's eyes narrowed.

Both Paco and Mike gazed down at their shoes, like parents caught arguing by the children.

"We just stepped out to get some air for a second." Mike glanced at the amber prescription bottle on the bedside table.

Jeff opened his mouth to protest, but his son called out from downstairs, asking his dad to come sit with him through the scary parts of the video, and he stalked off grumbling into the phone.

"Think he heard us talking before?" Paco looked out the door after him, making sure he was gone.

"I don't know," Mike muttered. "Let's just wrap this up."

It was taking more and more effort not to look over at the bookcase. Did she or didn't she? He could just leave the diary there and see what happened once they got a warrant. But that would be a little like leaving in a brain tumor and seeing whether it turned out to be malignant. Once it got vouchered as evidence, it would be part of the official record, and there'd be no pulling it back.

"Hey, man, *lo siento*." Paco raised a clenched fist to show solidarity. "I don't wanna fight witchoo. *No vale la pena.*"

"Whatever."

"We just have to learn to respect each other. Okay?"

"Yeah, sure."

Without warning, Paco suddenly grabbed Mike's right hand and snared his fingers in a soul shake, leaning forward to bump shoulders and clapping him heartily on the back with his free hand. Mike stiffened in the half-embrace, not wanting anyone this close right at the moment.

"Okay, we're good, we're good." He pulled back from the newbie and straightened himself. "All for one, and one for all."

"Todo sigue bien."

"Look," said Mike, "why don't you go downstairs and ask him if we can get access to both their credit card records so we can track their movements and purchases over the last few days. I'll be down in a minute to see if I can get the kids to talk to me while you have him occupied."

"What do you think it'll take for us to get real probable cause to give this place a good toss?"

"I'm not sure, but you'll let me know if you see a hacksaw with blood all over it."

"Yeah, right . . ."

He watched Paco leave the room, listened for the sound of his feet on the stairs going down, and then grabbed the diary off the shelf. He stuck it inside his jacket, zipped up the front, and started to look around for the laptop in earnest.

15

AS THE CAB made the turn into the driveway on Grace Hill Road, Barry was unpleasantly surprised to see the mailbox lying on its side with its little silver door wide open like a sleeping man's mouth. He cursed under his breath, remembering how he'd dug that hole deep in the dirt and pounded the post in with a sledgehammer. And then some suburban cretin knocks it down to impress his troglodyte friends. Brilliant. They couldn't have done it just by leaning out a car window with a baseball bat. Some genius probably stopped the car, got out, and strained his back trying to uproot it.

He gave the driver seven dollars for bringing him up from the station and then climbed out and shoved the post back in, thinking he'd fix it properly over the weekend. He trudged up the driveway, pausing inside the gate to pick up the pair of sunglasses that had fallen off Slam the garden gnome. Then he looked at his house, considering the distance he'd traveled. Crickets were just coming out, and streaming lights from the dining room softened the evening. He watched his family go through their familiar movements without him, like figures in an antique music box. Clay chugging Diet Coke straight from a twenty-ounce bottle; Hannah carefully spooning out wheat germ onto whatever meatless dairy-free vegan meal she was eating, while Lynn moved around the table, carrying heaping bowls and blue glasses. He wondered if that first man he'd seen falling from the North Tower that morning, his tie flapping silently in the wind, had had such a vision right before he hit the ground.

Taking a deep breath, he put the shades back on the gnome,

strode across the yard, and walked in through the front door, as if he was just coming back from a short practice.

"I have returned," his voice rang out as he closed the door behind him, put down his briefcase, and opened his arms.

With a slight pang, he remembered how the Munchkins used to scurry out to greet their mayor when they were small. Now, only Stieglitz trotted over to jump up and hump his leg.

"All right, down." He pushed the dog away. "Daddy doesn't need that kind of love."

They were arguing in the dining room just off the front hall. Hannah's voice a high tense pizzicato against her mother's low, patiently bowed counterpoint.

"You're such a hypocrite," his daughter was saying. "I haven't done anything that you didn't do when you were my age. I bet you went to the city every other weekend when you were a senior."

"I certainly did not."

"Hey, what's going on?" Barry walked into the room, stripped off his jacket, and draped it carefully across the straight-backed chair at the head of the table.

"Mom's being full of shit again."

"Hey." He rolled up his sleeve and drew back his hand, a halfhearted gesture toward Old World discipline. His father would've knocked him halfway across the room for talking to his mother that way.

"Your daughter wants to sleep over Saturday night in the city with some of her so-called friends," Lynn explained, looking sallow and drawn. "But she can't give me the phone number of the people she's staying with so I can talk to the parents and make sure someone responsible is going to be there."

"That's not true," Hannah said, flicking back her white streak. "I gave you Joanne's mother's office e-mail."

"Which, strangely, she hasn't responded to, even though I left her a message three hours ago."

"Well, *she* works."

"As opposed to?"

Barry gave a small groan, knowing there would be no peace once they got into the subject of work, the Bermuda Triangle of mother-child relationships.

"I think your mother's just concerned about you going into the city with everything else that's going on." He came over and kissed Hannah on top of the head, remembering how she used to sit on his lap and let him read *Go, Dog. Go!* to her. "She just wants you to be safe."

"Oh, Dad, we're not going anywhere near the bridges or the Empire State Building or any of those places. It's a Friends of the Earth organizational meeting. I don't think anyone's going to fly a plane into a building on Ninety-fourth and West End."

"You're still going to be coming through Grand Central Station." Lynn's jaw locked. "Barry, back me up on this *please.*"

He heard the scales tipping in her voice and was reminded he should've returned her call earlier today, instead of waiting until she was out picking Clay up from karate. "It's important," she'd said in her message. He looked over and was surprised to see that her face was puffy and a little warped-looking, as if he was seeing her through a rain-streaked windshield.

"Hey, what's the matter?" he said.

"I can't protect you all the time." She turned on Hannah, her voice choking as if there were stones in her throat. "Don't you understand? You have to learn to take care of yourself and make the right decisions."

Clay, never able to handle the sight of his mother upset, looked over at Barry, his little man's face on a big man's body scrunched up in confusion.

"I'm not always going to be there for you," Lynn was saying.

"Why? Where are you going?" Barry stood with a hand on the back of Hannah's chair, studying her and realizing something major had changed in the thirteen hours since he'd last been in the house.

This is how it happens. You're away at work five, six, seven days a week, and little by little the ones you love turn into other people while you're not looking.

"Is there something we need to talk about in private?" he asked.

Lynn nodded and started to rise, leaving a tangled pile of spaghetti puttanesca steaming on her plate.

"You had a diaphragm when you were sixteen," said Hannah, getting off a parting shot.

"And this is the thanks I get for being honest with you." Lynn wiped her eyes as she headed toward the kitchen. "*Very nice.*"

Barry saw Clay give him a blank look before he followed Lynn down the hall and realized there were some basic fundamentals about women that he needed to review with the boy.

"What's going on?" he said, shutting the kitchen door firmly behind him.

She ignored him, sprinkling flour on the counter and getting a ball of dough out of the refrigerator.

"Lynn? What gives?"

Fat tears began to drip down her cheeks as she slammed the ball down into the bed of flour.

"Sandi," she said.

"What about her?"

"That's whose body it was at the train station. They think they've identified her."

She suddenly turned and grabbed him in a puff of flour. He felt the dampness of her tears through his shirt as she buried her face in his chest. This was a woman who could straddle you like a cowgirl, haul fifty pounds of camera equipment uptown in sweltering New York heat, squeeze out two children, and build backyard jungle gyms without ever asking a man to lift a finger. But all at once, she was a fragile child.

"You've gotta be kidding me."

He gently took her shoulders and set her back a little, seeing her face crumble and the flour dotting her sweater like dried white tears.

"That's why I was trying to call you today," she said, pressing back into him. "But you didn't call me back. It was so horrible . . ."

He put his arms around her, letting the news sink in.

After all this time, he'd finally started to *get* Sandi. For years, he'd wondered why Lynn had put up with all this drama and lunacy. The crazy PR schemes, the extravagant children's parties, the ridiculous stiletto heels and low-cut shirts that seemed to force your eyes into the shallow valley of her cleavage, her wild frizzy hair, her severe angular looks and obsession with weight. But she'd grown on him. He'd started to see her friendship with Lynn was one with real stretch marks and dirt under its nails. They'd seen each other through tough childhoods, difficult pregnancies, and scabby marital patches. He wished *he* had a friend that loyal. Sandi was all right, he'd decided after seeing her weather the cancer scare with a kind of quiet stoicism that most guys he knew couldn't have mustered. And, in fact, watching her sail off the diving board into the pool this summer, legs flaring out straight behind her and red Lycra stretched tight over her breasts, he'd seen certain limber erotic possibilities in her that he hadn't noticed before.

"You tell the kids about this yet?" he asked, remembering Hannah had baby-sat for Sandi's kids two or three times last spring.

"No," she said, trying to find the drawstrings to pull herself back together again. "I wanted to wait until you got home. I didn't think I could handle it on my own."

"Shi-*ii*-itt." Barry stretched and laced his hands behind his head. "And so what's Jeff doing? Who's looking after the kids?"

"He was almost catatonic when I went there this morning. But when I came back to drop off some food this afternoon, the babysitter said Sandi's dad was there with her stepmom. They're assholes, but at least they can keep things running."

He remembered meeting the father once, a stumpy beetle-browed little white-haired guy who'd hit it big as a real estate developer, buying low in the seventies and selling high in the eighties. His second wife was like one of the apartments in his East Side buildings: cramped quarters, high maintenance, limited views.

"Jeff was taking a nap when I came back." She got a rolling pin out of one of the drawers. "He was apparently a mess after the police came there."

"What are you doing?"

"I just need to stay busy with my hands." She attacked the dough ball with the roller, trying to flatten it and smooth it out. "I'm too upset and nervous to stay still. I thought I'd make them a pie. I remember the kids liked my apple pie . . ."

"So has Jeff got himself a good lawyer?"

"I don't know." She put her shoulders into the task. "Why? Do you think . . ."

"It would just be standard for the police to take a good long look at him." He shrugged. "Especially considering what was done to the body."

"God, some of the things you say." She stopped trying to smooth lumps and just looked at him.

"I'm only thinking about it the way a prosecutor would."

"He just lost *his wife*, Barry!"

He asked himself what he'd be doing under the circumstances. The truth was, he might well be holed up in his office like a shell-shocked veteran, swilling scotch and watching *World at War* reruns on the History Channel. Jeff had never struck him as having a particularly flinty core to begin with. When you first met him, he seemed like a guy who you could have a beer with while the kids played in the pool. An army brat who landed in Babylon, Long Island, got himself into Harvard, and could name every Mets starting lineup of the last thirty-five years. Somebody you could tolerate at a cookout or dinner at a local restaurant every six weeks while the women huddled together like sequestered jurors. But once you really got to talking to him, a kind of gooey self-pity oozed out. Every other story was about how somebody had screwed him or failed to recognize his talent. Every slight was a grave insult; every bad break was a mortal blow. In a good mood, he could be even harder to take. Earlier this year, he'd bragged to Barry that he was going to celebrate the completion of their new house by bending Sandi over and giving it to her "doggie-style" — *doggie-style!* — over the new three-thousand-dollar WaterWorks bathtub they'd put in upstairs.

Just as bad, he had a competitive streak. Finding out Barry had rarely played tennis, he insisted they hit the courts at the Stone Ridge Country Club. But after losing the first set and wrenching his bad knee, Barry had gotten his groove on and beat Jeff easily in the next two sets, and Jeff had spent the rest of the afternoon sulking and watching golf on the TV in the clubhouse.

On the other hand, the guy had built his baseball card collection into a 12-million-dollar-a-year business selling souvenirs on the Internet. He'd bought himself a brand-new wine-dark Mercedes 320 SUV late last year while everybody else's business was tanking. So maybe it was just pure jealousy Barry felt toward him.

"You really think Jeff could've done that to her?" Lynn swiped more tears out of her eyes as she went back to making the pie crust.

"I don't know. You never get the real story just looking at it from the outside."

"I swear, I'll kill him myself if I find out he had anything to do with it."

She started pressing down harder with the roller, her eyes getting that fierce, almost scary, determination. He remembered this was one of the things he both loved and feared most about her. Her refusal to ever back down. He'd seen her bull her way past cops twice her size at crime scenes and browbeat fusty school administrators into getting more money for the children's art programs. She was unstoppable once she got going, but in part of his mind he always worried about what would happen if she ran into somebody who decided to push back.

"Listen, I'm sure the police have got this covered. You said they were over there already?"

"I saw Mike Fallon going in with another cop as I was leaving." She put the roller down and got herself a sharp knife off the wall rack.

"Well, there you go. I'm sure they're professionals."

"I saw something else there, though. I was in such a daze, I didn't think to say anything."

"What?"

She hesitated with the knife in her hand, as if she'd forgotten why she picked it up. "There was a little mark on the wall in the living room. At first, I thought it was a chocolate handprint or something, but now . . ."

"Oh, come on. You think it was a blood splatter?"

"Barry, she was *murdered*." She grabbed an apple from the fruit bowl. "Somebody slaughtered her. They stuck a knife in her throat . . ."

"All right." He patted the air, urging her to keep her voice down. "I hear you. Maybe you should call the station then and let them know, in case they missed it."

She started peeling skin off the apple in a long unbroken strip. "Christ, I can't get over this. It's so horrible to think this could happen to a friend of ours."

"I know."

"I mean, you come to a town with good schools and no crime, where you think you know all the people. And then . . ."

The skin broke before she was done with her peeling, and she dropped the knife on the floor. He came over and put his arms around her again, feeling the smallness of her bones moving under the skin and seeing the glint of the blade on the floor. Now would not be the time to mention the fallen mailbox or the potential disaster unfolding at work, he decided.

"It's gonna be all right," he said, resting his chin on top of her head.

"I know you keep *saying* that."

"Well, what else do you want me to say?" He stepped back again. "Honey, let's go to the mall and buy a gas mask and a MAC-10 this weekend."

A vertical crease appeared between her eyes. "I feel like we've lost our ozone layer."

"Look, I'll make some calls tomorrow about upgrading our home security system, but we both know that it's not going to turn out to be some random maniac breaking down people's doors. It's going to be somebody who knew her."

"*We* knew her."

"Come on." He touched her face, trying to smooth the line away. "Let's get back to the table. The kids are waiting."

16

RAY MARTIN WAS seventy-seven today and had long since given up hope of ever having a real relationship with his only son. The kid had ruined his life with drugs, burning through a half-dozen businesses and two marriages with nothing to show for himself except a job managing the broken-down Sunoco station on Route 12 and a son of his own named Kyle, a little reed bending in the wind. Five years old with a hapless smile and a gap in his teeth, but no one gave a damn about him. His mother was into drugs herself and relinquished custody, only visiting the condo on River Road often enough to ask for money and upset the little boy's delicate equilibrium.

But Ray loved the child. A couple of years ago, his wife had died, and he'd decided that instead of moving down to Florida and frittering away his remaining days on the golf courses, he'd try to hang on and raise Kyle as best he could without repeating the same mistakes he'd made with his own son. He lavished attention on his grandchild, feeding him, buying him clothes, and learning to play his insanely violent video games. Occasionally, with his hand on the joystick, he'd remember the clear blue clarity he'd had as a young pilot flying missions in the Pacific, and he would hint to the boy that he'd been in a great war. Other times, he would just enjoy Kyle's company in silence as they sat together on the fold-out couch in the living room, drinking warm milk and watching *Barnaby Jones* reruns on the satellite dish, a small yellow head getting drowsy on his lap.

For his birthday, Ray had decided to indulge himself a little. The UPN 9 weather last night had predicted it was going to be another day in the low seventies, and he decided to keep Kyle home from kindergarten for some early morning fishing.

He woke the boy just before sunrise and took him out on the river in the rowboat he kept down at the marina by the train station. A bumper sticker on the side said, "OLD FISHERMEN NEVER DIE — THEY JUST SMELL THAT WAY."

"Grampa, are we gonna catch a shark?" Kyle asked, after Ray pulled his oars in and dropped his line into the water, clear and gray as an Akita's eye in the morning light.

"Eels is more like it."

He perched forward on his seat, ignoring the boy's squint and the arthritic ache in his bones. He wondered how many fall mornings like this he had left in him. He remembered his own father taking him fishing off the end of the old coal pier when he was this age and seeing a sturgeon suddenly erupt from the water, seven glorious feet long with greenish-yellow sides and a shiny white belly. A living rainbow, the river showing its muscle. As the great fish arced and plunged back under the surface of his memory, a breeze riffled through his sparse gray wings of hair and a small sense of wistful melancholy fell over him, knowing that his grandson would never live in a world where such simple uncorrupted wonder was possible.

"Oh, you still have your striped bass and your white perch, but chances are all we'll catch are eels," he said, feeling a slight tug on the line as the current shifted. "You know about eels, don't you?"

"No." Kyle leaned against him, still not quite awake.

"Scavengers is what they are. Nighttime scavengers. They live at the bottom of the river, and they don't care how dirty and dark it gets; they just lie there, waiting in sunken old scows."

He felt the tension in his rod and started to wind the line in.

"Have you got something?" The boy sat up alertly.

The top of the rod bent as Ray pulled it. "Feels that way."

"Can I help you?"

"No, stay back."

The rod bowed and seemed to stretch like taffy in his hands. He felt the strain in his shoulders as he leaned back and tried to reel it in.

"Maybe it's a swordfish!" Kyle bounced up and down excitedly, rocking the boat.

"Nothing of the kind," Ray said.

He felt the weight tumble away and then surge back toward him. Too heavy for seaweed, too light to be an anchor. Maybe it was a fish. The truth was, he hadn't caught anything substantial in years, making it that much more important that he actually haul something in that his grandson could bring home. A memory he could hold on to, spray with polyurethane, and put up on a wall.

He cranked the reel in two more times and felt the weight start to fight him again. His grandson grabbed him around the waist as he braced a foot against the gunwale and pulled with all his might.

"Don't let go, Grampa."

He told himself he couldn't just cut the line and admit defeat. The boy was depending on him. He gritted his teeth and heard a crack in his lower lumbar as the boat drifted and the line went taut. He reeled in some more line, the translucent spool thickening, and twisted himself for leverage.

"Grampa, let me hold the rod."

"It's all right." He pushed the boy's hand away.

It was a pitched personal battle. The weight thrashed and tried to swim away from him, but he cranked it back, refusing to relinquish control. A tingling sensation began in the middle of his chest.

"Grampa, are you all right?"

"Of course, I'm all right."

He was aware of the tingling becoming a burning dullness. *Oh my God*, he thought. *I'm about to have a coronary in the middle of the Hudson, stuck with a five-year-old in a rowboat. I'm going to die and take my grandson with me.* All at once, the anger and bitterness that he'd been holding back for years bloomed forth. Damn his worthless son. Damn his own sainted thrifty wife, who never gave him a day's peace while she drew a breath. Damn the mortgage, the people he worked for at the bank, the fact that he hadn't made love to a woman in twelve years. And damn this child for needing him so badly.

"Grampa, please, let me help you pull it in." A little hand reached for the nylon string.

"I said *stay back*," he snapped. "Are you deaf?"

But just then the line slackened. He turned the reel a few times, making sure the tug wasn't completely gone. But there was still something on the hook. He cackled and gave the boy a gleeful sideways look, hoping the jagged edge he'd flashed a moment ago had been forgotten. *See what the old man's getting for you?* The boat rocked on a passing swell as he reeled in faster. Yeah, come on, mama. The river seemed ready to part with this prize. He felt it rise toward him, limp with defeat. He sat back in his seat for the last few victorious turns as regular color returned to his face.

There was a tug of resistance from below, and then he pulled the weight free of the water's grip and hoisted it high into the air. He only had time to register that it was a torn black plastic contractor's bag before it came plummeting back at him and landed with a heavy hollow *thonk* in the gritty skim of water at his feet. He heard his grandson scream before he looked down. The bag had spilled its contents on impact. A gallon can of Thompson's Wood Protector lay on its side, having obviously been used to weight down the bag. And next to it, the severed head of a woman with a long aquiline nose, a blackened tongue, and seaweed tangled in her hair stared up at him from the bottom of the boat.

17

THE CHAIR WAS what finally unhinged Lynn again the next morning. A straight-backed French Provincial with a maroon cushion. She'd been doing all right until she saw it sitting empty at the emergency meeting that Jeanine had called for their book group. She'd managed to get up clearheaded, shower and dress, make breakfast for Barry and the kids, and then run them to their various destinations before stopping by the house on Love Lane to take Isadora to school for Jeff. She'd even kept up a cheerful front when Izzy started to sing "The Piña Colada Song" from the backseat in her mother's exaggerated showy vibrato.

But the sight of that empty chair in the semicircle of friends who'd gathered that morning did her in. It made her grief as real and solid as an iceberg sitting right in front of her, daring her to get around it. She'd photographed dozens of crime scenes, but this was death outside the frame. Death was here in the living room. Death said, *Take a look*. Death said, *How do you like working with me?* Death said, *That's another one I got*. Death said, *You get a good eyeful, lady?*

"Sandi always used to say, 'I don't care that much about dying,'" Lynn heard herself begin. "'Just give me sixteen years to make it to the kids' college graduations. After that, you can take me away in a pine box for all I care.' She just wanted to hang on longer than her mother did."

The other four women in the room turned to her, ignoring the crackers and cheese that had been set out. Jeanine looking both coiffed and glazed, as if she'd managed to put herself together perfectly and then lit up an enormous spliff as soon as the kids were packed off to school. Molly Pratt, with her Dorothy Hamill wedge

cut and her copy of *The Corrections* on her lap, as if they were actually going to discuss a novel today. Dianne de Groot, wearing a
striped crew-neck shirt and pigtails just like her eight-year-old
daughter. And Anne Schaffer, grimacing and groaning quietly, her
broken leg still encased in plaster up to the hip, with huge Frankenstein bolts sticking out from the ankle.

"She was a nut, but we loved her," Jeanine commiserated.

"Remember Dylan's fourth birthday with the knights in armor
and the jousting in the backyard?" Dianne de Groot's face lit up.

"Didn't you think that was a little over the top?" said Molly, who
wrote a magazine advice column for single moms, wrinkling her
nose. "It must have cost them five grand. How were the rest of us
supposed to keep up with that for our kids' birthdays?"

"Oh, I thought it was wonderful," Lynn said, barely resisting the
urge to raise her hand. "I totally got it. It's like that when you lose
your mom and you're young. You feel like you have to make it up to
your own kids by getting everything absolutely right and perfect.
She had a lot of life in her, didn't she?"

"That she did," Anne Schaffer grumbled, washing down three
Advil with her Bloody Mary. "Among a lot of other things."

There was tension in the air this morning, with everyone vacil-
lating between the urge to get fucked-up and the need to be hyper-
vigilant and totally in control. For Lynn, it was enough just to be
around other women at the moment. The silence of the house,
which she'd yearned for all of last year when contractors were tor-
menting her and the school meetings seemed endless, was suddenly
oppressive and ominous. She'd needed to surround herself with
friends, not just to soften the blow but to dilute its impact. To hear
other voices in the wreckage, telling her she wasn't alone.

"Everything she did was ten times bigger than life," Jeanine
rasped into a glass of white wine. "Remember when she hired the
hot air balloon to publicize that new restaurant on the West Side,
and it almost got stuck between the Twin Towers?"

"Or when she broke up with that schmuck Scott Lewin and
played 'I Will Survive' over and over into his answering machine so
he couldn't get any messages from his new girlfriend." Lynn smiled
wanly, the gloom lifting momentarily.

"And what about the wedding at the Waldorf with five hundred
guests and Lester Lanin's Orchestra and the shoes for the brides-

maids all dyed matching robin's-egg blue?" Jeanine dangled her wrist as if her hand was dripping with diamonds.

"It figures she wouldn't just die like a normal person, in an old-age home," said Anne Schaffer, wincing as she used both hands to move her leg in its massive cast.

"What do you mean by that?" Lynn drew back in her chair.

"Anne's just saying that Sandi always took things to an extreme." Jeanine jumped in like a UN interpreter. "Right?"

"Exactly." Anne nodded.

Something about the dry click in her voice made Lynn sit up straight again. The other women in this circle had known Sandi for as long as twenty-five years and as briefly as eighteen months, but now it occurred to Lynn that perhaps they'd all looked on Sandi with a slightly more jaundiced eye than she had.

For Lynn, there'd never been as much critical distance. Sandi was her bud. Her running partner. They were the Gang of Two. To everyone else, maybe they'd always been a little suspect because they didn't belong to any particular group. They didn't belong to any of the local country clubs like Anne; they weren't on the PTA like Di-anne or the School Board like Molly; they weren't active in the local churches or synagogues; they didn't work with the Historical Society or the library; they weren't among the strollerati or the hard-core tennis ladies like Jeanine. They were just Lynn and Sandi doing their business and not really worrying about what anyone else thought.

Lynn looked at the vacant chair again and remembered how Sandi had defended her last year after she'd recommended *White Teeth* to the group and everyone else complained, *I can't identify with these people!* She'd never forget the way Sandi stuck her tongue out as she told Jeanine, *Stretch a little, honey; you won't snap.*

Lately though, Lynn realized, Sandi had withdrawn a bit from their little club, presumably to work on her house.

"I'm not getting what you mean," she said, turning to Jeanine. "She took things to an extreme? What things?"

"You didn't know?" Jeanine raised her eyebrows high.

"Didn't know *what?*"

There was a pregnant pause, a marshaling of forces, a restless an-ticipation like the beginning of a horse race.

"What are you saying? She was having an affair?" Lynn felt her blood pressure drop.

The four other women started speaking at once like people running for the train.

"Listen, *listen*, she was very cagey, even with me." Jeanine waved her hands, quieting down. "You know, Jeff and her had been having problems for a long time."

"But I thought they were past that." Dianne de Groot frowned.

"Oooooh, nooo . . ." Jeanine lifted her glass of Chardonnay. "His business is in a lot of trouble. He's been depressed for months."

"Had you been over to the new house?" Molly Pratt said in a hushed appalled voice, touching Lynn's knee.

"Yesterday was the first time I'd been inside." Lynn's shoulders drooped. "She kept telling me it wasn't ready yet. I thought there was supposed to be some big grand opening this fall so she could show it off."

"Oh, yeah, right." Anne Schaffer snorted.

"It's a mess, isn't it?" Jeanine rolled her eyes. "They almost couldn't finish one of the upstairs bathrooms because they couldn't afford to pay the contractor . . ."

"But how could I not know any of this?" Lynn looked back at the empty dining room chair, as if expecting an explanation. "She's been one of my best friends since we were six. She stayed with my family for a month after her mother died."

"Well, that's probably the reason why." Jeanine started to cut into the Brie wheel on the coffee table. "Shame. Embarrassment. She didn't want to look bad in front of you anymore. No one likes to be the poor little waif. And she thought you'd scored so big marrying Barry that she didn't want you to think she was falling behind."

"But that's ridiculous," Lynn protested. "Like *I* would've cared."

"She was very competitive with you," Jeanine said, fastidiously spreading Brie on to a thin table water cracker. "That's what *you* never got about her."

"Absolutely." Anne Schaffer nodded.

"What're you talking about?" Lynn looked around, bewildered. She felt like she'd flipped over a rock in her garden and discovered a council of wriggling worms.

"She talked about you all the time," Molly said crisply, loading a cracker of her own. "She was always measuring herself against you."

Lynn held on to the sides of her chair as if someone had tried to tip her over. Could this be true? Her grief doubled back on itself.

Not only had she just lost her best friend, she was being told that she'd never really known her. This felt like betrayal. No, like a conspiracy. *No*, it was just a terrible misunderstanding. They had it all wrong. Hot tears surged into the corners of her eyes again, and she had trouble catching her breath. The black circle was back from yesterday, throbbing and pushing back against her insides.

"Wow," she said, trying to shrink the circle down again. "And in the middle of this, you're telling me she started having an affair?"

"Hey, listen, people look for solace in different ways." Jeanine shrugged and wiped her mouth with a cocktail napkin. "You were known to smoke a doobie or two after your mom got sick. Marty hits the scotch every night after he gets home from the magazine because he's worried about layoffs. You know, Sandi was always kind of insecure about her big nose and the size of her ass."

"A man comes along and gives you a little positive attention after your husband's been going around feeling all sorry for himself, you tend to perk up." Anne Schaffer gave a weary knowing sigh.

Lynn took a deep breath, trying to focus on Jeff. She pictured him in his tux at the Waldorf, surrounded by his office buddies, drinking too much Cristal and talking too loudly about the strippers at Shenanigans. But when she watched him take Sandi for the first dance across the ballroom floor, she remembered thinking that this was a guy who'd come a long way to find love. When Sandi's father and Jeff's friends hoisted him up on the chair to carry him around for the traditional part of the celebration, his smile became a klieg light shining from face to face, and she could see exactly what had drawn Sandi to him.

"So do you think Jeff could've found out and killed her?" Lynn heard herself blurt out.

The book slid off Molly Pratt's lap as she was eating and hit the floor. The thud seemed to jar everyone else.

"Jesus, Lynn, you don't mince words, do you?" Anne tried bending down to pick up the book. "The man's supposed to be in mourning."

"Well, who else could've done it?" Lynn asked, remembering what Barry said last night.

"It couldn't have been him," Jeanine announced in the prescriptive tone she used when friends failed to listen to her instructions properly. "He's been away for a few days in Boston and Providence, meeting with venture capitalists to try to prop up his business. I saw Sandi with the kids on Saturday down by the skateboard park, and she said he was coming back at the beginning of this week."

"Did you tell the police that?" Lynn said.

"Of course. Some Hispanic detective with a shaved head and an earring came by yesterday. I tell you, this town has really changed. When I saw him coming up the driveway, I thought he was one of Eduardo's gardeners."

"All right, but if it's not Jeff, who is it?" Lynn turned back to the rest of the group, trying to enlist them. "Why wouldn't she tell any of us who she was having the affair with?"

"I think she was trying to break it off," Jeanine murmured.

"What makes you say that?" asked Lynn, hearing the others start to whisper.

"She just turned to me on Saturday and said, 'Why is it everyone always acts like it's women who are the ones who won't let go after a thing's over?'" Jeanine said, imitating Sandi's slightly adenoidal deadpan.

"Really?" Dianne de Groot's girlish features pulled back. "She said *that?*"

"Yeah." Jeanine sniffed. "It was one of those kid conversations when you never get to complete a sentence. Zak fell coming down one of the ramps and skinned his knee, and it was like an Oliver Stone movie at the skate park . . ."

"A . . ." A surprised laugh caught in Lynn's throat.

"You know: '*Shut up and take the pain, soldier!*'" Jeanine snorted, starting to crack up. Molly coughed. Dianne gave a little gasp. And then the floodgates opened, and they all began crying at once. The living room became a republic of tears in a country that hadn't stopped crying for two weeks. They cried for their friend, and they cried for themselves. They cried for the children who lost their mother, and then they cried because they were scared. They cried because they didn't know what was going to happen next, and they cried because they knew all the crying wasn't going to change a thing.

"God, I don't know how I'm going to be able to stand it." Lynn shuddered and dried her eyes.

"What's the alternative?" Anne Schaffer said, giving up on the fallen book and accepting a tissue from Jeanine to blow her nose.

"I don't know." Lynn hugged herself. "It just feels so useless to sit here *talking* about it."

"Honey, just let the police do their job." Jeanine tried to reassure her. "They know what they're doing."

"You think so?"

Lynn found herself staring once again at the empty velvet seat. She'd sat right there, hadn't she? Just a few feet away, with one leg curled up under her and both shoes parked beneath the chair. Her mind went back to a winter afternoon senior year of high school. A long train ride into the city, her breath fogging up the window, and a slender brown serpent of coffee spilling down the aisle. Her first time going to Manhattan without her mother. She and Sandi had made a promise to each other, that if they somehow got separated on the subway, one of them would come back for the other. Sure enough, at Times Square, the doors had closed and she'd seen Sandi's face receding on the downtown local, leaving her stranded among the platform prophets, the stumblebum bystanders, and the muttering angry creeps in dirty raincoats. The lurid carnival she thought she'd been looking for. She remembered how that one scary silver-suited freak with a video camera kept asking her to come back to his apartment and take off her clothes. But then she'd heard a shout and turned to see Sandi running up the stairs to rescue her, having just caught the local coming back uptown, keeping up her end of the deal. If one of us gets lost, the other always has to come back for her. Cross your heart, hope to die, no excuses.

"So," said Molly Pratt, finally bending down to get her own damn book, "anybody want to talk about the novel?"

18

MIKE GOT TO work a couple of minutes late that morning and found most of the officers in the squad room watching that ridiculous annoying *Riverdance* video again while Larry Quinn, acting as desk sergeant for once, accepted a package covered in duct tape from the distinguished citizen known around the station as Peculiar Clark.

"What's going on?" asked Mike, raising his voice to be heard above the clatter of tap shoes and the sawing of violins.

"There's nowhere to hide anymore," said Peculiar Clark. "It's everywhere."

He was an elegantly addled old man in a milk-stained double-breasted suit, who'd supposedly made his fortune back in the forties writing saccharine holiday homilies for one of the major greeting card companies. But these days he lived by himself in a huge old Victorian wreck up in the West Hills, and at least two nights a week he got himself liquored-up and slicked-back like a boulevardier to try to importune young soccer moms in the aisles of Stop & Shop.

"Mr. De Cavalcante says he may have been a terrorist target," said Quinn, the station's records officer and a character in his own right, twisting the waxed end of his mustache slyly. "He received a suspicious package."

"A pair of woman's lace panties and an obscene note in my mailbox this morning." Clark leaned on his battered wolf's-head cane, his face as corrugated as an empty scrotum. "I never asked for that."

"Oh, yeah?" said Mike. "What do you think that's about?"

"Biological warfare." Clark gave a sage nod as Larry slipped the package into a silver hazmat bag. "Anthrax-soaked panties. The terrorists test it out on the old people first because they think we won't be missed."

"Probably right." Mike took the bag from the sarge. "I think I better show this to the chief."

"Thank you, son." Clark shook his hand. "I'm glad somebody recognizes we've got an emergency on our hands."

Mike gave him a two-fingered salute and sprinted up the stairs to the chief's office, trying to remember the last time he'd gotten so much as a true laugh out of Harold. The panties were probably a pair of those old rayon drawers that you could fit a little elephant into. Chances were they belonged to some hooker Clark slept with in 1953. But maybe they could be an opening, a way to get into a more casual kind of conversation with Harold about Sandi. Having taken a look at a large portion of the diary last night, he realized he had to play it cool with the chief, find a way to artfully arrange some details ahead of time so Harold didn't go crazy and lop *his* head off.

He moved through the outer office, ignoring the finger Deb Ryan, the secretary, was holding up to delay him, and threw Harold's door open.

Harold and Paco Ortiz looked up in surprise, like Catholic schoolgirls caught smoking cigarettes in the bathroom.

"Hey, am I interrupting something?"

He clenched the bag to his side, deciding to shelve the gag for the moment.

"Case is starting to move." Harold set down his Mont Blanc pen. "Old man and his grandson fished a head out of the river this morning."

"Sandi?"

"Looks that way. The ME already picked it up. They did the autopsy on the rest of the body last night and said they didn't find any oxygenated water in the lungs."

"And when were you going to tell me about this? I don't rate a phone call?"

Mike noticed the stubble contract like iron filings on Paco's head, and he wondered what the two of them had been talking about just before he came in. There was a definite afterburn lingering in the air. Harold studiously avoided looking him in the eye. Did they know something already?

No. It was too early for them to be seriously onto him.

"I was going to tell you this morning, when you came in," said Harold carefully. "Nobody's keeping anybody out of the loop."

"Glad to hear that." Mike shot Paco a cold look, reminding him who was in charge here.

"So, what else is doing?" he said, as if the two of them were still holding smoke in their lungs.

"Working on putting together an affidavit for a warrant to search Lanier's house," Harold said. "Brian Bonfiglio from the DA's office is supposed to be here any minute to help us write it up."

"Hey, hey, what's this about?" Mike looked back and forth between the two of them. "I thought we weren't going to make a move until we all agreed we had probable cause."

He was sure he'd had everything under control when he left the Laniers' with the diary yesterday. But here he was being upended and forced to scramble for his footing.

"It was my call," said Harold.

"Your call." Mike stared at him over the sallow dotted orb of Paco's head.

"The phone rang five minutes ago. Somebody saw a bloodstain on the wall in Lanier's house."

"You're shitting me."

"Hey, bro, don't feel bad about not seeing it." Paco swiveled in his chair to face him. "We were just there to get the prints in the bathroom. It's better this way. Now we have a witness."

"Who is it?"

"Well, that's the sixty-four-thousand-dollar question." Harold steepled his fingers. "Judge always likes to see a real name, but we don't want to put anybody at risk unnecessarily."

"Fuck it," said Paco. "Put it in. He's gonna figure it out eventually anyway. How many other people were in his living room yesterday?"

"Yeah, maybe you're right," Harold said. "He won't see the actual affidavit with the name on it until we're closer to trial. And by then he'll have bigger fish to fry."

"Wait a second." Mike made sure he'd closed the door behind him. "This was Lynn Stockdale who saw this?"

Harold nodded.

"And she called *you* and not me?"

"It was a police matter, Mikey. She wasn't looking for a date or anything."

Mike stared in silence, a hard dark coal glowing in his head.

"This the lady we saw yesterday?" Paco palmed the top of his bald head.

"I just don't know why she would've called you instead of me," said Mike, trying to button up the hurt quickly. "It's just funny, that's all."

"Well, either way it's a break, and we have to move on it fast before he gets a chance to clean up." Harold picked up his pen again. "We want to get a look in his garage and basement too while we're there, and see what kind of saws he's got."

"I know how to do a search, Harold," Mike cut him off. "Who's going to take the warrant over for the judge to sign?"

On a Wednesday morning this early, old Highball Harper, the real estate lawyer who sat on the bench and heard local cases three days a week, would probably be out on the links at the Stone Ridge Country Club with all the other desiccated old WASPs, reminiscing about the Ford administration and trying to maintain their tenuous grip on the town's levers of power.

"I'm going to ask Paco to do it," said Harold, officiously clearing his throat and rolling his pen between his fingers. "He's the primary on this case. He's going to have to swear to the warrant and answer any serious questions that come up later in court . . ."

"But . . ." A hot protest started to spill out of Mike.

"I *said* Paco is the primary, and you're the supervisor," Harold said in that brusque stentorian tone he'd started using since he became chief. "I've thought about it, and I've decided maybe you're a little too close with too many of these people."

"So that's how you want it?"

"That's how I want it."

Mike took a beat, watching Paco scratch at the side of his goatee with his finger. That pumped-up little prick must've said something to Harold about the argument they'd had at the Lanier house yesterday. And these were the guys who held his fate in their hands?

Screw this.

He was thinking maybe some of the old-timers might've been right about Harold: that he'd suddenly decided he was a black man after all, once he got the chief's badge. Sliding Paco in ahead of men with more seniority. Going to that NAACP dinner after all those vicious protests over the Woyzeck shooting. Joking around in the locker room with the three other black guys on the job, making all these coded little references white people weren't supposed to get.

When did the Blue Wall get color coordinated? What about loyalty and fraternity? What about remembering the men who put their lives on the line for you? What about the fact that they'd known each other since they were ten? Moment by moment, though, the idea was hardening in his mind that this was no longer completely his tribe.

He sighed and put up his hands, knowing he had to keep stonewalling. He couldn't count on Harold for anything. No mercy for the white man once he's down on his knees.

"Okay, Chief, whatever. It's your bat and ball."

Harold sat back in his chair, hearing the bitter undertone.

"Look," he said, "nobody's trying to do an end run around anybody else here, Mike. We're all team players."

"I don't have a problem working with Paco if Paco doesn't have a problem working with me. You got a problem with me, Paco?"

"No, man." Paco draped an arm over the side of his chair, eyes moving warily. "We got an understanding."

"Fine, then we're all one happy family." Mike gave him a small scar of a smile. "Let's go catch the bad guy."

He saw Harold fidget and shift in his seat, deciding whether to bury the tension or have it all out at once.

He looked over at Paco, as if this was his new battery partner, and seemed to take the signal to take the easy way for now.

"So, what's in the bag?" He turned his attention to the hazmat bag Mike was still holding.

"Forget it." Mike opened the door to walk out. "Nothing important."

19

LISTENING TO NPR on the way back from Jeanine's that morning, Lynn heard the attorney general say more terrorist attacks were a virtual certainty, though he couldn't say when or where. She turned it off quickly as she pulled into the driveway, noticing the mailbox leaning a little to the left, as if the post had been pulled out and then shoved back in haphazardly. Dead yellow leaves crunched under her wheels, and a falling acorn ricocheted off her hood, the trees following autumn's usual narrative even as the sun ignored it. When she got out of the car, she saw that the plastic owl that was supposed to drive the crows away had fallen off the roof, and the gardeners had left a pile of pulled weeds by the garage.

She stood there for a moment, promising herself not to fall into a deep depression again. She'd already been down that route after her mother died last year. But right after her book group broke up, her mind went back into a tailspin. Someone pretending to be human had done this to her friend. Someone who went to the supermarket and probably filled his car with gas a couple of times a week. Someone whom she might have nodded to at a stoplight. Someone who might have sat near her at town meetings and watched her children cross the street. The thought choked and bulged inside her head, threatening to burst like an artery.

Breaking the paralysis, she went through the gate and out to the studio in the backyard, determined to stay busy and focused.

The studio stood white-shingled and cool in the shade of a leaning cedar. Her private sanctuary with a working bathroom. Part of the deal when they bought this house was that she'd finally get real work space instead of having to furtively develop her pictures in the bathtub like some amateur pornographer. So they'd spent more than twelve thousand dollars to convert the old toolshed, installing a fully equipped darkroom, bathroom plumbing, an iMac with a state-of-the-art scanner, and a comfortable outer office with cool Scandinavian-style furniture. A window cut into the wall offered a tantalizing glimpse of the river down the hill. Stepping into this quiet zone five days a week had allowed her to reclaim a bit of her life from the children. But now she felt isolated and hollow, wishing she could just pick up the phone and call her mother or Sandi.

She unlocked the studio and flipped on the lights, still feeling vaguely bothered by what Jeanine had said. *She was very competitive with you. That's what* you *never got about her.*

Could that be right? She prided herself on being the girl who never looked away. Even on the fifth-grade school bus, she'd make herself stare at the squashed squirrels on the road while the other girls were shrieking and the boys were making retching sounds. She was the girl who'd always climb the extra flight of stairs in the tenement to get the shot all the other photographers had missed. Now somebody was telling her she couldn't even see her best friend clearly.

She turned her attention to the coffee-colored file cabinets next to her tilted drawing table, thinking this couldn't be entirely true. Maybe there'd been more competition than she'd ever really acknowledged, but Sandi was in her corner. She'd been the first friend to say she liked Lynn's pictures. And she certainly wouldn't have wanted Lynn moping around the studio, gnawing on the butt end of a throwaway conversation. Get on with it. She'd meant to go through more of her old shots anyway for the retrospective, but she had put off looking through some of the files, knowing they were as jumbled and disorganized as her memories. She pulled out a drawer and got a faceful of dust motes. Blowing them aside, she picked up an old envelope, and a series of red-tinted negatives fell out like peeled-off scabs.

She turned on the halogen light and started examining the individual frames, realizing that these were the first pictures she took with the Kodak Brownie her father gave her on her seventh birthday. An off-kilter image of her mother's rosebush. Hampton, the beagle, moving toward his water dish in a blur. And then the impossible, a perfect family portrait of Mom, Dad, and her baby sister,

Carol, standing in front of the old house on Birch Lane, all the elements falling into place for one fleeting second. Mom before the MS, in her white-ribbed turtleneck, looking a little like Natalie Wood, with dark hair cresting on top of her head. Seeing it again brought back that old ache. Mom at least twelve years younger than Lynn was now, still slightly stunned to find herself back in the burbs, her bohemian painter years living with three other waitresses in a cold-water flat on Perry Street far behind her. Still thinking she was going to have more than half a life. Dad looking rakishly handsome in a Brooks Brothers shirt, with his initials monogrammed over the right breast, not yet staring off into the distance and contemplating divorce. Carol standing between them, shading her eyes, as if she was already shrinking from her parents and thinking of moving to a hippie commune in Oregon.

Looking at the shot reminded Lynn that like autumn leaves and Billie Holiday's voice, families were sometimes at their most achingly beautiful right before they fell apart. She remembered the warmth that flooded through her when that picture came back from the Fotomat and Mom and Dad stood on either side of her, quietly murmuring that, yes, she really did have *an eye*.

A year later, Mom took her to the Museum of Modern Art for the first time, to see the photo collection. She could picture herself standing before Diane Arbus's *Masked Woman in a Wheelchair*, transfixed, as Mom — not yet wheelchair-bound herself — explained that this was how this artist looked at the world. "And the things she saw made her want to kill herself," Mom said. "Can you imagine?"

Looking back, Lynn realized that that was the first nudge. The second was Mom giving her the old Roloflex a year later, as if she was handing over a baton. She held a different negative up to the light and saw that it was a series of later pictures. Mom alone at the kitchen table in the midseventies. *The Energy Crisis*. The "first presenting symptom," as the doctor called it, was a change in her perception of the color red. Mom noticing that a crimson line she'd drawn seemed to twang like a guitar string on paper. Then came the gradual loss of sensation — the inability to feel silk, sand, her husband's touch. Eventually, she couldn't even feel her own feet, making it almost impossible for her to walk. Not that Mom ever liked to dwell outwardly on the subtractions. She was happier talking about the new vibrancy of her vermilion strokes.

Lynn put the magnifying glass over the image and saw the blank easel in the background next to the old Amana refrigerator, where Mom tried to do some sketching before the tremors got too bad. A red pencil was on the floor, having rolled off the edge of the table. The fallen baton. Mom was too weak to pick it up. So it stayed there for almost five hours until Lynn came home. A hot wave of shame washed over her as she remembered Mom insisting she take the picture because it was a good image. *Mom, lemme help you; really, I don't mind. Really. It's okay, Mom. Don't cry. I don't mind cleaning up. I don't mind helping you in the bath. I don't mind cutting your food for you.* The daily tug-of-war between guilt and obligation. Life getting smaller and smaller. Until the day Lynn found what looked like a rough draft of a suicide note in the desk drawer and confronted Mom with it in the bathroom. *WHAT IS THIS?* And Mom, naked and abashed on the rim of the tub, looked up at the ceiling and said, *Your father's right. One of us has to have a life.*

Somehow, at that moment, Mom had made up her mind that she was going to go on. She'd forced herself back into the world, bit by bit, first taking on the kitchen, then getting back in the car, then navigating the A&P aisles. Trying to make that vibrating red into a stronger bloodline, as if she could will herself into remission. She'd staggered into Lynn's first high school exhibit, anarchy on a black cane, determined to see at least one of her daughters finish the race for her. Even as a teenager, Lynn understood that the only real way to honor her was just to keep going.

A knock at the studio door jarred her into the present.

"Who is it?" she called out.

Maybe it was the Dryer Man or the mythic Tree Guy, finally arriving to trim the maple branches that were threatening to break the bedroom windows. She hated it when contractors and landscapers showed up unannounced weeks after their supposed appointments.

"Hello. It's me," she heard Michael Fallon say.

Something in his voice made her think of the second drink of the night, the one where the novelty wears off and the potential for trouble begins.

She opened the door. "I wasn't expecting you."

"That was another song on the jukebox at the Copperhead." He stepped in. "'Hello It's Me.' Remember that?"

"What's up?" She pursed her lips.

"Just a couple of follow-up questions." He moved past her and looked around. "Hey, this is nice too. How much did it run you?"

"Michael, I'm a little busy. Is this about Sandi?"

"Of course. *Why else would I be here?*"

He put his face up close to a picture on the wall. A family portrait she'd taken of Barry and the kids at dusk in Yosemite, the sky dimming like a hand was over the sun and the mountains cloaked in black velvet behind them.

"You know, when I was down on the pile, at Ground Zero, there were a lot of photographers around," he said quietly. "You had all these guys in emergency gear, still trying to see if they could save lives. All these firefighters finding body parts and cops' guns going off in the heat. But then there were all these parasites with Nikons. I remember I saw a fireman's arm under a pile of rubble, and I was trying to get somebody to come help me move it. And then I turn around and this bitch sets off a flash right in my face. I swear, I almost punched her."

"She was probably just trying to do her job."

"Sure she was."

He put his face even closer to the picture, as if he was trying to smell the chemicals through the glass. She remembered how this part of him had gradually started to unnerve her when they were going out. That eerie stillness he had, an almost animal alertness.

"I hear you called Harold this morning," he said.

"I realized I had some information that might be useful after I left the house yesterday."

"Yeah, but you called *Harold*. Why would you do that?"

"I don't know. What difference does it make? You're all working together, aren't you?"

He adjusted the frame on the wall, even though it had been hanging perfectly. "So why didn't you tell *me?* You saw me when you were leaving the house."

"I don't know. I guess it took me awhile to realize that's what it could be."

"And what other information have you been holding out on?" He turned slowly, his eyelids drawn and darkened as if he'd been sitting in front of a fire for a long time. "Or am I supposed to get that from Harold too?"

"*Michael.*"

"Whatever you think of me personally," he said, "I am still the one working this case."

"I understand that."

"Then why can't I get a straight answer out of you? She was supposed to be your best friend."

She noticed a tiny blue mark at the bottom of his shirt's breast pocket.

"Do you have any leads?" she said.

"That shouldn't concern you right now. What should concern you is giving me the answers I'm looking for."

The blue mark darkened before her eyes. His pen had sprung a tiny leak.

"It's not like I've been deliberately holding anything back," she said, trying not to stare at it. "It's just that I was in such a state of shock yesterday that I wasn't thinking clearly."

"You thinking more clearly today?"

"I guess." She shrugged.

"Okay. Let's get on with it. What can you tell me about the marriage?"

"I don't know." She leaned against a file cabinet. "Not all that much more than I knew yesterday. They'd been under a lot of stress financially because of Jeff's business. But you could see that just walking around their house."

"What else?" he said brusquely.

The dot was gradually expanding, the indigo-blue ink finding its way along the network of white cotton seams.

"It could be there was somebody else who got between them."

"You saying you heard she was seeing someone?"

She nodded, wondering why he'd automatically assumed it was the woman at fault.

"And who are you hearing this from?" His eyebrows gathered.

"Do I really have to tell you?" she asked, reluctant to drag Jeanine into this.

"This is a homicide investigation."

She nodded, seeing the point but still not wanting him to hear all the secrets of their tribe.

"I just saw Jeanine Pollack at my book group."

"Okay. And what else did she say? Did she know who the guy was?"

"No. She just knew Jeff had been depressed and maybe Sandi was looking for a way to give him a little zap."

"Figures," he said, a corner of his mouth turning down.

"What makes you say that?"

"A woman gets a man to pull the plow for her. And as soon as he comes up lame, she goes looking for another stud."

"I think that's maybe a little simplistic," she said.

"Is it?"

The blue eyes regarded her warily, as if challenging her to one of those old staring contests they used to have. *Whoever looks away first loses.* People used to say they got together because they were both like owls, hardly ever blinking. She dropped her eyes and saw the indigo stain had grown to the size of a dime below the pocket.

"So did Jeanine say if he ever found out she was getting it somewhere else?" he asked.

"That wasn't my impression. But you'd probably have to ask her yourself. There's a lot I don't know."

"You can say that again."

"Excuse me?" She squinted.

"Never mind." He shook his head. "It doesn't matter."

The stain was expanding like a bullet wound.

"Michael, is this all really part of your investigation?"

"Why? What else would it be?"

"I don't know," she said, trying to take her eyes off the blot. "I just keep getting the feeling that you came here to talk about something else."

"Well, we still do have a lot of unfinished business, don't we?"

"I thought we'd decided to let that lie."

"Oh, did we?" His eyes locked on to hers.

"We were talking about Sandi." She looked away, trying to get him back on track. "And Jeff."

"I know what we were talking about. He stopped pulling down the Benjamins, and she started looking around. A man without his wallet on him isn't worth a damn. Same thing as what happened with you and me."

"Oh, boy."

She had a sinking sense of déjà vu as she watched the blot change shape, like a nova exploding.

"Come on," he said, "let's not sugarcoat it. You dumped me because my mother kept books of Green Stamps in the cupboard. And my father drove a Rambler with the windows up in the summer so people would think he had air-conditioning."

"I thought we were talking about *Sandi*." She tried to frost him with a level glare.

"We would be, but you already called Harold and told him everything, didn't you?"

He was less than three inches from her, closer than any man besides Barry and a few subway riders had gotten in eighteen years.

"Don't you think you're being a little unprofessional?"

She raised her eyes, calling his bluff. Who's going to blink first? Usually, you were asking for something if you looked at a man that long and hard.

"Maybe," he said.

"So why are we getting into all this?"

"I dunno."

He stared back at her, letting the silence form. As it went on, it became heavy, then uncomfortable, and then dangerous. She thought of the long agonizing buildup in a pirate movie in which two ships slowly, slowly draw close enough to lower their cannons and fire a broadside at each other.

"I mean, this thing with Sandi, it got me thinking about all this other old crap I got up in the attic," he said finally, tapping the side of his head.

"What are you talking about?" She stumbled back against a stool.

"I'm saying it didn't have to turn out the way it did." A muscle worked along the side of his face. "With you and me."

"I'm sure both of us have regrets," she said as calmly as she could. "But don't you think we both have more important things to worry about right now?"

He looked down, lost in thought for a half-minute. Letting the silence fill the room again.

"It's all right," he said, just before it became unbearable. "I've decided to forgive you."

"You've decided to what?"

"I've decided to let it go."

"Excuse me?" She blinked. "*You've* decided to forgive *me?*"

"Why? You got a problem with that?"

The threat in his voice was unmistakable. She remembered the time he hit her. That rattlesnake-quick backhand outside Gary Livingstone's party senior year. A flash of light and she was on her back, bleeding from the mouth, his silhouette smoldering against the backdrop of sycamores. What stayed with her wasn't so much the numbness in her jaw, the looseness of her bicuspid, or even the trickle from her split lip. It was the way he shut his eyes and twisted his mouth after he'd done it, as if he'd always known that this would happen but couldn't stop himself. And how he'd picked her up like a broken doll and gathered her in his arms, kissing her and begging to be forgiven.

"No, I don't have a problem with it." She noticed ink dribbling farther down his shirt like heart's blood.

"Good." He nodded. "Life's too short to hold a grudge. You've just gotta let that shit go so it doesn't poison you."

"I couldn't agree with you more." She cast a quick look toward the door.

"So gimme a hug," he said, starting the staring contest all over again.

"Oh, Michael, I don't think that's such a good idea."

"Just one little hug."

"Really." She returned his gaze, having reached the edge of her resistance. "I have to get back to work, and I'm sure you do too."

"Come on, one hug. It's not gonna kill you."

Before she could answer, he took her in his arms, nearly lifting her off the floor. He was a couple of inches shorter than Barry, but broader across the chest, and something about the way he held her suggested that he still had some rights to her body, like a former house owner walking through old rooms. For a moment, she let her chin rest on his shoulder, remembering how good this used to feel.

"Michael, come on." She tried to gently push him away.

His arms wrapped more tightly around her back, as if he were holding on to a mast. "It's okay," he whispered into her hair. "It's okay."

"No, Michael." She felt his breath on her scalp. "Really."

But he wasn't listening. "It's all right," he said. "Don't worry." His arms dropped down into a tightening loop around her waist, his ribs pushed against her breasts. She squirmed, trying to get away,

bringing her knee up, and he took the turning of her hip as an invitation. One of his hands eased its way into the back of her waistband, searching for the plush dimpled spot right above the cleft.
And as his musculature closed in around her, she caught a scent like
red wine and glue and realized that she was about to end up with an
indigo stain on her shirt as well.

20

JEFFREY LANIER SAT on his front steps in a Mets jersey and gray sweatpants, cradling a black mobile phone against his neck and disconsolately studying the search warrant before him.

"So, what time *can* you get here?" he asked the defense lawyer his accountant had recommended. "I'm twisting in the wind."

"I got an evidence hearing for Skeezy G. in Manhattan in five minutes," said Ronald Deutsch, his voice cutting in and out on the staticky line.

"Skeezy what?"

"He's a big rap guy. He does that 'Slap My Ass, Bonita' song my son loves. Just tell me what the warrant says."

A half-dozen Riverside police officers moved through the big house behind Jeffrey, collecting carpet fibers and hair samples in plastic evidence bags and cardboard boxes full of clothes and papers.

"Oh, God, let me look at it." Jeff adjusted his glasses and leaned to one side as a young sergeant with a unibrow and a premature double chin hurried past him carrying his wife's Dell laptop. "It says, 'In the name of the People of the State of New York,' blah, blah, blah, 'there is reasonable cause to believe that certain property, namely clothes, tools, tissue, hair, bloodstain on the living room wall, kitchen knives,' blah, blah 'will be found at twenty-two Love Lane.' Jesus, what *a fucking nightmare*."

He took off his glasses and put his wrist up to his eyes.

"Whoa, where'd they get that business about blood on the wall?" said Ronald Deutsch on the cell phone. "I thought they only went in the bathroom to get fingerprints when they were there yesterday."

"I don't know." Jeff shook his head. "The only people who've been in the living room are me, the kids, the grandparents, the baby-sitter, and her friend Lynn . . .'"

Putting his glasses back on, he watched a dull glint of sun on a squad car's chrome fender narrow into a hard white gleam.

"Well, one of them must've said something to the police," said the lawyer. "We're gonna have to deal with that if we want to get the search thrown out later."

"All right, so what time will you be done in court?"

Paco Ortiz came out of the house and stood beside him on the steps, waiting for him to take a break from the phone conversation.

"The earliest I can be out to your place is four-thirty, buddy," said the lawyer. "Sorry about that."

"Shit, that's two and a half hours." Jeff put his hand over the mouthpiece. "Yeah, what is it?"

"Sir, we don't want to be taking your house apart unnecessarily." Paco tugged on his earring. "So would you mind telling us if you have a workshop in your basement or some other place where you keep your tools?"

"What tools?"

"You don't have saws, hammers, pliers?"

"My wife said we were married almost ten years, and she never even saw me pick up a screwdriver." He took his hand off the mouthpiece. "Ronald, are you hearing this?"

"Only let them look in the areas specified by the warrant . . . ," the lawyer said, electronic interference starting to scrub out his voice. "And . . . can you hear me? Don't give them any . . . all right? And don't answer any other questions until I get there."

"Ronald, I'm losing you."

The signal cut out as commotion rose in the house behind him. Couches were being moved, rugs rolled up. Tremendous banging echoed from the second floor. Jeff heard officers yelling at one another inside like a bunch of Bavarian tourists who'd just stumbled upon a beer garden. And then a long slow creak of wood timbers ending in a sudden painful crack brought him to his feet.

"My children lost their mother two days ago and now they have to see their home torn apart?"

"We're being as careful as we can, but we need to be thorough." Paco nodded sympathetically. "You can understand that. We all want the same thing here."

"Yeah, yeah, of course, but . . ."

"In-laws got the kids?"

"Yeah, they took them to Rye Playland, but . . ." Jeff felt all the blood start to drain from his head.

He steadied himself against the railing. "You know, my little guy wants to have a party when Mommy finally comes back."

Paco raised an eyebrow. "You lay it out for him?"

"He won't believe me."

He heard the garage door being pulled open and pictured the apparatus of his breastbone lifting, revealing his raw beating heart.

"I'm sorry to be putting you through this, Mr. Lanier," Paco said. "We'll be out of your hair before you know it."

The sergeant with the unibrow and the double chin came around the corner from the garage, toting a white-and-brown paint can. "Hey, look what I found."

He hoisted it high so they could all read the label for the gallon of Thompson's Wood Protector.

"Well, how about that?" Paco pulled his mouth over to one side of his face. "Where'd you find it?"

"Sitting right there in the garage, when I first went in. I didn't even have to look for it."

The detective smoothed his goatee and looked down at Jeff. "You want to tell me about this?"

"What?" Jeff shrugged. "It belongs to one of your guys. Keeps the wood from rotting, I guess."

"'Scuse me?"

Paco looked from Jeff to the can and then back again.

"One of your guys was doing our deer fence this summer. The guy who was here with you yesterday. Mike Fallon. Old friend of my wife's. I thought you knew that."

Paco's head became a stubbly sphere of clefts and ridges. "So, what's it still doing here?"

"Beats me. I don't get that involved. He took two or three other cans with him when he came to pick up his tools last week."

The sergeant's mouth opened slightly.

"So Mike was by in the last week?" Paco asked, the skin wrapping tight over his skull again.

"Yeah, sure." Jeff stared at him. "Don't you guys talk to each other?"

21

"HE DID *WHAT?*"

Barry sat up quickly, as if he was about to choke. He'd started off doing one of those tender just-hold-me things with Lynn after the kids went to bed, but it somehow turned into a whole hot fleshy triple-X-rated adventure during which they were bouncing around the four-poster like pinballs, falling off the mattress, tonguing and humping wildly on the floor. Eighteen years and she could still intrigue and startle, still beguile and enthrall, still draw him in so deep and rock and roll him with such abandon that half his relatives, the School Board, and the Mormon Tabernacle Choir could all walk in the room and he wouldn't be able to tear himself off her. But then . . . a huff. A restless shifting of the hips, an upward tilting of the torso. A murmured "I'm sorry . . . I just . . ." Okay. He backed off: she needed time. Her best friend was dead. Come on, man. Call that dog back from the hunt.

And then she suddenly climbed off the floor and up into bed and laid this story on him about her ex-boyfriend showing up at the studio.

"You've gotta be kidding," he said, getting in beside her. "This guy's supposed to be investigating a murder. What's he doing coming by the house unannounced in the first place?"

"He said he had some more questions."

"I'm sure he did."

He propped up his pillow and punched it a few times as he pictured Fallon smiling down at him in the train station parking lot. *You trying to tell me she's never mentioned me?*

"You didn't let him think it was okay to make a play for you, did you?"

"Of course not." She pulled the linen sheet over her breasts. "I told him to go away."

"I just couldn't help noticing that you were a little cagey when I asked you about him before."

She sighed and started to tug a blanket away from him. "It's complicated."

"So you keep telling me."

He felt the shifting of her weight on the bedsprings. It had taken him years to truly understand that when you marry someone, you marry a whole history. Not just the bloodlines that give your son the big nose and your daughter high cholesterol. You marry close friends, old records, inside jokes, and long-standing Friday-night traditions. You marry into arguments you never made, deals you would've never agreed to in a million years, promises you could never hope to keep.

"Then are you going to fill me in on some of this deep background or am I just going to have to go blundering along, stumbling over my own dick?"

She sat up and fluffed the pillows behind her. In the bedroom candlelight, she looked like a portrait of one of those fair porcelain beauties who always turned up in the middle of tawdry nineteenth-century scandals that caused great empires to collapse.

"Well, you know, things got a little rough after the first time my mother got sick," she began.

"Yeah, okay."

"My parents had already split up, and my dad was living in the city, making the swinging bachelor's scene at Maxwell's Plum or wherever."

Barry snorted at the mention of her Deadbeat Dad, who'd stepped out on the family just in time to miss the tail end of the Sexual Revolution. The brilliant advertising mind that brought us the famous chimp Mr. Muggleby smoking a Winston in a Chevy convertible. Barry remembered the old man standing by himself in his groovy black turtleneck and tweed jacket at their wedding reception, trying to hit on young waitresses going by.

"So it was basically the three of us staggering along," said Lynn, tucking the sheet under her armpits. "I'd just gotten my learner's permit, and I had this ridiculous Chrysler Cordoba my father left us so I could get Mom to the doctor's and do the shopping . . ."

"Ah, Cordoh-bah," Barry purred like Ricardo Montalban. "Feel the rich Corinthian leatha-ar."

"Exactly. It was like steering the Love Boat."

It occurred to him that she'd never mentioned this car before. Not that he'd ever probed her that much about high school.

"Anyway," she said, "one day it stalls out in the school parking lot, and this Eric Clapton song comes on the tape player. You know, 'Sister will do the best she can . . .' And I just lost it. I couldn't keep it together anymore. My parents are divorced. My mother has MS. I just broke up with my boyfriend. And I'm sitting there, tears streaming down my face because we're like a boat taking on water every day."

"What about your father? Where was he?"

"He was being a schmuck," she said, giving the deli-counter Yiddish she'd picked up from him a certain WASPish élan. "Trying to pick up the coat-check girl, visiting about once a month, and chintzing out on child support payments."

He couldn't recall the last time she'd spoken with such heat about her father. But everything was sounding different tonight. He wondered if there was more to the story of her and the cop in the studio than she'd let on so far.

"So, what happened with the car?"

"So I look up, and there's Michael Fallon staring at me. And I'm like, *Oh, shit.*"

"Why?"

"Because I thought he was a lunatic. His older brother, Johnny, and him were like these local legends who'd go down to the river and shoot fish and give each other ink tattoos, like inmates. And we all knew their father was this prison guard who used to beat them and whip them up like rottweilers so they'd act even crazier."

"I went to school with guys like that." Barry shook his head. "The Lobrano brothers. Their parole officers came to our graduation."

"So I think I'm about to get carried off and raped, but instead he pops the hood, disappears under it with his big head, and bobs up again a minute later and says, 'Okay. Try it now. You had carbon on the spark plugs.'"

"The course of true love. He fixed your car."

"Listen, it was more than my father was doing." She picked up an elastic band from the night table to tie her hair back. "It was good to have a man around."

"I'll bet." He wagged his eyebrows, not wanting to appear to take this too seriously.

"It wasn't just this caveman thing," she protested. "He was really nice to me. I guess he kind of recognized that we were both damaged goods. I remember he asked me out for ice cream about a week after he fixed my car. And I just kind of mentioned that I was trying to figure out how to get Mom into the car for her next appointment. And so he just shows up the next day and literally carries her to the car, as if she was this precious vase. It was . . . sweet."

"Sounds like you were really into him," he said, noticing her face was still flush and warm.

"Yeah, but you know what? I wasn't so much into *him* as a guy. As a boyfriend. I was more into everything around him."

"What's that supposed to mean?"

He found himself pausing and pondering little details that he normally would've shrugged off and forgotten. He'd always just assumed that she was reticent talking about this time in her life because she'd got slingshot so abruptly into adulthood. But now he was beginning to wonder if there was another reason.

"I mean, I kind of fell in love with his whole world. *For a while.*" She gave him a worried look, wanting him to understand. "He was this real neighborhood guy, and I grew up on a street that didn't even have sidewalks. You know what I mean? His family was real bedrock in this town. Literally. They came over during the potato famine and helped build the old tunnels and aqueducts."

"*Sandhogs* they used to call them."

"They totally took me in," she said. "His mother would cook these big heaping trays of lasagna and ziti for me to take home to my mother and sister when we were all living on junk food and pizza. And then his dad would give Mike extra money to take me out to the really nice restaurants in town, like Florio's and . . ." She stopped and shook her head, silently recriminating herself. "I didn't get what a big deal that was. These were working people. They never even took themselves out."

"So why'd you break up with him?"

He found himself pulling back the layers, playing prosecutor, wondering exactly how it was that she'd managed to never mention these people in his presence before.

"I don't know. I guess I just started seeing around the edges too much. But it's not like I was totally naive either. I did some things that were maybe kind of questionable."

"Like what?"

He noticed lumps and hills appearing and disappearing under the covers as she fidgeted. Here a bent knee, there a crooked elbow. He found himself growing a little wary, as if he'd just realized she was concealing a jackknife under the mattress.

"Like I had this camera Mom had given me, and I started taking all these pictures of him and his family." She dropped her voice. "I mean, she always said that once you find your subject, hang on to it with both hands. So I kind of got to be the official photographer at their family functions and Knights of Columbus dinners. It was this whole other world, one great picture after another. Old drunks at christenings, laughing with a beer in one hand and a baby in the other. Volunteer firemen checking out patio furniture while the market down the street was burning. Then one day his father gave me a tour of the prison, and I got that picture of the guard asleep in the old electric chair."

"Well, I certainly know that one," Barry said.

One of his personal favorites. He remembered bursting out laughing the first time he saw it. But when you looked again, it be- came more haunting; the screw with his head thrown back and his mouth open, as if Old Sparky had just discharged him from this mortal coil.

"So that's when I really figured out what I was doing," she said.

"And what was so bad about that?"

"That I kept doing it even after I knew I was going to break up with him." The sheets were bunched up around her like clotted cream. "I mean, I always sort of knew it wasn't going to work out in the long run. He just needed to control things too much."

"Oh, yeah?"

All this scrunching down and covering up was starting to get to him. It was as if they'd never been naked together.

"See, I took all these great black-and-whites of him and his fam- ily. Really good grainy W. Eugene Smith, Dorothea Lange stuff.

They were just these amazing subjects. His mother was kind of a hefty Irish lady with big ankles, who kept house for the good families up the hill. But she was always carrying on like she was Jackie Kennedy. She had all these nice plates and bath towels that never matched, like they'd all come from different places. And so I got this picture of her at the ironing board, wearing these fake pearls and a helmet of sprayed black hair. And it's heartbreaking because you can see the distance between who she is and who she wants to be. She's all dressed up in this nice sleeveless blouse and Capri pants, but she's got this black eye and her husband's sitting at the kitchen table behind her, and he's like this bent steel pipe in an undershirt, cigarette on top of his Piel's can. And his arm is in a cast because it got broken in a fight with an inmate. It's just this study in frustration. I called it, *Someday My Prince Will Come*."

"So why haven't I ever seen it?" asked Barry.

He'd seen hundreds of her other pictures. In fact, he used to joke that he wanted to make love to her the first time he laid eyes on her, but actually decided to marry her after he saw her pictures and realized they'd still have something to talk about in sixty years.

"Mike made me destroy it."

"For real?"

"Yes. He couldn't stand to see his father that way, because he loved him. Even when I said I'd never show it to anybody, that wasn't good enough. He wanted me to burn the negative because he couldn't stand the way *I* made them look. As if I'd given his mother the black eye. So that's when we started having serious problems."

"How serious?" He found himself pinching a half-inch roll on his waist, thinking the time had come to start those sit-ups again.

"Well . . ." She tucked her chin in, looking embarrassed. "Some of it was my fault. I might've let him get the wrong idea about how things were going to be."

"What are you talking about?"

With a queasy stomach, he decided that he needed to know the general outline but not the more graphic details of his wife's past sex life.

"I mean, he thought we were going to get married. We even talked *very* seriously about having kids. And then when he realized that it wasn't going to happen, he got really upset."

"Are you telling me he hit you?"

"Just once," she said, almost as if she was rationalizing it. "And a lot of things led up to it."

"Oh, fuck this." He stood up and pulled on his boxers. "Where's the phone? I'm calling the chief."

"*Listen*" — she reached across the bed and grabbed his elbow — "I'm not saying I deserved it, but there was a lot going on then. His father ended up getting in a lot of trouble for that picture of his friend sleeping in the electric chair. They transferred him to a really bad unit, and the next time they had one of those riots, he almost got his throat cut. And in the meantime, I was off getting a scholarship to Pratt. And then there was this whole thing with his brother . . ."

"Doesn't matter." Barry cut her off, sitting back down on the edge of the bed. "I can't stand a man, hits a woman."

"I think I got over it faster than he did, to tell you the truth."

He studied her profile against the background of the white lamp shade. Dot by dot, a portrait was accumulating in his mind of a woman very much like his wife but somehow just slightly unfamiliar.

He hunched over, tension ratcheting its way up his spine, disk by disk. "So how come you didn't tell me any of this before we moved back here?" he said.

"It didn't seem important. It was all so long ago. Last I'd heard, Mike was working out in Arizona."

"You've had this whole little secret world going on here, and I'm only just finding out about it."

"That's not true." She drew her knees up, making a linen mountain between them. "I didn't call Michael and ask him to come by. Why are you accusing me?"

"I want him to stay away," he said.

"I don't think he'll come back. I was pretty definite with him."

"You don't *think?*" He stood up again and found his robe, experiencing a late-night rush of adrenaline. "Well, then why don't I pick up the phone and make sure he got the message? We'll have a sit-down, just him and me."

"I am seriously asking you not to do that, Barry. *Really.*"

For a moment, he was too angry to properly hear her.

"*Barry,*" she repeated, trying to retrieve him.

"*What?*"

"I know him. He's not going to like it if another man tells him to back off."

"So, what do you suggest we do?"

"Just don't provoke him. That's all I'm asking."

He looked back over his shoulder, wondering if there was anything else she wasn't telling him. *You'll be happy here*, the real estate agent had said when they first moved to this town. And he'd gone along with it, figuring he owed Lynn a chance to settle down and to be near her mom for the end after all the moving around they'd done for his work. And, of course, there'd been that apple tree. But now he had to wonder what he'd got himself into.

"Please," Lynn said, hugging her knees and raising her eyes.

"Ah . . . *fuck*."

He fell back beside her. He'd outmuscled players with thirty pounds on him in basketball and beaten lawyers with ten years more trial experience, but he'd never had any talent for fighting with her.

"Will you at least promise me you'll call the second he shows up again?" he asked.

"Sure." She pressed against him, slipping a hand under the sheets. "Now will you just shut up and hold me until I fall asleep?"

22

THE PARTY ACROSS the street was just getting going as Mike parked in front of his house on Regan Way. He smelled pork barbecuing, heard Marc Anthony blaring, and saw a Mexican flag draped over the porch railing of the tiny two-story where his father's cousin Brian Moran used to live. How the hell did these Hispanic guys do it? Every day, they were up the hill digging wells and mowing lawns, and every other night they were in the backyard, throwing back *cervezas* and celebrating as if they couldn't believe their good fortune winding up in America. Some of these guys didn't even live *inside* a house. At least four of them slept in the '89 Lincoln Town Car parked in the driveway. But as he listened to the raucous burble of their laughter and let himself into his own house, a drab twin sister with the same concrete driveway and the same lopsided porch built into the slope of the hill, he felt a rusty screw turn inside his heart.

The place smelled like Murphy Oil Soap and cedar chips from the hamster's cage. Piles of laundry sat neatly folded on the stairs. Down the short hallway, he saw Marie in the kitchen, still in her work clothes, making a pot of tea for herself. He closed the door behind him and heard the sound of water about to boil.

"What's the matter?" he said. "Doesn't the new girl put the laundry away?"

"She doesn't know where anything goes." The pot started to whistle. "I haven't had time to show her."

His shoulders brushed the walls as he came in to talk to her. Was the hall always this small? After being reminded of how big Lynn's place was from the outside, he found himself noticing the lowness of the ceilings here, the age of the wallpaper, the narrowness of the kitchen, the way the two of them could barely fit between the stove and the refrigerator.

"How's life among the deadbeats?" he asked, putting his brief-case down on the counter and seeing where caulk had worn away around the sink.

"Unbelievable." Her eyes registered the ink stain under his pocket. "These people have driver's licenses and bank loans. And zero sense of personal responsibility."

He tried to flash her the old Burt Reynolds smile. "You get a lot of those second and third notices out tonight?"

"Yes, but it's all at the point of diminishing returns. Every time we send out a notice, the percentage of people who pay goes down. We're going to end up sending half of them out for collection any-way, so I don't even know why we bother giving them another chance."

"Hmm . . ." He moved around her to wash his hands and saw a pile of sawdust on the windowsill over the sink.

Diminishing returns. Zero responsibility. Why bother giving them an-other chance? Not exactly encouraging words for a man to come home to. What happened to the devoted girl who used to rub his shoulders every night? He missed her gratitude. The way he could see himself grow bigger in her eyes instead of smaller, the way he did today with Lynn. He missed how the whole family used to climb over one another to get at him when he came home. And most of all, he missed the man he used to be around here.

He thought they were together on this story when they got mar-ried. He was a gift to her. He'd rescued her. She was living in a cruddy little two-bedroom above the garden supply store on Ever-green with her mother, two sisters, and her brother the schizo. He was taking her away from all that. He was going to be the hero, making up for her fuckhead father abandoning the family without a single support check. He was going to be the one who made up for all the failures and disappointments of other men.

But somehow that story got balled up. Yes, he'd screwed up mon-umentally. And yes, he'd had to beg her to take him back and give him another chance. But what was truly galling was that she'd decided that *she* was going to be the hero, going back to school, buying a couple of business suits from Talbots, getting a brusque little pixie cut, and landing herself a job in delinquent accounts at the hospital. She seemed to be saying that she didn't need him that much anymore. She could pay off their loans, cover half the monthly expenses, and still have time to wreak vengeance on all the other deadbeats in the world.

"How's the case?" she said.

"You know. Just trying to pull the threads together one by one."

"Still doesn't seem right, having you work on it. I mean you *did* know her."

His eye stayed on the pile of sawdust as he dried his hands. She hadn't found the diary he had hidden downstairs, had she?

"I know everybody," he said. "If I let that stop me, I couldn't even write a traffic summons."

"We have to talk." She turned the heat down under her kettle.

He tried to gather himself in as he watched the blue flames stop licking the underside of the pot.

"Timmy," she said. "I got another call from school."

He heard water still bubbling in the pot. "What happened?"

"Ms. Wagner said he's being aggressive in the yard with Lanny Taylor again."

"Shit." He heard the hot water hiss as she lifted the pot. "Well, what's he supposed to do if that other kid keeps picking on him?"

"Two weeks ago, you were supposed to spend the morning in school and help him settle down."

"Excuse me, but have you noticed what's come up in the meantime?"

"They want us to come in Friday afternoon for another conference about this impulse control problem."

He watched the steam rise as she poured the water into her cup.

"Great. I'm in the middle of a major homicide investigation. I need this like I need a fucking hole in my head."

"Well, I'm sorry Timmy didn't check with you before he decided to go berserk again."

"Why do you call it 'going berserk'? This other kid keeps stealing his lunch money. What's he supposed to do? Turn into a Maytag?"

He watched her get the honey down from the crowded cabinet shelf she'd spent forty-five minutes organizing. "So, what've you been telling him to do?"

"I tell him to work it out, but don't let anyone push you around. You don't know what it's like with guys. You can't accept disrespect. First they take your comb, next day it's your radio. Sometimes you gotta put a man on his ass and let him know what goes where."

"Yeah, that's brilliant, Mike." She ran the honey jar lid under the hot water, not even bothering to ask him to open it for her. "Is that another one of your father's pearls of wisdom?"

"The man survived thirty-one years in Owenoke. He must've been doing something right."

"Excuse me, but did it ever occur to you that what works on a cell block doesn't work in a schoolyard?"

"Sure, but did it ever occur to *you* that maybe this is about you going back to work?" he came back at her. "Maybe he thinks you're abandoning him."

"Well, maybe if you didn't spend twenty thousand on a new Toyota pickup when we're already fifteen hundred in the hole every month for *your* alimony payments, I wouldn't be working this hard in the first place."

"Thanks a lot, Marie. That really helps."

"Hey, I wasn't the one who let customers pay me in stock options for putting up their fences. It's not my fault you lost money on those jobs. I told you not to do it."

He turned away from her and caught sight of the little sawdust pile again. Carpenter ants. Wouldn't that just be perfect if they had an army of dark little carpenters gnawing away at the insides of their house. He already felt like he had a mass of them working their way through his head.

He yanked open the refrigerator door to look for a beer and saw the milk and orange juice cartons standing sentry on the top shelf, the labeled Tupperware containers on the second shelf, the jars lined up by size on the door shelves, the fruits and vegetables sensibly segregated in the crisper. *Impulse control.* One of those social-work phrases that made you feel like somebody was boring holes in your brain. Control all those nasty impulses. Don't look at another woman. Don't spend all that money. Don't get ahead of yourself. Don't fall behind. Don't lose your temper. Don't raise your voice. Don't raise your hand. Don't think about things going back to the way they used to be.

"So, what do you want from me?" he said.

"I want you to be where you say you're going to be. I want you not to humiliate me or the children anymore."

"When have I . . ."

"You know damn well what I'm talking about. I want you to make up your mind about whether you're going to be part of this family."

He stayed bent by the open door, trying to let the cool air roll over him. *Eggshell country*, he thought. *Ever since she took me back, I'm living on a continent made out of eggshells. Any wrong little movement can break off a state.*

"I think they want to talk about putting him on Ritalin," she said in a muted voice.

"Fuck." He grabbed a Coors and slammed the door harder than he meant to, jarring the tubes and bottles inside.

"I'm starting to think it's not such a bad idea." She looked at him.

"Yeah, yeah, great. Keep him doped-up all the time and turn him into a goddamn robot." The dewy silver label crinkled against his palm. "Where's my bottle opener?"

"Drawer next to the oven."

He pulled it open, noticing the handle was loose. One of these days he'd have to get the Phillips and tighten it. He used to be so good at fixing things around the house. She used to love that about him. If there was a shelf that needed to be put up above the washing machine, or a leak in the sink, they never needed to call anybody. And in those days, she had a way of showing a man he was appreciated. Thinking back, he realized that some of the best sex they ever had was after he'd just put in the fiberglass insulation or replaced a rusty pipe.

But lately he'd begun to notice drill bits and Molly bolts lying around when he got home, because she was doing the work herself.

"We've always known he had a temper," she said.

"At least we know he comes by it honestly."

"You're telling me."

He pried the cap off the Coors and heard the greedy little suck-gasp of air.

"How many times do you need me to say I'm sorry, Marie? You want to give me a number one of these days? Three thousand five hundred and twenty-seven? You want me to spend a week saying nothing but I'm sorry, I'm sorry, I'm sorry . . ."

"Keep your voice down. The children are sleeping."

He took a long hit off the bottle, trying to cool his gut. Christ, how long was she going to keep him dangling on this hook? He felt like he was on parole with stringent conditions. *No fraternizing with undesirable elements. No fraternizing with desirable elements. No more fucking around with other women. No more choir practice. No more unnecessary roughness with the wife and kids. No giving in to uncontrollable impulses. No Shit.* He knew he couldn't afford another divorce, financially or mentally. And she'd already made it clear this was his last chance.

He thought again of the passage he'd read in the diary yesterday (*Starting to think there's something the matter with M.*), and more of the carpenter ants fanned out in his head.

Half of what made it truly terrifying was how much he had to lose. Not just the kids and the marriage, but the respect of his fellow officers, the smiles of the moms on the soccer sidelines, the teachers and ladies at Saint Stephen's all knowing him by his first name, the Christmas cards from the town trustees, the Planning Board people coming up and thanking him for cleaning up downtown, the nod of recognition from the bartenders at the Gate who'd filled his father's and grandfather's glasses and still waved off his money.

"I'm really worried about him," Marie said, getting back to the main subject, her words too much like the ones in the diary.

"What are you talking about?"

"I've seen how he is. He'll just be playing and wrestling with one of his friends on the ground, and then all of a sudden a switch will go off in his head."

"I never saw that," he said, holding the beer in front of his chest.

"Yes, you have. He becomes a different person right before your eyes. You know exactly what I'm talking about."

He turned away from her and took another swig, cold fingers encircling his heart.

The other kids were fine. Mike Jr., his ten-year-old, was a fearless knucklehead like his dead uncle. Cheryl, his eleven-year-old, was more like her mother, always with her head inside a Harry Potter book. But Timmy, his youngest by a year, was the one most like him. They even looked alike: the same long groove between his nose and his lip, same big jaw, and same deep-set eyes. But there was also a dark spot in him that up until now he'd thought no one else had noticed. Something fizzing under the surface. He'd recognized it one afternoon at soccer last year when Timmy was pretending to fence with another kid on the sidelines. Almost in slow motion, he saw his son pick up a stick and jab it at the other kid's eye. Mike had managed to get between them before the damage was done, but he was scared shitless for weeks afterward. Because he knew what it was. He knew because he struggled with it every day himself. That fist that could never quite unclench. That red mist that seemed to fall over him sometimes, that shout always at the back of his throat.

"You know what this is really about?" he said. "It's about real estate."

"How do you figure that?" She tapped the lid of her honey jar against the side of the counter.

"They just want all the kids sitting there like little corporate drones so the reading and math scores go up and people will pay more for their houses. There's nothing wrong with Timmy."

"That's right, Mike. Just keep saying it. You don't have to come to the meeting. You don't even have to come home at all."

He had a sudden urge to strike her. The idea of a punch forming in his shoulder and working its way down his arm. Or maybe he'd just smash her over the bridge of the nose with the half-full Coors bottle, see if that shut her up. But then she twisted the top off the honey jar and gave him a look of girlish pride for not having asked him to help. He let the fist drop back at his side. See? *Impulse control.*

"There's nothing wrong with the kid," he repeated.

She dipped her teaspoon into the open jar and dandled a clear golden line into her cup.

"Three-fifteen, Friday," she said, licking the spoon when she was done. "I'm going to bed. I left some chicken in the refrigerator. You can heat it up in the microwave."

"Yeah, nice seeing you too." He gave her a limp salute as she took her tea and started to walk out.

"What happened to your shirt?" She stopped in the doorway and stared at his pocket. "Looks like you bled all over yourself."

"Leaky pen. I didn't have another shirt in my locker."

"Give it here." She sighed, holding her hand out. "Though what the hell you expect me to do about it I don't know."

23

BARRY DROPPED LYNN off early the next morning to get the Explorer back from Riverside Motors on Front Street and then continued on down to the train station in the Saab. As he parked in the lot, he saw Harold Baltimore get out of his navy Buick LeSabre across the street and amble toward the Starbucks around the corner. Almost immediately, Barry decided that he needed a third cup of coffee to really get the day on its feet.

He crossed the street after the chief, maneuvered his way through the milling pack of day laborers out front, and then went in through the tinted glass doors, seeing that Harold had already arrived at the front of the line.

"Gimme a *venti* cappuccino," Harold Baltimore was saying in a hoarse exhausted grumble.

"It's on the house," said the boy behind the counter, who had a shaved head and a small gold ring through his eyebrow. "Compliments of the manager."

"I don't need any compliments." The chief proffered a ten-dollar bill. "Just gimme the correct change."

"Isn't that something?" Barry took his place in line behind him. "Our fathers fought the wars in Germany and Korea, and our generation invented the five-dollar cup of coffee. Makes you wonder about civilization, doesn't it?"

The chief turned and grunted, so tired it looked like he had old damp grain sacks under his eyes.

"How's it going?" asked Barry.

"It's going."

He'd gotten to know Harold slightly from Lynn's mother's funeral last year, which the Baltimore family had handled with understated decorum and taste at their funeral home on Bank Street.

"You remember me, right? Barry Schulman."

"Sure. The son-in-law. Rosewood casket, eleven o'clock service, three limos to the cemetery."

The chief himself had sat in their living room beforehand, patiently going through the casket catalog with Lynn and sparing her the arduous task of going to the funeral parlor to pick one out.

"That's amazing," said Barry. "You remember every service?"

"Mrs. Stockdale was my fifth-grade art teacher." Harold accepted his cappuccino and dropped a few coins in the tip jar. "Great lady. Taught me how to draw sunsets."

"Ah."

"And, of course, your wife was in my high school class." The chief moved down the counter for sugar. "We've always had friends in common."

"Just give me a regular cup, black, please," Barry told the boy at the register before he stepped to the side after the chief. "So it sounds like you had a tough case drop in your lap. I saw there was a little story today in the Gannett paper."

Harold raised the sugar dispenser high, pouring a steady granulated stream into his cup.

"We'll put it down," he said.

"You catching any breaks?"

The chief kept pouring, lowering and raising the white powdered stream so it arced and stretched in midair.

"Good luck is the residue of careful design," he said. "Just like a proper burial plot."

Barry paid the counterboy and took his coffee, staring down at the smoky black surface and remembering that Lynn had asked him not to make trouble.

"How's your better half?" the chief asked.

"She's pretty upset, as you might imagine. Sandi Lanier was a good friend of hers."

"Huh," said the chief, managing to pack commiseration, grim acceptance, and cool professional distance into a single syllable.

One of the other boys behind the counter began tapping the grinder with a little hammer to get every last grain out.

"You know, one of your guys came by my house yesterday," Barry said.

"Oh? Who was this?"

"Your detective lieutenant there, the big guy. Fallon."

Harold carefully put a white plastic lid on his cappuccino, making it clear that he was taking it to go.

"I was kind of surprised to hear about that," said Barry, "since he'd already been out to ask my wife some questions the day before."

"He may have had a few things he wanted to follow up on since your wife was so close with the victim." The chief shrugged, not letting on if he was bothered.

"I understand that, but it also made it a little awkward since your detective knows my wife as well. I think they may have had a sort of . . . an uncomfortable exchange."

A part of him knew that he should just drop it as Lynn had asked him to, but walking away at this point would have felt neglectful, like leaving the dome light on in the car or letting a very small child alone in the bath with the hot water running.

"I'm not sure what you mean by that." Harold worked his fingertips around the rims of his eye sockets.

"I don't want to get into specifics, but my impression was that some things were said that didn't directly pertain to the investigation."

He could see that he'd made Harold deeply unhappy. The chief drew in his lips and lowered his brow, making his face look slightly squashed, as if someone were sitting on his head.

"Look, I appreciate that you've got a murder to solve and that you're just trying to do your job. And we'll do anything you need us to do to cooperate. Sandi was a good lady. Just, if it's *possible* . . ." — Barry tread carefully here, knowing he might have already overstepped his bounds by a half-mile — "it'd work better for us if you could give us a little more advance notice. My wife would be happy to come down to the station to talk to you."

The compression increased around the chief's mouth. He put his coffee cup down firmly.

"You're a lawyer, right?"

"You don't miss much, do you?"

"My wife sold you your house," the chief deadpanned.

"No kidding? Emmie?"

Barry found himself having to readjust his settings a little. All right, so the chief is married to a white lady. A very white lady. Cool. Emmie with the oversize round glasses, turquoise bracelet, and straight blond hair, who'd piled them all into her Navigator and driven them up to the farmhouse on Grace Hill Road less than twenty months ago. *You'll be happy here.* She'd announced it, as if it was a prophecy out of one of the sun-faded New Age books on her dashboard. Not just your typical suburban couple. He'd forgotten her saying she was married to a cop.

"We've been married almost twenty-one years," the chief said matter-of-factly. "My point is, is that this is a *small* town. All right? A lot of people know each other. I even knew the victim. So we may have some big-city problems, but we all have to co*exist.* You understand what I'm saying?"

"Sure, but . . ."

"Three weeks ago, one of my officers had to arrest my second cousin for selling marijuana less than a hundred and fifty yards from the high school. Was I happy about it? What do you think?"

"I think things might be sort of tense next time the family gets together for the holidays."

"You're damn right. But I have a job to do, and I'm going to do it. Now we got all kinds of folks living in our little town. We've got stockbrokers and bank presidents, heads of foundations and plenty of distinguished lawyers such as yourself. But do you think it would be right if I gave them special treatment over my second cousin trying to put a little cash aside to buy himself a new car?"

"Of course not," said Barry.

"Now I know my officers make mistakes sometimes — believe me, *I know* — but I also know that I owe it to the people of this town to do a thorough and complete investigation without fear or favor and that Michael Fallon is one of the best men I have."

"He tried to put a move on my wife."

"Well then, I will certainly speak to him on that," the chief said stiffly, clearly roiling under the surface. "But I also would appreciate it if you cooperated fully with any other questions my investigators have. You and your wife knew the victim, and you may have other key information we're going to need in this case."

"Of course." Barry covered his coffee with a lid and picked up his briefcase. "You can count on it."

He saw the chief take a deep fortifying breath and instantly understood the crux of his daily dilemma: how do you keep both your officers and your constituents in line when most of them probably don't trust you in the first place? Probably only by conscientiously pissing everyone off to precisely the same degree.

"Well, all right then." The chief dismissed him with a curt nod toward the front door. "Don't miss your train."

24

WHEN MIKE OPENED up the detectives' squad room that morning, the phone was ringing on Paco Ortiz's desk. Mike picked it up before the answering machine got it and found himself speaking to a state trooper named Cotter.

Sandi Lanier's red '99 Audi had been found in a Motel 6 parking lot some five miles outside of town. The doors were unlocked, there were no signs of struggle, and there were no obvious traces of blood anywhere in the vehicle. They'd already run the plates and come up with a photo ID of Sandi, but none of the motel staff could recall seeing her and there was no room registered in her name.

Mike took down the information in his notebook and thanked the trooper, saying arrangements would be made to pick up the car within the next few days. Then he hung up the phone and stared at his own handwriting, as cryptic as a doctor's prescription, wondering what to do.

Two days at sea and he still had zero visibility ahead. Shouldn't the fog have parted? Shouldn't the next move have presented itself? But the only thing that was clear was that he should've said more to Harold the other night. Just enough to spin the wheel a little and save himself from a head-on collision.

Of course, now that he'd read the diary from end to end, he knew there was no easy way to double back and make excuses for not owning up in the first place. All he could do was keep sailing straight off the end of the map. But in the dreary haze of his early morning hangover, he felt confounded, seasick, and hard done by all the women in his life.

Am beginning to suspect no one will ever really love me. Every man I've ever known has turned out to be a fraud. Shiiiit, baby! Look at your own damn self. None of the men you knew had their fat sucked or their hair colored.

He decided to put off making a decision about the trooper's message until he could at least sweat the toxins out. After checking to make sure he had no calls on his own machine, he changed into his shorts, T-shirt, and sneakers and went downstairs to the gym in the basement. A sign on the wall said, FATIGUE MAKES COWARDS OF MEN. Greaseman, the D.A.R.E. cop who spent his on-duty hours lecturing school kids about drugs and his off-duty hours popping steroids, was on the StairMaster, listening to his Walkman and watching stock prices fluctuate wildly on CNBC. Sweat stains darkened patches of the mustard-brown carpet and a Fedders air conditioner rumbled asthmatically.

Mike took a seat on the bench and adjusted the weight to 220 pounds. Then he lay back and shut his eyes, focusing all his concerns into the effort of raising and lowering those stacks of black steel plates.

His muscles felt sluggish and achy; he'd stayed up too late reading the diary in the basement, tooling around on the Internet, and drinking bourbon from a SpongeBob SquarePants glass. He tried to gather his strength in the middle of his chest and push it out, imagining himself as Atlas, holding up the world. He felt the strain in his lats, the heavy laboring of his heart, the poison starting to ooze out of his pores. His elbows locked, and slowly he tried to straighten his arms, tightening his grip even as every nerve in his body screamed for him to stop. It was just a matter of dead-center control. Life was about maintaining control.

I told M. that I didn't want to keep doing this, she'd written in the diary. *But he's so relentless. He won't let things just be. I'm really starting to get nervous about him . . .*

Screw her. He concentrated on the flickering light over his head, pulling down deeper into himself, trying to find the hard impenetrable core of his being, the part that could never be broken.

The other night I showed him the new tattoo on my ankle . . .

Two hundred and twenty pounds and he was about to pop a double hernia. His brother could hoist 250 and dive with 75 pounds of scuba gear on his back, no problem. But how could that be? Johnny didn't have any of his body mass. He was just a wiry little guy. So how could he have been so much stronger?

I made some stupid remark about how I hoped I didn't get hepatitis C from the needle they used, and he just went nuts on me . . .

His sinews burned, and an angry hiss escaped from the corners of his mouth.

He started screaming and yelling about how could I do this to him and his family. What if I got them all infected?

Slowly, his elbows unlocked, and the weights began to rise higher as if succumbing to some buildup of hydraulic pressure. I'm a man. I'm the son of a man who was the son of a man.

He shoved me down on the bed and put his hands around my throat. I really thought he was going to strangle me . . .

His arms trembled slightly as he thought of shutting the book as soon as he read that. It didn't happen that way. Yes, it did. No, *it didn't.* She was crazy. She was exaggerating. No one would have ever believed her if she was still alive. And not for nothing, she was kidding about that needle, wasn't she? Hadda be. Hadda be. *I'm a man. I'm the son of a man who was the son of a man . . .* He ground his jaw, pushing harder and harder, slowly extending his arms until they couldn't lift anymore. But just then, Harold's face loomed above him, eclipsing the flickering light.

"What do you think you're doing?"

"What does it look like?" Mike gradually lowered the weights, incrementally becoming aware of the sound of his heartbeat fading in.

"Are we having some problem understanding each other?"

"What's up?"

He sat up quickly, thinking somehow Paco had found out about the missing diary. Blood began pounding in his ears.

"You think this is some kind of joke that they made a black man the police chief?"

"Look, will you chill the fuck out and tell me what's bothering you?"

Mike mopped his face with a towel, feeling a throb in the base of his throat. He'd never been afraid of Harold before, and he didn't like it. The Greaseman had departed the gym, leaving the CNBC lady babbling about earnings disappointments and declining indexes.

"I told you I needed you to take a step back, didn't I?"

"Just tell me what I did wrong." A droplet of sweat eased down the bridge of Mike's nose.

"Lynn Stockdale's husband came up to me at Starbucks this morning and said you were by the house yesterday bothering his wife."

"That what he said?"

The drop fell off the end of his nose and landed at Harold's feet.

"You want to tell me your side of it?" The chief looked down at the spot it made.

"I came by the house to clear up a couple of details."

"After I told you Paco was the primary. *Twice.*"

"There are certain kinds of information he might not be able to get, being from outside the community." Mike dabbed sweat out of the groove in his lip. "Sometimes people are more comfortable talking to somebody they've known all their lives. Sets off fewer alarm bells."

"Well, that worked like a charm, didn't it? What'd you do, whip your dick out?"

"Nothing she hasn't seen a hundred times. She used to be all over me, in case you forgot."

"We are in the middle of a murder investigation."

The chief's voice echoed off the cinder-block walls and died in the middle of the room. On the television, a former presidential candidate was talking about erectile dysfunction.

"Look, nothing happened," said Mike. "Absolutely nothing. She gave me a little peck on the cheek when I was leaving."

"And that's it?"

"Oh, come on. You know how it is when you see somebody you used to be into. There's still a kind of energy. It doesn't all just dry up. So she wanted to give me a good-bye kiss. It wasn't any big deal."

"Then why'd she tell her husband about it?"

"Who the hell knows? Maybe she felt guilty afterward. Or maybe somebody saw me leaving and asked her about it later. Whatever. Listen, it'd be the exact same way if you saw Sharon Carson again."

With the mention of his first white girlfriend, the chief's eyebrows relaxed and his features softened. It had taken him a good six months to get over the way Sharon's mother broke them up senior year, determined that her Bryn Mawr–bound daughter wasn't going to throw her life away dating one of the local black boys who washed dishes at the Copperhead Diner after school.

"You still put my back against the wall, Mikey," the chief said, renewing his determination. "I told you to step off."

"What're you gonna do, Harold? Wrap me up in Tyvek and fiberglass insulation? I live in this town. I'm still supposed to be running day-to-day operations for this department."

"And I am your chief," Harold told him coldly. "I already saved your career once. I can't do it again."

"And I saved your life when Brenda Carter came at you with a butcher knife. I didn't hear you complaining when I pumped a round into her."

Almost unconsciously, Harold's hand went to the right side of his abdomen.

"I haven't forgotten," he said. "I owe you a lot, but if I have another problem with you in this investigation, I'm gonna have to ask you to take more than a step back."

"Understood. I hear you." Mike stood up, wiping his face again. "You the big man now, Harold."

The chief squinted, trying to decide whether he'd been dissed with his own father's line.

"By the way," said Mike, playing it light and casual, "you ever get the tox results back from the state crime lab?"

Harold's face got small, as if he was going to start barking again. "You said you'd keep me in the loop," Mike reminded him.

The chief looked down at the hand still hovering near the old entry wound, notice of a debt outstanding.

"Yeah, we did," he said reluctantly. "She was eight weeks pregnant. But do me a favor and keep that under your hat, will you?"

25

AN IVORY-WHITE BMW 525i sat glowing in Sandi's driveway, looking as if her big white house had somehow given birth to it.

Lynn parked the Explorer behind it and got out with three full Corning Ware bowls of food that she'd spent the morning cooking for Jeff and the children. The BMW had to belong to Sandi's father, she realized. Every time she saw him, he had a different car, much in the same way other well-to-do men always had a new wife.

She heard his familiar phlegm-and-gravel voice as she walked up to the door and rang the bell.

"Oy, *Gottenyu*, Lynn." He flung open the door and stood before her, shaking his head. "What did they do to my baby?"

"Saul, I'm so sorry."

She put the food down and threw her arms around him. He was a short, blunt, unreflective cigar-smoker, who most people took to be a self-made millionaire. In fact, his own father had amassed a small fortune in the carpet business just after the Depression, most of which Saul lost on bad investments in the late sixties after his first wife died. But he'd found his touch in the seventies, snapping up Manhattan properties in decline, fixing up the lobbies, slapping faux-European names on the canopies, and charging exorbitant rents as soon as the market turned and people were desperate for two-bedrooms.

"Look at you." He closed the door and stood back, appraising her. "You look just like you did when you got out of high school."

"It's very kind of you to say that, Saul."

"I always said if my Sandi had half your poise, she'd be beating the boys off with a stick."

She cringed a little, remembering how Saul had been a bit of a lecher for as long as she'd known him.

"She was a beautiful girl, Saul. I'll never have another friend like her."

He nodded his great white mane sagely. "She looked fantastic when she lost all the weight before the summer," he said. "'Pretty as a shiksa,' I told her."

Okay, thought Lynn, *that would have been worth five years of psychotherapy right there if Sandi were still alive.*

"Is Barbara here?" She asked after the second Mrs. Feinberg.

"Upstairs, taking a nap. This has been very hard on her too. She was very close with Sandi."

Actually, Sandi always despised her stepmother and referred to her as Queen Botoxica. Barbara had been serviced and overhauled more often than a nuclear submarine, and if Saul had had a mind to do it, he could've made himself a third wife out of all her cast-off parts.

"How are the kids doing today?" Lynn asked, wondering if Jeff had finally got up the nerve to break the news to them.

"Who knows?" Saul raised his great bushy eyebrows. "I don't think it's even sunk in yet."

She heard clattering and yelling from deeper in the house and peered down the hall to see Dylan and Isadora back by the stairway, wailing on each other and their baby-sitter, Inez, with wooden swords and plastic baseball bats. To the casual eye, they were just children playing wildly. But then Lynn saw Dylan take his sword with both hands and smash it as hard as he could against the flimsy cardboard shield Inez was holding. This was the fury of a little boy who understood perfectly well that he would never see his mother again.

"See what I mean?" Saul waved a weary hand. "They're okay."

Lynn looked askance, thinking what an old obtuse dope he was and how Sandi must have suffered growing up with him. No wonder she'd always been throwing herself at men, trying to get attention.

On the other hand, Saul was *here*, wasn't he? He'd managed to raise Sandi and her two brothers mostly on his own, and now he was here to help keep an eye on his grandchildren. The man had lost a wife *and* a daughter in one lifetime, but he was in far better shape than Jeff was yesterday. So maybe obtuse and insensitive wasn't such a bad thing to be.

"What about Jeff?" Lynn asked. "Is he around? I didn't see his car by the garage."

"Ach, he's off making *arrangements*," said Saul, his face etched in craggy contempt. "What arrangements do you have to make? Pick up the phone, call the rabbi. Get the body in the ground and say the Kaddish. You're not rebuilding downtown. You're trying to make a funeral."

"Is he using Harold Baltimore's funeral home?"

"I don't know *what* he's doing."

Lynn realized she'd never really sounded the depths of Saul's true feelings about his son-in-law before.

"You don't sound happy," she said.

"Hey, what's it my business? She was only my daughter."

In his bitterness she heard an invitation to pry.

"Saul," she said cautiously, "had you got the impression that Sandi and Jeff weren't getting along?"

"You think they tell me anything? I'm just the father who writes the checks. That's all . . ."

He closed his mouth, appearing to masticate on his words for a few seconds.

"I'll tell you one thing, though," he said, deciding to spit the rest of it out. "If I thought he wasn't treating her like an absolute princess, I would've cut him off years ago."

"What do you mean, 'cut him off'?"

"Who the hell do you think helped pay for this house?" He turned his palms up. "You'd think they'd at least be able to furnish it themselves."

"Wait a second. *You* paid for this house?"

"That's my name on the deed. Unless my brilliant son-in-law has decided to change his name to Feinberg as well."

"But I thought Jeff's business was *good*." She put her hands on her hips.

"Sure it is. And I look just like Cary Grant."

He grunted like an old garbage disposal, and for a moment she'd felt sure that he was about to spit on the onyx floor.

"Then who paid for the old house?" Lynn asked. "Didn't they sell that before they moved here?"

"Mine too. Picked it up for thirty thousand less than its asking price and sold it for almost twice as much. You think I went into real estate so I could lose money?"

"But I still don't understand." She blinked as if a fly had just gone past her face. "What about Jeff's company? I thought they were making ten, twelve million dollars a year."

"My love, do you know what the first great lesson of the Bible is?" He looked at her with a kind of fatherly indulgence. "It's not Do unto others. It's If something looks too good to be true, it probably is. For five years, I've been helping float this kid and telling him his business plan doesn't make sense on paper. I keep asking him, 'Where does the profit come in? What's your revenue stream?' And he keeps telling me that I'm out of it, that I don't know what I'm talking about, that there's a new — he crooked his fingers to make quotation marks — 'paradigm' with the Internet. Ha!"

"So you've been helping to underwrite Jeff's company this whole time?"

"You call it *underwriting*; I call it *bloodletting*. By this spring, I told him enough is enough. I said he had to cut his overhead by fifty percent and come up with a new plan to take this company public in a year or I was pulling the plug on him."

"Oh." Lynn swallowed. "I guess that's understandable."

She wondered how Barry and she would handle having their backs up against the wall this way. She told herself that they'd be strong and stick together. But then again, she'd noticed the way Barry seemed to get quiet and tense lately whenever she asked him how Retrogenesis's stock was doing.

"Listen," said Saul, "I loved my daughter, but I have other children and grandchildren and a wife with stepchildren I have to try and help support. My name is not Warren Buffett, and my pockets are not the Grand Canyon. You have to set limits, even with your children. Otherwise, they never learn to do things for themselves."

"Of course. You're right, Saul."

She listened to the sounds of the kids' swords and bats beating against the baby-sitter's shield, noticing how much emptier the house seemed now that she had this information. Almost like a movie set deserted by the cast and crew.

She saw Inez retreat from the force of the blows, each one seeming to say, *You're not my mother; you're not my mother.* The baby-sitter backed into the kitchen and let the door flap shut after her, a light breeze ruffling the children's hair. Dylan and Isadora looked at each other and then gazed toward the front of the house.

"Grandpa, come play with us!" Dylan raised his sword, the little warrior beckoning. "I'll be the bad guy."

"Can you believe I gotta start this shit all over?" Saul sighed and reluctantly started to take his jacket off. "At *my* age."

26

"WHAT'S UP?" Ross Olson asked as Barry walked into his office. "I'm sorry I wasn't around to return the call yesterday. Chiropractor appointment in the afternoon and Curriculum Night at Dalton. The perils of being an old husband with a young wife."

Kara, honey-haired, golden-thighed, and thirty-two, grinned from a picture on a side shelf next to framed finger paintings by the kids and a photo of Ross with his old artillery unit in Vietnam.

"I went to see Mark Young," said Barry.

Instead of sitting down, he stood before Ross, hands deep in his pockets, flexing slightly at the knees as if he was getting ready to jump on top of the desk.

"And what was on his feeble mind?" Ross swiveled sideways in his black leather office chair.

"We got problems."

"Do tell."

"He knows how badly we're stuck in Phase Two trials for Chronex. I think I scared him off using any more information about the Monkey Suit, but there's nothing I can do to move our drugs through the pipeline faster. If the FDA moves up our deadline for filing results to December fifteenth, like they're threatening to, we're not going to be ready, and he's gonna be all over us again, saying we misled our investors."

"I'll call Paul Fleming down in Washington," said Ross, referring to the former Florida congressman who'd done lobbying for Retrogenesis. "Maybe he can buy us a few more months."

"There's something else." Barry cocked his head to the right, looking past Ross for a moment to the exact spot where he'd seen the American Airlines plane coming in low.

"Okay."

"Why didn't you tell me you sold four thousand shares of your stock this summer?"

Ross's face became taut in the middle and wrinkled on the sides, like a tarpaulin stretched by a baseball ground crew on a rainy day.

"Who told you that?" he asked.

"Young did. His researchers caught it."

"And why is it any of *your* business?"

"Ross, I just made a speech to the executive officers of this company, telling them why they shouldn't abandon ship. And now I see the captain's already in the lifeboat."

"Oh, that is just a pile of thoroughbred shit." Ross's chair gave a small insulted squeak. "You knew I was buying a summerhouse on the Vineyard."

"I thought you'd already closed on it."

"Kara and I agreed that we should lay out a bigger down payment and reduce the monthly mortgage. Nothing wrong with that, is there?"

"Of course not." Barry put his shoulders back. "But I just want to remind you that there are a lot of people risking almost everything they have on this enterprise staying afloat. And they have a right to know if the ship's going down."

"The ship is not going down," Ross said. "We're going to be outlining a new 'Path to Profitability' report to the investors in the next six months. Coridal is coming on three new Asian markets in January. And I didn't want to say anything premature, but I just set up a meeting with one of the major pharmas next week, who might be interested in giving us some extra support to finish off our R-and-D work on Chronex."

"These aren't the same guys Steve's been talking to, are they?"

"Shit, no." Ross gave a barbed chuckle. "He's got a friend at Pfizer who he thinks is going to put him in my seat. That boy's got more ambition than sense."

"Then who are you talking to?"

"Well, I don't want it getting around, but you know Bill Brenner and I are still close . . ."

"Oh, come the fuck on." Barry winced. "Brenner Home Care?

Bill Brenner's a psychopath. I worked on that pesticide case for five years with you, Ross. I know how he works. He'll surround himself with yes-men and ease the rest of us out one by one . . ."

"I've already made it clear to Bill that he wouldn't be the Grand Pooh-bah of this particular lodge. I told him we were envisioning more of a supporting role."

"You mean, he'd become one of our creditors?"

"That's one possibility." Ross angled his chair. "But I wouldn't make any definitive moves without consulting the rest of the executive committee."

"Look" — Barry found himself fingering the coins in his pocket like worry beads — "all I'm asking is that you give the rest of us a little heads up if you're seriously considering a move like that. It's going to be hard as hell finding another job in this economy."

"Barry" — Ross stood up — "it's like I told my men in 'Nam. I may ask you to take risks, but I'll never ask you to do anything I wouldn't do myself."

"Keep me in the loop," Barry said tersely.

But as he walked out of the office and headed down the hall, he remembered that Ross's company had lost more than half its men in a firefight near Da Nang.

27

LYNN WENT INTO Sandi's kitchen to put away the lasagna, apple pie, and salad she'd made and found Inez, the baby-sitter, leaning against the counter, trying to catch her breath.

"Hoo, boy." Inez put her cardboard shield down and wiped her brow. "They wear me out."

"It's a good thing you're here for them." Lynn opened the Sub-Zero and shoved the food in. "They must need a lot of attention right now."

"Please, God, *tell* me about it. I was here all day and all night Sunday and then all day Monday until *midnight*, please, God, when Jeff came back from the police station," Inez said, emphatic Jamaican accent bobbing and weaving among her words. "Then I had to get my granddaughter ready for school and go by Jeanine at *ten* the next day, please, God, because I'm only supposed to be here *three* days a week. Then I had to come back here at *four* yesterday so Jeff could go out. Do you know I'm beginning to wonder if I ever get back home?"

Inez was the Holy Grail of suburban nannies, a fabulous cook with a driver's license. She was a compact woman in her midforties with quick darting eyes in a round pleasant face. A woman who could keep her own counsel but never miss a thing. Lynn had met her while she was baby-sitting Jeanine's kids and always found her a gas to talk to, not only because she was wise about children but because she was tart, discerning, and undeluded in a way that most white middle-class people in the suburbs couldn't afford to be about themselves.

"And in the meantime, Jeff needs all his shirts *with* starch on a hanger, not folded, in the drawer. Do you know he needs *all* his suits back from the dry cleaner so he can look at them and *then* decide which one to wear to the funeral?"

"Hmm."

Lynn watched dry ice smoke tumble out of the freezer, still thinking about the conversation she'd had with Saul. So odd that he'd been carrying Sandi and Jeff financially for such a long time. What must that have done to their marriage? She remembered Sandi confiding to her right before the wedding that one of the things she loved most about Jeff was that he'd given her a way to stop being so dependent on her dad.

"Inez" — she turned around — "were Jeff and Sandi fighting a lot right before she disappeared?"

"What do you mean *a lot?*" Inez busied herself, folding dish towels. "He was always after her for spending too much money on the house, and she was always after him about those *nasty* habits he has. Please, God. I hate to talk about *some* of the things I've bundled up in the trash."

Good old Inez. You could always rely on her to come across with the dirt. A couple of years ago, Jeanine had gone back to work part-time and Inez had matter-of-factly told Lynn that she was the one personally providing the clean urine so Jeanine could pass the company's drug test.

"What kinds of things?" asked Lynn.

"Oh, you know, *man things.*" Inez wrinkled her nose. "They have their *nasty* ways. I hate to tell you about some of the videos up on the shelf in his study."

Though how Inez would know what was on the tapes if she hadn't looked at them pretty carefully herself, Lynn wasn't sure.

"Do you think he ever hit her?" she asked instead.

"Oh" — Inez turned on the sink and started washing glasses by hand — "*I* never saw *that.*"

"Well, had anything changed between them?" Lynn looked around, realizing there was no dishwasher in the kitchen.

"You know? I'll tell you *the truth* what I saw happen," said Inez, never one to resist the chance to tell a story. "Sandi was always asking him to clean those rain gutters outside the house. You know? But he was *always* upstairs watching his sports. And then one day, a few weeks ago, she wouldn't leave him alone, and so he finally got high up on a ladder to do it and he *slipped*. I was in here, and all of a sudden I hear all kinds of bangin' and yellin' and cursin' from outside. Because he's hanging on to one of them aluminum gutters to keep from falling, and she's standing under him, yelling for him to let go before he tears the gutter off the house."

"Really?" asked Lynn, the image of Jeff dangling by his fingertips burning directly into her visual imagination. "So, what happened?"

"So he let go and fell in her rosebushes, and then all that yelling started up again. He comes in this house, limping and cursing *the hell* out of her because she loves the house more than she loves him. And she's rushing around, telling him that's not true and trying to get him ice for his leg. And the kids are upstairs covering their ears. Oh, Lord, that was *something*."

Lynn shook her head, still framing the scene in her mind. Portrait of a marriage under pressure.

"So have the police talked to you about this already?" Lynn asked.

"Ye-*esss*," said Inez, trapping the word in her teeth. "They've been by last night and again this morning."

"I didn't realize that."

"Yup. I talked to a couple of them. Big white one and a little bald Spanish one."

"I guess they must've asked you if either Jeff or Sandi was seeing other people."

Inez cut the water off with a quick muscular turn of the wrist and stood there watching suds circle the drain. Lynn had the sense that a faint but unmistakable social boundary had just been transgressed.

"Mrs. Schulman, I *need* this job," Inez said evenly. "My family *needs* me to make this money. I've got one daughter on public assistance and another who's HIV positive and won't take her drugs. I've got *four* grandchildren I'm helping to take care of. I *don't need* to have a problem with the police or the people I work for up here."

Lynn looked down and saw Inez squeezing a Brillo pad so hard in her fist that pink soap oozed out between her knuckles.

"I'm sorry," Lynn said. "I didn't mean to upset you."

Inez turned the sink on again, letting the water run hot enough to make vapor clouds rise toward the ceiling.

"So who was it?" asked Lynn.

"I don't know. Mrs. Pollack already asked me about this."

"Did she?"

"Oh, I tell you, she give me *the third degree!*"

Lynn snorted, remembering how critical Jeanine had been yesterday. *Let the police do their job.* Sure. Now it turned out she'd been snooping herself. And she called Sandi competitive?

"So you told her you don't know anything," said Lynn, not above doing a little scorekeeping of her own.

"I *don't* know anything." Inez rinsed out a highball glass and a Pikachu juice cup. "It's none of my business."

"I don't believe you. I know all the extra hours you gave Sandi. I saw you out there sword-fighting just now with the kids. So I know this isn't just a job to you."

She could see Inez fighting with herself as she started drying the glasses with a dish towel more vigorously than she needed to, the drain slowly pulling the remaining suds toward the middle of the sink.

"You didn't hear anything from me," she said finally, opening the cupboard to start putting the glasses away. "Please, God."

"What is it?"

"I came home early one day with the kids because the library was closed, and I saw the man who put up the deer fence had his truck in the driveway but no one was working in the backyard. I started to come in the house, and then I heard *these noises* from upstairs in the bedroom . . ."

Inez turned over a wineglass and looked at it from the bottom, leaving no doubt about the kind of noises she meant.

"So, what'd you do?"

"I took the kids and went to the supermarket for a half-hour." Inez carefully placed the glass on the shelf above the children's cups. "And when I came back, the truck was still there. So I took them to the video store until it got dark, and then I called to make sure it was okay to bring them home."

"And did Jeff ever find out about it?"

Lynn felt a little electric surge up the back of her legs as she heard Jeff's voice right outside the kitchen door, talking patiently to the kids. He must've just got home.

"I don't know." Inez dropped her voice. "*I* never said anything."

She shut the cupboard and wiped her hands on a dish towel.

"So who was he?" whispered Lynn, determined to grab any last scrap before the baby-sitter fled. "The deer fence guy. Was his name on the side of a truck?"

"He was a cop," Inez muttered as she slid past her to start setting the dinner table. "One of the same ones who talked to me. He didn't know I'd seen him that day."

28

JUST AS THE train pulled out of Grand Central that night, Barry looked over and saw a familiar figure come chuffing and staggering red-faced up the aisle. His guy. His traveling companion. The keeper of the cubicle, the lord of the saltbox, the ignorer of the river. His doppelgänger, who he hadn't laid eyes on since the Eleventh. At that moment, Barry was so elated to see him alive that he actually blurted out, "How you doing?" after the guy collapsed in his usual seat and caught his breath. The man froze with his laptop half-opened, slightly aghast that a stranger was trying to pick him up, and then quickly turned away.

By the time he reached Riverside Station just after eight, Barry's relief began to evaporate as he seriously considered the future of Retrogenesis. A CEO secretly selling four thousand shares of his own stock did not inspire confidence. But thinking about going back into corporate litigation brought back memories of those blinding migraines. Something had shorted out in him in the five years the Brenner Home Care case dragged on. It wasn't idealism that kept him from doing it all again; he'd never been afraid to throw a few sharp elbows under the boards. It was the sense that he was dedicating his working life to running around making sure all the lights were off.

He found the Saab in the darkened parking lot and thought about sending Lisa Chang an Instant Message. Long-term options needed to be mulled over. Too many lab hours, late-night pizza party / bull sessions, disputed patent applications, and brain-damaged monkeys had been poured into this project for it all to come to naught. And in the back of his mind, Barry quietly had to admit to himself that he'd started to like the way Lisa looked without her glasses.

He gunned the engine and swung out of the parking lot, hoping Lynn would still be eating dinner with the kids. When he spoke to her on the cell phone this afternoon, she was over at Sandi's with the children and their grandfather, waiting for Jeff to get home. Again, he'd heard that tiny hitch in her voice, that little pause that let the static in, suggesting all manner of disturbance going on in the background.

He made the left onto Prospect and started up into the hills, still wondering what else she was holding back. It bothered him that she'd waited so long to tell him this whole tortured story about her high school boyfriend. On the one hand, who cared what happened twenty-five years ago? On the other, the story didn't quite gel. It sounded like an awful lot of emotion to be stirred up by a bunch of old pictures. Maybe a key detail or two had been cropped out.

Of course, that might be his own guilty conscience, he thought, noticing a pair of headlights intensify behind him. It was going to be a helluva conversation when he told her the company might be going down the tubes along with most of their savings. And having Bill Brenner involved just made it worse. Lynn had always despised the man, referring to him as "that greedy little bridge troll."

He sped up as the car behind him put on its high beams, making a glaring white spot in his rearview. *Why is this guy riding my tail?*

Near Indian Ridge, he tried to slow down and let the other car pass, but it stayed stubbornly in the single lane behind him. The high beams switched off and then flashed on again, a blink in the middle of a long cold stare.

Barry stepped on the gas and shot past the golf course construction project and the Van Der Hayden estate, doing a hair over forty, trying to lose him. But the glow from the headlights just seemed to heat up on the back of his neck.

He glanced up at the rearview, trying to glean what the guy wanted. But there was only a stark silhouette behind two blinding lights. Barry's suspension squealed as the Saab listed on the turn. *Gimme a break.* He raised a hand. He was just thinking of veering onto the detour past the cow pasture, when the other driver suddenly reached up and put a revolving cherry top on his roof.

"Pull over," said a voice over a loudspeaker, as if it were addressing Barry from the heavens.

"Oh *shit*." Barry slowed down and pulled off on the deserted stretch right before the old millpond, realizing he should've seen this coming both literally and figuratively.

The cherry top kept pulsing behind him, throwing Maraschino-red waves over his windshield.

Naturally, Michael Fallon was taking his time getting out of the car behind him, as if he had to arrange some special transport for the ungainly size of his balls. Barry pulled out his cell phone and tried to call Lynn. The answering machine picked up after two rings.

"Honey, I think I'm about to have a serious problem with your old boyfriend," he began.

Fallon climbed out slowly, his shadow narrowing and lengthening on the desolate road as he approached the Saab.

"Call me back right away . . ."

"Sir, put that phone down." Fallon stood by his open window.

"If you can't reach me on the cell, try the police station . . ."

"Sir, I asked you to put that phone down . . ."

"He just pulled me over on Prospect without due cause." Barry started to talk faster, determined to get as much of this conversation on tape as possible.

"Sir, a police officer is giving you an order . . ."

"I love you," Barry said, staring at the cop and making sure he heard every word.

His authority ignored, Fallon suddenly reached through the window and tried to grab the phone. From old athlete's instinct, Barry pushed the hand away, as if he was protecting the ball. Instantly he knew he'd made a serious mistake.

"Get out of the car with your license and registration." The lieutenant drew back, no longer a man to be trifled with. "Keep your hands where I can see them at all times."

Mechanically, Barry turned the phone off and got the proper cards from the glove compartment. "Why is it, pray tell, that you had me pull over, Officer?" he asked, trying to keep his temper in check.

"You were doing forty-two in a thirty-five zone. I clocked you with the radar gun."

"After you almost ended up in my backseat because you were so close on my bumper. That's great professional police work there."

"Get out of the car, please."

Barry remained at the wheel. "I believe I have the right to say no."

Though it had been so long since he'd been a criminal attorney, he wasn't sure exactly what the law said at the moment.

"Sir, you've already put your hands on me, so I can charge you with obstruction and resisting arrest if I feel like it," said Fallon. "Now get out of the damn car and give me your license and registration."

Moving deliberately, as if every gesture was being filmed, Barry climbed out, noticing that it was distinctly chillier up here in the hills than it was closer to the river.

Fallon took the cards and stood there studying them in the revolving light. He looked bulkier tonight, and it dawned on Barry that he was probably wearing a Kevlar vest under his windbreaker as well as a Glock in his shoulder holster.

"I understand you had a talk with the chief this morning," Fallon said, without taking his eyes off Barry's ID picture.

"We ran into each other buying coffee. But I guess you already knew that too."

"I know a lot of things."

A silver Nissan Pathfinder whipped by hard, nearly sideswiping both of them, but Fallon didn't bother to look up.

"You'd think that if a man has a problem with somebody, he'd take it up with him directly instead of whining to the boss." He put the license and registration on top of the Saab, where they could easily blow away. "I'd tend to say that's a little on the chickenshit side. Wouldn't you?"

"All right" — Barry raised his chin — "then let me take it up with you personally. *Stay away from my wife*. Is that direct enough?"

"*Your wife* may be a material witness in a murder investigation. I'm entitled to ask her anything I want."

"Well, what she described to me didn't sound anything like legitimate questioning."

"Maybe she didn't supply you with all the pertinent details. Ever think about that?"

"I heard enough," Barry said. "Next time you want to talk to her, I think an attorney should be present."

He started to reach for his license and registration as a GMC Safari came rushing by, blaring prime-time Rant Radio.

"Excuse me," said Fallon. "I didn't say you could take those back yet, did I?"

"Why? You have something else you want to say?"

"Turn around and put your hands together."

"You've gotta be kidding me. I'm *a lawyer.*"

"I don't care what you are. You interfered with a police officer doing his duty. Now give me your hands before I have to use the pepper spray."

"Jesus Christ." Barry turned slowly and presented his hands as if he was humoring an unreasonable child.

He heard the jangle of cuffs coming off Fallon's belt and then felt cold steel biting deep into his wrists.

A Volvo station wagon cruised by slowly, and three children stared out at him through the back window. He felt a drizzle of embarrassment as their puzzled expressions receded and the Volvo's brake lights flared in the distance.

"You have the right to remain silent." Fallon took him firmly by the elbow and marched him back toward his unmarked Caprice. "Anything you say can and will be used against you . . ."

In the chill, Barry's old knee injury started hurting, a painful throbbing in the cartilage that reminded him that the most powerful man in the United States at any given moment was not the president, not the head of the joint chiefs of staff, not even the chairman of GE, but a police officer with a loaded weapon and full discretion.

Fallon finished with Miranda, opened the back door of the Caprice, pushed Barry in, and slammed the door after him. Then he leaned against the side of the car for a moment as if he needed to catch his breath and clear his head. Barry watched the little condensed clouds come out of the lieutenant's mouth and evaporate, thinking, *I am fucked.* He put his head against the window, resolving to try to stay calm.

The car sprung up as Fallon stopped leaning against it, walked to the front, and got in the driver's seat.

"You know, you're really about to make a huge mistake," said Barry. "It's not too late to put the brakes on this."

"Excuse me, but *I'm* driving." Fallon looked over his shoulder as he started the motor.

Lights surged across the dashboard, and Barry saw an orange cursor blinking on a small Motor Display Terminal. The car made an abrupt U-turn, leaving the Saab by the side of the road as if it had broken down.

The backseat of the Caprice was hot and stuffy. Despite the fragrance tree dangling from the rearview, there was an overwhelming odor of oil rags and gasoline. Barry felt his stomach turning before they'd even reached the first stop sign.

"You wouldn't consider cracking the window, would you?"

"I'm fine," said Fallon.

"You're not going to call this in?" Barry rested his head against the glass, as if this was no matter of pressing concern.

"We're five minutes from the station," Fallon said sharply. "You gonna start telling me what to do?"

"No. Just curious. That's all."

As they cruised past the old Victorian on Birch Lane, Fallon shoved a cassette into the tape deck, and the winsome old 10CC hit "The Things We Do For Love" came on.

"Your wife used to like this song." Fallon tapped two fingers on the wheel, keeping time. "You know that?"

"Doesn't sound like her taste."

"She used to make me play it for her over and over on the jukebox. I lost track of all the quarters I spent."

Barry looked out the window, studiously ignoring him, as they joggled over a rough patch of road, the small lit-up porches of Indian Ridge appearing to extinguish in the dark as they passed.

"She used to like French Fries with mayonnaise too. Did you know that? She had to stop eating them because they made her skin break out."

Barry bowed his head, trying to will himself to get into the Zone mentally, that place where you seemed to be both in the middle of the play and somewhere above it at the same time. But the rattling of a crowbar at his feet kept bringing him back.

"See, I know a lot of things you don't know," said Fallon.

The Zone. Stay in the Zone. Don't let him get to you. Concentrate. Pretend you're alone on a mountaintop. Or on the foul line. Make the rest of the world fade away, so there's only a hoop and a net floating in empty space. The crowbar clanked as they hit a pothole.

"She still like it rough?" Fallon grinned back at him.

"What?"

"I said, *does she still like it rough?*" They picked up speed, heading into the low-slung neighborhoods closer to the river.

All at once, Barry was out of the Zone and imagining himself taking the crowbar in both hands and splitting Fallon's skull with it.

"Why don't you shut the fuck up?"

"Oh, yeah," said Fallon, beginning to enjoy himself, "she used to be up for anything. Absolutely anything."

Barry's wrists strained and bulged from the cuffs cutting off his circulation.

"Of course, that's probably all over now. You probably never got any of that. It's never the same after the first go-round. Especially after they have kids. It's like seeing the Yankees in '71 or the Stones in '89. All the juice is gone. After that, it's just going through the motions, isn't it?"

Barry felt rage bubbling in his gut, threatening to boil out of him. Of course, that was what this cop wanted. To have an excuse to beat the balls off him.

"I'm sitting here, trying to decide which is sadder," he said, staring at the tendons in the back of Fallon's neck. "The fact that you're still talking about this twenty-five years later or the fact that you thought it was that big a deal in the first place."

"Oh, it was a big deal. Believe me. It was a big deal."

"Then how come I never heard your name before?" he asked, focusing on the razor line where the hair was shaved. "Sounds to me like you've spent a lot of time making this into something it wasn't."

Fallon suddenly became very quiet, and a thin roll of skin appeared on the back of his neck. They'd reached a stop sign at the bottom of the hill. Moonlight rippled on the river ahead like floating wreckage. The police station was a sharp right. But on the left, Barry remembered, there was a series of abandoned old factories, a little RV park, and big vacant tracts with FOR RENT signs. He remembered Lynn warning Hannah never to go down that way, saying that no one would ever hear her scream if she was in trouble.

He watched the roll on the back of Fallon's neck slowly expand like baking dough.

"Is that what *she* said?" Fallon asked, adjusting his rearview.

"My wife is a photographer. She always gives me the full picture."

"Oh, she does, does she?" He turned the mirror a little more to study his passenger. "She ever talk about my family anymore?"

Barry looked out the window, trying not to take the bait and drive the hook any deeper into his own mouth.

"So are we going to the station?" he said. "Or you got some other idea?"

Fallon turned down the music abruptly. Through the underbrush of his bristle cut, Barry saw a faint second roll of skin, just an inch or so above the first one.

The lieutenant gave a surly grunt. "Hey," he said quietly, "you don't know shit about the full picture."

I hurt him. Barry watched the two rolls disappear. *Sitting here with both hands cuffed behind my back, I somehow managed to put a hurting on him.*

"Excuse me." He leaned forward. "You need to check your map? Because I know the way to the police station if you don't."

A northbound train passed before them, its windows lit up like the sprockets of a film running through a projector.

"Okay, fine. Let's go your way." Fallon dutifully put on the signal and turned the car right. "Maybe I can get you there in time for the last bus over to the county jail."

29

AS SHE WALKED through the glass double doors, Lynn remembered the last time she'd visited the town's police station was senior year, right after she got stopped with Jeanine trying to buy beer with fake IDs. At Jeanine's insistence, Lynn had stuffed the bag of pot she was carrying down the front of her pants in the squad car and then spent five minutes in the ladies' room trying to flush it down the toilet while a matron waited outside. She could still recall the horror of the seeds and stems welling up over and over in the dank water that kept returning.

Now that same sense of dread welled up in her again as she approached the sergeant's desk.

"Hi, I'm here about my husband, Barry Schulman," she said. "I believe you have him in a cell downstairs."

The sergeant had a soft chin and a fuzzy little caterpillar of hair connecting his eyebrows, which made him look stern and unforgiving. A purple-haired troll wearing an "I'd Rather Be Golfing" T-shirt sat atop his computer monitor. Four other officers worked in the dispatch room behind him, answering phones and hunting and pecking at keyboards. Lynn noticed two fishing rods in the corner next to the enormous white sector map of Riverside.

"I'd like to post bond for him," she said, reaching into her bag for her wallet. "I was told I could do that on the phone."

"It's all right, Eddie." Mike Fallon appeared in the doorway of a small office on the right. "I'll take care of this one."

There was something official and impervious in his voice that made her think of a bank manager calling in a loan. The sergeant went to answer a ringing phone as Mike took his place at the front desk.

"It's bad, Lynn," he said, shaking his head. "It's bad."

"What happened?"

She'd already braced herself, knowing from Barry's message that she would probably have to deal with Mike at some point tonight.

"Your husband was speeding near an area where children play, and when I pulled him over, he tried to get physical with me. We're giving him an Intoxilyzer right now."

"Oh, for God's sake, Mike. He'd never drink and get behind the wheel."

"We have a serious DWI problem in our community," he began sententiously. "And then he tried to put his hands on a police officer, which is a serious offense in this town . . ."

"Oh, come on, Mikey . . ."

He gave her a grave admonishing look. Barry must have broken his promise to her and confronted him about what happened in the studio yesterday.

"All right, so what do I owe here?" She opened her wallet, trying to get it over with. "The sergeant I spoke to on the phone said the cash bond would probably be set at about twenty-five hundred dollars. So I hit the ATM and got the ten percent . . ."

"Not so fast." Mike raised a meaty slab of a hand. "He's already in the system."

"What do you mean? What are you talking about?"

"He is already *in the system*," Mike repeated the words more slowly, as if he was addressing a half-wit. "I already entered his paperwork on the computer."

"So, what does that mean?"

"What does that *mean?*" He seemed incredulous. "It means there's nothing anybody can do about it. He's *in the system*. The bus is going to take him to the county jail in less than twenty minutes."

"And then he'll have to spend the night in jail?"

"Hey, court is closed here. Highball Harper's probably tucked up in bed already with a nice warm bottle."

She pictured Barry in the county pen, packed in among the gang-bangers, rapists, and street crazies from all over the jurisdiction.

"I can't let this happen," she said, trying not to panic. "What can I do to get him out tonight?"

"Nothing." He glanced over at the one-browed sergeant, who was talking on the phone and gesturing at him with great animation.

"Once somebody is in the system, they have to go *through* the system," he said with a kind of grinding vindictiveness. "Your husband's a lawyer. He understands."

"All right, will you stop saying that!" Her voice cracked. "You don't have to keep talking about *the system* like it's something that can't be controlled!"

Everyone in the room stopped talking and stared, as if she'd just fired a starter's pistol at the ceiling.

She realized she had no idea who Mike was anymore or what he was capable of. She was still trying to process the idea that Sandi had been having an affair with him. It was like learning that a house you'd visited a hundred times had a torture chamber in the basement. How had the relatively straightforward kids she'd known become such morally baroque, recklessly perverse, and frighteningly untrustworthy adults?

"Look" — she stood on tiptoe and leaned across the desk, trying to maintain her composure — "is this about what happened between you and me?"

"And why would you think that?" He looked down at her, his face a mask of indifference.

"I know you keep wanting something from me that I can't give you," she whispered. "But I don't want you to take it out on my husband."

He lurched suddenly forward as if he was about to take her face in his hands. "Are you going to start telling me how to do my job too?"

"No." She felt his breath on her lips. "I just don't want to have any more problems *with you.*"

She stopped talking and looked over his shoulder, seeing all the men in the room still riveted as if this were in a sports bar and they were watching the last inning of the World Series on TV. The sergeant was gesturing madly, trying to get one of them to tap Mike on the shoulder.

"Let me ask you something, Lynn." Mike leaned farther across the desk, his breath almost in her mouth now. "Did you really never care about me?"

"Excuse me?"

Again, her eyes roamed past him, and she saw the sergeant holding the phone up and saying, "Mike?"

"You heard me." Fallon ignored him.

She dropped back onto her flat soles, convinced that he'd lost all sense of propriety. "I really don't think this is the place to discuss this."

She saw the other cops pretending to go about their duties, trying to look and not look at the same time. Small-town chain-of-command types, men whose respect Mike obviously needed. Now they were like mountaineers seeing the top of Everest melt just a little.

"Mike?" The sergeant held up the phone. "I got the chief on the line."

"Yeah, what does he want?"

Mike kept staring at Lynn, as if she'd disappear the moment he looked away.

"He says kick him loose." The sergeant waved the receiver.

"What?"

"He says we should release the guy downstairs. Cash bond is acceptable."

Mike looked over his shoulder, muscles rising and clenching in his neck. "And how is it that he happens to know about that guy, *Eddie?*" he said fiercely.

"We called him as soon as you brought him in through the bay doors. That's how the chief wants it from now on. Call him at home whenever there's an arrest."

She saw Mike start to seethe behind the desk, leaning heavily on his elbow.

"You wanna talk to him?" asked the sergeant, cradling the phone to his ear.

"No, you can tell him I got the message."

Mike started breathing heavily through his nose and shuffling through papers on the desk, as if this had all just been some minor inconvenience.

"Well, I guess that's that," he said. "You can take the old man off our hands. He doesn't have to wait around to be arraigned. You'll get a letter telling him when he has to come to court."

"Okay, good." She exhaled in relief as the sergeant hung up the phone and shook his head at his fellow officers. "I just want to get him home. That's all."

She quickly started laying down the $250 she'd got from the ATM, eager to get out of this place.

"You can still pick up the car by the side of the road; we didn't impound it yet." Mike scooped the bills up preemptively. "By the way, you understand that you are assuming responsibility here, and if he doesn't show up for his court date, you forfeit the bond and we come looking for him."

"It's all right. I don't think he's going anywhere."

She looked at him, meaning to share a lighter moment, but instead saw that a certain wounded, dangerous male intransigence was still in his eyes.

"Just keep him out of trouble in the meantime," he said.

30

THE DOORBELL RANG a half-hour later, followed by a series of angry insistent raps rising steadily in force and volume until they sounded almost like thunder on the threshold.

"All right, all right." Mike went to answer it. "Put your nightstick away, will you?"

He opened the door and found Paco and Harold looking somber and resolute, a fly circling the porch light behind them.

"Now you know you done fucked up, don't you?" Harold moved past him into the foyer. "I don't have to tell you that, do I? I don't have to tell you shit."

"Come on in." Mike forced a smile as Paco followed and closed the door behind them. "Good to see you too."

"How long do you think you'd last in any other department after the stunt you pulled tonight?"

Mike didn't bother making excuses right away. He knew as soon as he put the cherry top on the roof that he was going to have to answer for chasing Schulman. But his foot was already on the gas. He was in full hunt-or-be-hunted mode. The only thing he would've got by stopping short was whiplash.

"Let's talk out back," he said, leading the two of them down the narrow hall and past the kitchen.

"Hey, handsome," Marie, making her late-night tea at the stove, called to the chief. "Can I fix you gentlemen a drink?"

"No, thank you, m'dear." Harold did his courtly bow in the doorway. "We won't be long."

"Could you get me a beer?" Mike looked in after him, knowing he was going to need some fortification.

"Why don't you get it yourself?"

He saw vapor leaking from her teapot and wondered how she'd like having it poured over her head.

He decided to skip the beer and led them through the tiny living room, where Timmy was awake an hour and a half past his bedtime, jabbing at the hamster with a pencil through the bars of its cage.

"Hey, didn't I tell you to knock that off?" Mike saw the rodent dance away from the sharp end. "You keep torturing that poor animal, he's gonna turn around and bite you one of these days."

"Big Tim, what's the word?" Harold offered him an upraised hand.

"What up, dawg?" Timmy reached up to high-five him.

Great, Mike thought resentfully. They're happier to see him than they are to see me. Maybe he can stay and I can go, and there'll be another minority family on the block.

Instead of stopping to introduce Paco to his wife and son, he continued to the screen door and held it open for his visitors.

"After you guys," he said, thinking it was time to put the storms in.

"Well" — Harold waited for the door to close after them — "you must think you're a hell of a man."

"Remind me what we're talking about here."

The night itself felt aggravating. Cold enough so you could see your breath and wear a sweater but warm enough for some insects to still be around. The yard seemed particularly small and paltry with three grown men standing in it. There was barely enough room for the deck, the grill, Marie's wilting annuals, and the rope swings he could never get to hang right because of the slope of the hill.

"You knew he was a lawyer when you pulled him over, right?" Harold's left eyelid twitched slightly. "You couldn't slow down for just a second to think about that?"

"The law is the law, far as I'm concerned, Harold. The man was speeding, and then he laid hands on me after I told him to turn off his phone . . ."

"He's probably going to sue the town and the department. You know that, right?"

"I got him on resisting and obstruction, Harold."

"Twelve hours after he came to me about you and his wife? Forget it. I'm dropping the charges."

"You're what?" Mike bent a little, as if he'd been cracked across the rib cage with an aluminum baseball bat.

"Tell me again why I didn't suspend you this morning when I came to talk to you?"

"Three oh five Bank Street." Mike reminded him of Brenda Carter's address. "That's a good place to start."

"Man, when are you gonna stop cashing that chit in?" Harold grimaced. "Don't you think that's getting kind of tired?"

"I don't know. Are you getting tired of your life?"

They both fell quiet for a few seconds, remembering the aqua-green housing project kitchenette. Could it really be ten years ago? A call about an EDP coming over the radio. The neighbors complaining somebody's grandma had snapped. Didn't sound like much. Until they showed up and found a three-hundred-twenty-pound wild woman swinging a butcher knife around and jabbering about Rockefeller impregnating her niece. Harold, who knew her from church, gently tried to talk sense to her. And then that sweet fat old lady came roaring at him like a garbage truck. She caught him with the knife right up under his Kevlar vest, driving it hard into his abdomen just barely short of the vital connections. She was about to bury it deeper when Mike raised the twelve-gauge and blew her brains all over her gas range.

"I told you to back the fuck off." Harold jabbed a finger at him. "Why wouldn't you listen?"

Mike put his hands in his pockets. "Same reason I didn't back off with the shotgun."

"Ah, that's bullshit." Harold swiped the excuse out of the air. "One thing don't have nothing to do with the other."

"Yeah, that's what you think."

He noticed Paco staring at the side of his face. What did these motherfuckers know anyhow? You pull a trigger. You step on the gas. It's all the same thing — survival instinct. You can't take it apart any more than you could unravel strands of DNA.

"Why'd you bring *him* here?" he asked Harold. "You don't have the balls to talk to me on your own?"

"Paco's got a few questions for you," said the chief. "I thought you might be more comfortable answering them away from all the surveillance cameras and microphones we've got set up around the station."

Mike blinked at the mention of all the hardware that had been installed after the Replay Washington shooting to make sure suspects weren't having their precious rights violated.

"So, what can I do for you, *Paco?*" He glared at the detective.

Paco's bald head seemed to glow a little in the evening chill, as if he'd been saving energy by not speaking.

"Hey, man," he said in that mongrel city accent that was truly starting to grate on Mike, "how come you didn't tell me the state trooper called me this morning about finding Sandi's car at the motel? I only got the message after he called me back again."

"Sorry. I got tied up," said Mike, flushing.

"And how come you didn't tell me you'd been back at that house on Love Lane a week before we went to search it?" Paco crossed his arms like one of those macho rappers you see on billboards.

"I told you. I knew her." Mike shrugged. "We all knew her. Harold knows I did some work on their fence."

Mike sensed a shadow moving in the depths, underneath all the little minnows swimming back and forth.

"We're having some problems with the chain of evidence in this case," said Paco.

"What are you talking about?" Mike looked over at Harold.

"You see a diary when we were over at the victim's house the other day?" asked Paco.

Mike heard the day laborers' pit bull starting to bark across the street, a throaty yelp above the merengue din. "No. Did you?"

"We have information from people close to the victim that she kept a detailed diary. Friends saw it around the house recently."

"Well, maybe the husband got rid of it. Maybe there was something in it that he didn't want us to see."

Jesus. He was flailing here.

"Maybe," said Paco, giving him the hundred-watt stare right back. "Except the husband noticed it was missing too and mentioned it to us. He said he'd seen it on a bookshelf right before the two of us came over the other day."

That crazy bitch. She must've put it there deliberately, as if she wanted the whole world to know.

"Obviously, he's lying." Mike gave a half-strangled laugh. "Did he happen to say what was in it?"

"No," Harold interrupted. "But, Mike, I'm starting to think you haven't been a hundred percent straight about some of the things I've asked you . . ."

"Like what?"

Some part of his mind was retreating to his childhood bedroom, hearing his parents' voices in the kitchen.

"Part of the reason I'm here is to tell you that we're opening an Internal Affairs investigation into the way this all went down," Harold said.

"Get the fuck outa here. *I* do the Internal Affairs investigations."

"Not this time, partner."

The rush was like diesel fuel filling up his mouth. Too fast. It was all coming apart on him too fast to make a rational decision. The body washing ashore, the diary turning up, the fact that she really was pregnant like she'd said. He was a pilot losing altitude, his dials spinning wildly. When do you bail out?

The screen door opened behind him, and he whirled around.

"Yeah, what the fuck do you want?"

Timmy stood in the doorway, eyes glistening and lower lip sore from being chewed. "I just wanted to say good night to you and Harold," he said in a shaky voice.

"Get back in the house."

He saw the boy back away and let the screen slowly close, a dense gray rectangle of tiny wires between them.

Regret drenched him like a freezing rain. "Hey, come back here . . ."

But the boy had already bolted back into the living room and up the stairs, his bare feet thumping unsteadily on the wooden treads.

"Thanks a lot, you guys." Mike turned back to his guests, still feeling the scorch marks on his tongue. "See what you made me do?"

Harold was wearing his deeply etched solemn face, as if he was about to present the bereaved with their bill. "Mike, I want to ask you one more time: Is there something about your relationship to the victim that you haven't told us yet?"

Mike began to shrug, heaving weight off his shoulders. *Okay, so I was doing her.* He tried the line out in his head. *Okay, so I lied about it. Okay, so I took the diary. Okay, so there's a couple of things in it I didn't want you to see. Okay, so I might have roughed her up a little sometimes.*

Okay, I might've put my hands around her throat. Okay, so that might've been my kid she was carrying. Okay, so where do you stop saying *okay?*

"I can't believe you guys are wasting time on this bullshit," he said, trying to deflect them. "We should be sweating the husband, going over his financial records, sending a guy up to Boston to try and shake his alibi. He's the one that did her."

"What makes you say that?" Paco tugged on his earring.

"She was scared of him."

"And how do you know that?" asked Harold pointedly.

A slant of light fell over Mike's face. Marie turning on a lamp upstairs.

"I don't think I want to answer any more questions without a lawyer around," he said abruptly.

"Then I'm afraid I'm going to have to ask you to take a leave of absence." Harold bowed his head as if he was about to lead them all in common prayer. "I checked before I came over, and you've got a week of paid vacation that you have to take before the end of the year . . ."

"What the fuck are you doing?" said Mike. "You're suspending me? I haven't done anything wrong. My only problem is I have an old girlfriend with a big mouth and a jealous husband."

"No, your only problem is you're about to become a material witness in a murder case, and you could be sued by a member of this community for harassment. Other than that, you're doing a hell of a job."

"I'm sorry I *embarrassed* you, Harold. Is that what you want me to say?"

"I'm not the one you need to apologize to."

"Oh, screw this." Mike slapped a mosquito on the side of his neck. "You guys are going to let this case slip right through your fingers."

"You're not giving me any choice." Harold lowered his voice. "There's going to be a disciplinary hearing if Lynn and her husband press charges. But if you start cooperating with us right now, you can count on it all going down a little smoother."

"I made you, Harold. You would've never got to be chief without me."

"I know that. But I am not going to jail for you."

"Let me tell you something." Mike stood back, his voice scrounging down in the gutter. "You try and drown me, I'll pull everyone else down with me."

"Then I take it you already have the name of a good lawyer." Harold gave him a circumspect look.

"Don't worry. I can take care of myself."

He saw Harold shake his head at Paco, as if they were a couple of gravediggers rubbing their hands. Thirty-two years. So this is how you bury a friendship. You bring a stranger with you.

"Look," said Harold, reaching into his back pocket for a white business card, "I brought along Dr. Friedman's phone number at County Psych Services, in case you lost it. I remember how she helped you out after Johnny died."

"Just what I need. A *professional* friend."

Mike took the card from the chief, tore it in half, and handed it back to him.

"There. Now you can say you tried."

Harold stared at the torn pieces in his palm. "Can't make a man take a lifeline if he doesn't want it." He said it not so much to Mike, or even to Paco, but to himself.

"No, you certainly can't," said Mike, hitching up his chinos and drawing up to his full height.

"Fine, we'll do it your way." Harold sighed in resignation. "Go get me your gun and badge. We'll wait out here. No one wants to humiliate you in front of your family."

31

WITH EACH THUMP and scatter of dirt hitting the coffin lid, Lynn felt the hollowness inside her chest.

A breeze swept across Green Hill Cemetery as she watched the ritual of mourners taking turns shoveling dirt into Sandi's grave, having heard Saul and Rabbi Heyman from B'nai Israel recite the burial Kaddish.

"Yisgadal v'yiskadash sh'mei rabbaw . . ."

The words still seemed to circle in the wind. But a different recitation was going on in her head.

That's my friend down there in that rosewood box. That's real dirt they're throwing on top of her. These are three dozen people we both knew dressed in black, gathered in a circle around this hole in the ground. Those are her children back in the rented Lincoln Town Car by the entrance with their step-grandmother. Those are her feckless brothers at the back of the crowd. That's the man she married, looking ashen and anemic. That's my husband standing beside me in a black yarmulke, holding my hand and bowing his head.

Amen.

Grief kept reinventing itself and finding new ways into her. She remembered a woman she'd met at Sloan-Kettering with Sandi last spring, an old lady with Alzheimer's and a double mastectomy. Every night she forgot what had happened to her, and every morning she woke up and started crying again.

She saw Saul, his hair brilliantined and his eyebrows trimmed, take the shovel and stare bitterly at his son-in-law. With a grunt, he stooped and stuck the blade into the mound and then ladled the dirt lovingly into his daughter's grave. A decommissioned old warship adrift on a dark river. She understood that he needed to do something with all this pent-up rage, but this seemed wrong. Not a half-hour before, Jeffrey had delivered the eulogy at B'nai Israel and spoke so movingly of how Sandi had been his soul mate and conscience that tears burned the corners of Lynn's eyes like kerosene. So weren't they all part of this growing province of grieving people?

She looked up the hill toward the grove where she'd buried her own mother last year. Harold and Paco Ortiz stood in the shade of an elm near the grave, with their heads lowered but their eyes conspicuously alert. Something about seeing them here broke the mood. Were they paying their respects or on the job?

She turned back, watching Saul daven, rocking back and forth over the grave. Lost in bereavement, he closed his eyes and began to recite the Kaddish all over again, having forgotten he'd already done it. Marty Pollack came to the head of the grave and took the shovel from him. He bent over to stick the blade into the pyramid of dirt and then stopped and delicately touched the small of his own back as if he'd injured himself. Jeanine came up quickly and took the shovel from him, tossing a coffee cup's–worth of soil down on the lid and fulfilling the family's obligation. Again, the thump felt like a depth charge going off inside Lynn. The finality of it. The grain-by-grain reality of covering someone she'd known all her life. The surrendering of flesh to the earth. She decided that when her turn came she'd have to pass.

Barry let go of her hand and went to take the shovel from Jeanine. Something about watching him unbutton his suit jacket and get down to business made Lynn feel slightly distant from him. He could say he understood what she was going through, but really he couldn't. Just as she couldn't quite get to him after his father died. Grief put a velvet rope around you. People could come and look, but they couldn't touch. Barry turned the shovel over, and a hard lump of dirt fell and broke on the coffin lid. The sound caused Saul to look up from his davening.

"*V'yis'halawl sh'mei d'kudshaw b'rich hu . . .*"

Slowly, all eyes went back to the grave, except for Harold's. Lynn saw him staring into the mid-distance, that look of alertness beginning to pull his heavy features together.

"*L'aylaw min kol . . .*"

Barry handed the shovel to Jeffrey with a solemn man-to-man

nod and then went back to Lynn's side. "He'll be all right," he muttered. But she was distracted, seeing Harold give Paco a small nudge.

"*B'all'maw, v'imru: Amein.*"

"*Amein,*" the men in the crowd answered.

Jeffrey sniffed, dug into the pile, and started to bring out an unsteady scoop. But then the shovel stopped and hovered over Sandi's coffin, a few shaky grains spilling over the side and pouring down on the lid. Something was not right here. His mouth opened slightly, and the lenses of his glasses turned into opaque white circles. Following his gaze, Barry looked over his own shoulder. Then Jeanine started to whisper to Marty and point urgently.

"*Y'hei shlawmaw rabbaw . . .*" Saul's voice trailed off.

Lynn turned and saw Mike Fallon lumbering up the hill toward them, over the low-lying tombstones and the paling neatly trimmed grass. He seemed to bring a highly charged ion field with him. The sight of his thick wrists dangling from the sleeves of an ill-fitting dark suit only heightened the sense of a man out of place.

"*Min sh'mayaw, v'chayim . . . ,*" Saul began to recite the prayer again, oblivious to the disturbance.

Lynn saw Paco Ortiz's chest swell as he started down the hill to intercept him. But then Harold took his arm and pulled him back, waiting to see what would develop. Saul's bewildered eyes found Lynn's, requesting explanation. But all she could do was dip her shoulders helplessly.

"*Awleinu v'al kol yisroel . . .*"

Jeffrey turned over his shovel full of dirt and then lowered the blade as the circle of mourners parted. Mike stepped between them and boldly walked right up to Jeffrey, the interloper confronting the bereft. They stared at each other blankly, like species encountering each other for the first time.

It was, Lynn decided, the most uncomfortable thing she'd ever seen.

Mike, a good two inches taller and thirty pounds heavier than Jeff, firmly seized the shovel from his hands and looked around the circle, daring anyone to try to take it back from him. His eyes lingered on Barry, doubling the challenge. Lynn squeezed her husband's hand, silently begging him not to rise to the bait again.

"*Oseh shawlom bim'ro'mawv . . .*" The rabbi joined Saul in running through the prayer a second time, trying to complete the ancient words of a tribe used to burying its dead while under siege.

Satisfied that no one was going to try to take the shovel from his hands, Michael loosened his tie, bent his knees, and dug into the mound as if he was about to heap coal into a steam engine. Dirt cascaded over rosewood. Most of the other mourners had only tossed a small ceremonial amount in. But Mike pivoted and threw another load down and then another, a small rivulet of perspiration appearing by his temple, glimpses of scalp reddening vividly through his bristle cut. Several of the women in the circle stepped back, not wanting any part of this confrontation. Saul looked at his useless sons and then at each of the other men in the circle, imploring one of them to intercede. But then Mike suddenly stopped, having completed his tribute. He turned and handed the shovel back to Jeffrey, as if to say, *See, that's how it's done.*

Then he walked out of the circle and back down the hill again.

32

THREE DAYS LATER, Lynn picked up the small bronze coffin that sat at the edge of the chief's desk and turned it slowly, noticing its craftsmanship — the tiny hinges on the side, the minuscule indentations representing nails in the lid, and the name of the funeral home etched on the side.

"So, what'd you think of Sandi's funeral?" she asked Harold, who sat before her, half-tilted back in his leather chair, bifocals riding down his nose as he reviewed her complaint against Mike.

"Can't go wrong with understatement," he said, turning a page and still not quite meeting her eyes.

"I meant what Mike did at the graveside."

Instead of answering immediately, Harold just rocked in his chair, flipping back and forth between one page and another as if trying to understand an abrupt transition.

"We all grieve in our own way," he said finally.

Poor Harold. His office was starting to feel like a reinforced air lock with all the pressure building up outside. In the week since Sandi's headless body had been found, there'd been emergency town meetings, Neighborhood Watch Groups formed, beefed-up security around the schools. A hot line number for anonymous tips had been set up at the police station, and blue and red signs for ADT and Slomin's Shield security systems had begun popping up in front of houses like crabgrass. But none of it was enough to reassure anyone, especially with the backdrop of local Activist Moms complaining that not enough was being done to safeguard the nuclear power plant twelve miles up the road from terrorist attack. All at once, the tag line of every other conversation in the parking lots and driveways seemed to be *But when are they going to do something?* And obviously Harold could not have missed the unspoken implication: that everything had gone to hell as soon as a black man was put in charge.

"I guess you must've heard they were seeing each other, Sandi and Mike," Lynn offered tentatively.

"And where did you hear that?" Harold replied cautiously, staying in neutral.

"Hmm, people who've been around the house." Lynn lowered her voice, not wanting to expose Inez as her source and betray a confidence.

"Well, then I can't comment to you about that," Harold said. "It would be prejudicial."

"Of course."

She put the little coffin back down on his desk and brooded for a while, still seeing the image of Mike shoveling dirt into Sandi's grave. Had Harold known about the affair already? He would have been hard-pressed not to have suspected it after the funeral.

"So how's it going with Sandi's case?" she said, changing the subject.

"As well as can be expected."

"Is there a lot of talk about the state or the county police coming in to help out?"

"We have most of the resources we need within our own department," he said curtly.

"I'm sure that's true."

She folded her hands on her lap, hoping she hadn't offended him. Her affection for Harold had been one of the real constants for her in this town. Even as a teenager he'd had a kind of stolid patience beyond his years, always listening to everyone else's arguments to the last intemperate word and then talking sense to them. Always knowing just the right thing to do and say to calm everyone down, whether it was in the middle of a schoolyard brawl or a funeral with two hundred and fifty guests waiting in the chapel.

He suddenly brought his chair upright and took his bifocals off.

"Lynn, may I speak with you?"

"Yes, of course. That's why you asked me here."

"No, I mean, can I really speak with you? Plainly and honestly. About this *other* matter."

He looked down at the double-spaced two-page complaint Barry

had made her type out about Mike coming in to her studio and trying to kiss her.

"Sure." She felt her ears pop as if the room had changed altitude.
"I realize it seems awfully trivial compared to everything that's going on . . ."

He cut her off. "I asked your husband to wait outside while we
talked because you've put me in a difficult position."

She looked back at the door, wondering how Barry was doing in
the outer office with the year-old *Sports Illustrated*s and *People* maga-
zines. At least a half-dozen cops had wandered past the doorway while
they were waiting, blatantly checking out the skirt and the stiff who'd
brought charges against the number-two man in their department.

"Normally, Mike would be the one running an Internal Affairs
investigation into an officer, but since he's the subject in this case,
that's obviously not an option."

He put his glasses down on the statement, and through the lenses
she saw the words *at that point, Michael tried to put his hand down the
back of my pants* magnified beyond fourteen-point type.

"My other main detective, Paco Ortiz, is running the homicide
investigation, so I can't ask him either." Harold rubbed his eyes,
plunging blindly ahead. "That leaves me. And I've known both of
you most of my life."

"Harold, if there was any other way . . ."

"Wait." He held up a hand. "Now, I am not in a position to tell you
not to press charges against Michael. That would be an abuse of my
position. My job is to take the statements from you and your husband
and then turn them over to a prosecuting attorney appointed by the
board. And once that happens, the entire matter is out of my hands."

"What do you mean?"

"There'll be a disciplinary hearing put on the schedule, and
you'll be called upon to testify in open court. And once that ball
starts rolling, there's no way to stop it."

She felt a dry leathery spot crack at the top of her throat and realized that she hadn't swallowed since she'd walked into the office. *I
don't want to do this,* she'd told Barry last night. *We have to live in this
town.*

"Are you condoning what he did and telling us to just let it go?"
she asked cautiously, licking her lips and wondering if she'd worn
too much makeup today.

"No, I am not. But I want to make sure you have the full picture before you decide to move forward."

"Harold, that sounds a little bit like a warning."

He gave her the famous tombstone eye, a look that said, *Go no further.* "I don't need to tell you how long the Fallon family has been in this town. Michael is an important part of this community. He raised eighteen thousand dollars last year organizing a bowling tournament for Sergeant Quinn and his wife after their daughter got leukemia. He took the Little League team to the county finals three years in a row and helped pay for the runner-up trophies out of his own pocket. And the truth is, you wouldn't even be sitting here if he hadn't cleaned up the crack problem down by the train station. Because you wouldn't have wanted to buy a house in Riverside . . ."

"So does that mean the law shouldn't apply to him?"

One corner of his mouth jerked, threatening a quick smile. "This is not an opinion," he said. "This is stating facts."

"But you're telling me that everyone's automatically going to be on his side."

He sighed and hunched forward, his fingertips forming a kind of triangle. "I'm saying this is a situation involving two people I care about. And both of you could get hurt badly."

"Oh?"

She crossed her ankles and stretched back into the confines of her chair, trying to look guiltless.

"If you get up on the stand, you're gonna be subjected to all kinds of ugly questions. The normal rules of evidence and procedure don't apply in a disciplinary hearing. A defense lawyer can ask you anything he wants."

"I see."

She was aware of a small pain starting to grow, very much like a flathead screwdriver wedging in under one of her shoulder blades.

"They might dredge up all manner of things from the past that might be very painful for a person with a family to hear discussed in public."

"You're not blackmailing me, Harold, are you?"

She saw something flare white-hot in his eyes and only cool slightly with the hooding of his lids. And for just an instant, she sensed the sheer physical exertion and strain of his life, all the effort it took to keep other people from ever glimpsing the true depth of his anger.

"I am trying to give you the information you need to make an intelligent decision," he said, as if he had a steel bit clenched between his back teeth. "What you do with it is up to you."

The digging under her shoulder blade sharpened. She should have told Barry more before they came in here today. But there were parts of her old life that she'd barely even admitted to herself, let alone tried to explain to anyone else. They were like pictures that sat at the bottom of a chemical tray for too long, dark and undeveloped.

"Barry said there was a good chance that Mike would fold and take a plea once he saw our statements rather than go through the whole process."

Harold shrugged. "I can't predict the future. I'd have thought you might've dropped these charges after your husband's arrest got voided."

"You don't know Barry. His gears don't do reverse."

"And neither do Mike's. He's pushing to get this hearing over with so he can get reinstated right away. And the mayor's thinking the same thing. He doesn't want this mess hanging over the whole department while we're trying to solve a homicide and restore confidence. They're talking about putting this trial on next week."

She hesitated, not realizing this would all happen so quickly. "Does that give anyone enough time to prepare?"

"That's not for me to say." He stood up, signaling this meeting was just about over. "So, what's it going to be, Lynn? It's not too late to jump off."

She looked up at him, realizing that the days when he would casually refer to her as a friend might be passing right before her eyes. She already felt the loss in her bones.

"I'm sorry," she said quietly. "This isn't just about me anymore, Harold. Mike pulled Barry off the road and put the handcuffs on him."

"I understand." The chief nodded, as if he'd known she would say this all along. "So I'll pass both of your statements on to the board and the prosecuting attorney."

"I guess that's the way it has to be." She stood and offered her hand. "I wish I wasn't the one making your life more complicated."

"Believe me" — he smiled in spite of himself — "you're not the only one."

33

"DADDY, who's the scariest monster in the world?"

"I have absolutely no idea."

Mike sat at the kitchen table, mobile phone and pile of papers at one elbow, SpongeBob glass half-filled with bourbon at the other. He tried to studiously ignore his youngest son, Timmy, in the doorway and the plucky merengue music blaring from the house across the street as he read the charges against him one more time.

Michael tried to put his hand down the back of my pants . . .

"Who do you think would win in a fight between Voldemort and Spawn?"

"What?"

He looked up and saw Timmy in rumpled cowboy pajamas, staring at him saucer-eyed, a ragged old comic hanging limply from his hand, the splayed toes of one bare foot awkwardly massaging the instep of the other.

"Cheryl says no one can defeat Voldemort but . . ."

"Timmy, gimme a minute, willya?"

At that point, I asked the lieutenant to leave my studio . . .

He picked up the phone and dialed his union rep, Frank Murray, pretending not to hear the wild shriek and rumpus of his older children arguing over what video to watch upstairs. Almost eight o'clock on a school night. Shouldn't these kids be doing their homework and getting ready for bed? Jesus, maybe they all needed to be on Ritalin. Fucking Marie. Working late again and throwing him to the wolves. *Somebody's got to bring the money in*, she kept saying.

By the end of next week, his vacation time would be all used up, and Harold would have the option of officially suspending him without pay. Another piece breaking off the eggshell they lived on.

Of course, she *said* she was staying with him for the time being. It only took half a night of him carefully explaining that the charges against him were obviously horseshit, that everyone was freaking out because of this sicko murder, and that Lynn was taking advantage of all the rampant paranoia to exaggerate a few things he'd said to her so her sleazebag husband could sue the town for harassment. *The oldest scam in the book*, he told her. *And Harold's just knuckling under because he wants to keep his job.*

But three days later, the thought still nagged at him that he could've maybe given her a little more of a heads-up. Not a full weepy confession or anything. Just a few strategically placed mumbles and grunts to soften up the ground a bit and make sure he didn't get dragged away in the backwash. The last thing he needed was his wife publicly abandoning him on the eve of a hearing.

The dull burr of the phone ringing vibrated the little bones deep in his ear canal.

"Dad . . ."

"Just gimme another second, Timmy." One finger extended, begging for indulgence.

He'd been desperately trying to make amends since that night Paco and Harold came by. Even before he'd had kids, he'd sworn he'd never lose control and start screaming the way his parents did. But they wear you down; they really do. A hundred little fights a day over things that couldn't matter less. A thousand little questions posed at the exact wrong moment.

"Daddy, Cheryl says Voldemort could beat Spawn . . ."

Obviously, the kid just wanted to hang out with him. They'd had a nice talk the other day in the car about monster movies — the first time in months, really, they'd connected. Just two guys going to the hardware store in the middle of the afternoon, sharing a black-cherry soda on the porch afterward. You couldn't blame the boy for wanting to stay in that little pocket of time. But now the line was clicking, and Frank's answering machine was coming on.

"Hey, Frankie! Mike Fallon again," he said once the outgoing message had played. "I just got the file from the chief, and it's time to stop screwing around. They really lowered the boom on me, buddy."

Timmy stayed in the doorway, paralyzed, as if he understood exactly what was being discussed. Mike waved for him to go sit in the living room.

"I already talked to Duffy Springer, and he's just not going to cut the mustard this time," he said. "I need a real lawyer."

Sure, Duff was a grand old fixer when it came to wheedling auto insurance and medical coverage for the family, but for the love of God this was *his life* they were talking about. As soon as Mike mentioned the words *disciplinary hearing* and *homicide investigation* in the same sentence, Duff started sputtering and pulling all the wrong law books down off his shelf. This was not a man capable of cutting the miracle deal Mike needed at this point.

The next time I saw the lieutenant was when I came down to the station to post bond for my husband. He asked me if I'd ever really cared about him . . .

His insides squirmed. No, this had already gone too far. He had to find somebody to help him put a stop to it. He put the phone down, took another sip of bourbon from the SpongeBob glass, and then reached for the address book to get Frank's cell phone number.

"Daddy, why do you need a lawyer?" asked Timmy.

"Why are you listening in on my phone calls?"

"I'm waiting for you. I thought we could play checkers."

"Isn't it time for you to be in bed?" Mike raised his eyes to the ceiling, hearing the other children sounding as if they were running from bulls on the second floor. "What are they doing up there anyway? Are they in their pajamas?"

"I dunno." The boy shrugged innocently.

He looked at the clock on the stove, praying for Marie to get home soon. Weird thing. As soon as he realized that there was a chance of losing her for good this time, he found himself wanting more attention from her. He'd started doing a few of the old chores again, so she'd notice. Regrouting the bathtub, fixing the cupboard doors she was always bitching about. Little things she hadn't gotten to herself. Just to remind her it was useful to have a man around the house sometimes.

"I gotta make another call," he said, dialing the cell phone number quickly.

His eyes fell on Lynn's statement again as the phone began to ring.

The lieutenant seemed upset when the chief ordered my husband to be released. . . . Gradually, reluctantly, he was beginning to understand how hard it must have been for his father to maintain control. *Brrrrrp.* The noise from the cell block still ringing in his ears when he came home at night. *Brrp.* The fights in the commissary lines, the turds tossed out between bars, the razors taped to the ends of toothbrushes. *Brrp.* The need to win every fight, no matter how small. The cold fact that you could never let them see you weak or wavering.

Brrp. The wife nattering at him because the only vacation they could afford was a crappy cabin without proper toilets or heat in New Hampshire. *Brrp.* His sons refusing to stop grab-assing in the backseat. *Brrp.*

Didn't you hear me when I said to keep your fucking hands to yourself? What part of that didn't you understand?

Johnny sassing, *How can your hands be fucking?*

Mom asking, *You let him talk to his parents like that?* The car suddenly veering into a Howard Johnson's parking lot off I-95, late on a Friday night, and Dad ordering everyone out of the car, making his sons stand side by side as though they were inmates in the exercise yard. Johnny refusing to back down. Mom telling Dad to make the boy mind his manners. Wanting to see the mick beaten out of him. The stumpy digger's fingers and the surly sandhog squint. The parts she was ashamed of. *For the love of God, give it to 'im, Pat. Teach 'im he can't talk to his parents that way.* Johnny raising his chin and grinning. *Yeah, show me who's the boss in this house, Dad. Let me know who's really wearing the pants.* Dad slapping him across the face even as Mike pleaded for his brother to stop. *Come on, Johnny, you're just making him madder.* Johnny defiantly wiping his nose on his sleeve and smiling right in Mom's face. *Jaysus, izzat the best ya can do, Dad? Gimme another.* Mike wincing and looking away as Dad finally lost it once and for all and broke his big brother's collarbone.

Brrp. He gave up on Frank and dialed the number at the station.

"Riverside Police," Larry Quinn's old-time soft-shoe-and-sarsaparilla voice came after two rings.

"Quinnman! Quinnasaurus! What's shaking, buddy?"

There was a pause so long you could almost feel the chill leaking through the receiver holes. "Oh, hey, Mike . . ."

"How're things going there?"

"Fine, *Mike*." His name said a bit too loud, as if someone else in the room was being alerted that he was on the line.

He plowed ahead anyway. "So, what's the good word? I feel like I'm on a desert island. You hearing anything from upstairs?"

This pause was just a little longer. "No. Not much."

"You guys haven't forgotten me, have ya?"

"No. No one's forgetting."

"So how's our friend from south of the border doing?"

"Who? Paco?"

"We got any other imports?"

"Come on, Mike," the sergeant muttered.

"Come on what? We're just talking here."

"Yeah, I know. But *you* know I can't talk to you about *this*."

"Why the hell not? I help you; you help me. The river flows both ways. Am I right? We all want the same thing."

"Can't do it, Mike."

"Sarge, don't cut me off. I mean it. I'm just looking to do right by that poor girl. Two kids left alone in the house with that miserable fuck . . ."

He heard a joist-shaking thump upstairs and Cheryl starting to cry, a high piercing feminine keen that made those tiny bones in his head tremble once again.

"Can't do it, Hoss," said Larry. "It's not that I don't want to."

"Sure you don't." Mike sighed, a billiard ball falling through his chest.

"Tell you something for nothing, though. That other girl that knew her was in with the chief yesterday . . ."

"Who? Lynn Stock . . . Schulman?"

He heard a burst of *Lord of the Dance* fiddle music and Harold's dour tones in the background. "Mike, I seriously gotta go."

"Lar?"

But the line was already dead. He put down the phone and spread his hands out on the table before him, trying to get a grip.

"Dad . . ."

"Just give me another minute, Timmy." He took a deep breath. "Please. I need another minute."

He started to reach over for the blue book of bylaws, wanting to make sure the union would pay for his lawyer and all the expenses of mounting a defense. But his left arm suddenly shot out straight, and his fist banged the table.

The sound startled him, and from the corner of his eye, he saw Timmy, cross-legged on the floor, lower the comic book he'd been reading. For a fraction of a second, he felt a kind of relief, as if he'd coughed and cleared his throat. But then the tension spasmed up in his gut again, and he hit the table hard enough so that the phone jumped. He closed his eyes and opened his fist, trying to settle himself.

"Dad?" the boy asked him cautiously.

"What?"

"Who do you think is the scariest monster in the world?"

He squeezed his lids. "You really want to know?"

"Yyy-yeah."

Okay, Timmy, you wanna know who the scariest monster is? He saw himself swiping his arm across the table and flinging the glass and papers across the kitchen floor in scalding fury. *You really wanna know? It's the Shit Monster! That's right! The SHIT MONSTER! You try to hold him in for as long as you can, but he wants to come out. Yes, he does! He comes rushing out of a long dark tube and gets all over everything. He covers you in brown runny turds so no one wants to get near you. And once he's on you, you can never get him off because he's full of disgusting germs and worms and invisible bacteria. He infects you for life, and you can never wash him away. Okay? You get the idea?*

He looked over at his son and realized that his own eyes had started to tear up from the effort of keeping all this inside. You spend your whole life telling yourself you won't end up like your old man, and then one day you look in the mirror and *there he is*. Biology's mean little private joke. It's worse than awful. It kills you a little. Because it means nothing you've ever tried to do changes anything.

"Dad? Why're you looking at me like that?"

The boy's head tilted to the side a little, as if he was seeing the open space around his father for the first time. This is where it begins, Mike thought. This is where you start thinking you might actually be able to run away.

"The Wolfman." He gathered up his papers. "He's the scariest."

"Why?"

"Because he knows what's going on, but he can't make it stop."

34

LYNN HESITATED as she stood facing the vast deserted garden supplies aisle at the back of Home Depot.

Where did everybody go? At the front of the store, there were long lines of burly contractors, nervous women in flannel shirts, and excitable Hasidim from upstate with carts full of building materials. But back here, by the chicken wire and fifty-pound bags of fertilizer, the place was as quiet and forbidding as a mausoleum, save for the occasional nerve-shearing whine of a buzz saw a few aisles away.

What was the matter with her? She used to be so brave and heedless. Back at the *Daily News*, she wouldn't think twice about walking into a crack house with her expensive cameras. But ever since Sandi's funeral the other day, she'd been on edge, flinching even when Barry came up from behind to put his arms around her.

Slowly, she pushed her cart forward, its hard rubber wheels wobbling over the concrete floor. Her eyes searched the shelves for mesh to hold the rosebushes down and deer-repellent spray. It was late in the season, she knew, but she hoped she could at least protect the tender shoots for the spring thaw. Coyote urine was good, Jeanine said. Nothing scares them away like the scent of a fiercer animal.

Another cart clattering nearby, its stainless-steel lattice rattling loudly. She looked up and down the aisle but saw no one. Again, she wished she'd made a date to go shopping with one of her friends. These in-between moments of solitude had an ominous gravity lately. She pushed on, past the bags of ammonium nitrate. Wasn't that what terrorists sometimes used to build bombs? God, paranoia was really getting the best of her.

The metal shiver of the other cart grew louder. She found herself picking up speed, noticing the sound was coming from nearby, as if she was being shadowed from the next aisle and watched through spaces in the shelves.

The buzz-saw whine filled her ears, reminding her of Sandi again. She started pushing her cart toward the end of the aisle, trying to remember if she'd recharged the cell phone battery this morning. Why didn't she listen to Barry? The tremor of the other cart's cage was so close she could feel it in her molars. She realized that she'd gone the wrong way and was headed right into his path. He was about to turn the corner and cut her off at the end of the aisle. Her wheels skittered as she tried to turn.

But then dapper old Clark De Cavalcante appeared before her in his spats and three-piece suit, a ghost from 1948 with a wolf's-head cane dangling off the end of his empty shopping cart.

"Good afternoon, madam." He made a gentlemanly show of tipping his fedora to her.

"Good afternoon, Mr. De Cavalcante." She nodded, allowing herself a small sigh of relief.

"You're looking very erotic today."

"How . . . kind of you." She demurred, wondering how far the prerogatives of old age really extended.

"Might I ask you to accompany me back to my studio?" He smiled, displaying a row of Indian-corn teeth.

"No, not today, thank you."

"Ah, well." He shrugged as if his proposal had already been turned aside a half-dozen times today. "I suppose I'll just have to try my luck in the kitchenware section."

"I suppose you will."

"Adieu, my dear."

She watched him shuffle off and then turned to find herself face to face with Michael Fallon.

"Let me ask you something," he said. "Are you proud of yourself?"

His voice was like a chest defibrillator, shocking her back a step. He must have been following her around the store, waiting to get her alone.

"Did you hear what I said?" The frame of his face tightened. "I asked you if you're proud of yourself."

She was still trying to recover from having him sneak up on her like this. "Hello, Michael."

His lip curled. "I saw that piece of shit you handed the chief. Your *statement*."

He looked older and perhaps a little heavier since the day of the funeral. Three deep lines creased his forehead, and five-o'clock shadow darkened his jowls. His upper lip seemed wider, as if it was strained from the effort of holding back his words. His work shirt smelled of fresh-cut lumber. Beside him was an orange pallet carrying a pile of two-by-fours and a couple of fence posts with sharp points on their ends.

"Michael, I really don't think it's appropriate for me to talk to you like this . . ."

"Oh, you don't think it's appropriate? Well, fuck me then. Do you think it's appropriate for you to have got me suspended when I have a wife and three children to support? Do you?"

The buzz saw screamed, going right into her cranium. He stared down at her, awaiting her reply. *Who's going to look away first?*

"You did what you did, and I did what I felt I had to do," she said, trying to make it all sound neutral and impersonal.

The sawdust odor began to make her throat itch. *Where were all the other shoppers?* Had there been some evacuation siren that she'd missed, leaving her alone back here?

"You're a fucking liar, Lynn. You know that?"

"I'm not a liar. I just said what happened."

"According to you! According to you!"

A fleck of saliva hit her cheek as he yelled. She suddenly remembered the time he choked her. His thumbs pushing through the soft tissues and into the hard cartilage of her voice box just as she rolled him off. He'd said it was an accident, that he didn't mean to do it, but she'd always wondered.

"There's two sides to every story." He jabbed a finger in her face. "Even your fucking wonderful pictures can lie. You cut things out. You show a man picking up a gun, but you don't show he's in the middle of a war or that his friend's lying dead at his feet."

The buzz saw tore into another piece of wood, the whine sinking into a deep growl.

"Well, I guess you'll have your day in court," she said, trying to draw herself up straight against a rack of dangling garden shears.

Don't show him that you're scared. That will only make him stronger.

His eyes went back and forth, strafing her face, as he leaned in on her, bracing himself with a hand on a shelf above her head.

"You're really going to do this, aren't you?" he said, shaking his head in ragged disbelief.

"I don't see where I have a choice."

"You know, it's not just my life you're going to be ruining."

"And what's that supposed to mean?"

His finger retracted. "Think about it."

"Hey, buddy!" A chunky Home Depot clerk in an orange shirt and an Everlast weight belt called to Mike from the far end of the aisle. "You still want that pressure-treated wood?"

"Yeah, I guess I'll look at it," Mike grumbled, slowly simmering down.

"We got it piled up for you in aisle nine."

"All right, I'll be there in a minute."

Finally, more shoppers strayed into their aisle as he withdrew his attention from her face one degree at a time. It was as if they'd been locked in a dark private dream for a few minutes while the rest of the world was going about its daily business.

"I want you to know I was starting to get somewhere with Sandi's case when you got me suspended," he said quietly. "I was going to nail that bastard's head to the wall."

She held her own tongue, literally against her teeth. He's insane, she thought. He's truly lost it. She'd known it as soon as she saw him take the shovel out of Jeffrey's hands and start flinging dirt into Sandi's grave.

"You know, she was a friend of mine too." He took his great barge of a pallet and shoved off. "Stupid *bitch*."

35

THE TOWN ADMINISTRATOR, Beverly Crawford, was a vaguely Prussian-looking woman with hair the color of tarnished brass and a face like something drawn hastily on the back of a cocktail napkin. A People's Bank calendar and a dark-purple vase with two wilting daffodils stood sentry at the front of her desk. A page taped to the back of her Compaq monitor advised: "I Can Only Please One Person a Day and Today Is Not Your Day." Small letters below added: *"And tomorrow is not looking too good either."*

"What can I do for you?" she asked in a voice that would have made strong heavily armed men flee their capital cities in despair.

"I came to check on my Freedom of Information Act request." Barry leaned an elbow on the Formica counter between them, having rushed out of work early to get here before the office closed. "This is the third time I've tried to follow up on it in four days."

"Remind me what this is about again."

Mrs. Crawford tapped a single key six times and pushed her face at her computer screen.

"I was asking for the Civilian Complaint Review Board's records on Michael Fallon."

Barry smiled, more out of habit at this point than any sincere conviction that he could truly ingratiate himself.

"You've had my formal letter making the original request since last week."

"Well, I'm not sure where that letter is right now. I've probably passed it along to the Town Board and the police chief. I'm sure they'll take it up shortly."

She pulled a typewritten sheet from the in-box on her desk, examined it cursorily, and then dropped it into her green aluminum wastepaper basket.

"Actually," said Barry, "there's nothing for them to discuss. Those records are public information. If I ask for them, you have to turn them over to me."

"Excuse me."

Mrs. Crawford slowly slid her eyes across his face, as if she'd lost whatever small interest she'd had, and picked up a ringing phone.

"Yeah?" she growled, wrinkling her nose.

Barry stayed by the front of the desk, as if waiting for the ball to carom off the boards.

"You know, I don't know what you expect me to do with that memo," she said. "He just pulled all those numbers out of a hat."

Barry cleared his throat and stared at the top of her head, fully aware that like one of the mythic creatures in the medieval fantasy novels Clay and Hannah used to love, this was an entity that derived its power in direct proportion to the amount of frustration it could provoke in the questing hero.

"Just bill him again and see if he pays twice," she said. "But don't make it my problem."

She pressed down on the hook and started to dial a number.

"I'm still here," said Barry.

"*I know that.*"

"I'd like to leave here with those files."

"And I'd like to wear a size six." She stabbed at the Flash button with a stout wattled finger. "What do you need these records for anyway?"

"We've been over this. It's not necessary for me to tell you that."

As if they couldn't have guessed part of what he was up to already. Even a small child could have discerned that Fallon had pulled that little number with the radar gun before. The first question was whether there were previous complaints on file about him doing it. The second question was whether he'd harassed other women in the past the way he'd harassed Lynn. From six months handling domestic violence and police corruption complaints at the DA's office, he suspected that the answer was yes.

He'd decided he had to come up with other witnesses for the disciplinary hearing on his own since the town attorney had yet to contact them about their statements. The possibility of a cover-up had started to take shape in his mind. He didn't want to leave Lynn dangling as the only other witness against her ex-boyfriend. Already he noticed she was starting to look distinctly wan and uneasy whenever the subject came up, preferring to talk about Christmas in Paris or her gallery show in the spring.

"How far back do you want these records?" Beverly Crawford asked.

"Starting whenever he came on the job." Figuring Fallon was around the same age as his wife, it had to be the early eighties when he was a rookie. "At least twenty years."

"Yeah, good luck. Most of those old CCRB records are probably warehoused with Iron Mountain in Wisconsin. It's going to take at least six weeks to track them down."

"Then you better try to find a way to speed things up . . ."

A police sergeant walked into the office, whistling, and waggled his monobrow as he came around the counter to drop a file on Mrs. Crawford's desk.

"Hey, good lookin' . . ."

He stopped beside her and looked over to see whom she was talking to.

On recognizing Barry, the whistle trailed off abruptly, and the monobrow came down like a riot gate. The officer looked from Beverly Crawford to Barry and then back again, slowly doing the math in his head.

"How's it going?" said Barry, realizing this was indeed the same officer who'd fingerprinted him the night Michael Fallon pulled him over. The smell of the ink pad seemed to linger on him.

"Yowza," the sergeant muttered, turning with his shoulders hunched, carrying the burden of this knowledge back to the station across the street. Barry wondered if it would be seconds or minutes before Fallon knew what he'd been doing here.

"There's a town meeting coming up soon, isn't there?" Barry said.

"I think there's one scheduled for the end of the week." Beverly Crawford looked after the sergeant, the embers of smoky romance gradually fading in her eyes. "The mayor is just trying to keep everyone up to date on the situation as it develops."

Ah, the *Lanier situation*. So that's what they were calling it this week. As if actually using the word *murder* would inflict further damage.

"You know, I'd hate to have to take this matter up with him in a public forum."

She pursed her lips, finally giving him her full undivided attention.

"I'm not sure what you mean by that," she said.

"I mean I could stand up at the next town meeting and ask him why his administration is withholding information about police misconduct that's supposed to be available to the public. I'd think he might find that a little embarrassing to hear in front of all the truth-in-government types up from the city who voted for him last time around."

She paused for just a moment and then continued about her business, pulling staples out of thickly stacked documents.

"I suppose that's your right as a taxpayer," she said.

"And I could also ask him about that piggy little deal he has with Northern Coastal Developers for the new golf course and the condos they're building on Prospect. My understanding is that the mayor's son is settling in very nicely as a vice president over there. I noticed there wasn't much of a debate when the Town Board approved that particular arrangement. In fact, I don't recall seeing any public announcement about the vote coming up at all."

He'd only heard about it on the train platform afterward when Marty Pollack mentioned it in passing, four weeks ago. This type of sleazy little real estate quid pro quo would make for screaming *Daily News* headlines in the city but barely raised an eyebrow up here since most people cared only about low taxes and good schools. But next year was an election year, and given the current circumstances, the mayor was under especially harsh scrutiny, his every misstep potentially providing evidence of deep subcutaneous moral rot.

"I'm sure there was some notice in the local newspaper," Mrs. Crawford said more mildly, realizing she was losing ground here.

"If there was, it was probably buried among the used car ads, and the print was so small you would've had to have been an ant with bifocals to read it. I'm sure the town charter says these announcements are supposed to be 'prominent' and 'easily accessible.' So do you want me to keep making a stink about this, or are you going to give me what I've been asking for?"

Her eyes were already taking on the cloudy far-off look of a snake about to start shedding its old skin. She reached for her phone.

"How many years back did you say you wanted those files for?"

"Twenty, at least. And don't skip any years. I'd hate to have to come back and start this whole process all over again."

She began to dial a number. "Well, you don't have to be nasty about it."

36

"'ONCE THERE WAS A LITTLE BUNNY who wanted to run away . . .'"

Still shaken by her run-in with Michael, Lynn kept her promise to stop by Sandi's house and read to the kids after school.

"'"If you run away," said his mother, "I will run after you."'"

Dylan reclined against her on the bed, his head heavy against her chest. How much she missed having this comfort from her own children. The way she'd grow drowsy reading to them, her eyelids getting leaden, her voice slurring conscious and unconscious thoughts together as she noticed herself referring to "John Sununu" and "silver gelatin prints" in the middle of *The Runaway Bunny*. She sniffed, finding herself unreasonably upset by the sight of the mother bunny fishing for her child in a trout stream.

"Go on," Dylan prompted her, his head going back and bashing her between the breasts like a bowling ball. *"Read!"*

"See?" Lynn turned ahead. "When he becomes a crocus in a hidden garden, his mother becomes a gardener and finds him . . ."

She heard her nose clogging, a prelude to tears. God. Why did he insist on *this* book? An author who'd died suddenly at forty-two. A child separated from a parent. This constant sense of loss and search. *Controlling Mommy fantasy*, Sandi used to joke.

"Oh, look" — Lynn wiped a fallen tear-spatter from the corner of a page — "she's become a tightrope walker."

"Mommy said she'd always come look for me," said Dylan.

"What?"

"Mommy said that if I ever got taken away from her, she'd always get me back."

Again, there was that eerie unchildlike harshness in his voice.

"Who did she think was going to take you away?" She took him gently by the shoulders and tried to turn him. But he made his body rigid, refusing to let her see his face.

"Dylan?"

His head turned toward the door.

"Did Mommy think someone was going to try to steal you?"

Once more, she felt that spindling sensation on the back of her neck. An awareness of being observed as acute as a spider's thread touching her skin.

Dylan's head lifted from her chest.

"Daddy!" He got up and ran for the doorway.

Jeff stood there, in a white Polo shirt and navy Dockers, looking slightly less shell-shocked than he did the day of the funeral.

"Hey, Lynn," he said, gladly receiving a hug around the knees. "I'll take over for you."

"Jesus, I didn't even hear you come upstairs." She took a deep breath as she swung her legs off the bed and looked around for her sneakers.

"That's me," he said. "The strong silent type."

So this is what it's coming to. Even a childrens' book can unnerve me. She slipped her Keds back on and gave Jeff a quick kiss on the cheek as she passed him in the doorway. "I better get going. My guys will be getting out of school any minute."

"You're a champ, Lynn." He touched her elbow. "Sandi always knew she could count on you."

She hurried down the steps and into the empty foyer, still hearing, *If you run away, I will run after you.*

37

"AM I MISSING SOMETHING HERE?" asked Harold, looking over the open containers of Chinese food arrayed on his desk and the reports Paco had written up for him.

"That's everything I've put in the system."

Paco sat on the other side of the Great Wall of Takeout, toying with the orange Nerf football with huge foam gouges taken out of it that Harold kept in his desk drawer for times of extreme stress.

"Sandi Lanier's husband is away all weekend, having business meetings in New England." Harold lowered his bifocals. "That makes sense to you?"

"It all checks out." Paco tossed the ball from hand to hand. "Lanier lands at Logan Thursday morning, registers at the Four Seasons hotel by eleven. Spends the next three days tooling around in a rented Tempo, meeting with venture capital people. Goes sailing with two college friends on Sunday in New London. Goes to two more meetings Monday in Providence. Returns the car to Avis at Logan by three-thirty. Lands at LaGuardia at five. Walks in the front door a little after seven, almost twelve hours after his wife comes floating down the river without her head."

"You pull his cell phone and hotel bill records?"

"Called home twice over the weekend and made about half a dozen work calls from the hotel. I think he might've been blowing smoke up our asses about how well his business is doing, but that don't make him any different from most folks around here."

The chief folded up his bifocals and put them in his vest pocket as the two of them took a moment to contemplate the moral lubricity of white people and their money.

"Still think there's any way he could've done it?" he asked his detective.

"If there is, I'm not seeing it." Paco let the ball rest on his lap. "I've talked to people who saw him every one of those days. The only gaps are when he's sleeping and a few hours Sunday night when he says he went to see *Moulin Rouge*. And he would've had to drive something like a hundred-fifty miles to be back in time for his meeting Monday morning. It's possible, but . . ."

He opened his palms, indicating to the chief the precise amount of hard evidence he would have to present to a jury at this point. A second-year law student could tear apart this circumstantial a case.

"What about paying somebody else to do it for him?" the chief asked.

"When we think he's low on cash?" Paco shrugged. "I'll look into it, but I gotta tell you, Chief, hit men don't give preholiday discounts, even in this economy."

"Shit." Harold pushed aside the round tin of beef lo mein he'd been picking at indifferently, wishing he could go home early and eat with the family one of these days. "So I guess we've gotta start looking at the other guy. Is that what you're telling me?"

"Hey, bro, I don't like to talk bad about another cop, and I know you guys go way back together. But do the math."

"Let's hear it."

Harold wiped his hands with a paper towel and sat forward in his chair, revealing a small tear in the leather behind him.

"He knows the victim from the old days and does work around the house when the kids and the husband are out," Paco said.

"Mmm." Harold grumbled, brooding again on what Lynn had said about those two "seeing" each other. *Damn.* They'd have to nail that down, get a real source. Not that he hadn't figured it out already, but what else did the women in this town know? And how could you subscribe to be part of their closed-circuit twenty-four-hour news network?

"He's at the crime scene the first morning at the train station," Paco went on, laying it out piece by piece, as if he was putting together a bike, "so his footprints were all over the riverbank by the time I started to take shoe impressions. Then he's all hinky about what kind of relationship he had with Mrs. Lanier when I ask him about it. And he keeps bothering Mrs. Schulman, wanting to know if

Sandi ever said she was having an affair. Then a can of the same wood protector he uses turns up in the bag with the victim's head . . ."

"You don't think that could've been someone setting him up?" Harold raised his eyebrows.

"I ain't done yet." Paco shook his head. "He has access to all the physical evidence in the locker, so I don't even know the rest of what we're missing besides the diary. There could be fingerprints, carpet fibers, and hair samples I never got a chance to look at because he got to them first."

"Damn . . ." Harold eyed the open container of white rice, deciding the last thing he needed was more starch in his life.

"And then there's the laptop."

"The laptop?"

"The one we collected from Mrs. Lanier's house. It's got a bunch of e-mails from an AOL account called Topcat105."

"So?" asked Harold, remembering the old cartoon character Top Cat, who was always giving people a dime on a string and then yanking it out of their hands.

Top Cat was probably working for the federal government now.

"The last e-mail from this Topcat was asking Mrs. Lanier to meet him at the same Motel 6 where the state trooper found her Audi a few days later. It says, 'I have a few things of yours that you might want back. You miss that earring?'"

Harold glanced over at his office door, making sure it was firmly closed. "And who's this Topcat?"

"His member profile gives the name J. C. Martin and says he's a law enforcement professional with an athletic build and a movie-star smile."

J. C. Martin. Harold took a second to close his eyes, trying to drop the name into his memory bank. It rolled around and then hit the jackpot, sending him back to the Samuel R. Walker Middle School lunchroom. He was in the pack with white kids gathered around a little Panasonic transistor, listening to Lindsey Nelson call the fourth game of the '69 Series. *And the ball hit Martin in the wrist as he was running up the first-base line!* A journeyman back-up catcher for the Mets, having his one moment of glory because an errant Baltimore throw struck him and allowed a run to score. He remembered the whole lunchroom exploding with joy, everyone jumping up and cheering, slapping him on the back as if he'd finally become one of them just by being a Mets fan. The more he thought about it, the more he was sure that Mike had been one of the white boys who'd put an arm around his shoulders.

"It's a fake name," he said.

"I figured as much too, even though I'm a Yankees fan." Paco squeezed the ball on his lap. "It don't look good."

"Can you prove it's Mike's account?"

"I'm working on it with the company's legal department. They got all kinds of privacy laws to protect people's identities."

Harold threw his bulk back into his chair, a jagged lightning bolt of rage shooting across his brain. Long ago, he'd acclimated himself to the fact that this was an imperfect world and that there was little to be done about it but to accept the bitter immutable facts. When he was seventeen, he'd learned that his father, whom he dearly loved, was having an affair with a local widow and had never told his mother. But at this moment, he felt his tie slowly constricting his throat.

"You got a theory why he would kill her?" he asked, reaching up to loosen it.

"Not yet, but it's pretty goddamn obvious something's up with him, after all that crazy shit with Mrs. Schulman and her husband. And then that John Henry number at the cemetery. I thought he was gonna hit water the way he was digging . . ."

"I kept telling him to leave it be," Harold muttered, pulling on the fat end of his tie in rhythmic frustration. "I said it once, I said it a hundred and fifty fucking times."

"You cut him a lot of slack."

"He saved my life, Paco. Not just with that crazy old woman, but a hundred thousand other nights out on the street. You know what it's like trying to get some little punk-ass motherfucker in the back of a squad car with fifty of his relatives and best friends surrounding you and yelling, 'Get their guns'?"

"So what? I'm trying to save your job."

Harold grimaced and touched his right side again, feeling the old knife wound starting to burn a little.

"I'm not seeing it," he said.

"You're not seeing what?"

"I'm not seeing him kill Sandi. I see a husband killing his wife because she's stepping out on him. But the boyfriend as the doer?"

"I've seen it." Paco shrugged. "He's a control freak. Maybe she was trying to break it off with him."

"It still don't make sense to me."

Harold pulled open his top desk drawer and looked for the Motrin. At least he didn't have to take those nasty antibiotics that had him running to the bathroom every five minutes while the wound was still healing.

"How's he get along with the ladies generally?" asked Paco, trying another angle.

"Fine . . . okay . . . not bad." Harold heard the confidence in his voice ebbing as he cast his mind back. "Better than some, worse than others. What are you getting at?"

"I'm just saying, I worked Sex Crimes a couple of years in the Bronx. I know how the play goes. Has he got a history with this?"

"Listen, the man's no saint." Harold picked up the Motrin bottle and started wrestling with the lid. "I'm not defending the way he acted with Lynn Schulman. Or the fact that he was having an affair with Sandi. But I don't see him cutting off anybody's head and throwing the body in the river. You're gonna have to connect those dots for me."

"Some guys they start small and then they escalate." Paco shrugged. "It's like a drug, bro. You gotta go a little further, hit that shit a little harder every time so's you can still feel it." He smacked his fist into his palm for emphasis. "Maybe a couple of times he hit it a little too hard."

"I still don't see it."

"Then maybe you're too close to it. Lemme ask you something else, Chief: If he was screwing Sandi, but he didn't kill her, why wouldn't he just tell us that?"

"I don't know." Harold pulled the cap off the Motrin bottle and saw it held only cotton. "Chain of command. He was afraid I'd take him off the case and bust him down to patrol. Problems at home. He thought Marie would give him the heave-ho and take the kids away. Say what you will about the man, but he loves those children."

"Then the best-case scenario is that he was impeding an investigation and tainting the evidence against whoever killed his girlfriend."

"Maybe he thought he could keep control of the wheel and steer us around the problems." Harold tossed the Motrin bottle across the desk in disgust. "Who knows what he was thinking? The man's seen more fucked-upness in his life than veterans of two world wars. Maybe it started to get to him."

Should a friend have tried to help out more? Harold was reluctant to absolve himself too easily. In his new job as chief, he'd told himself he couldn't afford to get too close to any of the officers anymore, but at the same time he knew you couldn't be so distant as to have no idea of what they were up to.

"So have you entered all of this evidence into the system?" he asked.

"What, are you kidding?" Paco let the ball roll off his lap. "So a defense lawyer can subpoena all of it as Rosario material if we end up arresting somebody else? We'd be fucked if they got their hands on all these notes. That's why I wanted to talk it over with you first."

Harold saw the orange Nerf ball appear under his desk and roll up to his feet.

"What do you want to do then?" He bent down to pick it up and felt a small tearing in his side.

"I want to take a run at him."

"For real?"

"We've almost got enough for a warrant," Paco said. "And he's already gotta be sweating about the disciplinary hearing. I say we lay it all on him. Go at him hard. Straight on. Lying about the relationship. Stepping on the evidence. Not answering our questions. The e-mail account. Ask him to give us a DNA swab so we can compare the fluids on the body and then see if it was his baby she was carrying. Make him think he'd be lucky to catch a break from us."

"Won't work." Harold shook his head.

"Why not?"

"It's not enough. I know this man. Some of his wiring may not be up to code, but the lights still go on. He'll see right through us. If we're only going to get one shot at him, we have to make sure he doesn't get up and walk away."

"So how do *you* want to play it?" asked Paco.

"Keep digging. Get us a little more leverage. See if you can prove it's Mike's Internet account on the laptop. Recanvass for witnesses who might have seen the body dump. Give it a few more days."

"All right." Paco nodded.

"One thing I do worry about, though." Harold cocked the ball back by his ear, feeling the burning like a lit cigar stuck in his side.

"What's that?"

"If we can trust Mike to keep his hands to himself in the meantime."

"I don't know." Paco got up. "You know him better than I do."

38

"I SAW HIM AGAIN TODAY," said Lynn.

At half past midnight, she was sitting up in bed, listening to branches scrape the window and watching the play of moonlight on her husband's profile.

Barry's eyelids fluttered. "Who?"

"Michael. He was in the aisle at Home Depot."

Barry rolled onto his side, suddenly wide awake.

"Why didn't you tell me this before?" he said.

"I didn't want to mention it in front of the kids."

"Did he try to talk to you?"

"He was pretty upset, as you might imagine."

"What exactly did he say?" She heard a hint of impatience in his voice, a former prosecutor's demand for precision.

"He kept asking me, 'Are you proud of yourself?'"

"Are *you* proud of *yourself?*" He flipped each word over as if carefully inspecting its underside. "What the hell is that supposed to mean?"

Here it is, Lynn. Here's your opening.

"I guess what he meant was, we've known each other a long time," she began cautiously.

"Yes. And?"

Listen to me, she thought. *Don't just hear the words. Hear what I'm not saying.*

"I was close to some of the other people in his family too." She pushed it a little further. "Did I ever tell you about his brother?"

"No," he said, remaining male and frustratingly obdurate. "I'm sure he was wonderful. But so what? Attila the Hun probably had a nice sister too. Is that supposed to be an excuse?"

No. He'd missed the signal. There used to be this subfrequency between them, a silent way she could prompt him to ask the right question, but they weren't hearing each other as well anymore. Too much static on the line. The noise-to-signal ratio was off. Even their sex life was phasing in and out lately. For a while there, they'd been in a real groove, not just having boring Married People Sex, but Rock-'Em Sock-'Em Post-Apocalypse Sex. The last few days, though, they'd been having Refugee Sex, furtive and uncomfortable, as if they were doing it in steerage among hordes of other starving immigrants.

"So did you call the police to report it?" Barry pushed back the covers.

"I spoke to one of the sergeants. Larry Quinn. He said there's no law against talking to somebody in the aisle of a chain store."

"Bullshit." He pushed back, knocking the headboard against the wall. "You're a material witness against an officer in a disciplinary procedure."

"They said somebody would have an informal conversation with him about keeping his distance."

"And that's supposed to make us feel better?"

They both fell quiet for a few seconds, watching maple-leaf shadows on the ceiling.

"I really don't want to do this," she said. "I don't want to testify against him."

"Great," he said. "We keep our mouths shut, and he skates? Is that the idea?"

"Would that really be so terrible?"

"Hell yeah. I just spent the afternoon pulling his old CCRB complaints. The guy's got a file like the Sunday *Times.* Harassment complaints from at least two other women and four brutality complaints out of the drug sweeps they did down by the waterfront. If we let him off the hook, what'll we do next time he comes by the house?"

She heard a distant sound in the woods like the tensing of a dock rope. You should tell him. He'll understand. Unless he doesn't.

"We could move again," she said, rubbing her chin against her kneecap. "Our old apartment in Manhattan's probably renting for a couple of hundred dollars less since the Eleventh."

"You're serious?"

"Halfway. What if we just stayed in Paris after Christmas vacation? Remember how we used to talk about moving there?"

"Yeah, before we had kids and high cholesterol."

She felt around for his hand in the dark. "You really wouldn't consider moving?"

"Lynn" — he sighed, his knuckles lightly brushing hers — "all our money's tied up in this house. We can't just pick up and move tomorrow. We'd lose our shirts if we tried to sell it in this market."

"I thought you said our company stock was going to come roaring back any minute."

She felt him go rigid beside her, a center of gravity sinking into the mattress. "It's late," he said, starting to roll away. "We should talk about all this tomorrow."

He was shutting down on her, like the old local television stations used to. *This concludes our broadcast day.*

"Did you make sure all the doors were locked before you turned in?" She watched him pull the covers up again, his silhouette curving away from her, becoming an indistinct lump.

"I did."

"Did you tuck the kids in?"

"Hannah's seventeen," he muttered. "If I tried to tuck her in at this point, she'd call child welfare on me."

"They're still very young."

"Lynn" — he reached back, feeling around for her tentatively in the darkness — "everything's going to be okay. You know that, don't you?"

"That's what you keep telling me." She turned back the quilt and started to slip out of bed. "I'm going to check on them again. I can't help it."

Parquet cold against the soles of her feet, she padded out into the hallway, grabbing the blue flannel robe from the closet on the way. The thermostat reported it was 68 degrees in the house, but that seemed unlikely. Even with pajama tops and bottoms on under the robe, the chill went right into her bones.

Call me Cleopatra, Queen of Denial.

She stopped in Clay's room first and found him curled up under the "Raw is War" quilt, little Stone Cold Steve Austin action figure clutched in his pudgy left hand, like a talisman to ward off evil spirits.

Almost thirteen years old. Should she be worried? Hannah had put most of her dolls away by the time she was ten. Shouldn't he at least have something more appropriate for his age, like a stroke book hidden under his pillow? She smoothed back his hair and moved on to her daughter's room.

The den of iniquity. The door gave a long drawn-out groan as she pushed it open, and she found herself cringing, awaiting the contemptuous hiss and the inevitable exasperated question — *What are you doing?* It felt as though it had been weeks since she'd entered this space uninvited. Light from the red gamma-globulin Lava lamp illuminated the Marilyn Manson poster and the faux-Egyptian amulet dangling from a nail above the bed. She felt a pang, remembering the old kindergarten finger paintings and crayon scrawls they used to tape to the apartment walls. Back when she wanted to make pictures like Mommy. She stepped carefully, knowing there were stacks of Anne Rice novels and CDs by the Cure somewhere in the dark. For some reason, the Goth obsession was lasting longer than her other phases. Odors of patchouli and recently extinguished incense lingered vaguely. Hey, what happened to the little bottle of Chanel Number Five she bought for Hannah's birthday last year at Bloomingdale's? Her daughter lay faceup on her pillow, the full moon melting away her baby fat, a thin black camisole strap slipping off her bare shoulder, as if she was waiting to be ravished.

The time was near for another one of their *talks*, if it hadn't already come and gone. Seeing that soft white shoulder, she sensed with a reasonable degree of certainty that Hannah had begun having sex with Dennis Paultz, and all she could do about it at this point was make sure her warnings about protection had been heeded and prepare Barry so he wouldn't need four-point restraints when he found out.

She sat down on the side of the bed, wondering if she'd missed the moment. More and more these days, she was looking around and asking where her children went. The details of their daily lives were no longer second nature to her. There were friends, places, and habits popping up in the middle of conversations that she'd absolutely never heard of before.

She touched the satiny side of Hannah's face, a privilege she was no longer permitted to enjoy in waking hours.

Are you proud of yourself? Why didn't she say something to Barry just now? The shot was right there. The light was perfect. But somehow she missed the chance to frame it and click the shutter. Why couldn't she just come out with it? Instead, here she was, rambling at midnight, the little disturbances of the house echoing and amplifying the disjunction of her thoughts.

It occurred to her that secrets were like a town sometimes, with their own social hierarchy. The Arrivistes sunning themselves at the top of the hill, having bootstrapped their way up into semirespectability. The Status-Seekers in the middle, trying to stay busy so no one will question them too closely. And at the very bottom, the Unmentionables, the things you tried not to think about, the memories you could barely admit even to yourself. They labored like a mutant workforce under the surface, toiling in the fuming, grinding infrastructure, pushing the millstones, loading up coal carts, digging deeper and deeper into the sediment, and occasionally hitting a vein and sending spumes shooting up into the Overworld.

Realizing she wouldn't get back to sleep easily, she prowled back out into the hallway. From the master bedroom, Barry was snoring along obliviously like the distant surf. *Everything's going to be okay,* he'd said. And she'd let that stand. *Are you proud of yourself?*

She noticed that the door to the vest-pocket study at the other end of the hall was half-open. A soft beacon glow spilled out. Her heart tripped on the off beat, thinking someone was in there. But when she cautiously pushed the door open, she found the room empty and the desktop computer left on. She went to turn it off and found a gray-blue grinning devil's head on the Gateway screen, a window in its mouth asking, "Are you sure you wish to be released from the dark realm? Yes / No." Jesus, another one of Clay's games about creating your own world and then torturing its inhabitants like a malevolent god. She turned it off, wondering if Barry had pushed him too hard on this Bar Mitzvah business and given the kid an angry Messiah complex. The devil's head scrolled away, leaving the America Online sign-on greeting in its place. Were they affiliates?

From outside, she heard a tiny *chp-chp* sound, like two wet marbles being tapped together. A woodpecker? A cricket? She'd always had an overstimulated imagination in the late hours, telling her younger sister, Carol, bedtime stories about headless horsemen and dismembered schoolgirls that scared both of them so badly they'd need to sleep in the same bed. She sat down in the chair, regretting they'd never regained that closeness. In becoming an instant grown-up after Mom got sick, Lynn had turned into one of the people that Carol had to get away from. And so she'd gone all the way out to Oregon to join a commune and then marry an architect and start a family of her own, having had more than enough of MS, her bossy older sister, and Riverside in general. Maybe she had the right idea, Lynn thought, making a clean break instead of stumbling back into town like the prodigal daughter.

Lynn looked at the clock in the corner of the screen and saw it was almost one o'clock, but still a few minutes before ten in Portland. Her nephews would be asleep, and Carol would almost certainly be dog-tired, but she needed to touch base with somebody. A kind of desperate loneliness had come over her, a yearning for connection without consequence.

The chair's struts gave a little cry as she tucked a cold foot under her butt. Her fingers danced across the keys, entering her name and her secret password, *Weegee*, as the computer made that odd flickering sound like a fuse burning up, a reminder that they needed to get a DSL line one of these days. She hit the sign-on button and waited for the connection, the whine and squeal of electrodes shooting through miles of fiber-optic cable and branching out like vines across the country, searching for something or someone to latch on to. And just before that bright impersonal male voice announced, "Welcome!" she'd heard a light drizzle like someone pissing against the side of the house.

She froze for a moment, trying to find a benign explanation. An animal. Deer and raccoon go to the bathroom too. Why shouldn't they do it right outside? Maybe she should've gone back for that bag of coyote urine this afternoon, to keep them away.

"You've got mail!" announced the voice on the computer, like the world's most ambitious flight attendant.

She clicked on the yellow envelope and saw she had three messages from François at the gallery, probably wanting to talk about their lunch on Thursday and the most recent set of prints she'd sent him for the spring show. The immigrant laborer series from in front of Starbucks. She knew he was going to hate them. *Too drab*, he'd say. *Too gritty. Isn't this sort of 1930s social realism old hat? Where's the cutting edge? Where's the beauty for beauty's sake?* She had half a mind to beg François to postpone the show for a month. How could she think about work at this point anyway? It would be like trying to take a picture in the middle of a dust storm.

She clicked to open the first e-mail, and just as she started to read the words *Union Square Cafe, twelve-thirtyish?* a fierce rustling began outside. A thin gust blew into the room. Hugging herself for warmth, she got up to close the window, the floorboards giving a mournful sigh, as if there were a song trapped beneath them.

Wind slapped hard at the glass. She saw the ceaseless tumbling of treetops in the moonlight. A chill crept over her. The *chp-chp* was coming from right under the window. She shut it quickly and backed away. Easy there. Mike wouldn't just show up at your house in the middle of the night. Would he?

The lunch proposal was where she'd left it on the screen, dutifully awaiting her answer. No, Mike wouldn't dare. Larry Quinn said someone would talk to him. But there was still an undeniable presence in the vicinity. She'd felt it strongly right by the window, a stillness in the air, a coppery taste in her mouth that reminded her of this afternoon.

Enough. She was scaring herself. She hit the reply button and typed, "see ya then," back to François, with what she hoped sounded like plucky confidence, and started to turn the computer off. But just before she clicked on the X in the upper right-hand corner, the screen winked. A slightly cheesy-sounding wind-chime sound issued from the speakers, and a small white space appeared in the left corner, signaling an Instant Message.

Stark black words filled in the top line.

I KNOW WHAT YOUR DOING

Her heart jammed. How would anyone even know she was up at this hour? Could he see her?

She started to rise from her chair. Then a second line appeared.

WATCH YOURSELF.

The whole room pulsated in time with her breathing.

In a panic, she blanked out the screen before fully registering the name of the sender. She couldn't allow this to go any further. The threat was already stamped and burning in her head. She slowly backed away and knocked over her chair, as if a hand was about to reach out of the screen. *"Good-bye!"* said the ambitious flight attendant. She turned and ran, her bare feet thumping hard on the landing, sounding hollow spots below the boards. The master bedroom door was still half-open, and she dove in beside Barry, seeking refuge against his frame. Shivering in the dark, she realized that in her rush to get rid of the message she hadn't considered how to track it back to its source.

Watch yourself. Something about seeing those small black letters against the plain white background made her think of bodies lost in a snowstorm.

She huddled in a semifetal ball, listening for further disturbances. But the great outdoors had fallen quiet again, except for that one owl hooting what sounded like "how true!" over and over. She tried to rest her head on his chest, but that special upholstered place where she could always hear his heart was no longer there. Instead there was just unyielding bone, as if the dimensions between them had somehow changed since she left the room.

"What's going on?" he said, starting to wake up.

39

AS HE EMERGED from the beige-tiled thrum of the Holland Tunnel the next morning and saw the greasy clump of gas stations and hourly-rate motels packed tightly before him, Barry felt an odd mixture of nostalgia and chagrin. New Jersey: his natural state. He veered right onto the turnpike, catching a glimpse of the diminished Manhattan skyline across the river, and remembered that sense of predestination he used to have, that rock-solid conviction that one day he would carve out a place for himself among the skyscrapers and brownstones.

The Statue of Liberty oxidized at the edge of the horizon, and jets leaving Newark Airport slanted up into the sky, leaving faint trails of black fumes. On the car radio, 1010 WINS was reporting that American forces were about to begin gathering in Afghanistan.

Barry changed the station, feeling a small barracuda wending its way through his guts. *Watch yourself.* Something about using that bit of wordplay on a photographer made the threat even more palpable. The author had thought about it carefully, considered his options, and calibrated his words for maximum impact before hitting the Send button. *i know what your doing.* This didn't sound like a harmless crank. This sounded like someone sticking a foot in the door.

So Barry had called in late for work this morning after asking Chris from Operations if there was any way to retrieve Instant Messages from a hard drive, and then set off for his hometown.

"We should just carpet bomb the bastards back into the Stone Age and then build a McDonald's on the rubble," said a young man's voice on a call-in show.

Newark. Twelve years since he'd driven through town for his father's funeral. New skin had formed over old bruises. Decals for the
Newark Downtown Facade Improvement Project covered boarded-up
tenement windows on Halsey Street. A new minor league baseball
stadium sat beside the Passaic River, and a respectable new performing
arts center stood in the heart of downtown. But on Central Avenue
where his father's deli once stood, a dusty old poster in an abandoned
storefront window declared, THERE ARE A LOT OF PEOPLE IN AMERICA
WHO DON'T CARE ABOUT YOU. DON'T BECOME ONE OF THEM. VOTE.

So this was his point of origin. People who grew up just a few
miles away in Nutley and Livingston would have to have a gun put
to their heads before they'd admit to having ever set foot in Newark.
But he'd never felt that way. He had a soft spot for the old men playing boccie in Branch Brook Park; the cherry blossom display; Bam-
berger's afternoons with Mom; doo-wop twilights in front of the
Diary Queen; *La Traviata* and Jimmy Rosselli wafting out of door-
ways on Bloomfield Avenue; the old court with the rusty hoops over
by the Colonnade; Friday afternoon helping out at Dad's deli; jars of
fresh olives and cherries in brandy on the counter; Dad cooking
kasha *varnishkes* for just the two of them on the stove in the back.
And, of course, the apple tree that Dad had tried so hard to grow in
their little dried-up backyard on Clifton Avenue. They were one of
the last Jewish families left in their part of the North Ward. Dad had
come up from the Prince Street shtetl and paid twenty-eight thousand dollars in 1953 for a two-story with an actual yard, so he'd be
damned before he sold it for almost a third less after the '67 riots. *If
I go now, when do I get my apple tree?* he used to say.

So twice a week Barry got beat up for his lunch money on the
way to Barringer High School, just across the street from the Cathedral Basilica of the Sacred Heart. The only thing that saved him, day
after day, was basketball. Other guys were faster, taller, more graceful. Other guys had better jump shots, better instincts, better eleva-
tion. But no one put in more hours at practice. No one stayed
longer shooting fouls. No one dove for more loose balls. No one
scrapped and hustled and took as much punishment. They called
him Celtic because he was all blocky white-boy moves, skinned
knees, and bruised elbows. He got his nose broken and turned his
hamstrings into boiled linguini. But he kept going because no one

had more faith that the hard work and long hours would pay off, that it was all leading somewhere, that sheer determination, force of will, and emotional intensity would be enough to lift him above the crowd.

It's all right, I know how to do this, he thought as he parked in Don Frederico's lot in the Ironbound District and cut the ignition. *Don't give up the high ground.* He popped the front of the Pioneer radio unit out of the dashboard so it couldn't be stolen and locked the bright-orange Club over his steering wheel.

The restaurant looked back to the glories of old Spain. Murals depicted bullfight scenes and conquistadors riding high in the saddle. Flamenco guitars strummed and castanets clacked on the stereo as the unlovely Passaic rolled outside the windows. His cousin Richie Marcus was at a table near the back, digging into a plate of seviche and wearing a gray knit sweater with a bold black zigzag pattern across the front.

He was a pudgy man in his early fifties with a shiny brow, thick rubbery lips, and a crimped black knot of hair on top of his head that made him look a little like a suburban samurai.

"What're you wearing, Armani?" he asked as Barry sat down opposite him.

"Davide Cenci." Barry flipped his lapel lightly, hoping his cousin wouldn't recognize the name of the Madison Avenue tailor.

"Nordstrom." Richie tugged on his collar as if it wasn't quite wide enough for his neck.

"So, what do you say, Rich? You're looking good."

"You kidding? I'm turning into Dom DeLuise. I haven't seen my dick since the Reagan administration."

"Well, thanks for showing up on such short notice. I've been kicking myself for not staying in touch."

"Hey, what am I going to do? My favorite aunt's kid says he has a problem." Richie shrugged. "I had to go see a guy anyway this afternoon, so I figured we could meet near the old neighborhood. Easier than Bloomfield for you."

"How's your daughter doing at Rutgers?"

Barry had decided ahead of time to just make glancing reference to the letter of recommendation he'd written to the dean of admissions on Chloe's behalf.

"She's dating a Dominican kid, and she wants to be an interpretive dance major." Richie speared a scallop. "Isn't that great? Remind me to celebrate by shooting myself in the head."

Barry tapped his water glass with his long fingers, keeping time with the music. "Maybe she'll learn flamenco."

"The art of applauding your own ass. Just what she needs to go to college for."

"And how's the store?"

Richie studied the fish on his fork for a moment. "What can I tell you? The sporting goods business sucks. Sales are down for everything except guns."

"Is that so?" Barry opened his menu nonchalantly.

"Yup, permit applications are up like four hundred percent since the Eleventh." Richie popped the scallop into his mouth and started chewing on one side. "Beats me why anybody thinks having a piece is gonna save them from a plane crashing into a building, but what am I going to do, not take their money?"

Barry let that sit for a moment, as a pompadoured beige-jacketed waiter came over to read off the specials with a slight Castilian lisp. He'd had to think long and hard before he picked up the phone to call Richie, making sure this was the best of all the bad options. It wasn't that he didn't get along with his cousin, but even after all these years there was a kind of no-man's-land strewn with explosives between them.

"You know what?" He handed the waiter back his menu. "I think I'll just have a club soda for now."

His cousin's eyes narrowed, as if he'd just realized he might end up getting stuck with the check today. "You not hungry?"

"My stomach's been bothering me a little lately."

"Really?" Richie leaned across the table and lowered his voice as the light scent of shrimp wafted through the air. "Look, Barry, I know you didn't come all the way out here to ask about my house or my family. You said you had a problem on the phone that I might be able to help you out with."

Instinctively, Barry found himself looking around the place to see who might be listening. But it was still a bit before the regular lunchtime crowd came in, and the only other diners in the restaurant were a middle-aged black woman wearing a baseball cap that said "Impure Thoughts" and an old white guy with a matinee idol mustache and a green velour running suit.

"It's okay, you don't have to be shy with me," Richie said. "I always knew you never wanted anything to do with my side of the family."

"Come on, Rich." Barry feigned exasperation. "You know what that was about. It wasn't anything personal."

Richie held his eye just long enough to show he wasn't wholly convinced. The truth was, Barry had always been a little skittish about his mother's side of the family, even before Richie started acting as a front for Bobby "Gaspipe" Caglione's crew, buying up real estate in Cherry Hill. Back when they were kids, he used to notice that the Marcuses never had any books in the house and spent all their time at the dinner table picking their teeth and ridiculing other people for not being as materialistic as they were. He remembered his father storming out of a Seder one year in disgust because he wouldn't go along with a plan Richie's father had to defraud the company that insured both their stores on Central Avenue after the riots.

"All right, fuck it." Richie rocked back and wiped a hand down the front of his sweater. "Let's just let bygones be bygones. What do you need from me?"

"I was thinking of buying a handgun."

"*Were you?*" A hint of mockery played on Richie's lips. "And why a handgun? Why not a rifle? You wouldn't need a license for one in New York State."

"You know, it's not something I'd want to leave lying around for the kids to find." Barry exhaled. "A pistol might be a little easier to keep out of sight."

"I see. And have you talked to Lynn about this?"

"Not so specifically. But I think we're both feeling kind of concerned about security these days."

Sandi Lanier dead. His wife getting stalked by her ex-boyfriend. *i know what your doing.* Yeah, *concerned* was a fair word.

"So, what, are you having a problem with somebody?" Richie's eyebrows peaked.

"You really need to know all the details, Rich? I'm just looking to buy a little extra protection for me and my family."

The last thing he needed was word about this whole *mishagas* getting around the New Jersey side. He remembered Richie's sisters bitching about having to drive into the city for their wedding at the Loeb Boathouse in Central Park eighteen years ago and then standing around the reception making fun of Lynn for having only two bridesmaids.

"It's just interesting, you end up coming *to me* for help after all this time," Richie was saying. "So have you tried to get a carry permit in New York?"

"It's a three- to six-month wait to get your application processed. And my understanding is that in my town, the local police chief is allowed to review all handgun applications. And that's something I'd like to avoid as well."

"And why is *that?*" Richie chewed with his mouth half-open.

"Politics. It's just awkward, having people know your business."

Fallon's suspension had done nothing to reassure Barry, especially after last night's e-mail. They'd reported the message to the police first thing this morning, but the facts remained that Fallon's good friend Harold Baltimore was still the chief and that at least a half-dozen previous complaints against the lieutenant had been swept under the rug.

"I remembered something you said at Chloe's Bat Mitzvah, about being able to expedite things." Barry stared at his cousin's gold bracelet. "You mentioned you had some contacts who could move the paperwork along in New York."

Richie picked absently at one of his incisors. "Let's just say I have a certain understanding that allows some of our applications to rise to the top of the pile."

"I'd like to take care of this situation right away."

"Hey, if a gun is all you want, you can walk into a thousand places around the city and buy one illegally."

"I'm a lawyer, Richie. I need to keep my license. God forbid I ever have to use the thing to defend myself, I better have the proper registration for it."

Richie smirked, the side of his mouth twisting up like bundled wire. "You know, my mother used to drive me nuts talking about you. It was always Barry this, Barry that. She used to bring home clippings from the *Star-Ledger* about you playing basketball for Barringer. And then when you went to law school, it was 'Why can't you be a scholar like your cousin? Why're you hanging around with those idiots on the corner? When are you going to make something of yourself?' Man, I just wish she were alive to hear this now."

Barry fixed him with a cold level stare. "So are you going to help me or not, Richie?"

His cousin sighed, not really wanting to relinquish the moment. "What is it exactly that you want me to do?"

"I was thinking we could try to speed up the process. What difference does it make if the date on the application is today or three months ago?"

"You want me to falsify a date on a permit application?"

"Don't look at me like I've got three heads." Barry unfurled his napkin and set it on his lap, dropping his voice into a low tense whisper. "You've done a helluva lot worse in your life, and we both know it. Remember that little tip I passed on to you about the raid at Dr. Feelgood's?"

Richie blanched slightly at the reminder of how close he'd come to getting arrested for trafficking in heroin and underage North Korean prostitutes. "Barry, I swear on my mother's grave, I never set foot in that place again . . ."

"Listen, I don't give a shit. You're my cousin. I was looking out for you. Just like I know you're here to look out for me."

Across the table, his cousin's face became a kind of gauge, measuring resistance against obligation.

"You're not going to use this piece to go do something stupid, are you?" Richie said quietly, realizing he'd lost the advantage.

"What do you mean?"

"I mean, you're not going to go shoot a cop with it or anything."

Barry felt a tiny fatigue crack spread out from the far edge of his smile. "What the hell would make you say a thing like that?"

"I just don't want this coming back to bite me in the ass someday. I've got enough problems with the legislature."

"Don't be ridiculous."

"Fine. How much were you looking to spend anyway?"

40

"*FLORIO, FLORIO.*" Mike murmured the name like an incantation as he sat in his new lawyer's office in White Plains, rubbing his thumbs together on his lap. "Used to be a nice Italian restaurant on River Road called Florio's."

"Oh, yeah?"

"I remember it had a penny fountain and a little statue of the Venus de Milo up by the cash register."

Late-afternoon sun sliced through the venetian blinds, making white stripes across the orderly surface of Gwen Florio's heavy mahogany desk.

"Venus de Milo lost her head," she said, crossing her black-stockinged legs. "Given the current atmosphere around your town, maybe it would be a good idea if you didn't remind anybody about that."

She was a middle-aged lady in glasses, whose degree of fuckability had probably declined precipitously in the last couple of years, he decided. She wore a cranberry-red suit and chunky high heels, a crop-dusting of makeup with claret-red lipstick and dark mascara. Gray streaks shot through her stringy black hair, but there was still something kind of hot and avid about her, like maybe she looked better with her clothes off.

Law books and pictures of teen-aged children lined the bookshelves behind her, alongside framed letters of thanks from various fraternal organizations and local Police Benevolent Associations her firm had done work for.

"Sorry," he said, "I was just trying to make the connection. You aren't from Riverside, are you?"

"My father was a cop in Mount Kisco; my late husband was a detective in Yonkers." She tilted forward in her seat, quickly establishing her bona fides. "And I was an officer myself for several years in Larchmont before I had children."

"I was just surprised when my union delegate told me I was getting a female lawyer, that's all. You don't mind me saying that, do you?"

"Not at all." She arched her back. "But what's important for you to know is that I've represented over a hundred officers in the twelve years I've been doing this, and I've gotten acquittals or the charges dismissed in over eighty percent of those procedures, with officers getting reinstated with full back pay and benefits. And in cases like spousal abuse or harassment, where the chief complainant witness is female, my percentage is even higher. So sometimes it doesn't hurt to have a good woman out front fighting for you. *Capisce?*"

"*Capisce.*"

"So, what's your story, Lieutenant?"

"You got a couple of days?"

Her smile said you wouldn't want to know about her frown. "The union is paying for my services at the moment, Detective, but I'd appreciate it if you didn't waste my time."

Okay. A tough bitch. He could handle that, as long as she was taking a hunk out of someone else's ass.

"You have the statements from Mrs. Schulman and her husband," he said. "So you've got the gist of their case. And then you have the notes that I typed up right after the interviews, which is the real story. I was just doing my job."

She flipped back and forth between pages in the file he'd given her, her mouth relaxing as she concentrated.

"You used to go out with the wife, and you nailed the husband for speeding and resisting arrest. That's it? It's just a he said / she said / he said?"

"Don't sneeze; you'll blow their whole case away."

She pushed the glasses up on top of her head, and he saw there was still something frisky and youthful in her eyes.

"Then why did Chief Baltimore pass these disciplinary charges up to the Town Board?"

"Politics. What else? The two of us were both up for the job last year, and he got it and I didn't. So now he's all insecure because he thinks the white guys in the department are all on my side, trying to undermine him."

He pressed his thumbs together, thinking about that message he got from Larry Quinn this morning. *Chief's not happy about you bothering your ex at Home Depot.* He'd almost thrown the phone across the kitchen. Like anyone had a right to tell him where to shop.

"He's just threatened by me and looking for any excuse to get rid of me," he said. "He's trying to move his own people into place."

"Is that all there is to it?" She smiled tolerantly, used to naughty boys playing hide-and-seek with the truth.

"Well . . ." — he twiddled one thumb over another like a turbine — "there might be one other thing."

"Yes?"

"This new guy, Paco Ortiz. A detective I trained, up from the Bronx. Hispanic guy." The thumbs circled each other more quickly. "He's running the homicide investigation for Harold, and I think he's got some crazy ideas about where he wants to take it."

"Are you telling me you're a suspect in this case?"

"Nothing official yet. Just, he's said some things that sounded a little . . . off the beam to me. I'm thinking maybe this whole disciplinary hearing is an excuse to go after me for the murder. Like it's part of a pattern or something."

She looked at him in silence, as if she were breathing him in through her eyeballs. "I have to tell you, Lieutenant," she said, "if criminal charges develop, I won't be able to represent you for free. The union only covers you for disciplinary charges. Defending a murder would break most people. Financially."

"I understand that." The thumbs rose up, forming an X on his lap. "But I could look into this on my own time and clear myself. This woman, Sandi, was a friend of mine . . ."

"I'm not sure I like the way that sounds."

"Why not? I'm the best investigator this department has. I can make some phone calls. Track people down. I can take apart witnesses in two minutes that the rest of them couldn't break in a week."

"You try anything like that and I walk," she said. "Let's understand each other, okay? You are the defendant here. If winning your job back in this disciplinary hearing helps you in the criminal case, then so be it. But if I'm representing you in this disciplinary matter, I'm your watch commander. And I'm not going to have you running around trying to play pin the tail on the defendant."

"So I'm just supposed to sit tight?" The chair he was in seemed to shrink down to kindergarten size, bringing his butt closer to the floor. "I'm totally innocent."

"Gee, I've never heard that before." Her lips thinned. "Look, Lieutenant. If you want to play games and blow smoke up your lawyer's ass, go pick up the phone book and find another one."

"You learn to talk that way in Larchmont?" he asked glumly, trying to keep his back straight.

"I've been around cops all my life, Lieutenant. I've seen the best, and I've seen the worst. Which one are you?"

He made a fist, noticing how the tracery of veins changed. "I'm a good cop," he said slowly. "I've given half my life to this job and all my life to this town. My brother lost his life in the line of duty. My father was a C.O. And *his* father guarded the aqueduct. And on and on. I'm not perfect by a long shot, but I would never bring disgrace to the uniform."

"Are you telling me no one else is going to come out of the woodwork?"

He willed himself to sit up and look her straight in the eye, remembering everything he'd ever learned about interrogation technique and turning it on its head. Don't fidget. Don't evade. And for God's sake, don't look away.

"If they do, they're liars," he said, maintaining the steady beam of his stare. "Go back and look at my service record if you want to see what I'm about. It's right there in your file. Two awards for valor, three citations for bravery in the line of duty, and one for saving the life of a fellow officer. Who happens to be the chief now."

"You saved the chief's life?"

"It's right there in the jacket. The letter he wrote to the Firearms Board, saying it was a good shooting. That's gratitude, huh?"

As she glanced down at the file again, he saw something begin to change in her face. It reminded him of the moment when a woman decides to stop ridiculing a man on the next bar stool and consider maybe going home with him.

"Well, perhaps that does give me a little more to work with," she said, fingertips gently brushing the page.

"I hope so."

"All right, let's think about how we can attack the witnesses in the disciplinary hearing." She uncrossed her legs and leaned across the desk. "What can you tell me about Mrs. Schulman?"

41

AS SOON AS Barry opened the front door, the brand-new alarm sounded, a deafening lunatic *bloooop! bloooop!* that made the dog jump up and whine frantically.

"Aperture!" Lynn shouted from the dining room. "Aperture!"

"What?" Stieglitz started to hump Barry's leg.

"That's the new password they put in this morning! You have to punch it into the keypad."

"*Aperture?*" Barry turned to the green-lit unit on the foyer wall, his fingers clumsily searching for the right buttons to push.

"You have to do it within thirty seconds or the light goes off at the security company's monitoring center."

Normal. The goal here was to act like everything was relatively normal. They'd made a mutual decision this morning to talk to the kids together about what was going on. Present a united front. Reassure them that everything was going to be okay, even as they upgraded the security system, talked about imposing a new curfew, and told Hannah and Clay that they couldn't be on the Internet without an adult in the room.

"You couldn't have picked an easier word to spell?" he said, entering the dining room as the alarm died away and the dog slunk back to the table.

"What about *Mankind?*" asked Clay.

"Or *redrum,*" suggested Hannah, imitating the little boy from *The Shining* with his creepy netherworldly voice.

"Somehow I don't think that would be entirely appropriate," Barry said, cutting a quick glance over at Lynn to see if she'd gone ahead and started *the talk* without him.

This kind of stomach-knotting tension must be what other couples go through when they're about to tell the kids they're getting a divorce.

"Hey, what's that you're holding?" Lynn's eyes dropped down to his side.

"Oh *this?*" He casually held up the head of Slam the garden gnome, as if he hadn't been disturbed to discover it lying in the driveway. "I found it like this. I was wondering if we could glue it back together."

Right. Keep it loose and normal.

"What happened?" Lynn looked stricken.

"I dunno." Barry set the head down on an empty chair and took his place at the head of the table. "Maybe the dog knocked it over."

Hannah and Clay stared at the head and then looked at each other across the table. They'd have to have the approximate intelligence of woodchucks not to notice something was up.

"I tried you around lunchtime on the cell phone," Lynn said, passing him the spaghetti bowl and the tongs, trying to slip back into the role of Regular Mom.

"I had to make a quick little trip to New Jersey. I guess our regional plan doesn't extend to the end of the Holland Tunnel. Cheap bastards."

"Everything okay?" All the concern she kept out of her voice went right up into her eyes.

"Yeah, fine. We're just looking for a little more tech support."

He was still trying to decide what to tell her about the .38 he'd brought home in his briefcase and planned to hide in the old Nike sneaker box on the top shelf of his closet. On the one hand, he knew she'd be apoplectic when she found out that he'd brought a gun into the house. Especially one with the funky registration his cousin had provided. On the other, what was the good of having the piece around unless she knew where to find it if she needed protection?

"Everything all right here?" he asked, pouring himself a glass of Cabernet.

"I was a little late picking up the kids, but otherwise nothing significant to report."

Her eyebrows rose like accent marks, alerting him that she hadn't told the kids anything yet but that the time was upon them.

"So, Hannah, what's the good word?" he said, deciding to lead into it slowly. "You get the first draft of that college essay written yet?"

She rolled her eyes back into her head so that only the whites showed through her kohl-tinted lids.

"What's that supposed to mean?"

"It means I'm still working on it." Her shoulders slumped under the straps of a red tank top that said: *I Know Victoria's Secret: She's Anorexic.* She'd consumed a piece of tofu the size of a hotel soap and a cup of alfalfa sprouts.

"You ever notice she doesn't smile anymore?" Barry gave Lynn a sidelong glance.

"I'm too tired to smile," said Hannah, one of the straps slipping off her shoulder. "I don't see what there is to smile about."

"Clay, my man" — he turned to his son for relief — "what are you up to?"

The boy looked up from the business of carefully segregating the meatballs from the pasta on his plate, like a postwar governor dividing up the Balkan states.

"Nothing much," Clay said glumly. "I got a karate tournament tomorrow."

"Then you better stop playing with that food and start eating it."

The Stone Cold Steve Austin T-shirt was looking a little big on him these days. Barry had laughed it off a couple of weeks ago when Lynn said she was worried the kid was turning into a bulimic and making himself throw up in the bathroom, but now with this sudden weight loss he wasn't so sure. Clay looked like he'd dropped ten pounds in a week. Maybe big sister was trying to clue the parents in on a secret with that shirt she had on.

"How's your Torah portion?"

"It's okay."

Barry looked over at Lynn as if she could interpret this terseness. Did they know already?

"So have you been practicing?" he asked his son.

"We were just talking about it when you came in before," said Lynn. "I was asking him why he thought God asked Abraham to sacrifice Isaac."

"I think it's a story about not waiting too long to have children." Barry turned his fork, raveling his pasta. "What was Abraham, a hundred?"

"I think it's about learning to have faith." Lynn filled her own wineglass almost to the brim.

"Then why don't you have enough faith to let me go to the city with Dennis?" Hannah made a surly show of pulling her strap back up on her shoulder, refusing to take part in this sham of family togetherness.

"I guess all politics is local," Barry muttered.

"Honey, we just weren't sure it was safe," said Lynn, creating an opening for the main subject.

"As opposed to being *here?*" Hannah raised her voice. "Oh, yeah, Mom, that makes *a lot* of sense."

She threw her napkin down and let the strap fall off her shoulder again, a deliberate provocation.

"I just think it's so ridiculous," she said, seizing control of the moment.

"What?" Barry felt the dog's wet nose nuzzling into his lap, looking for scraps.

"The way you both keep telling us to act like everything's fine when it *isn't.*"

Barry watched Lynn's knuckles turn white around the stem of her wineglass. *Our fault. We waited too long to say our lines. It wasn't just Hannah grabbing center stage. The girl had an eye, like her mother.*

"I'm not sure what you mean by that," he said, testing her.

"Oh, you're not sure? How about the fact that one of Mom's best friends is dead? How about the fact that no one knows what's going on? How about the fact that we're about to go to war? How about the fact that Mom's going to court next week, and neither of you said anything to us about it?"

"Who told you that?" asked Lynn.

Hannah tossed her black molasses hair over the vanilla scoop of her bare shoulder as Barry realized that he wasn't even around when Lynn broke the news to the kids about Sandi.

"Jennifer Olin in organic chem," Hannah said, clearly relishing the opportunity to capture her parents in their full hypocritical glory. "Her father's a town trustee. She overheard him telling somebody that both of you were fighting with the police."

Lynn and Barry both started speaking at once. "Well, that's not really . . . We were going to tell you . . . If you want to be accurate . . . I thought I mentioned . . ."

Hold the front lines. Man the barricades. The children were an invading army trying to get at the stockpile of secrets. God help us all if they ever got ahold of them.

They both went quiet again, and Lynn kicked him under the table as she crossed her legs, accidentally he assumed.

"I think what we're trying to tell you," Barry started again, measuring his words judiciously, "is that an unusual situation has come up."

The dog scrambled out from under the table, noticing that there were no longer as many ankles to lick or scraps to feast on.

"An old friend of your mother's has decided he has a problem with the two of us," he said. "It's not necessary that you know all the details. Just that this man is not right in his head and not acting . . . *responsibly*."

The children took a moment to absorb that, Clay looking to his sister for cues about how to react. And Hannah directing her searchlight gaze right back at her father.

"I guess I should also tell you that this man is a police officer," Barry continued, trying to sound calm and reasonable. "He's been suspended, but he obviously still has friends on the job and around town. So I think it would be wise for all of us to be very careful over the next few weeks."

"Oh, that's just great," said Hannah. "And what exactly does it mean?"

"It means that you're either going to have to come straight home after school or go directly to a friend's house where I can pick you up," said Lynn. "And we're going to need you to be home by eight every night."

"Now it's an *eight* o'clock curfew?" Incredulity crushed in Hannah's mouth. "Are you kidding me? None of my other friends have to be home until ten."

"Honey, whaddaya want me to do? We can't afford to just go move in to a hotel somewhere indefinitely." A half-dozen spaghetti strands slid off Barry's fork. "I'm sorry you guys have to go through this, but things come up in life. You're forced to make adjustments sometimes."

"But what about karate?" Clay piped up.

Something small and plangent in his voice reminded Barry of the nights when the boy would show up over and over in their doorway with the quilt around his shoulders, like James Brown with his cape, begging please, please to be allowed into their bed.

"I have to have lunch in the city, but I'll make sure I'm back here in time for your match," Lynn said, thinking fast and trying to make last-minute adjustments. "Jeanine's heading over there, so she'll give you a ride."

She tried to give him a reassuring smile, but Barry saw the effect fall short. Clay's chin lowered. He nudged his plate away. And somehow that small look of boyish disappointment wounded Barry as much as anything he'd seen since the day his father's deli burned down. *My son thinks his parents can't take care of him.*

"Look, it's not going to be like this forever." Barry pushed his chair back from the table. "We're going to get through this hearing, this man's going to lose his job, and then everything's going to go back to the way it was."

"And what are we supposed to do in the meantime?" said Hannah. "Just sit around and stare at the computer screen?"

"Um, that's another thing." Lynn sighed. "I kind of only want you guys going on-line when one of us is in the room. We got a bit of a weird Instant Message on the computer."

"Oh, shit," said Clay, lending credence to his mother's suspicion that he was downloading porn off the Internet.

"Watch your mouth," said Barry.

"Nice town you brought your kids to." Hannah folded her arms, fed up with both of them. "Anything else?"

"Well, we certainly don't want to make you any more over-anxious, but you both have cell phones." Lynn cleared her throat. "You should call us if you see something that makes you uncomfortable."

"Then who will you call?" asked Hannah. *"The police?"*

Barry touched his tongue to the roof of his mouth, not having devised a ready answer.

"Never mind." Hannah got up and started to clear the dishes, showing some vestige of the good-girl manners that she used to have in such abundance. "I think I'd like to be excused."

42

ALL THE WAY DOWN to the train station that morning, Lynn was jumpy, seeing things out of the corner of her eye that weren't really there: stop signs, flashing lights, children crossing. The sight of a young cop standing by the side of the road pointing a radar gun at her car almost made her veer off the road.

Given her druthers, she would've skipped the trip to the city altogether and hunkered down at the house, waiting for school to be finished so she could pick up the kids. But François was threatening to cancel the gallery show if she didn't come in for lunch to discuss the pictures, and the rest of the family had admonished her to go about her business. On the car radio, the president was exhorting people to keep going to ball games and taking their kids on vacation, as if nothing was wrong.

Nevertheless, she'd pored carefully over the schedules, making sure Hannah had her after-school study group and Jeanine would pick up Clay for karate, so there wouldn't be a single moment when they'd be left alone and unattended before she arrived back on the 4:02.

She took the portfolio case out of the Explorer, locked the car behind her, and started up the steps to the overpass above the tracks, having decided it was safer to take the train than risk traffic getting in and out of the city.

Down below, a lone figure in a khaki Burberry coat loitered in front of the HBO *Sex and the City* billboard at the far end, staring out at the ripples that moved like veins under the surface of the river.

Something in his solitude brought her attention into fine-grained focus. The wind seemed to whip around him without quite touching him, only lightly riffling his light-brown hair, as if an invisible force field surrounded him. From above, she saw a telltale patch of pink scalp exposed and then covered at the back of his head.

Jeffrey turned and waved when he saw her coming down the steps to the platform.

"There she is," he called out, the wind whisking his words out over the water.

"What are you doing here?"

She came down to his end of the platform and gave him a hug, the portfolio under her arm getting between them.

"Oh, you know, business in the city," he said. "Taxes on the estate and all that crap. It's terrible, having to deal with all these lawyers. Parasites."

"Well, not all of them."

"Of course, I didn't mean Barry." His nostrils flared in embarrassment. "I meant these bastards who are trying to keep Sandi's money from going to the children, like it's supposed to. I really don't know how some of these people sleep at night."

"I understand."

She noticed how clean-shaven and comparatively bright-eyed he looked today. That looked to be a good brown wool suit under his coat, possibly Canali, and he was wearing black-tasseled loafers, an ironed white shirt, and a red silk tie with tiny yellow octagons that couldn't have cost less than a hundred and fifty dollars at Barney's.

"So how are you?" she said.

"Hanging in. It's been very tough. I'm still not sure the kids really get it. Maybe it'll just sink in over time."

She felt the wind whipsaw through her bones as it dawned on her that this was where Barry must have been standing when he first spotted the body. *Watch yourself.* And she was going into the city today? Already the thought of being separated from the children was causing a painful pulling in her chest, as if she'd drifted off her moorings.

"Lynn, can I ask you something?" Jeff stood close to her, blocking the wind.

"What?"

He bowed his head. "I know how women talk. Did Sandi ever tell you she was having an affair?"

"Oh, Jeff, I don't know . . ."

"Listen, it's all right. She's gone. You're not betraying anybody. I just need to know."

She winced at the abasement, the utter humiliation. He might as well have dropped trou on the platform and asked for her frank assessment.

"She never said anything to me," she answered scrupulously.

He looked out toward the palisades, where the morning mist was burning off.

"I know she'd been unhappy for a long time," he said.

"I think she always appreciated you for the man you are, Jeff."

He startled her with a pinched dry laugh.

"I'm sorry." He wiped the corner of his eye. "I didn't mean to put you on the spot. It's just some things the police said have got me thinking."

"Like what?"

"First they ask me if we were having financial and emotional problems in our marriage. Then they want to know if either of us had started seeing other people. I said of course not, but . . ."

A southbound express blew by, sending a gust through her clothes.

"What do I know?" he said. "Then they come to my house and start ripping things up and making all kinds of strange insinuations to me until they find this can of Thompson's Wood Protector in the garage."

"Wood protector?"

"This cop was using it. The guy we hired to put up our fence. Fallon. He went to school with Sandi. You must know him too."

"Uh-huh."

The wind tore through her pea coat, a sudden blast of winter pebbling her skin.

"And then right after they found that, they all clammed up," said Jeffrey. "It was like everything shifted, and they all started looking the other way. I mean, they kept asking questions and taking out evidence in cardboard boxes, but I had this feeling like they weren't really that interested."

The front page of the *New York Post* blew off the platform and drifted down to the surface of the river, the president's picture darkening on the water.

"You know, my mind's been such a mess that I haven't been able to focus on anything." His hair flapped wildly about his head, clawing his brow and flailing all over his crown. "But after that crazy thing at the cemetery, the fog's been starting to lift. This guy took the shovel right out of my hand. What were people thinking? I mean, Sandi's home all day while this cop's out there working on the fence, and when Inez took the kids out, it was just the two of them . . ."

Lynn felt a trap start to open at the bottom of her stomach, remembering the last thing Mike had said to her at Home Depot. *You know, she was a friend of mine too.* It sharpened that dire sense of possibility she'd been feeling since that day she talked to Inez in the kitchen. That he wasn't just investigating Sandi's murder or mourning her. He was the original source of the agony.

"Everyone must think I'm a fucking idiot," said Jeffrey, the wind raking his thin patches of hair mercilessly.

"Don't say that."

"But it's true, isn't it? Halloween's coming up, so I might as well wear a pair of cuckold's horns when I go trick-or-treating with the kids because everyone already knows."

"Jeffrey, stop . . ."

"The thing is," he said, spreading his nostrils again as he struggled for control. "The thing is, I *know* everybody does it; everybody cheats. Everybody has secrets. So that's not the point anymore. Whatever problems there were between Sandi and me died with her. But this was the mother of my children. And somebody killed her. And they *should not get away with that.*"

"What makes you think they're going to?"

"I'm just saying, things are starting to come together in my mind. There are questions that aren't getting asked."

"Are you saying there's a cover-up?"

"I'm saying, people look after their own."

He glanced over his shoulder at the patrol car waiting by the station entrance.

"It's pretty damn obvious this cop was doing my wife. So who knows? Maybe she tried to break it off and he didn't want her to. Maybe he got rough with her. All I know is that he's the one they ought to be looking at. And if they aren't prepared to do the right thing, then I will."

She turned as if a firecracker had just gone off next to her ear.

"Jeffrey, don't talk that way." She touched his arm. "The children don't need you to do anything crazy."

"Everyone can't keep looking the other way. Someone has to pay."

"I understand, but I really don't think this is all going to get swept under the rug. I've known Harold Baltimore most of my life. He's a good, honest man."

"He damn well better be."

She realized that this was as far as she wanted to go in this conversation. There was something fetid and bacterial in the air.

"Jeffrey," she said, "I promise you, I'll call you the second I find out any more about what's going on. But what you have to focus on is putting one foot in front of the other and letting the kids know that you're still holding steady for them."

"Of course. I know that."

"So, what are you doing with your Web site in the meantime?" she asked, just to change the subject. "Are you going to shut it down and regroup?"

"What are you talking about? Things are going great." Half-smiling disbelief broke across his face. "Why would we be shutting down?"

"I don't know. I thought . . ."

"The business is growing so fast we can hardly keep up with it. Did somebody tell you otherwise?"

"No, of course not."

You call it underwriting. I call it bloodletting. She tried to put Saul's exact words out of her mind so she could stay in this conversation.

"It's just so weird that you would say that." He pushed back the centerpiece of his glasses. "We got Honus Wagner's mitt the other day. You know what that could be worth?"

"No idea."

"We're talking mid–five figures once it's authenticated, minimum. And we're supposed to be getting one of Rogers Hornsby's bats next week . . ."

"Sounds great."

She averted her eyes in pity, realizing how much he needed this at the moment, a woman's look of encouragement, a sign that someone still believed in him, a little wink of light at the end of the tunnel.

"I guess you're cruising then," she said.

"Yeah, we're rocking and rolling."

He checked his watch and looked up the tracks, starting to lose momentum.

"Hey, wasn't there supposed to be a nine-fifty-five?"

"That's what my schedule said."

"It's nine-fifty-seven already. You know, I just realized I left my PalmPilot at the house, and it's got all my appointments in it."

"Uh-oh." Lynn pulled a sympathetic face.

"Yeah, I guess my head is still in the wash. I better go back and get it." He belted up his Burberry. "There's a ten-thirty-five, isn't there?"

"I think so. My schedule's back in the car."

"Yeah, maybe I'll get that." He edged toward the stairs. "I'll call the lawyer and tell him I'll be late."

"I'm sure he'll understand."

Okay. She got that this was an excuse. That this conversation had stripped him of so much of his dignity that he couldn't bear to ride the train into the city with her for the next thirty-five minutes. A kind of squalid, grimy guilt backwashed over her as she realized that she hadn't properly helped him sustain the illusion he needed.

"Hang in there, Jeff," she called after him. "We're all right behind you."

"I know." He waved. "And no offense, what I said before about Barry and lawyers. I didn't mean anything by it."

43

GRRRRIGGGGGGG. Grrrrrrrriggggggg.

The ground was starting to get hard from the lack of rain, Mike noticed, as he leaned over the power auger, digging a hole for a fence post on the de Groots' property.

Grrrgg. Grrrrg.

Pieces of dirt and stone went flying as he gripped the handles and heard the buried industrial rut of blade hitting schist. *Grrrrrgggg.* He pulled the gas-powered engine closer, beginning to think that this was as deep as he could drill in this spot, that he was only trying to bore into solid stone.

He stopped for a moment to wipe his brow and swig lemon-lime POWERade. The sun was just beginning to seep through the brittle fried circuitry of trees, and the first real hint of winter's sawtoothed bite was in the air. A part of him was still not quite wide awake, but he'd decided he had to get out here early today to finish the job and get some money coming in. He picked up the auger again and continued his digging, the vibrations going right up his arms and into his shoulders, tremoloing his spine and rib cage. *Grrrg.* He noticed the soil getting darker and wormier as he burrowed under the surface.

Would you like some ice tea?

That was how it began last spring. The chard in Sandi's vegetable garden starting to pop up through the soil. New growth on the rose canes around the deck, the blackberry brambles putting out their leaves.

I'll leave it in the refrigerator so it stays cold. Come in and help yourself anytime you feel like it. Just make sure you take your boots off.

For Chrissake, could she have been more explicit, short of ask-ing, "Hey, Fallon, would you care to step in the house and lick my pussy?" *She wanted it.* It was obvious from the second she'd hired him. She was tired of that limp-dick husband of hers, who paid him in stock options from his crappy dot-com to put up the fence. She was wondering what it would be like to get a righteous drilling for once.

Grrg. Gritty fragments flew back in his eyes, and he cursed him-self for forgetting his plastic goggles this morning.

Grrrwwwwwwwww. The grinding steel into soil slowly became the swoosh of the upstairs shower in his mind. For a few seconds, he was halfway up the stairs again, hesitating on the landing. Not want-ing to cheat, knowing damn well that he was going to. A rigid digit has a mind of its own. Once again, he remembered looking down and having a melancholy moment, seeing her children's galoshes in the front hall, their bright-yellow slickers hanging from hooks with the same black fireman's stripe around the hems that Timmy had on his FDNY coat. You'd think that would slow a man down, wouldn't you? The prospect of losing the things that were holding him to-gether. But then he'd heard the shower cut off, the pipes giving a squeak of anticipation, and he knew it was too late.

Grrrrr, the blade purred underground as he remembered how eagerly he'd bounded the rest of the way up the steps to meet his ruin, almost stepping on a yellow Pokémon figure with its arms raised and its tail in a lightning zigzag.

The shadow of sadness broadened. She'd been in the bedroom at the end of the hall, drying herself before the wall mirror with one foot up on the bed, naked, dewy, and vulnerable, as if he'd just come upon her in a wooded clearing at dawn.

He'd stood in the doorway, watching her, the moment threaten-ing to crack open and swallow him. At first, it was that same gnaw-ing in the pit of his stomach that he'd felt at Angelo's Candy Store and in the Castlemans' bathroom. But then it became something else. She became young for him right before his eyes. Her body seemed to slim and ripen. The laws of gravity reversed, wrinkles smoothed, her belly flattened, her breasts lifted, presenting them-selves in all their splendor to the slant of sunlight streaming through the window.

And for a few seconds, he became young as well, no longer a man who'd disappointed his wife and been passed over for the chief's job. He was seventeen once more, seeing Lynn Stockdale stand naked for the first time before him. He remembered how he'd felt at that moment, that a door was opening, that another kind of light was shining on him.

Standing in Sandi's doorway, he'd felt that readiness again, that hunger. And Sandi had lowered her hands, her modesty fading, her hip jutting out like the bend in a question mark.

When they fucked, her eyes opened wide as if she was in awe of him. It had been months since Limp Dick Jeff had touched her, she said. Mike was rescuing her. Same as he was rescuing Lynn. And all the others. He lived for that vulnerable awestruck look. He was always trying to get it back again. As he was giving it to Sandi from behind, he kept seeing Lynn's face looking back over her shoulder. Somewhere, somehow, she must've known what she was missing.

He put the auger aside and slammed the post into the ground. A yellow pine four-by-four. He was charging the de Groots the full price for cedar, but that was almost two dollars extra a foot and he was entitled to peck at the margins a little, wasn't he? A man had to live. He started shoveling loose pieces of rock and gravel to hold the post in the hole so he could measure it against the other posts he'd put in. He remembered how Sandi had rolled over on the pillow next to him that one time. How she'd looked up and said, *You'll watch over me, won't you?* Shit, it all should've ended right then. He used the yellow plumb line with the leveler's bubble attached to make sure this post was even with the last one. But then she had to go and get herself pregnant and put everything on the line. His marriage, her marriage, the job, the kids. She was a crazy bitch, no doubt about it.

He saw that the new post was an inch or two higher than the last one. He got the short-handled sledgehammer off his tool belt to try pounding in the difference.

Swwwkkk. The thin pine sound echoed through the woods. He'd let himself get confused. *Swwkkk.* He had to try not to think about it anymore. *Swwk.* His problem was that he'd let things get mixed up in his mind: thinking Sandi could make him feel better about what happened with Lynn all those years ago, and then that Lynn could make him feel better about what happened with Sandi in the end. *Swwk.* It was only when they didn't need to be rescued that his problems with women started. *Swwk.* The post started to lean, and he tried to hold it in place as he drove it in. *Swwk*. He smashed himself hard on the thumb, and for a few seconds everything went dim.

"Hey, man, you all right?"

Paco Ortiz was coming across the yard toward him with Mike's customer, Dr. Richard de Groot, trailing in his blue bathrobe, a steaming Weather Channel coffee thermos in hand.

"What are you doing here?" Mike bit his lip, trying not to black out.

The thumb was just beginning to throb, only slowly waking up to the damage he'd done.

"Following up on a couple of calls we got at the station." Paco glanced over at Dr. de Groot, waiting for him to walk back toward the house so they could begin this conversation in earnest. "Seems somebody's been harassing Mrs. Schulman."

"Is this about Home Depot again? Jesus, I already talked to Larry about this. What are we turning into, a police state? I can't even go shopping anymore?"

The pain began to pulsate out in waves. He felt the thumbnail buckling from the amount of swelling underneath.

"If I were you, I'd keep my distance from that lady." Paco half-smiled at Dr. de Groot, who'd gone back inside and was watching them through the kitchen window.

"Listen, I didn't say anything out of line to her. I just ran into her in the middle of the aisle and made it clear that I wasn't happy about what she's putting me through. Next time I'll go the other way. All right?"

"We got another call from her yesterday." Paco's newly shaved scalp furrowed as if some unseen hand was molding it.

"Yeah? And?"

"She said she got a message over the Internet. Some kind of half-assed threat."

Mike took a quick look at his thumb and saw that the nail was, in fact, starting to turn the color of an eggplant.

"I don't know a damn thing about it," he said.

"I thought you'd say that." Paco pressed his lips together, not in the least intimidated by Mike being five inches taller. "So here's what I want to say to you, *muchacho*. Are you listening?"

"Yeah, I'm listening." Mike seethed, gritting his teeth.

"I don't know you, man." The goatee circled Paco's mouth like a noose. "I didn't go to school with you. I never played football with you. I never dated your sister. When I look at you, I don't think about whether you saved my life or whether your aunt knew my uncle. I just see what's right in front of me."

"What's your point, *Paco?*"

The thumb was starting to throb so much that it felt as if it were drawing breath.

"My point is, is that there's no credit line here. You start shit on my corner, I'm a do more than just write you a ticket. *Comprende?* I'm a come over your house, and this time we won't worry about embarrassing you in front of the kids."

"Now what am I supposed to do with that?" Mike squeezed the handle of the hammer, trying to restrain himself.

"You suppose to take that shit to the bank, *compañero. Estar sobre sí.* I got my eye on you."

He turned on his heel and walked away, leaving Mike resting the hammer on his shoulder, the nail pressing down on the bone. *Yeah, I got my eye on you too*, compañero.

Having seen the conversation ending, Dr. de Groot came out through the glass doors and passed Paco on the lawn.

"Heh, heh." The doctor pulled back his lips as he ambled over, showing broad purplish gums. "A little off-duty consultation?"

"Yep. Crime never sleeps." Mike blinked back the tears of nausea.

"You guys must be working around the clock these days. Awful about Sandi Lanier. She was in my wife's book group, you know."

"Yeah." Mike dropped the hammer to his side. "I guess I did know that."

The doctor was an orthopedic surgeon with Nutty Professor glasses and surprisingly crooked teeth. His wife, Dianne, was that flake who wore her hair like Pippi Longstocking, coordinated her outfits to match what the kids were wearing, and blasted Britney Spears and 'Nsync from her Blazer every time she went to the supermarket.

"Listen, Mike, we've been having some second thoughts about the fence." Air passed loudly through the doctor's septum.

"What?"

"We've been thinking we might want to put money toward upgrading our security system instead."

Mike looked over at the fence post he'd left leaning like the Tower of Pisa. "Where's all this coming from?"

"Look, Mike, I want to be honest with you. We have some concerns. I should've called before, but I didn't know you were coming today."

"Concerns?"

"Dianne already heard from somebody at the School Board that you were having a problem with the police department. Apparently there's going to be some kind of disciplinary hearing?"

"Yeah, what about it?"

The hammer pulsed in time with Mike's swelling thumb.

"Perhaps it would be better to put off finishing the job until everything gets cleared up."

"Put it off? I'm not sure I understand, *Dick*."

"Heh, heh." Dr. de Groot made a wheezing sound as he eyed the hammer nervously. "Mike, you have to understand. It's a difficult position we're in. I'm at work all day, and my wife would be alone in the house while you're working here. I'm sure you can appreciate how awkward that would be."

"So she asked you to speak to me?"

"Mike, would you mind putting that hammer down while we're talking?" The doctor pursed his lips. "It's making me a little uncomfortable, and I'm sure that's not what you want."

Mike jammed the hammer back in his tool belt, accidentally jarring the thumbnail again.

"You know, we're supposed to have something called the presumption of innocence in this country," he said, grimacing and holding back a raging torrent of curses.

"I know." The doctor nodded. "It's terribly unfair."

"So, what're you gonna do about the fence?" Mike said, resisting the urge to suck the end of the thumb. "You gonna leave it half-done?"

He'd been in their kitchen and seen their magnificent granite countertops and Swedish energy-efficient dishwasher. These were not people who left things half-done.

"We might have somebody else come in and finish the job."

Mike glared at him, and for a moment the pressure was so strong that he thought about taking the hammer and hitting the doctor so hard on the tip of the nose that blood shot from his eye sockets.

"I guess that's your right," he said.

"We weren't going to ask for the money back. You've already done part of the work."

"Yes, I have. And I'd hate to come back and pull it all out."

"Heh, heh." The doctor wheezed again, not sure if Mike was serious.

Mike had half a mind to do it right now. Just tear out all the fencing and leave gouges like teeth marks all over the property.

"Take your time cleaning everything up," said the doctor, glancing down at the auger and the wheelbarrow that Mike had brought along today. "I'll be here all morning."

"Yeah, let me just finish the footings for the last four-by-four."

Other contractors had told him not to use concrete to secure the posts because it could trap the water and make the wood rot faster, but did he really care at this point?

"By the way," said the doctor, "what happened to your thumb?"

44

"JACK DAVIS?" Barry, on the phone, stood by the window, watching scattered fires still spitting and a yellow crane slowly removing pieces of wreckage from Ground Zero.

"That's my name, don't wear it out," said a voice on the other end, so phlegmy and clubbable that Barry could almost hear the faux-wood paneling on the walls of the office from which it issued and see the law degree and Rotary Club awards in Lucite on the bookshelves.

"This is Barry Schulman. I'd been expecting to hear from you."

"Have you now?" The bonhomie thinned just slightly. "Well, I've been busy as a fox in the henhouse. What can I do you for?"

"I'm supposed to be your client. As is my wife."

"You don't say."

"I do. The Michael Fallon disciplinary hearing in Riverside?"

Jack Davis made a quiet *wup, wup,* sound like an old computer trying to read a warped floppy disc.

"Of course," he said finally. "Your statement to the chief is right here on my desk. And I think I must have your wife's statement too. Somewhere."

"I can certainly fax you another copy if that's necessary," Barry replied evenly, having already decided to exercise more patience than he did with Mrs. Crawford at Town Hall. "But really I was hoping to have a chance to speak to you before the hearing."

"Glad you caught me in, then. I can be harder to get ahold of than a greased pig. You understand, naturally, it's not my full-time job, being the town's prosecuting attorney. I'm doing this as a favor to the mayor, old Tom Flynn, who's a dear friend of the family."

"What kind of law do you usually practice, if you don't mind my asking?"

"Oh, I putter around in insurance and real estate development a little. I've done some work for Olympia and York, Douglas Ellman, Northern Coastal, a few local outfits . . ."

The tinny bell went off in the back of Barry's head. Northern Coastal, the golf course developers who gave the mayor's son a job as a VP. As Buddhists and ward politicians alike understood: we are truly all part of one great whole.

"So have you ever prosecuted a case before?"

"Of course. I put in a few years at the Westchester DA's office, back before the Civil War. Heh-heh-heh."

Political appointee, Barry thought. In the DA's office, something like ninety-seven of the one hundred assistants were Republicans. The man might not know how to work a case, but he could certainly work a room. Not that there was anything wrong with a little patronage now and then. As a famous Southern governor once said, "What would you expect me to do, give contracts to *my enemies?*"

"Well, sir," Barry said, trying to keep it friendly, "I know you've been preoccupied like everyone else, but I was trying to make sure you knew that both of us are available so you'd have a chance to talk to us and adequately prepare your case."

"Damn kind of you, Mr. Schuler."

"Yeah . . ." Momentarily disconcerted, Barry reached for the legal pad on his desk. "I also wanted to pass on some phone numbers to you for potential witnesses, in case you hadn't had a chance to look them up."

"Excuse me . . ."

There was some manner of kerfuffle on Jack Davis's end of the line. A flap of papers, a side-of-the-mouth mutter at a secretary, a groan of a creaky drawer opening, and a door shutting noisily.

"You were saying?"

"I have the numbers of some potential witnesses who could do serious damage to Lieutenant Fallon's credibility and help bolster my wife's testimony." Barry tapped his legal pad with a Cross pen.

"You do?"

"To begin with, I found a series of complaints from people who say the lieutenant beat them with a radio in his patrol car after they were handcuffed in Operation Ivory Snow a few years ago . . ."

"Old news." Jack Davis cut him off. "Those charges were already dismissed by the Town Board. I'm sorry, Mr. Schiller, but I don't see the relevance. Until that unfortunate incident with the Three Musketeers bar, that little campaign probably cut the crime rate in this town by three quarters and doubled the value of the house you're living in."

Unfortunate incident? Nice way to talk about an unarmed black kid getting shot in the back. Nobody's a liberal when he's talking about the price of his house. Barry flipped the page, deciding not to push it.

"And then there are these two young ladies who've filed papers with the Civilian Complaint Review Board saying the lieutenant harassed them. I thought at least one of them might be a credible enough witness so that the hearing wouldn't just be our word against his . . ."

"I'm sorry, Mr. Schulman" — Jack Davis's chair gave a squeak loud enough to be heard through the phone line — "but how exactly did you come into possession of these phone numbers?"

"Freedom of Information Act. Standard stuff. No burning of incense or bowing down before graven images, I assure you."

He decided to omit that unpleasant bit of arm-twisting he'd had to do with Mrs. Crawford at Town Hall. Davis would certainly hear about it soon enough.

"Are you an attorney?" said Jack Davis.

"A humble consort of the devil, just like yourself."

"Then do you really think it's appropriate for you to be both a witness *and* a witness wrangler in this particular rodeo?"

"I'm not sure how else these witnesses are supposed to appear if nobody calls them. Is this court a *magical* jurisdiction?"

Jack Davis paused as if he was seriously considering the question.

"I'm sorry," said Barry, "but this is more than a matter of passing concern to me and my family. This man has posed an ongoing threat to us. My wife had a disturbing run-in with him at Home Depot the other day. And that night she got a rather threatening message over the Internet."

Barry noticed a subtle change in the air quality of the room and realized that a door had opened behind him.

He turned and saw his secretary, Shameequa McPherson, from Do-or-Die Bed-Stuy, waiting by the Styrofoam NCAA backboard next to his bookcase. Cornrowed hair framed her delicate features like a beaded headdress, and thin yellow Walkman headphones rested on her clavicle like an Egyptian princess's necklace. You could never be sure if she was listening to Master P or *Mastering Italian*. She raised a fingernail as curved and carefully adorned as a Grecian urn.

"*Attenzione*," she said sotto voce. "Mr. Olson wants you."

Barry lightly covered the mouthpiece. "Tell him I'll just be a minute."

"Mr. Olson wants you *pronto*."

Something in her voice produced a tug in his side, and he was reminded once again that a good secretary could do as much with nuance and intonation as a great musician could.

"Mr. Davis, I'm going to have to call you back later today," he said into the phone.

"Call me anytime you like, just don't call me late to supper."

"Thank you." Barry put the phone down with a grimace and stepped away from it.

"The ways of white folks," he said.

"You're telling me."

"What's up?"

"The message was: 'The coach wants to see you. Bring your playbook.'" She held the door open wide for him.

"That's what they used to say in football when they were about to trade you." He felt a tiny crick in his neck as he snatched his suit jacket off the back of his chair.

"And it's what I told my last boyfriend when I broke up with him. 'Don't you try those moves on anybody else.'"

She looked him up and down as he buttoned the coat and brushed off his lapels.

"*Bello*. Not bad for an old guy," she said. "If you were a couple of years younger, I might be giving you *un occhio sessuale*."

"Or if I had a couple more dollars in the bank."

He heard the joke land with a thud and realized something serious was afoot.

"What's the matter?" He followed her out of the office.

The back of her dress drew taut over her hips. "I didn't say anything."

"Which is the same as saying *something*. I know you."

"Maybe you don't know as much as you think you do."

He stopped in front of her desk, where the gondoliers of Venice drifted across her computer screen. "You trying to scare me?"

"*Honi soit qui mal y pense.*" She sashayed on ahead of him.

"That's not Italian. That's French."

"I know. It means Evil be to him who thinks evil."

Before he could ask her to explain, she doubled back to answer a ringing phone on her desk, leaving him to walk the rest of the way on his own.

The floor between here and Ross Olson's office seemed to roll out before him like a long red velvet tongue. For the last two weeks, Retrogenesis stock had continued to plummet downward to five dollars a share — *five dollars!* — as other money managers began to follow Mark Young's lead in shorting the stock. Every other day, a rumor tore through the office about a white-knight investor coming along to rescue them — on Tuesday it was the Japanese; on Thursday, it was Merck — but Ross just insisted everyone needed to take a Coridal and be patient while he searched for the best deal possible.

In the meantime, Barry had had lunch twice with Lisa Chang, ostensibly to prepare for her deposition in the Monkey Suit, but in reality to talk about future prospects. In her subdued, indirectly seductive way, Lisa had encouraged him to take heart and hold the course. There'd been a couple of unexpected breakthroughs in the lab on Long Island lately, having to do with manipulating the genetically altered squirrel monkeys by raising and lowering their body temperatures, and the potential long-term implications for the Alzheimer's market were staggering. *If we can hang in there just a couple of more years, this could be bigger than the polio vaccine*, she'd told him over goat cheese salad and pad Thai noodles at the New Economy Café around the corner. *Unless we fuck it up and kill all the monkeys with pneumonia.*

Barry put his shoulders back and strode purposefully down the hall, trying not to think about liquidity. Five dollars a share. His equity had lost more than two thirds of its value since he'd joined the company. Less than seventy thou — that's what he'd have if he cashed in now. The numbers came rushing into his head, just like his old shooting percentages. Less than seventy g's in the savings account, *clank;* freshman-year tuition at college for Hannah would take care of half that, *clunk.* Taxes would get a chunk of the rest, and he was still looking at three-thousand-dollar mortgage bills coming at him every month like rotating knives in an abattoir. No wonder it was easier thinking about gathering witnesses for court. At least there he felt that he was having some effect.

As he crossed through the main open work area, noticing the unusual number of empty cubicles even for lunchtime, his eyes fixed on another computer monitor up ahead, just outside Ross's office. An animated screen saver showed Magritte's *petit* bourgeois umbrella men raining helplessly through the sky in their hats and overcoats.

"Come on in, Baairr." Ross cracked the heavy door and stuck his head out. "We've been waiting for you."

Barry noticed his CEO's southern accent sounding ominously more pronounced, the way it did whenever he talked to somebody down South with access to eight figures. The last time he'd heard this much twang out of Ross was at the end of a long late-night drinking session with a couple of Houston bankers at 21.

"What's doing?" He stepped in as the door closed with a thunderclap behind him.

Instantly, his heart sank as he saw the reason why Ross was talking like some unholy combination of Bear Bryant and Minnie Pearl.

There in Ross's black leather office chair sat Bill Brenner, like the Sun King, light glaring off the top of his bare freckled scalp and a pair of black stitched cowboy boots resting comfortably on top of the CEO's desk.

"Hey, good buddy, long time no see." He opened his arms. "Welcome to the New World Order."

"Eh *bien*, I can see why you went back," said François Gortner.

"What are you talking about?" Lynn perched at the edge of her stool, the angst of being apart from the kids growing by the minute.

They were sitting in the office on the second floor of the Gortner Gallery in Chelsea, a set of work prints spread out on the table before them. François, ever the curator, had put two of the pictures side by side: a shot Lynn took twenty-five years ago of the old textile factory juxtaposed with the morning shape-up of immigrants last week outside Starbucks at the same location.

"*Tout le monde*, it's all here, yes?" said François, a round-bellied bearded Satyr in rimless glasses, a black blazer, and a white Turnbull &

Asser shirt buttoned snug at the collar. "This light. This *caractère*. *C'est formidable*. Everything your other pictures are not."

Lynn frowned, distracted from her worries for a moment and smarting from the swift backhandedness of the compliment.

"*Regarde*."

François moved his magnifying loop over the older scene of tough-fingered sewing-room ladies in hair nets, taking their cigarette breaks in the parking lot while men in sleeveless undershirts unloaded giant spools of thread from trucks with white outlines of naked women on the mud flaps.

"Everywhere else you go, these pictures you take, they are like the Weegee. This is, how you say, *gawking*. But when you go home — *bon!* — you are Cartier-Bresson."

"Really? Cartier-Bresson?"

"Eh . . ." — he reconsidered — "perhaps Ruth Orkin."

She'd always had a hard time getting a precise fix on François. Everything about him seemed a little indeterminate: his weight, his nationality, his social background, his gender preferences. He wore bulky clothes even though he appeared slim at times; he claimed to be Parisian but sometimes his accent was about as exotic as 2nd Avenue; he called himself frugal but took her to only the most expensive restaurants; he could be feline and languid and annoyingly partial to Mapplethorpe but always surrounded himself with pretty young assistants. The one thing that was absolutely reliable about him was his eye.

"But you know what I like best?" he said, adjusting the halogen lamp. "Even if you hadn't told me, I'd be able to tell these pictures were taken in the same place, twenty-five years apart."

"How?"

"*Je ne sais quoi*." He magnified a corner of the newer shot. "Something that comes through. *L'esprit du place*."

"Maybe it's because the same photographer took the pictures."

"Ah *bébé*, you are a lot better now. Though you still have a long way to go."

Bitch. She smiled, restraining herself, remembering how much she wanted this show to work.

"No, this is not the technique," he said, setting the loop aside. "This is the *sujet*. Some people have only one, like the fat naked ladies or the bullwhips in the *derrières*, and this is yours. You look at this place, and you open your eyes a little wider."

She studied the pictures more closely, asking herself if this could be true. She'd taken good pictures elsewhere, hadn't she? Not just the splatter shots, but the full panoply: parades on 5th Avenue, marathon runners on the Brooklyn Bridge, country estates in Greenwich, dunes in the Mojave Desert, even the swirling unfinished Gaudi Cathedral in Barcelona. But in the back of her mind lurked the suspicion that he might be right. Somehow all those other images seemed a little fuzzy and undefined; anybody could have taken them. It was only in Riverside that everything came into sharp focus, the textures and details almost bursting out of the frames. And she wondered if she'd put something at risk trying to get that clarity back.

"I like this one," said François, touching the work print of George urging his ragged friend to take heart as the contractor's Suburban pulled away. "I like to see a bit more of this guy."

"Oh, you would, would you?"

"You're starting to get closer."

"You think so?"

She cringed a little, remembering how she'd ducked behind the Dumpster to change her lens that day.

"Robert Capa said, 'If your pictures aren't good enough, you aren't close enough.'"

She checked her watch, realizing she'd have to hustle to get the 3:28 leaving Grand Central. The dark storm cloud of guilt passed over her again, reminding her of the terrible risk she'd taken leaving town for just a few hours. *i know what your doing*. A part of her mind had remained back in Riverside, fretting over the minutiae of the kids' day even though they were carefully guarded and accounted for with the new security procedures at school. She still couldn't shake this dreadful image of someone watching them from across the street.

"Is still not *suffisant*, though," said François.

"What?"

"*You need to get even closer. Something's still missing. I'm not see-ing the image that pulls it all together.*"

You aren't close enough. Is that what someone was saying to them-selves in Riverside right at this moment?

"What do you want?" she asked, feeling a surge of panic and re-alizing that by dividing her attention into such minuscule fractions she might have failed as both a mother *and* a photographer.

"I don't know." He pulled on his beard. "Just . . . closer."

"Ross . . . what . . . is . . . *this?*" Barry asked in a voice like a slowly clenching fist.

"This is the new deal. Sorry, pardner. We've got no choice."

"What about the 'Path to Profitability' we were talking about? What about the three new Asian markets for Coridal?"

"You got to know when to hold 'em," Bill Brenner sang, "know when to fold 'em."

In his own mind, Bill was the essence of virile robust frontier manhood, a kind of plainspoken Marlboro Man of the free-market economy. In truth, he *did* look more like a bridge troll, with stubby legs, pudgy hands, furry arched eyebrows, and a strikingly round head with gray-black horseshoes of hair around both of his ears. His third wife, a tall blond former Pirelli Tire model who called herself Taffy, never wore high heels and looked noticeably depressed one night when Bill half-jokingly announced he was going to take part in his company's clinical trials for a Viagra knockoff.

For five years, Barry had labored to keep this man from destroy-ing himself and his own company. He'd literally found stacks of lab reports and e-mails explicitly saying that Brenner Home Care's top executives knew that Virulant, the pesticide they were aggressively marketing, could cause birth defects, even after Bill had sworn up and down that no such documents existed. Bill lied on the stand, he lied in the boardroom, he lied in restaurants, on the company Lear-jet, at barbecues, at quail hunts, at ski lodges, at corporate retreats, at shareholders meetings, and at depositions. He lied on the putting green. He lied when you were standing next to him at a urinal. He lied when there was no conceivable reason to lie. On at least one oc-casion, he lied so blatantly in court that the judge threatened *Barry* with possible disbarment for allegedly suborning testimony. He lied, and when he was confronted, he lied some more and intimated that he would not pay Barry's bills and expenses, telling him, *If you don't like it, you can kiss my ass sideways and sue me.*

In the end, Barry had given up some of the best years of his own life and his children's lives to put in the countless hours required to reach a settlement in this epic of a case. The one thing he'd thought the experience was good for was giving him the absolute determination to strike out on his own. But now here was Bill's smiling face, bobbing into view again like a child's helium balloon freed from under a chair.

"I thought we were going to have a discussion with the full executive committee before Bill came on board here." He turned to Ross. "You can't just impose this on everyone. The equity partners have a right to a vote. How much of the company are you proposing to sell Bill anyway?"

"We're not," said Ross.

"What?"

"We're not selling him a piece of the company. We're going to start bankruptcy proceedings. And Bill has decided to buy some of the assets off us so we're not just left with the shirts on our backs."

"But none of the goddamn liabilities." Bill rocked back too far in the leather office chair and found that his boot heels barely reached the desk. "If I need another ball and chain, I'll get divorced and married again."

"You can't do this," said Barry.

"Well, obviously it's a long process, Baairr." Ross cleared his throat. "We have to start filing papers for Chapter 11 protection and then . . ."

"No. I mean, you *can't* do this. Almost all of the employees of this company have their savings and 401(k) plans tied up in stock. You're going to wipe them all out."

"That's always a risk with a start up. If you want security, go work for the post office."

Barry flashed on the image of a mail-sorter turning on his supervisors with an Uzi. "But you sold off *your* shares in August."

"As was my right," Ross said, his face somber and indifferent. "I was just exercising my options."

"Which most of the people under us weren't allowed to do according to the company's bylaws."

"But you're not in that boat, Barry." Ross raised his top lip like a curtain, revealing two squarish bonded front teeth. "You could've sold out anytime, just like me. You still could. Maybe your stock isn't where it was back in April, but as a founding partner you might be entitled to some of the revenues from our selling the patents to Bill."

"As long as I go along with helping you structure the bankruptcy plan so we can't be sued by any of the rest of our present employees, right?"

"You're either on the bus or you're under it." Bill Brenner flexed his leprechaun eyebrows. "I know a half-dozen first-rate litigators in Houston who'd be happy to help us put this baby to bed without you."

Barry closed his eyes and once again saw Magritte's umbrella men raining from the sky. Gradually, their faces changed into people he knew. Steve Lyons, Bharat, Lisa, Chris from Operations, all plummeting past him, their eyes sad and steady, stoically accepting the fact that no one was going to catch them.

"I can't do it," he said.

Ross touched his shoulder lightly. "Think about it."

"I am thinking about it, believe me." Barry swallowed. "I'm breaking the Guinness world record for most rationalizations per minute while I'm standing here talking to you. But this isn't the ride I paid for."

"Nobody gets exactly what they pay for, Barry. That's why we all end up needing lawyers."

"Well, you probably don't need this one anymore." Barry took a step toward the door, letting Ross's hand slide off him.

He had the sensation of the room disintegrating around him. All the surfaces — the polished black desktop, the leather chairs and couches, the windowpanes, the white bookshelves and computer screens — melting away. Another reality had been lurking behind the scenery all along. He was back in front of his father's deli the day after the riots, as if he'd always been there, the storefront looking like a blackened empty eye socket with the front window smashed in and a befouled dead-animal odor wafting from the charred meat inside. All the way over in the car, Mom had fretted about what they'd find. But Barry would never forget the way his father had simply stooped his shoulders, kissed her, and picked up a broom. *So now we know*, he'd said, starting to sweep up.

So now we know.

"*Fine.*" Bill clapped his hands. "I'm happy to give the work to old Cyrus Miller. Our wives were sorority sisters back in Austin."

"Naturally," said Barry. "You can't forget loyalty."

"*Touché,*" Ross parried as he went to pick up the phone on the desk and punched a button. "You always know just what to say under the circumstances."

"That's why they used to pay me the big money." Barry smiled modestly.

"Is this Dan in Security?" Ross nodded as he spoke into the phone. "Please lock down Mr. Schulman's desk and escort him from the building. Make sure he doesn't take any papers or discs from his computer. And call my office if he tries to get back in."

45

ONE WORST-CASE SCENARIO after another fomenting in her mind, Lynn caught the 3:28 off a dead run through Grand Central and still didn't feel she'd completely caught her breath even when the train pulled into Riverside Station thirty-four minutes later.

She bolted for the car and drove maniacally to the Holly Farms Family Martial Arts Center between the Radio Shack and the Dress Barn on Evergreen, not even allowing herself a moment's satisfaction over François's praise for her more recent photos.

The dojo was full of anxious mothers by the time she arrived and doffed her shoes at the door. The women sat cross-legged around the canvas mat, trying to ignore gray hairs and extra pounds in the pitiless floor-to-ceiling mirrors. The children, in their starchy white outfits, warmed up on the far side of the room, kicking and punching at the air, pretending their mothers weren't present.

"Hey, babycakes, you're right on time." Jeanine jumped up to give her a hug.

Her white Liz Claiborne sweater reeked of pot and pencil shavings. *That's one way of dealing with all the stress*, Lynn thought. She'd noticed a kind of continental drift among her friends these last few days. After the initial burst of emergency meetings and neighborhood patrols, some of their gang had begun to withdraw, hunkering down in their homes and peering out from the drapes as if they were avoiding a contagion. No one had even called to set up the next Tuesday-night book group.

"How's everything going here?" Lynn settled onto the spot that Jeanine had made for her on the floor, glad and relieved to be among other mothers again.

"You're not going to believe the kid Clay's decided to fight."

"Why not?"

Jeanine pointed to a boy across the room. A close-shorn young wolf with long legs and pointy elbows. His brow was a bony ridge over pale-blue eyes. Was it just her imagination that he looked a little like Mike? A white foot lashed out and shattered a half-inch-thick plywood board held by another boy.

"Oh, shit." Her mouth dried as she watched the boy who'd been holding the split board brush splinters from his lapel.

She waved to the sensei, Rick Webber, doughy, ponytailed, and slack-faced yet utterly convinced that every single Karate Mom in town was madly in love with him.

"Rick," she said as he came trotting over in red-white-and-blue Gore-Tex, "is Clay going to be all right with that kid?"

"Whaddaya mean?" He glanced over dully. "They're both orange belts. Clay's up for it."

"But he's not in shape. He's lost all this weight lately from not eating. He can't even kick his sister's butt."

"Don't let him hear you say that." Jeanine tapped Lynn's leg. "You'll undermine his confidence."

What confidence? She watched Clay staring down at the canvas as he adjusted his headgear, her fragile little boy trying to play Stone Cold Steve Austin in front of all his friends.

"So how are *you* doing?" Jeanine asked meaningfully as Rick went back to center-mat to help the boys get ready.

"Okay . . . a little shaky . . . pretty nervous if you want to know the truth."

"Oh, I know." Jeanine sighed. "It's such a shame."

There it was again. That sound Lynn noticed when she'd first talked to Jeanine about filing disciplinary charges against Mike a few days ago. A certain polite cautious reserve.

"You haven't heard from Mike lately, have you?" Lynn asked.

"No. Just to wave at him picking the kids up the other day." Jeanine pulled her hair back. "I think he's having a tough time too."

"Do you?"

The wolf boy had put on his pads and his red Everlast headgear, making him look pinched and engorged. By contrast, Clay appeared exposed and lopsided in his protective wear, and Lynn had to fight the urge to go over and embarrass him by fixing it.

"It's too bad you guys weren't able to work things out before it got this far." Jeanine suddenly leaned over, not able to keep her own counsel.

"Jeanine, believe me, we did everything we could to avoid it. The last thing we wanted was a public hearing."

"All right, ladies" — Rick had gone out to the center of the mat to address the mothers in the round — "we've been over the rules before, but one more time . . ."

"Look how cute Zak and Brawley look," Jeanine whispered as her twins stood in the corner and tried to punch each other in the nuts.

"This class is about learning to have control and discipline," Rick explained in a booming voice, as if he was talking to a roomful of marine recruits. "But this is sparring, so there will be some *moderate contact.* Three-point match. Whoever fails to block three times loses. Everybody okay about that?"

"Yesss," a dozen reluctant women replied.

"Well, then I don't know why the whole thing couldn't have been put off awhile," said Jeanine.

The two boys bowed stiffly at each other in the middle of the mat, a formal little ritual that somehow seemed to mock the grown-up world of good manners and superficial niceties around them.

"You think I'm looking forward to this?" Lynn whispered.

"Hajime!" Rick stepped between the boys as they shifted down into stylized fighting stances.

In an instant, all the mothers in the room disappeared, their presence negated by a kind of fiercely concentrated energy in the middle of the mat.

"Every morning I wake up with this weight on my chest," Lynn murmured, still feeling the need to explain.

"Honey, you don't need to tell me."

The other kid struck first, a pistonlike punch straight from the shoulder. Lynn heard herself give a gasp as Clay turned sideways and danced away with an agility she'd never noticed before.

"See that?" Jeanine clapped her hands and touched Lynn's arm.

Lynn hunched forward, seeing something of Barry in how the boy moved. A way of tucking his chin in and keeping his shoulders squared. The low center of gravity, the side-to-side movement of the eyes searching for opportunity. She'd had mixed feelings since she'd signed him up for karate last year. On the one hand, it got him out of the house and moving. A body at rest with a Sega Dreamcast tended to stay at rest. On the other, it was a step farther into that realm where mothers and sisters had no coin.

"I was just saying it's too bad it all had to come out *now*." Jeanine turned to her, keeping her voice low.

"What do you mean?"

"I mean, we're all looking for the police to *protect* us. You hate to see one of them on the spot."

Clay suddenly lunged, a quick rabbit punch that the other boy caught in the crook of his elbow.

"It sounds like you're blaming me," Lynn muttered.

She realized several of the other mothers were staring at her as well, perhaps starting to make some judgments of their own.

"*Yame!*" Rick the sensei stepped between the boys, separating them briefly.

"I'm not blaming *anyone*," Jeanine said.

But in that last word, Lynn heard sympathy being put on an even higher shelf, just out of reach.

What did Jeanine think had happened? That she'd tried to seduce Mike? That Barry was just a jealous husband? Did she seriously believe that this was some plan the two of them had cooked up to deprive the town of one of its guardians?

"Look, Lynn, the main thing is you know I'm on your side," she said. But somehow these words just made Lynn hunch down farther.

"*Hajime!*"

She was distracted by the boys going at it again. The wolf boy striking out and drawing back as if there were coiled springs inside him. Lynn tried to catch Clay's eye, to let him know there would be no shame in quitting. But Clay adjusted his hand chops and shook his head furiously, wanting to continue.

"I wish I could just get in there and make them stop," Lynn said, protective instinct scratching at the walls of her chest.

"If you did, he'd never forgive you." Jeanine put a hand over Lynn's wrist. "Don't embarrass him in front of his friends."

A white foot landed just below Clay's rib cage, and all the other mothers gave a sympathetic *ooooooffffff*. But instead of doubling over, Clay danced away and raised his hands, showing everyone he was okay.

My brave man. Lynn felt her heart start to rise. In some way, seeing her youngest child refuse to back down gave her courage. Yes, I can do this too. I'm going to hold my head up.

"We'll all be there for you," said Jeanine.

"I know."

In slow motion, Lynn saw a closed fist come straight from the wolf boy's shoulder and find its way through the opening in Clay's headgear. She felt the impact of fist and face as if she'd taken the blow herself.

A slaughterhouse squeal went up from the boys in the class, whose voices hadn't changed yet. Clay's hands flew up to his face, and his body wilted. A thick red clot of blood hit the beige mat.

Lynn ran over to her son and saw that the nose wasn't quite broken, but two streams of blood were guttering down onto his lip. She threw her arms around him and glared over his shoulder at the sensei.

"Why didn't you stop it?" she said. "Couldn't you see someone was going to get hurt?"

"I thought he was doing all right." Rick shrugged.

46

"HEY, LARRY, you got those time sheets I was looking for?"

Just before six that night, Paco stuck his head in to see Sergeant Larry Quinn, the records officer.

"You're not gonna leave me alone about that, are you?" Larry sat behind his desk with his pant leg rolled up to his knee, examining a nasty red scrape on his shin.

"What happened?"

"Fell off my goddamn bike. Can you believe they've got a fifty-seven-year-old man riding around town like a twelve-year-old?"

"I thought you'd like getting out of the patrol car and riding a beat. Seems like something they would've done back in the day."

"If we're going to turn the clock back, give me a horse. Give me a fine Arabian steed. I'll ride it through the hallways of the housing projects. That'll get rid of your loitering problem."

Larry was Old School, so Old School that he had a handlebar mustache and combed smelly pomade into his steel-gray hair like a cop from the turn of the *previous* century. So Old School that he still hadn't quite succeeded in getting the department's time-card system computerized like he was supposed to by last summer, making it necessary for every officer to sign in and out by hand.

He was the department's history buff, and he'd turned his corner office into a kind of minimuseum of Riverside. His walls had pictures of the town's first police department from the 1890s, with its six bewhiskered officers in matching long coats and soft felt bobby hats. An authentic 1902 mahogany nightstick lay across his desk, and a plastic replica of the department's first mascot, Horatio, a Jack

Russell terrier with a black ring around his eye, sat atop the row of black file cabinets.

"What were you looking for anyway?" Larry said, wincing as he tried to stand up. "'I Forgot to Remember to Forget.' You know that old song?"

"All of June. All of July. All of August. All of September."

"'Try to remember the kind of September . . .'" Larry limped over to the file cabinets, switching songs and singing in a broad operatic baritone.

Paco watched him, holding a tolerant smile for as long as he could.

"You trying to find out when the loo punched in those days?" Larry cast a wry knowing look over his shoulder.

"Just putting in the roadwork. Crossing my t's and dotting my i's."

"You know, some of the other guys, they wonder why the chief put you in charge of this investigation." Larry slid the top drawer all the way open until it banged loudly.

"Do they?"

The muscles in Paco's cheeks began to tire from the effort of grinning at all these *blanquitos*.

"A lot of us go back a ways with Mike. Some of the young patrol guys he taught everything they know, so they still feel pretty loyal to him."

"Maybe that's why the chief doesn't want them working the case."

Fingering his way through the files, Larry nodded sagely, as if he saw the wisdom here. "Not that I have much of a dog in this fight myself, but they just want to make sure the loo gets a fair shake here."

"A fair shake is what he's getting."

Paco looked at one of the other old prints on the wall, trying to contain his restlessness. Bunch of gaunt white nineteenth-century motherfuckers in shirtsleeves, 'staches, and suspenders, their faces smeared with grime and muck, boots the size of marlins up to their knees, canvas tents, and the river gray and molten behind them.

"So who're the *chico viejos* here?" he asked.

"Them?" Larry glanced over, pleased that he'd noticed. "That's my great-great-grandfather in the middle of his crew. He was a sandhog."

"Say what?"

"You know, a tunnel digger. A river rat. Some of the loo's relatives did the same. Shanty Irish just off the boat."

Paco studied the picture for another minute, picking out Larry's ancestor with no trouble. The same receding chin and beady mole eyes, the hard-man stance with legs and arms folded, even the same little country-dude spit curl falling on the brow.

"They look like Pancho Villa's gang."

"I know." Larry chuckled. "Bunch of hungry bastards, aren't they? They built this town. They really did. They built the aqueducts so all the toffs on Park Avenue could have drinking water and then they laid the railroad tracks so the toffs' grandchildren could move out to the burbs and get away from the grubby masses and still commute to their jobs at Morgan Stanley."

"Is the lieutenant's great-great-grandfather one of these guys?" Paco adjusted the frame.

"Might be him on the far right." Larry shrugged. "He was supposed to be the hardest of the hard."

A big-shouldered guy with deep shadows under his eyes and a neck like a redwood.

"They say one of the local farmers got pissed because sparks from the trains passing through set his cow pasture on fire. Story is, he started pulling spikes out of the tracks so the next train going by went sailing off the rails, killed about twelve people. So supposedly Old Man Fallon went by with a repair crew. And I guess they had a bit of a row. Because the next day the local constable found that farmer facedown on his own pitchfork. Must have had a farm accident."

"Country life can kill you, man." Paco grimaced.

"Well, he was apparently a good man to have on your side, Robbie Fallon. They say he dug most of the first quarter-mile of tunnel three by himself because the rest of the crew was too shagged from working six days a week. And what'd he have to show for it in the end? Pile of mud."

"What do you mean?"

"I mean, he died in a cave-in. They couldn't even get the body out. He's part of the foundation. We're probably standing on him."

Without thinking, Paco found himself looking down at the linoleum floor. "Damn."

"Exactly. You know, sometimes I think there's a curse on families that gets passed down."

"You getting anywhere with those time sheets?"

Larry seemed to walk his fingers through the files more slowly. "I'm getting there," he said. "Yep. And you know about his brother, right?"

"He died?"

"Makes you sick just thinking about it." He nodded. "His wife and kid don't even get a full pension because he was out of his jurisdiction. He was a city cop, come up on a Saturday night to have dinner with his parents. On the way home, he sees this mope having a fight in the car with his girlfriend on River Road. Rolls down his window, says, 'Hey, easy there, chico. That's a lady.' Guy pulls out a .357. *Mind your own fucking business.* Bang! Good-bye, Johnny. And they wonder why Mike was so aggressive about making us all do traffic stops after that."

Paco watched the sergeant kneel down and lean farther into the file, as if he was about to go headfirst into it.

"I just need those summer months," he said.

"I know what you're looking for." Larry pulled a bulging folder out. "Here's August and the first two weeks of September. Mike was out part of that second week because he took sick days to help out at Ground Zero."

He dropped the file on the floor with an angry splat and shoved the drawer shut.

"You wonder what the point of it all is sometimes." He yanked open a higher drawer. "You give your life to a place, and then your children give their lives and then their children give theirs. And what do you end up with? Shitty little two-story down in the Hollow while the toffs keep climbing over you and on up the hill. Sometimes I wonder why I bother studying history when all it does is keep repeating itself."

Paco scooped up the folder. "'Those who do not remember the past are condemned to . . .'"

"Yeah, yeah, right. Look, don't necessarily think you're getting any higher yourself. Back in the twenties, the Reverend Philips's great-grandfather and some of Chief Baltimore's relatives raised a half-million to buy a couple of hundred acres near Indian Ridge to set up their own little suburban community. Last minute, bunch of white bankers from up the hill swooped in and bought it for three hundred thou and kept the lots empty for thirty years. I can show you the headline from the *News* in my archives. It says, 'NEGROES FOILED!'"

Paco tucked in his chin, feeling mildly insulted. He'd never thought of himself as dark-skinned in the first place. His family were aristocrats from Cuba. It was just a quirk of history that they'd lost the plantation in Havana after *La Revolución* and had to go to San Juan for a few years. He'd never bought into this *tocarle a uno la suerte*, crushed-under-the-wagon-wheel-of-destiny sorry-ass bullshit. *Sucede lo que sucede*. A man took the future in his own hands and shaped it every day because otherwise, what made him a man?

"I got June and July." Larry plucked out another file and slammed the drawer shut. "So you're really looking to nail him, huh?"

"I'm not looking to nail anybody. I got a dead body and two tax-payers filing harassment complaints. The chief's got the Town Board and the state police breathing down his neck. You do the math."

Larry hobbled over to hand him the second file. "You know, some of the guys are saying that in the old days, it didn't matter if you were black, white, or brown. You gave a man the benefit. The only color that counted was blue."

"Can't turn the clock back, Sarge."

"Hey, Paco, this isn't me talking. I'm just telling you what I'm hearing from the rank and file."

"Yeah?" Paco flipped the folder open. "Well, here's what I'd like you to tell them: You don't love me? *Fine.* I don't love you either. But I am still the primary that your commanding officer put in charge of this investigation. And if you got a problem dealing with that, go get a security guard job at a museum. Because this is how it's going to be. And by the way, Larry, the Spanish made it to America a long time before the Irish did. But being a guy who studies history, you probably knew that already, didn't you?"

Larry's mustache drooped. "You don't have to chew my head off, Detective."

"I'm sure I don't."

Paco quickly paged through the file and saw the pattern almost immediately. Fallon had signed out early and often on his day tours the last two months, up to and including the night Sandi Lanier dis-appeared.

"So how's the case looking anyway?" asked Larry, trying to read his expression.

"Great." Paco snapped the file shut and put it under his arm. "Thanks for asking."

47

THREE PAIRS OF GRUBBY HANDS grabbed for the same bright-yellow dump truck, and a cry went up like an air-raid warning siren.

Barry saw the baby-sitter spring into action, rising from the park bench, stepping into the sandbox, and getting between the children to play mediator without missing a beat of conversation among her friends still sitting over by the strollers.

She was lovely, he thought, watching her from the playground entrance. One of those ageless Latin women with smooth copper skin, a tiny waist, and a heart-stopping smile. Somehow she managed to crouch among the toddlers without dirtying the knees of her white Levi's, stroking unruly heads, distributing her smile evenly, while deftly extracting the contested toy from the area of play without any of the children noticing.

By the time she stood up, they'd all turned their attention to a labor-intensive joint project, attacking a giant hole with pails and shovels. A lawyer who could resolve conflicts on Wall Street that quickly and painlessly would be making five hundred an hour easy.

He fixed his collar and came moseying over, intercepting her three steps short of her friends, the group of older nannies who gathered for early lunch just about every day at this time at the Eisenhower Park playground in Indian Ridge, a half-mile down the hill from his house.

"Muriel?" he said, raising his eyebrows, as if they were old friends just running into each other. "Muriel Navarro?"

"What is it?" Hearing her own name from a stranger's lips dimmed the wattage in her smile instantly.

"My name's Barry Schulman. I'm an attorney. I was wondering if I could take a few minutes of your time."

Her eyes danced from the children in the sandbox to her friends on the benches, who were cautiously watching this scene unfold while still opening Tupperware containers of fresh fruit and talking loudly to one another in machine-gun Spanish.

"You from Immigration?" asked Muriel.

She had the deep husky voice of a much older, heavier woman. A smoker's voice. *Tremont Avenue in the Bronx*, he mentally placed her. He'd taken dozens of statements from women who sounded just like her when he was a DA. Except that so many of them looked worn out beyond their years, with baggy eyes, junk-food figures, and phlegmy asthma coughs from crappy housing-project ventilation systems. Somehow this girl had made it out into the sun.

"No, I'm not from Immigration," he said. "I'm a private citizen."

"Then what do you want? How'd you find me?"

"You used to work for Kim Roseborough, whose daughter Allison went to the same school as our son, Clay. I got Kim's number out of the school directory, and she gave me the number for the lady you're working for now. She told me I might find you here."

If he'd hoped to allay her suspicions by throwing around familiar names and casually outlining the route he'd taken, he saw now he was sadly mistaken. She was looking at him as if *he*, not Fallon, was her stalker.

"You don't have to worry. I didn't get you in trouble with the boss," he said. "I told Mrs. Lockhart we were thinking of hiring somebody to help out with some baby-sitting on the weekends. She told me you were busy with your classes at Hostos Community College, but that we could talk to you . . ."

She shook her head, not buying it. "What do you want?"

He turned, subtly using his size to encourage her to walk alongside him. "I know you filed a complaint against Sergeant Michael Fallon a few years back."

"Oh, no."

She took two steps and then stopped, gold hoop earrings swinging and winking in the daylight.

"Look, you're probably not eager to get into all this again. But my wife and I were also harassed by him. And we've filed charges too."

"That was a long time ago," she said.

"I understand. But we've got a little disciplinary hearing coming up the day after tomorrow, and so I'm just trying to rally a few more support witnesses in the meantime."

"How'd you get my name in the first place?" Her eyes narrowed again, seeing through that breezy *so* and *just*, right down to the shifting unstable core of their case.

"You filed your complaint with the Civilian Complaint Review Board. I looked it up in the old records."

"*Qué batingue!*" She looked back in frustration at the sandbox, where a towheaded girl was mashing a Korean boy's face into the dirt. "Chiara, leave your brother alone!"

He suddenly became aware of just how unwelcome his presence was here. A white man at a playground in the middle of a working day. Even his size marked him. He had to squat to sit on a low jungle-gym bar so he wouldn't keep towering over her.

"So, what happened?" he said, trying to sound solicitous. "He pulled you over when you were driving your boss's car?"

"I can't talk about this."

"I understand. You're nervous. You don't know me. The man's a police officer . . ."

Slow down, he told himself. You're violating your own rules of the road. The moment a witness knows how badly you need him is the moment he pulls away.

"No, you don't understand," she said. "I'm this close to getting full citizenship. I don't even know the family back in San Salvador anymore. I haven't lived there since I was nine."

"I seriously doubt Immigration is going to come after you just because you testify in a local cop's disciplinary hearing."

"Yeah, thanks a lot. I'll wave to you from the back of the boat."

He watched the children rocket down a long wiggly aluminum slide and wondered what else he could do to gain her trust. As always, time was the enemy.

"So why'd you withdraw the complaint after three days?" he asked. "Did somebody say something to you?"

"You know, my life is good now." She brushed a fringe of dark hair, almost the same shade as Lynn's, out of her eyes. "The kids are nice. The lady I work for lets me borrow the Honda twice a week to drive down for my classes in the city so I can get my RN license. Why you wanna mess me up?"

"I'll take that as a yes then. So did he threaten you?"

The texture of her skin seemed to go from butter cream to distressed leather right before his eyes.

He realized he'd come on far too strong. "Look, I didn't mean to pressure you. All we'd need is a brief statement."

She looked back toward the sandbox, where two of the little girls were beginning to bury the Korean boy up to his neck, sunbursts of fine lines appearing around both of her eyes.

"I'm sorry." She turned. "I have to get back to work."

"What about all the other women?" he called after her. "You know if he did it to you and he did it to us, he's probably done it to other people."

Her shoulders seized up under her bright-yellow sweater. It was like watching his own shot at the buzzer arc high and hopeful in the air, begin its descent on target, and then somehow bounce uselessly off the back rim. He'd let it go too soon. His timing was gone. He'd lost the soft touch.

"You trying to make me feel *guilty?*" she said.

"Well . . ."

She glanced back, taking in his Italian loafers, his Brooks Brothers khakis, and the cut of his blue Custom Shop shirt. All this studied hey-I'm-just-another-dad-at-the-playground casualness that suddenly felt like an ill-fitting costume.

"You know what the police used to do in San Salvador?" she said. "I have an uncle who doesn't have ears anymore because he left them in the interrogation room. There's just a hole on either side of his head."

"That usually doesn't happen in your average East Coast suburban town."

She needed only the mild lowering of her eyelids to remind him that a woman's decapitated body had washed ashore less than a mile down the hill from here.

"Well, it doesn't happen very often . . ."

"I think you should go," she said firmly, her eyes roaming past his shoulder and finding the black Saab, newly washed, parked alone across the street. "The police patrol here all the time now."

Nothing in her expression gave him any indication whether she was warning him to be more discreet or telling him that she was about to call the cops herself.

"Forgive me for bothering you." He dug a business card out of his wallet, scribbled his home number on the back, and slipped it to her in a handshake. "But call me if you change your mind."

"Okay." She dropped the card into her sweater pocket as if it was of no great importance and then went back to referee the children.

He watched her go, a gentle knowing sway in her hips, sunlight spreading like quicksilver in her hair. From behind, she looked a little bit like Lynn. And in that instant, he saw why Michael Fallon had pulled her over in the first place.

48

"GOOD AFTERNOON, Mrs. Schulman." Gwen Florio faced the witness stand, a stiletto-thin figure in a dress-blue skirt and jacket with official-looking white piping along the lapels that seemed to strongly suggest some kind of police affiliation for the benefit of the judges hearing this case.

"Good afternoon."

The disciplinary hearing had gotten off to a relatively uneventful start this morning. Lynn had been sworn in by Tony Shlanger, the six-foot-nine court officer who spent every Saturday morning outside abortion clinics in the city, screaming himself blue in the face and waving tiny plastic fetuses at frightened young pregnant women rushing by. Her right hand wavered slightly as she swore to tell nothing but the truth. The members of the Town Board stared down at her from the dais. But even the so-called friendly questioning by the prosecuting attorney, Jack Davis, a stumpy old codger with hair the color of a striped bass and a worsted plaid suit, had left her feeling exposed and shaky on the stand.

For almost an hour, Mike had sat at the defense table, less than fifteen feet away, glaring up at her and jotting down the occasional note to help arm his lawyer for this cross-examination. His anger emanated toward her in waves, defining her like the shadow on a sonogram. Even more disturbingly, his thumb appeared to have swelled up to twice its normal size and had turned a livid purplish shade that reminded her of an erection.

And just to ratchet up the general anxiety level, right after lunch the courtroom doors swung open and Jeanine, Molly Pratt, Anne

Schaffer, and Dianne de Groot from her book group filed in, giving her A-OK signs and warm supportive smiles.

"You know my client, don't you, Mrs. Schulman?"

"Just as I told Mr. Davis right before lunch."

Lynn had dressed demurely for her appearance, in a blue blazer, a gray skirt, and a white shirt with a subdued Chanel scarf and simple pearls. Her hair was pulled back, starkly revealing the grip and release of sinews in her throat.

"How long have you known my client?" asked Gwen Florio, stepping from behind the lectern.

"I think I've testified that I've known him since high school."

Barry sat two rows back on the right side of the spectator section, arms spread wide across the back of the pew, trying to look open and relaxed.

She felt as though she was seeing him across a busy avenue, cars and trucks speeding back and forth in between. In the middle of watching *Charlie Rose* in the living room the other night he'd suddenly announced, *I quit today.*

She didn't even wait to turn the sound down. *You what?*

You heard me, he'd said. *They wanted to do something like a Mafia bust-out. Pull the furniture out, burn the place down, and scam the insurance company. They wanted me to hold the matches. I couldn't do it.*

So you just quit? she'd asked, trying to get over the shock.

He'd studied the separation of his scotch and water. *Why am I not hearing the kind of support I expected? All these people I work with are going to get screwed out of their savings.*

But what about us? she'd said.

Gwen Florio stood before her, smiling. "Can you tell us a little more about the nature of that early relationship? You seemed to gloss over that very quickly this morning."

"We were close." Lynn gave up trying to make eye contact with Barry and concentrated on speaking in a strong loud voice. "At the time."

"*Close?*" Florio's eyebrows lifted. "Is that how you characterize it?"

"Yes."

Lynn noticed a woman in the first row staring at her with the kind of pinpoint attention that made her aware of every pore on her face, every little catch in her throat. A lady with a kind of severe composure, wearing earth tones and a short sensible haircut. This had to be Mike's wife, she realized. She'd positioned herself to be dead center in Lynn's field of vision when she stared straight ahead into the spectators' gallery.

"When you say *close*, you are of course referring to a romantic relationship, aren't you?"

"Of course. I mean, I was." Lynn heard herself stumble, trying to sort through her tenses, and saw a slight droop in Barry's lip. "I mean, I was referring to back then."

Gwen Florio approached the stand, her heels clicking on the floor like a Geiger counter.

She was a woman who'd carried off middle-age with a certain seasoned smoky elegance. Her hair was a little wiry and her eyelids were weary, but she had legs like a Bob Fosse dancer and there was a hint of husky amusement in her voice, a throaty forthright quality that Lynn found both admirable and intimidating. She seemed like the kind of dame who would tell her lover straight-out when she didn't consider a job done right.

"Now, during the course of this romantic relationship, Detective Lieutenant Fallon would do things not just for you but for your family from time to time." Florio held her in the green-eyed tractor beam of her glare, slowly pulling her in. "Is that correct?"

"Yes."

"Your mother was sick then. Wasn't she?"

"She had MS."

"Mrs. Schulman, can you speak up please?" Mayor Flynn cupped a hand behind his ear. "Some members of this board — and I'd rather not say who — are at the age that they need hearing devices."

A gentlemanly chuckle rippled down the dais. The mayor was a chalky thin man in his midsixties, with a bow tie knotted neatly over a large Adam's apple. Lynn's mother used to call him the "most thwarted man I've ever met," back in the seventies when he was a local accountant just starting to run for office. And Lynn had captured a rather harshly lit Robert Frank–style picture of him standing alone in the canned goods aisle of the A&P with his campaign literature, looking for someone to shake hands with. *The Candidate*, she'd titled it. She'd been planning to use the shot in her gallery retrospective, but now she hoped that he wouldn't remember it from her high school exhibit and hold it against her.

"She had multiple sclerosis." Lynn raised her voice, trying not to sound strained or strident.

"I see. And isn't it true that Lieutenant Fallon helped take your mother to many of her doctors appointments?"

"I don't know if you'd say it was *many*, but he certainly helped us out. I would never deny that."

Lynn cast a quick look over toward Barry, hoping for guidance. But he was studying her with a sort of clinical detachment.

"So this was more than some puppy love," the defense lawyer pressed on. "Your lives really became enmeshed at some point. Isn't that right?"

"I'm not sure I'd go that far."

"But isn't it true that during the time you were involved with the lieutenant, you got to know all the members of his family intimately?"

"I guess so."

"You guess so?" Florio cast a foxy squint up at the dais, shaking her head in wry disappointment. "Isn't it true that his mother cooked meals for you and your sister when your own mother couldn't make it to the kitchen?"

"Yes, that happened on a few occasions."

"And the lieutenant's father helped your career as a photographer, as well," said Gwen. "That's true also, isn't it?"

"He helped me get access to things I wanted to take pictures of. Yes, that's right."

The board members began muttering to one another, obviously remembering a few more of the unflattering pictures she'd taken of the town in the seventies. In the back of the courtroom, a familiar old man with a hawkish face and an unevenly mowed gray crew cut leaned forward on his cane.

"Isn't it also true that you had a very close relationship with the lieutenant's older brother, Johnny, who went on to become a police officer in New York City?" Gwen Florio asked.

Lynn froze for a second and stared down at Mike, not quite willing to believe that things were going to move in this direction. She'd been warned that the normal rules of evidence didn't apply in this kind of hearing, that the defense lawyer could ask her literally anything. But surely there were *some* limits. She looked to Jack Davis at the prosecutor's table, waiting for him to object. But he seemed lost in the fields of thought, reading documents with his legs crossed and his pale shins and old-fashioned black elastic sock garters exposed.

"I've already said they were all very good to me," she said. "Though I'm not quite sure what that has to do with what we're talking about *today*."

She saw Barry give a slight encouraging nod, as if to say, *You go, girl.*

"I'm coming to that. Shortly." Gwen Florio smiled, the warning shot as a courtesy call. "Did there come a time when the lieutenant asked you to marry him?"

Lynn raised her eyes to a water-stained ceiling panel, ignoring the frantic whispering among her reading-group friends in the third row. "We were both about seventeen."

"Mrs. Schulman, I'm standing right here, in front of you."

"I'm sorry, but I'm going to have to object." Jack Davis finally roused himself and got to his feet, pant cuffs dropping over his garters. "What does any of this have to do with the price of beans? I can't see any relevance."

"It's relevant because it has to do with the credibility of this witness and the particular history she has with my client."

Gwen Florio looked back at Mike, who was brooding at his swollen thumb, a bloodred tie knotted thickly at his collar. Lynn shuddered a little, thinking about the conversation he must have had with his lawyer to prepare her for this line of questioning.

"I'm going to allow it," said Mayor Flynn, with a cursory rap of the gavel. "We're not in an actual trial here. Ms. Florio has a lot more latitude in what she can ask."

Jack Davis gave a small shrug before he sat down, as if to say, *So I tried.* Lynn girded herself, adjusting her scarf, wishing she'd found the nerve to tell Barry exactly what was coming.

"Yes, he did ask me to marry him."

"And did you consider the possibility?"

She focused on a burl in the wooden balustrade before her. "Only very briefly."

"And can you tell us why you considered the possibility?"

"I thought I was in love with him."

She looked down, the tightrope walker realizing she didn't have a net. How does she do it, ladies and gentlemen? *Why* does she do it? What had possessed her to think this would be anything other than the most heinous and humiliating public disaster of her life?

Of course, it was all her fault. She'd let shame nudge her out onto a high wire one hundred feet above safety. Shame had kept her from telling Barry the whole truth about who she used to be. But shame had kept her from backing out and not testifying today. So now she was stuck between the two points, wobbling and swaying above the gaping crowd.

"Was there some other urgent reason that made you consider his proposal?" Gwen Florio pressed her.

"Yes. I was pregnant."

The courtroom fell dead quiet. Barry's drawn face seemed to come rushing up at her from the second row and then quickly recede.

"And did there come a time when you decided to terminate that pregnancy?"

"Yes."

"And so you had an abortion."

"Yes. I did."

She looked over as the court officer, Tony Shlanger, cleared his throat. His ears had turned bright pink, revealing an embryonic-looking network of veins within the thick cartilage.

"And did you consult Lieutenant Fallon about that decision?"

"I did." She was transfixed, watching the color of the court officer's ears darken as she spoke. "He wanted me to keep it. He thought we could have it and live with his parents. But then I decided it was all a little too much for me."

"So, what did you do?"

Lynn looked forlornly at Barry. She'd tried to tell him, hadn't she? She'd said, *We talked* very seriously *about having kids.* But she couldn't even justify that excuse to herself for more than a half-second. She was a coward and a prevaricator, and this was precisely the punishment she deserved.

"I asked my mother for the money," she said. "And then I went into the city with my friend Sandi to get one at the Eastern Women's Clinic downtown."

Her stomach dropped, and for a split second she was seventeen and back on the subway platform at Times Square with Sandi. The crowd separating them before she saw the doors close and Sandi speeding off on the downtown train without her, fingers pressed against the scratchiettied glass, mouth open in a silent wail.

Then she was back in the courtroom, being gawked at, the tightrope walker starting to lose her balance. Jeanine pointing and whispering behind her hands to the other book-club ladies, as if she alone could explain what was happening. Mike's wife turning beet-red in her dark-green business suit. The mayor waving his hands, trying to get the other board members to stop whispering at him.

A kind of humidity filled the courtroom. The water stain seemed to spread across the ceiling. And gradually it dawned on Lynn that she'd altered the temperature just by mentioning Sandi's name, reminding everyone of the case lurking just beneath this one.

Gwen Florio approached the stand again, holding the legal pad out in front of her as if it were a young swimmer's Styrofoam kickboard.

"So you disposed of my client's child without asking his prior consent?"

"Last I checked it was my body as well," said Lynn defiantly.

"All right, all right." The mayor gaveled them both into silence, broken blood vessels lighting up like small red wires in his nose. "We're not going to reopen the Supreme Court *Roe v. Wade* case here. Ms. Florio, move on please."

"Certainly, Your Honor." She nodded sympathetically at Tony, the court officer, acknowledging his pain, before turning back to Lynn again. "Now, Mrs. Schulman, can you tell us what happened to your relationship with the lieutenant after you had this procedure."

"I believe we broke up shortly after that."

"Can you tell us why?"

Lynn rubbed her eyes, seeing Barry turn slate gray, thinking he'd already heard the worst of it. "Michael became very possessive and controlling of me. He started wanting to know where I was all the time. Who I was with. He started following me around, telling me how I should dress, and what I should be taking pictures of . . ."

"But isn't it also true that you'd started seeing somebody else?"

"Oh my God." Lynn sank in her chair.

She felt herself become physically ill. She looked down at Michael, as if to say, *Is this* helping *you?*

But he kept his head down, scribbling notes on a Post-it pad that seemed to throb and turn a sickening shade of bright yellow before her eyes.

"Do I really have to answer this?" Lynn looked up at the mayor.

"I'm afraid so," Tom Flynn said. "She can ask anything she likes, within reason."

"Mrs. Schulman?" Gwen Florio prompted her.

Lynn's chin drooped, and her chest became a groaning concave space bowing back against her spine. "Yes," she said.

"Yes what?"

"Yes, there were others."

The gorge started to rise in her throat, knowing there was still even more to come.

"Can you tell us who they were?"

"Objection." Jack Davis clambered to his feet. "Have we really degenerated to the point where all we're doing is retailing lukewarm gossip?"

"Just a little more leeway, Your Honor." Florio looked up at the dais, her navy jacket opened enough to reveal the stark womanly drama of her hips.

"I'll give you about three more questions to establish some relevance, and then we're done with this line of questioning," the mayor rebuked her.

"Thank you." She nodded. "Mrs. Schulman? We're still waiting."

Lynn sucked her lips, slightly dazed and dehydrated. "This was all so long ago."

She looked over at Barry again, hoping for some sign of understanding, but he was a black hole to her, gathering light in and giving none out.

"You were seeing other men," Florio prodded her.

"I had Michael stalking me." Lynn tried to sit up and defend herself. "He wouldn't leave me alone . . ."

"Who were these other men?"

Florio honed in on her, moving close enough so that Lynn could smell her perfume.

"He was just trying to protect me," Lynn said. "We didn't mean for it to happen."

"Mrs. Schulman." The lawyer's lip cocked back. "Isn't it true that one of those men was my client's brother, John Fallon?"

Lynn heard the first sharp intake of breath.

"It's not the way you're making it sound." The tightrope walker flailing her arms, trying to keep her balance.

"Yes or no?"

"Yes."

"Yes what?"

"Yes, one of them was John Fallon."

She was falling now, bracing for impact.

"What'd she say?" one of the Town Board members asked from the dais, hearing aid squealing with feedback from being turned up too loud.

People in the gallery began to whisper to one another, their voices light and sulfurous, like a hundred little match heads igniting at the same time.

"So you slept with my client's older brother while you were still going out with my client?" Gwen Florio plumped her lips, as if she was impressed with this as a feat of athleticism.

"I didn't sleep with him," Lynn protested weakly, already lying facedown in the sawdust. "We were friends and then . . ."

"Isn't it true that the two brothers physically fought over you?"

"Johnny was just trying to get Mike to leave me alone . . ."

"Oh, for God's sake." Jack Davis threw down a paper clip in disgust. "Are we reliving *High School Confidential* here? Is this a disciplinary hearing for Lieutenant Fallon or an attempt to pull the witness's pants down in public? Frankly, I'm embarrassed and I suspect the witness is as well."

Lynn tried to offer him a grateful smile, as if he were an anesthesiologist arriving halfway through her open-heart surgery.

"What I'm trying to establish is that this witness caused the breakup of a previously close-knit family that's been an important part of this community for generations." Florio turned to address the board. "She isn't just this innocent victim being stalked by my client. There was a complicated history here. It's no surprise that she was tense and ready to misinterpret anything he said when he showed up to investigate Mrs. Lanier's homicide. She was feeling guilty."

Lynn opened her mouth to argue, but Jack Davis cut in.

"I did not realize that along with being lovely and skillful as an attorney that Ms. Florio was also a talented mind reader," he said. "Perhaps she could rent a turban and a booth at the upcoming county fair to supplement her practice."

"All right, both of you, stop it," Mayor Flynn spoke up, forced into the role of beleaguered parent. Clearly, this was not what he had in mind during all those years he'd spent trawling through the local Kiwanis clubs and senior centers, looking for votes. "I hate this kind of thing. Mr. Davis, holster that famous wit of yours. Ms. Florio, finish up quickly and please spare us the graphic details."

"I appreciate your patience, Your Honor." Gwen Florio nodded sweetly. "Mrs. Schulman, can you tell us what happened to the relationship between my client and his brother after your little episode involving the two of them?"

Lynn searched for her voice. "I believe they stopped speaking for some years afterward."

"Would it surprise you to know that they never spoke again before John Fallon was killed?"

"I . . ."

This time, the gavel and Jack Davis's objection arrived simultaneously.

The mayor told Gwen Florio: "I believe we've heard enough about this."

But it was too late. Lynn had already been scraped off the ground, broken and bloodied. The book-club ladies were staring with a mixture of sympathy, embarrassment, and ill-concealed titillation.

Mike's wife stood up and walked out. Barry was motionless. To anyone else, he looked like a man watching a game from the sidelines. After all these years, though, Lynn was attuned to the more subtle indices: the tiny narrowing of the eyebrows, the minute thrust of the jaw. He was homicidal.

"Mrs. Schulman, in your earlier testimony and your statement to the chief, you said that Lieutenant Fallon came to your house twice in connection with the Lanier murder. Is that correct?" Gwen Florio rested her hand on the witness stand's railing, ready to finish her off.

"Yes, it is."

"And did he, in fact, ask you questions about Mrs. Lanier?"

"Yes, he did."

"Mrs. Schulman, I understand that your husband was a prosecutor and you yourself have some experience as a newspaper photographer taking pictures at crime scenes. Is it your understanding that sometimes investigators will try to engage a witness in conversation instead of just asking question after question?"

"I guess I've heard that."

"And did Detective Lieutenant Fallon try to do that on the two occasions that he stopped by your house?"

"Yes, but . . ." She felt pitted, exhausted.

"Didn't he try to talk to you about whether Mrs. Lanier had any enemies?"

"Sure, but . . ." She tried to rouse herself and put her guard up.

"And did he ask whether Mrs. Lanier and her husband were having any problems in their marriage?"

"Of course, but can I give a fuller answer?"

Having found a new rhythm, Florio lunged ahead. "And didn't you say, 'Who hasn't that's been married this many years?'"

Lynn flushed, hearing her own words being wielded against her. "I didn't mean it that way."

Barry kept staring at a spot just over her head, his mouth slowly hardening.

"And hadn't you recently talked to the lieutenant about 'getting together' outside work?"

"*Socially.*" Lynn turned to the board members, trying to make herself understood. "With the families."

But any sympathy that she'd hope to get from these dry gray men was quickly ebbing away. It didn't matter that she was a middle-aged woman with an SUV, two kids in the local school system, and a big house on Grace Hill. They knew an ungrateful little whore when they saw one.

"Over here, Mrs. Schulman. I'm the one asking the questions."

Gwen Florio bared her lower teeth in disdain. "So isn't it fair to say your relationship with the lieutenant wasn't just the usual one between investigator and material witness?"

"Of course not." Lynn drew herself up, deciding she'd had enough. "He hit me when I tried to break up with him," she said.

Gwen Florio smiled thinly at the counterpunch. "Was that before or after he found out you were sleeping with his brother?"

Lynn heard a reedy whisper and then a cymbal-like hiss from the spectator gallery. She looked up just in time to see Barry half-closing his eyes.

"I wasn't sleeping with him," Lynn insisted.

"Before or after you'd had *sexual contact*," Gwen said blandly. "We needn't get overly technical."

"Before," Lynn conceded. "And it wasn't . . ."

"So was it really entirely unexpected you wound up kissing the lieutenant when he came by your house?" Florio cut her off again.

"*I* didn't kiss him. He tried to kiss me."

"Uh-huh." Florio gave the men on the board a knowing look. "Wasn't it actually a magnanimous gesture that he hugged you back, a sign that he was trying to forgive you for what you'd done to him and his family?"

"No. It was something I didn't want."

"Sure you didn't." Gwen Florio strode over to a wall and leaned against it, striking a pose of coquettish impudence. "Isn't it true that you're a woman worried about getting older?"

"No. Not particularly."

"*Sure* you aren't."

Lynn caught Mike staring at her and glared back at him, acknowledging his cleverness in hiring a woman lawyer. A man would have to think twice about going after her this aggressively in open court.

"And isn't it true that there have been strains in your marriage lately?"

"No, not at all. I love my husband."

"Right." Gwen Florio nodded. "But isn't it true that after you came on to the lieutenant and he spurned your advances, you told your husband that you'd had an encounter in order to make him jealous?"

"Do I seriously have to answer this?" Lynn looked at Jack Davis.

The old lawyer gripped the sides of his chair and tried to hoist himself up again.

"Never mind." Gwen Florio turned her back to the witness stand and the dais. "I think I already know the answer."

"Ms. Florio, do you have any other questions?" The mayor massaged his temples.

"I'm almost done, Your Honor."

"Please be brief."

She wheeled on Lynn with a refreshed smile. "Mrs. Schulman, isn't it true that until recently your husband was vice president of legal affairs at a new company called Retrogenesis?"

Caught off-guard by the sudden change of pace, Lynn needed a second to answer. "Yes, he is. I mean, he was."

"Isn't it true that there was a short article in the *Wall Street Journal* yesterday about that company having to declare bankruptcy?"

"I guess so."

Obviously, Gwen Florio had done her homework on the Internet. A corner of Barry's mouth twitched.

"So wouldn't it be fair to say that your family has been going through quite a few emotional stresses and financial strains lately?"

"We're doing okay," Lynn said stiffly, in a voice that sounded unconvincing even to her own ears.

"But clearly you're having a bit of a shortfall, aren't you?"

"I don't know anybody who isn't . . ."

"But you have a substantial mortgage on your house and a child who's going to college next year, don't you?"

Lynn blanched as if the contents of her garbage cans had just been emptied onto her lap. "We'll be fine." She stared at Jack Davis, waiting for him to object.

"But until your husband finds another job you don't have any money coming in. Isn't that right? You're surviving on your savings, aren't you?"

Barry shook his head, knowing that there wasn't a damn thing he could do about this.

"Yes," Lynn admitted. "Yes, we are."

"So isn't it true that this entire hearing is a pretext for you and your husband to set up a civil suit against the Riverside Police Department for harassment and drain the town coffers because his business failed?"

Florio cast a sly tongue-in-cheek look at the board members, making sure that they understood that their interests were at stake as well.

"No, that's not true," Lynn raised her voice. "That has nothing to do with why I'm here."

The mayor banged the gavel wearily. "All right, Ms. Florio. That's enough. Do you have any other relevant questions?"

"No, Your Honor," the attorney said. "I do not."

For a few seconds, there were no more muttered asides, no coughing, no whispers. Just the uncomfortable squeak of people fidgeting in wooden pews as air leaked out of this case.

"Then, thank you, Mrs. Schulman." The mayor gave Lynn a terse nod without quite looking at her. "You may step down."

49

"WELL, that was fucking great." Barry slammed the driver's side door of the Saab and started the engine. "Is there anything else you might've forgotten to mention to me, like having syphilis or a half a million dollars in gambling debts?"

"Barry, I'm sorry. I tried to tell you before, but . . ."

They were in the parking lot behind Town Hall, watching the court buffs stream out the back of the building as the dusk fell over town and the sky turned the color of a raw bruise.

"Did you seriously think all of this wasn't going to come out?" He shook his head, barely able to look at her. "Did you really believe that you could get up and lie in court, the way you lied to me in our home? Are you crazy?"

"Can we go pick up the kids? It's getting dark, and people are leering at us."

Jeanine and her other friends rubbernecked as they walked to their own cars.

"Fine. Let them. See if I care. They can charge admission far as I'm concerned. Because I've gotta be the biggest sucker in the tristate."

A burly photographer with hair like a swatch of brown shag rug glued to his scalp and a green laminated press pass dangling from his neck stepped in front of the car and started shooting them through the windshield.

"Oh, terrific." Barry stepped on the gas and gave him the finger. "Where the hell did he come from? So was there a reporter in the courtroom as well?"

The car lurched forward, and the photographer jumped out of the way. Local stringer, Barry told himself. The major metropolitan dailies were probably still too busy covering 9/11 to send anybody up here to cover a measly disciplinary hearing. On the other hand, maybe having a story in the regional paper would be worse because more space would be devoted to it. From the corner of his eye, he saw Lynn fish a pair of Ray-Ban sunglasses out of her bag.

"You must really think you're something," he said, steering the car toward the lot's exit. "You fooled around with both of these guys and never told me about it?"

"We're talking about something that happened twenty-five years ago. Are you proud of everything you did when you were seventeen?"

He hesitated a moment, not quite able to rid himself of the memory of tipping Richie about the raid at Dr. Feelgood's. And that was when he was almost thirty.

"Well, what happened anyway?" he said, finding himself in a bottleneck behind at least a dozen other cars trying to get out of the lot. "How long did you manage to keep this little juggling act going with the brothers?"

"It wasn't a juggling act," she said fiercely, putting on the shades. "It only happened once. Okay? *Once*. And I've been sorry about it the rest of my life."

"I feel sick."

"Do you want to hear what happened, or do you want to keep berating me?"

"I'd like to hear the truth. That's what I'd like."

"It was senior year. I was burned out. I'd just had the abortion. The whole world was falling in on me."

"That's a convenient excuse, isn't it?"

"I'm not making an excuse," she said. "I'm telling you how it happened. I didn't know someday this was all going to come out in open court."

"Go ahead."

"So Mike was all over me all the time because I got rid of 'his baby.' He had this whole idea that we were going to get married. And at first it seemed okay because my mother had been so sick and I didn't know what else to do. And then she got better, and I realized that it was going to be this nightmare. That he'd never let me be out of his sight. And then after I had the abortion, forget about it. It was like dating the Taliban. No taking pictures, no short skirts, no going out on my own."

"Why didn't you just break up with him?"

"I tried, but he wouldn't let me alone. We were in the same school, so he could follow me everywhere. Or I'd wake up in the middle of the night and see him standing under my window, looking up at me from the lawn. Or he'd see me talking to another guy at a party, and he'd start smacking the guy around, looking for a fight. And then he hit me. It really started to get crazy."

"So, what'd his brother have to do with any of this?"

"Johnny tried to get in between us, kind of like a human shield. He kept telling Mike to leave me alone and get a grip. He was my bodyguard. And then after a while, I started feeling like I was closer to him than I was to Mike."

"Yeah, how did that work?"

"He used to come by the house sometimes to talk after his shift volunteering at the firehouse. Or we'd go out for a ride just to let some steam off. I really liked talking to him. Everyone else thought he was just this maniac, but he had this whole other sensitive side too. He loved his family and all that, but he also saw that they were strangling him. He had this Bruce Springsteen eight-track he used to play over and over in the car, the one with the song that says the door's open but the ride isn't free. And that's what he always used to say to me. That I had to get out, no matter what it cost in the long run."

"And so that's why you fucked him?"

"I didn't fuck him."

"All right. You blew him. Whatever. I don't need to hear all the grisly details."

"I don't know why it happened." Her face started to buckle behind her shades. "I guess those rides home just kept taking more and more detours. Sometimes, we'd go park by the river and get high and just talk. It was very . . ." She sagged, despairing of making him understand. "He was just this really strong guy, but you knew he wouldn't be around for very long . . ."

"Oh, so *that's* why you fucked him."

"I didn't — I . . . forget it. I'm not saying I'm glad that's what happened." She gathered herself up, refusing to be shamed any further. "I'm just telling you."

"Yeah, but you were going out with *his brother*. Didn't you think about what that was going to do to the two of them? Hadn't you ever heard of the word *consequences?*"

"I was an idiot, Barry. Okay? Are you happy? I was a complete fucking idiot. Or do you need me to say I was a little slut too?"

He quietly seethed, watching the mayor climb into the front of a navy Buick over on the right with an accordion-size court file under his arm and a look of strained exhaustion. In one part of his mind, Barry knew that he should be cool and rational. His wife was telling him about an indiscretion committed in another century, literally. But the middle of his brain remained stubbornly Neanderthal, not accepting that a woman of his could be so reckless.

"So why did you do it?" he said, tensing his shoulders and squeezing the vinyl-covered wheel.

"I don't know." She looked away in self-disgust. "Boredom. Stupidity. Maybe I just wanted to show Mikey he couldn't tell me what to do. Or maybe I was just trying to close that door behind me."

"Say what?"

"I'm saying, maybe once I made this big decision to get out of town, I had to make sure I couldn't come back too easily. So I had to slam the door behind me. I know that's what Johnny wanted to do. And then Mike and him had this terrible knockdown drag-out fight. I don't even know how Mike found out in the first place. But then they never spoke again. Johnny got killed."

"What happened?"

"I guess he was telling another idiot not to hit his girlfriend, and the guy pulled a gun on him." She shook her head. "I couldn't believe that when I heard it. He was this guy trying to break the chain, and it killed him. It literally killed him."

The tall red-eared court officer eased in front of them, driving a Chevy with bumper stickers that said "ABORTION KILLS" and "AN ARMED SOCIETY IS A POLITE SOCIETY."

"Shit." Barry pumped his foot up and down on the brake. "And you never had the decency to tell me about any of this? Didn't I ask you to level with me? Didn't I ask you to tell me what was going on so I wouldn't make a complete ass of myself?"

"I'm so sorry. I never thought I'd have to get back into all this again."

"Well, that's about the millionth thing you were wrong about, isn't it?" He hit the wheel in frustration, accidentally sounding the horn. "Along with thinking you could just come strolling back into this town . . ."

"I didn't know. I thought people would forget . . ."

"Well, obviously not everyone has as selective a memory. Seriously — what were you thinking? That they were just going to automatically forgive you because you're all grown-up now?"

"Maybe," she murmured, a single tear rolling out from under her Ray-Bans.

"Stop it," he said.

"I can't help it."

"Yes, you can." He rolled forward after the "ABORTION KILLS" car, heading for the guardhouse by the gate, where his ID had been checked earlier. "You know, it really doesn't bother me that you slept with this guy and his brother. Or at least I know it shouldn't bother me. What bothers me is that you lied to my face about it. You lay in bed next to me, looked me right in the eye, and lied your ass off when I asked you a straightforward question. You lied to me in the house I bought for you. Under the roof I paid to have re-done in slate. And you know what? It turns my stomach. How can I ever believe anything you say again?"

"Oh shut up, Barry."

"What?"

"I said, shut the fuck up."

"Excuse me?"

"You heard me. You've got a lot of nerve, talking to me about lies. When were you going to tell me about the stock falling and the company collapsing?"

"That's not the same thing." He stepped on the brake and pushed against the back of his seat.

"Like hell it isn't. We had most of our life savings tied up in that company. And most of the kids' college tuition. We sat at the kitchen table after we went to Windows on the World and *we* talked about *our* future. This was supposed to be a decision we made *together* with our eyes wide open. How long were you going to wait to tell me it was all going down the toilet?"

"That's different. I was trying to protect you from worrying about it."

"Bullshit. You were trying to protect yourself. God forbid anybody should ever think Barry Schulman was ever a failure at anything."

"Hey!"

"It's just win, win, win all the time with you. No wonder Clay has so much trouble talking to you . . ."

"Fuck you," he said.

"Fuck me? Fuck me?" Her voice broke. "How dare you. How dare you talk to your wife that way."

"You accuse me of letting our family down. What else do you want me to say?"

"How about, 'We've both made mistakes . . .'"

"Oh, how wonderfully feminine and compassionate. Well, screw that. Your lying has got us in this courtroom and the shit we're up to our necks in now."

"And your lying has me worrying about how we're going to make our next mortgage payment. I saw the last statement from Citibank . . ."

"Who asked you to open my mail?"

"And who asked you to put a joint account in your name alone?" she said. "I put money into that account too."

"Yeah, about three thousand dollars in the last three years."

"That was a low blow." She turned away from him. "You know I'm just getting my work going again."

"And who's been paying the bills in the meantime? Huh? The Ford Foundation? The National Endowment for the Arts? The United Way? No, it was me. Me. Barry Schulman, the *failure*. From Clifton Avenue in Newark and Barringer High School. You know what I'd like to hear for once? Not just oh, Barry, you don't spend enough time with the kids. Not oh, Barry, you never make time for us. Not oh, Barry, you don't know what goes on at this house and all the work I do to keep things running when you're not around. You know what I'd like to hear just for once? *Hurray. Good for you, Barry. You done good. Hurray for you, Barry. You did right by your family. Maybe you're not such a schmuck after all.*"

"I tell you that all the time."

"No, you don't. You make me live my whole life like I'm in debt."

"Well, you know what I think?" Lynn rounded on him, ready to defend herself. "I think that lawyer was right about one thing today. And I think she hit it right dead-center bull's-eye. This is a marriage that's in trouble. And I didn't see how serious it was until right now."

"Well, wake up and smell the coffee, baby. You're the one who left the fucking stove on!"

He stopped, realizing not only that they had been shouting, but that Michael Fallon and his lawyer, Gwen Florio, were standing just a few feet away from the car, staring at them through the streaky windows like newlyweds swearing they'd never end up this way.

"Oh, shit." Lynn blanched behind her sunglasses.

Barry honked his horn. "Come on already!"

"You think they could've heard us?"

"Must've made their day if they did."

"Do you think maybe we could put the swords down for a minute?"

"Yeah," Barry grumbled. "Maybe that would be a good idea."

The cars in front of him moved, and he cruised by Fallon slowly, keeping his eyes locked on the cop, letting him know that he had a bead on him.

"So, what do you want to do?" asked Lynn, sounding sober and subdued. "Do you want to continue this fight later?"

"I'm not sure what the point would be."

"It sounds like we've both been saving up ammunition for a while."

"Yeah, but this isn't the time to use it." He tried to relax his shoulders. "You turn on each other in the middle of a trial and you're dead."

He watched Gwen Florio rise up like a Degas ballerina on tiptoe to whisper something in Fallon's ear as she pointed at their passing car.

"So, what really happened that day anyway?" he said, taking a deep breath.

"Which day?"

"The day you were testifying about. The day he came into your studio and tried to kiss you."

"What are you asking me? It happened the way I said it did."

"Yeah, yeah. Yesterday I was lying, today I'm telling the truth."

"Today I *am* telling the truth. *Jesus!*" She balled up her fists. "I thought we were trying to *de*-escalate."

"Listen," he said, struggling to sound calm and judicious, "we're just talking like adults here, okay? Whatever the truth is, I'm going to have to find a way to live with it. But I *need* to know. I need the correct information to know what I'm supposed to do next."

"What is it that you're planning to do?"

"I just need you to give it to me straight, because it's not too late to say we've made a mistake."

"Barry, look at me."

She took off her Ray-Bans and stared at him. Her eyes were red and still brimming. The last time he'd seen her so completely cored was after she'd squeezed Clay out of her body and he tenderly laid the baby on her heaving chest. He sensed that this was another place where their marriage would either break or bend into a new shape.

"I was wrong not to tell you everything about Johnny the first time," she said. "I thought I could get away with it because I'm not the same person I was then. But you have to know that I've never been unfaithful to you. Not even for one day. I'm not saying I've never thought about other men, any more than you can honestly say you've never thought of other women . . ."

For a split second, he pictured Lisa Chang smiling and brushing her long black hair out of her eyes and then quickly banished the image from his mind.

"But I am saying that when it's counted, I've always been there for you. And you damn well know it."

He eased forward in silence for a few seconds, watching an old man with a cane pat Fallon on the back before the cop went to join his wife in the front of their Caprice. He saw them lock their doors and put on their seat belts without looking at each other. And in that instant, he decided he did not want to live the rest of his life that way.

"Okay," he said with a sigh.

"Okay what?"

"Okay. I'm going to believe you."

"Gee, thanks . . ."

She checked her eyes in the mirror and then decided that perhaps sarcasm wasn't quite the appropriate response here. She took a second to let the relief set in.

"I'm sorry," she said. "I should say I'm glad. And I should say I'm going to believe in you too."

"Yes, you should."

"Though how we're going to get through the next few months, I don't know."

"I'm more worried about the next few days." Barry took one quick look back at Fallon's car and then made a right turn out of the lot.

50

WHAT BOTHERED GWEN FLORIO MOST as she sat in the Riverview Diner with the client and his wife was not so much the quick craven stares from the old ladies in the booth across the aisle, the brusque pen-on-pad skitter as their waitress took their order without looking at Fallon, or even the grim tight-stitched expression Marie wore as she kept looking at her watch and dipping her tea bag nervously into her cup. It was the Thomas's English muffin with a light smear of butter that sat untouched on Mike's plate.

He'd skipped lunch to help her prepare for cross-examination this afternoon, and now she was urging him to eat something to keep his strength up.

"Marie, I know it's hard for you to take time off from work, but your presence is so important in the courtroom at this point." Gwen smiled at the wife in a show of womanly sympathy. "All you need to do is sit in the back for a few more minutes at the next hearing. Just to let the mayor and the rest of the board members know that you're still there for Mike."

Fallon bowed his head, still staring pensively at his plate. Probably meant nothing, Gwen tried to reassure herself.

"Because what you're doing is sending a strong message to the board," Gwen went on, not daring to break eye contact with Marie lest she get up and walk away. "You're saying, 'This is a family. This is my man. I believe in him. We're standing together in the storm. You will not break us apart.'"

Marie kept giving little nods, as if she were a dashboard figurine going over a bumpy road. She was shaky, but she was going to be all right. She was a good girl, Gwen realized. A truehearted girl. The type who'd always said her prayers, scrubbed the toilets at midnight, organized the closets on weekends, and never contradicted her man in public — even when he was making a total fool of himself. Someone, in short, she could never be friends with in her own private life. But she wasn't going to be the problem. She'd sit in the back of the courtroom and smile bravely and do whatever was necessary to keep up appearances.

Mike, on the other hand, was starting to scare her a little. He was getting the "dog face." That sunken resentful expression that seemed to suggest he expected a good whipping. He was writing too many feverish notes to her in court as well, which did nothing to convey the appearance of confidence to the board members. His thumb looked hideous, almost incriminating all by itself. She kept telling him to get it looked at by a doctor, that it wasn't healing properly. And finally, there was the matter of the uneaten muffin. Even as she kept up her spiel to Marie, Gwen found her eyes being drawn to it, thinking of how it was growing colder by the minute.

"I'm glad you were able to be there for this afternoon's testimony, because we scored some real points on Mrs. Schulman . . ."

Her eyes nipped over again quickly, trying to see if there was anything obviously wrong with the muffin. A fly circling. Green mold. Rancid butter. Probably meant nothing. But Florio's Grand Self-Indicting Cheeseburger Theory kept bothering her. Something her husband, Shep, used to say back in the old Yonkers days. Get a suspect in a room with a bag of White Castle cheeseburgers. If he starts eating, he's guilty. If he leaves them alone, he probably didn't do it — because what innocent man could stand to eat after he'd been falsely accused? As she did with most things her husband said when he was alive, she'd dismissed it out of hand.

Of course, now that he'd been dead five years, she'd started to admit there might be something to it. In the handful of cases she'd had in which the defendant was truly not guilty of all charges, she'd seen officers go on a kind of de facto hunger strike, picking disconsolately at their club sandwiches and potato salad like a bunch of bony-hipped schoolgirls. It was the part of the job she truly hated, watching substantial-looking men waste away like that. The guilty ones were always easier to represent. She never lost any sleep worrying that one of them was going upstate. You gave it your best shot, picked up the check, went home, and never thought about them again.

"So when do you think you'd need me?" Marie fumbled for the appointment book in her cloth handbag. "I have the kids out of school at three and meetings most of the day tomorrow. Are you still thinking this hearing is going to go for a full three days?"

"Hard to tell at this point. I'm supposed to have twenty-four hours' notice before any new witness is called who wasn't on the original list. Court is going to be closed tomorrow, and the chief and Mr. Schulman are on the schedule for the next day. But Jack Davis left the door open a little this afternoon, saying there might be some last-minute additions."

Mike touched his silverware tentatively, not daring to look at either woman.

He was a fool, Gwen told herself. Probably guilty of all charges, *in this case*. It was only her sly brilliance and legal brinkmanship that would get him an acquittal. *All hail Gwen Florio, queen of all strategists, defender of the boys in blue! The guiltier they are, the better I am for getting them off!*

But something had alarmed her in court this afternoon. A look that crossed Fallon's face when Sandi Lanier's name was mentioned. It wasn't the phonied-up outrage or even the fraudulent solemnity she would've expected. It was a sudden flinch in the eyes. No one else would've been close enough to see it. And even if they did, they might have taken it as the flinch of a guilty man confronted with the truth. But in that tiny spasm of muscle above the eyes, Gwen saw something else far more upsetting: a man facing a lie. And expecting *her* to do something about it.

"So do you think other people might come forward?" Marie put her appointment book away and leaned over her steaming cup of tea.

"That's always a possibility in a public hearing like this." Gwen lowered her voice. "Especially with that jingle of money from a civil suit in the background. Anybody can say just about anything, up to a point."

She cleared her throat, trying to get Mike's attention. But he was busy gazing off into the mid-distance, watching a long gray sliver of the Hudson churn past the restaurant windows.

"We're still going to win this, though, aren't we?" Marie asked. "We still have to live in this town. My children talk to their friends at school."

"I know how hard this must be for you, Marie." Gwen covered

her hand for a second. "That's why it's so essential to show the board that you haven't taken a step back from Mike."

"You didn't answer my question, though."

Marie took back her hand and scooped the tea bag out of her cup. "Are we going to *win?*" she said.

As Gwen watched Marie wrap twine around the sodden brown bag on her spoon, squeezing drops into her cup, she realized that she might have misjudged this woman. There was solid titanium under those pixie bangs and apple cheeks.

"I think there's a good chance we'll prevail," Gwen said, weighing her words carefully.

"I see."

Gwen watched her daintily wring out the last of the droplets and then set the flattened tea bag down on the side of her saucer. And in that instant, she understood that this was a woman who would know when to cut and run.

"Marie, I wonder if you could give Mike and me a few minutes to talk on our own," Gwen said. "There are a few minor points I need to go over with him."

"Of course, I understand." Marie signaled to a passing waitress. "Maybe I can get this tea in a cup to go. I have a few phone calls to make anyway. I can sit in the car outside."

"Thanks, hon," Mike said.

The first words they'd spoken directly to each other since they sat down. As Marie leaned over to give him a quick perfunctory kiss on the cheek, Gwen saw Mike's hand go up as if he was about to grab her wrist and hold on to it. But she was on her feet and out of reach before he could touch her.

For a moment, Gwen felt a small warm tickle of compassion for him. But then her eyes fell back to the uneaten muffin on his plate, reminding her of the terrible burden of trying to save what might be a falsely accused client, and her pity cooled into a cold hard lump in the pit of her stomach. *Don't worry about him. Just do your job and let the court decide.* But now he'd infected her with his misery. God-damn the innocent.

"Okay," Marie said. "He's all yours. See what *you* can do with him."

51

"BELIEVE ME, I understand your reluctance," said Barry, sitting at a wobbly kitchen table with a neatly folded napkin under one of the legs.

"You do, do you?" Muriel Navarro set down a cup of microwaved Sanka before him and lowered her eyes.

The three other nannies who shared this cramped little third-floor apartment above the recently closed Genovese drugstore on River Road were gathered in the other room, eating chips and watching a videotape of a television show called *Survivor*. With grave misgivings and icy courtesy, Muriel had invited him upstairs after he approached her on the street a few minutes ago, just so she wouldn't have to be seen talking to him out in the open.

"My wife was reluctant about testifying as well," he said.

She put a pink botanica bag down on the kitchen counter. "You don't want any milk with that?"

"No, thank you."

"You know I'm not doing this, right?"

"I completely understand your reasons."

"I only let you come up for a minute because I'm polite. It doesn't mean anything. Once you finish your coffee, I'd like you to leave."

"Of course." He carefully turned the cup on its saucer. "Maybe I would like a little milk to go with this."

She opened the buzzing old refrigerator, took out a quart, poured it into a delicate white pitcher with flowers around the border, and lightened his coffee for him. He sensed that there was a small chance here.

"She really took a beating in court today, my wife."

Muriel put the milk back in the refrigerator and closed the door.

"They brought up all kinds of things that she's never even told me about. Abortions, old boyfriends. They ripped her to shreds."

She turned her back to him and started taking newspaper-wrapped packages out of the bag. One by one, she carefully unfolded them, revealing a series of brightly colored candles poured into tall glasses.

"Whaddaya got there?" he said, studying the lettering on their sides. "Votives or prayerlites?"

She gave him a bemused look. "You know about botanica?"

"I used to work in the Bronx. We had one right around the corner on Gerard Avenue. I lit a nice fat *Causa de Corte* and an orange Chango for good luck every time I tried a case."

He didn't mention that it was the idea of a secretary in the office or that his supervisor, Sean Heffernan, always bitterly complained about the smell they left.

"So, what'd you buy?" he asked.

Muriel pursed her lips, looking faintly embarrassed. She seemed like the kind of young woman who'd spent her teen years smoking blunts and hoisting forties on the corner and had only begun to admit that there might be something to that old-time secret religion Grandma practiced in a back room on Southern Boulevard.

"Is that a Saint Michael?" he asked, pointing to a red candle.

"Saint Anthony," she corrected him.

She moved a long red-painted fingernail to the other candles in the row. "Infant of Prague," she said, reluctantly enumerating the names one at a time. "*Virgen Milagrosa, Sagrado Corazón de Jesus,* Seven Angels. This here is for Elegua, keeper of the crossroads" — she paused on a pink candle — "because my cousin's traveling. And this one . . ." She stopped on a green candle that said "Lotto" and had dollar signs on the glass. "This one is for me."

"What's that blue one on the end?"

"Saint Lazarus." She let her finger trail along the rim of the blue candle's glass. "Chiara, the little girl I look after, has been sick a couple of days. I'm praying for her. You're not supposed to fall in love with them, but you do. Bet you think that's dumb, right?"

"I won every single case when I lit a candle." He shrugged. "And even I wasn't *that* good."

She smiled in spite of herself and turned around to get some kitchen matches out of a drawer.

"Look" — he sipped the coffee slowly, finding it bitter on the back of his tongue — "I know testifying against the lieutenant is taking a risk . . ."

"You're damn straight. I don't have a husband who's a lawyer or a house in the West Hills. If I wind up in the river, ain't nobody gonna care except them kids I look after."

He watched her light the candles one by one. As each small flame sparked and slowly flickered up to its full height, he felt hope sputter and then revive again. He'd gotten no response to the twelve messages in four different locations for Iris Lopez, the other woman who'd filed a complaint against Fallon and then suddenly withdrawn it. If he didn't get this Muriel, he wasn't getting anybody.

"You know, my wife really surprised me today."

From the next room, he heard the other nannies groaning and gagging in unison, with one of them yelling, "*Ay dios mío!* I can't believe he ate that fuckin' rat!"

"I mean, at the time, I was furious with her because I thought she'd been lying to me all these years." Barry raised the coffee cup again. "But then, when I was outside waiting for you to show up, it occurred to me: she really went all the way out on a limb. Because she had to know she was going to take the hit. But she did it anyway. She got up and let them take their shots. Because she knew it was the right thing to do. It was an act of faith."

She took a step away from the counter and turned around, somehow still holding the candlelight in her eyes.

Keep going, he told himself. *This is your last shot.*

"You know what I mean? It was like she was sending up a flare. Saying, *Here I am. This is what happened to me. Is there anybody else out there?* It was like lighting a candle to draw people out of the dark."

She tucked a strand of hair behind her ear, studying the blue tips of the flames.

"So, what is it that you want me to do?" she said.

"I want you to go to the chief and the prosecuting attorney and give them a statement about what really happened between you and the lieutenant. And I want you to explain why you withdrew your original complaint. Because you know there's probably other women out there in the dark."

She looked back at the candles beside the sink, watching the flames waver and sway in the evening breeze through the half-open window. He almost missed it when she gave a tiny little nod.

"You want a fresh cup of coffee?" she asked.

52

AS HE GOT BACK from dropping all three kids off at school the next morning, Mike saw Harold's dark-blue LeSabre parked in his driveway. There was an instant pungency in the air, a bad smell about to reveal its source. He'd been in a foul mood to begin with. All this sitting around was starting to get to him. His body turning to mush: his face looking like a shucked oyster, his upper-body muscle dribbling down to his love handles. His thumb throbbing and changing colors with the season, the nail peeled back just enough to cause him constant discomfort without falling off.

He parked curbside, got out, and slammed the door behind him, taking an angry hunk out of the morning.

A pile of black pit-bull nuggets sat on the path to the front door. So this was how the neighbors welcomed him? Fine. He'd reckon with them too when the time came.

He stopped to pick up the mail on the porch and noticed he had a letter from his first wife, Doris, along with all the bills, probably complaining that he'd fallen behind on alimony again. Somehow she could sniff his wounds from three thousand miles away. *Women.*

He came up the steps and noticed that the door was already open. He went in and felt a pigeon fluttering inside his rib cage. The laundry had been put away. The refrigerator rattled, threatening to become the next appliance to turn on him. From the living room, he heard the hamster running on its treadmill, claws tumbling the steel bars over and over.

He came toward the kitchen and heard water dripping in the sink, reminding him about his latest failure with the plumber's wrench. When he turned it off, he saw Marie's teacup on the counter, with a bright scarlet lipstick stain still on the rim, as if she'd put it down in haste. The caulk gun was lying beside it. More evidence of her taking on the little projects he couldn't complete because of his bad thumb.

"Honey, what's going on?" he called out.

The door to the basement was wide open, deepening his sense of profound apprehension. The tensile roll of the hamster's treadmill faded, and his heart began to thump. He heard men talking calmly just above the grunt and rumble of his boiler. "You couldn't have got rid of it that easy," one was saying.

He came to the top of the stairs, and the smell of gas filled his nostrils.

"Hey, Harold!" he called out. "Is that you?"

"Anything?" Paco watched the chief broom Luminal powder across the surface of the table saw, checking it for bloodstains with the infrared light.

"Not that I can see." Harold, wearing special tinted glasses, scanned each shark-fin blade carefully. "No blood at all. You think he would've cut himself using it. People lose fingers all the time."

The two of them had been searching the basement for almost twenty minutes, armed with a warrant signed by Judge Harper and a statement from Muriel Navarro saying that Mike had blackmailed her into withdrawing her original complaint a couple of years ago. When the call came from Jack Davis just before midnight, saying that Barry Schulman had tracked the girl down, Harold was furious, smelling a setup. But after actually *hearing* the evidence for himself, he'd done a complete one-eighty. So here he was, searching his former best friend's basement. He tried to let his funeral director instincts take over. He was a servant of this community, he told himself. There were dire matters that needed to be attended to. No one ever said this was work for the faint of heart.

"Maybe he knew we were coming eventually and washed it down," said Paco.

"Nah, man. Look at this place. It's been years."

The basement was a mess. The rest of the house showed Marie's fastidiousness and attention to detail, but here, she'd given up trying. This was Mike's domain. An unfinished workshop with a dirt floor, an ancient octopus boiler covered in friable asbestos, and rusty ceiling pipes left half-insulated. It smelled of oil, sawdust, and airplane glue. On the work table, there was a cheap ProGen computer surrounded by bolts, hinges, and pieces of old radios taken apart but never put back together. Time got lost here. It rolled into corners and seeped into tiny spaces in the brick wall. It got covered in grime and soot and stacks of bundled old newspapers and sports equipment. It got buried under greasy bicycle wheels, bags of blacktop patch, paint-can lids, dismantled gearshifts, tangled fishing reels, and shoe boxes filled with Monopoly pieces, seashell soaps, spent shell casings, football trophies, Boy Scout merit badges, and, mysteriously, dozens of blue Corgi police cars and Tonka train engines.

"Here's what I'm thinking." Paco unplugged the computer and started to wrap up its power cord. "She's already dead when he brings her down here."

"Sandi?" Harold pushed the glasses up on top of his head.

"Yeah. Let's just say manual strangulation, for the hell of it. She wants to break it off. He doesn't. Whatever. We *know* they were fucking. They argue. They fight. Maybe they're just having too much fun. *Oops.* He chokes her. She turns blue." Paco let his head loll and his tongue hang out. "He's like, 'Oh shit, now what am I gonna do?'"

"Leave her in the motel parking lot where her car was." Harold carefully removed the circular saw from its groove, holding it daintily by its edge in his rubber-gloved fingertips. "Make it somebody else's problem in another jurisdiction."

"Maybe he thought someone saw him in the motel parking lot and figured they could ID him later. Maybe he just wigged."

"Come on, Paco. He's a cop."

"I know he's a cop, but he's human. We're all human. Right?"

Tiny specks from the ceiling drizzled down on Harold's head as he looked for a bag to put the saw blade in.

He wondered if maybe he shouldn't have begged off doing this search. Just before he'd left the house this morning, he'd finally broken down and called the state police to ask for help. They'd said they might be able to spare a senior investigator in about an hour and a half to help out. Perhaps he should've just waited outside for the guy to get here. But with Mike due back at any minute, he figured that they had to start to secure the evidence as soon as they could.

"I'm thinking he does her in the car and then maybe throws her in the trunk and drives her back here 'cause he doesn't know what the fuck else to do." Paco put the computer in a cardboard evidence box.

"Okay. I'm with you so far."

"He remembers that dump job from last spring, where they found the dealer's girlfriend floating in the river with her hands cut off so they couldn't ID her. So, what does he do? He decides to make it look like one of those by mutilating the body and throwing it in the water."

Harold looked up, not sure if he'd just heard a footstep.

"You don't like it," said Paco.

"He's got four people sleeping upstairs and a set of squeaky wood steps leading down to the basement." Harold lowered his voice. "The body's over a hundred pounds. He's going *thump, thump, thump,* carrying it down the stairs. And nobody wakes up?"

"We don't know if nobody wakes up. We haven't interrogated the rest of the family."

"It's got holes in it. That's all I want to say."

"Everything has holes."

"Not that many." Harold went to look at the slop sink in the corner. "Drainage would be a real issue down here. You ever see how much blood there is when a head gets severed? I'll show you the system we have at the funeral parlor one of these days."

Paco shrugged. "So he took his time and did it right."

"And then there's the river." Harold knelt down to study the underside of the sink with a flashlight.

"What about it?"

"Why would he dump the body in the river so close to town if he didn't want any of us to find it right away?"

"Whaddaya mean?" Paco rubbed the back of his ear. "He thought the tide would take it down toward the city."

"Are you out of your mind?" Harold took off his glove and touched the pipe to see if it was dry. "Have you ever looked at the way the current moves?"

"Chief, I'm from the South Bronx. All right?"

"It's an estuary," Harold explained. "It's constantly changing direction. If you dropped a stick off a bridge, it would go back and forth at least seven times before it made up its mind where to go."

"How am I supposed to know that? I'm not from around here."

"*Exactly*. Because if you were from around here, you wouldn't just roll a body into the water at low tide and expect to never see it again. You would know it would come back at you eventually."

The sides of Paco's head seemed to bulge and contract as he processed the idea. "You're telling me it has to be somebody from outside here who did it?"

"I'm not saying it has to be." Harold stood up. "I'm just saying that if you're from here, you'd know you couldn't get rid of it that easy."

They both heard the squeal and groaning press of a floorboard above them at the same moment. And then Mike calling down the stairs, "Hey, Harold! Is that you?"

Heart pinned up between his lungs like a piñata, Mike started down the steps and saw Paco standing by an open cardboard box with his computer inside.

"The fuck you think you're doing?" he said.

Men were in *his house*. Going into *his basement*. Touching *his things*.

"We got a warrant, Mike." Harold stepped into the light of a bare bulb, wearing one white latex glove, a liberal sprinkling of gray dust in his hair. "Marie saw it before she let us in."

"Marie let you in?"

"She said she had to get to work. And you'd be home soon."

"Let me see that warrant."

He trudged down the stairs, the treads creaking and threatening to snap under his weight. She'd let them in. *She had to get to work.* That's what he meant to her. On the last step, Harold handed him a warrant, still warm from his back pocket.

The words were a jumble before his eyes. He saw the name *Muriel Navarro* and the date *1998*. Slowly his eyes scanned the rest of the page, trying to make sense of it, stopping on the phrase *harassment and intimidation*.

"What IS this?"

"That baby-sitter you pulled over," said Harold. "She's decided to press charges again."

The warrant started to slip between his fingers. "Why?"

"Schulman FOIA'd her complaint and turned her up. She's saying you threatened her and made her drop the original charges. Said you were going to report her to the INS and send her back to El Salvador if she gave you trouble."

"Oh, fuck this and fuck you too. Fuck you twice." But his original rush of fury was already slowing to a cold trickle. "She's a greedy little bitch looking to get in on a civil suit with that shyster. And you know what? I don't blame her. I blame you. Thirty-two years and you don't have the balls to give me a heads up."

"She says you left messages on her answering machine."

"So what?"

"She kept one of the tapes."

Mike felt carbon soot fill up his lungs, slowly blackening his insides. "You've heard it?"

"She gave the tape to Schulman last night, and he gave it to Jack Davis, who played it for me. It ain't Dolby stereo, but a jury would get the idea. It's clearly your voice saying, 'You make trouble in my life, I'll make trouble in yours.'"

"I think I gotta call my lawyer." Mike sat down on the bottom step.

A distant rumble began in the back of his mind, like water rushing through a long dark tunnel.

"That's okay," said Harold. "But in the meantime, you need to understand that I'm going to have to turn over a copy to the DA's office so they can file charges . . ."

"Jesus Christ."

The cave-in. This was what a cave-in must feel like.

"Mike." Harold put a gentle hand on his shoulder. "You know, it's not going to end there."

Mike looked up and saw that Paco had opened one of his old shoe boxes and found his collection of squad cars and train engines.

"There are going to be others who come out of the woodwork," Harold said. "Aren't there?"

Mike probed the inside of his mouth with his tongue, finding a new canker sore in the wetlands of his cheek. The walls were narrowing on him. He had to give himself some breathing room.

"All right, so I had a thing with her," he said. "Is that what you want to hear? I got her doing sixty in a forty-five zone."

"This is when you were doing road stops?" asked Paco.

"Right after my brother got shot." Mike nodded. "Totally legiti-mate tactic. You never know when you're going to pull somebody over and find a gun in the glove compartment."

He saw Harold and Paco exchange skeptical looks, but in his heart he knew it was true: a part of him still dreamed of pulling over the Chevy his brother stopped that night on River Road.

"You thought that little baby-sitter was carrying a gat?" Paco arched one eyebrow.

"Okay, I caught a rap with her," Mike admitted. "I told her my mom looked after other people's kids too . . ."

"You banged her in the car and then tore up the speeding ticket," Paco interjected.

"Was it a chocolates and roses romance? No, probably not. Was she pissed about it later? I guess, maybe. She filed paper on me. Is it my proudest moment? Hey, I was going through a hard time."

"What about that answering machine tape?"

"Shit." Mike looked down at his thumb, seeing the nail hanging halfway off. "I made mistakes. I MADE SOME FUCKING MIS-TAKES. I knew I had a shot at the chief's office, and I freaked when her complaint came in. And then Marie got wind of it, and I was hanging by a thread. So I left this stupid message. Was I actually go-ing to do anything? Come on, Harold. Don't you know me better than that?"

Mike looked up at the chief, trying to find some small shred of understanding or fellow feeling to grab on to.

"I thought I did." Harold's eyes went cold. "But then you started doing all this crazy shit again. What about Sandi?"

"What about her?"

"Why didn't you tell me you were doing her?"

A hard lump of mucus lodged at the base of Mike's throat. "Who says I was?"

"Come on, Mike," said Harold. "We were all at the funeral. I saw you take the shovel out of the husband's hands."

"I was just paying my respects to a friend."

"Sure." Paco stepped up, crowding him a little more on the stairs. "Look, man, *de verdad*, I got you working on her fence. I got you signing out early all summer to go see her. I just went back and got Sandi's baby-sitter telling us she heard you upstairs while your truck was in the driveway. And now I got your computer."

He nodded toward the unplugged ProGen in the open cardboard box.

"What about it?" Mike swallowed hard, noticing the table saw had been pulled out and was lying on its side, teeth gleaming. "I use it to help the kids with their homework sometimes."

"Yeah, we'll see about that, Topcat," said Paco. "We're going to confiscate it and see what kind of e-mails you sent her."

They had him. Brick by brick they'd been building a wall around him, hemming him in. They moved closer as they stood over him on the stairs. Paco's belt buckle was level with his eyes, and the sight of the silver tongue poking through leather made him think of torture.

"All right, so what?" Mike said, realizing he'd waited far too long for this. "She wasn't getting any from the old man, so I helped her out a little. You gonna lock me up for that?"

"No, not for that," said Harold.

"Oh, come on. Everybody lies about sex. You know I've been trying to get back with Marie and the kids. I didn't need her to know I'd slipped up a couple of times. I'm a dog. I'm sorry. I'm a goddamn dog. But that doesn't make me an animal."

"Down at the train station," Harold murmured, studying the dust on his wing tips.

"Come again?"

"Down at the train station. You never said anything. When the body washed ashore. You saw the tattoo on the ankle. You saw the surgical scar on the breast and the liposuction scar on her ass."

"I wasn't sure."

"Of course you were sure. *You were fucking her, and you never said a damn thing to me about it!*"

They'd moved in so tight around him that he could barely breathe.

"I panicked, all right?" Mike shouted, trying to get them to back off. "I'd been fucking her and then she was dead. I knew how that was going to look when it all came out."

"And how's that?" Paco half-smiled.

"Listen, I'm not going to bullshit you anymore." Mike ignored him, appealing to Harold directly. "I got a wife and kids who I don't wanna lose. I kept thinking I was going to tell you, but things kept coming up."

"Like what?" asked Harold.

He thought of explaining about all the little mistakes he'd made, all the opportunities he'd missed. How he'd choked that first time Harold asked him about Sandi, how he'd been all set to come clean until he'd found that thing in the diary about strangling her. But then he stopped himself, realizing that he was in enough trouble.

"I made some bad decisions. By the time I was ready to turn around and give it to you straight-on, it was too late."

"So you deliberately impeded an investigation? Is that your story?" Paco tugged on his earring, playing the wiseass. "Tell me something: is that your baby she happened to be carrying?"

"Huh?"

"You said the old man wasn't giving her none. You could save us the expense of a DNA test right here."

"I don't know." Mike buried his face in his hands. "I seriously don't know."

"So why'd you kill her?" asked Harold.

"I didn't! It's the husband. That's what I've been trying to tell you all along. He must've found out about us."

"But then why are you the one who's been covering up all along?" asked Harold.

"*I'm telling you*, I thought I could stay on top of it. I thought I could keep my name out of it. I fucked up, okay? I didn't want to lose my job *and* my family. I was fighting for my life."

The red mist had fallen over him. His brain had locked up. He was off-balance, not fully in control of what he was saying. There was a part of him that knew he should stop talking immediately and call his lawyer.

But then Harold took the hand off his shoulder and hunched down so they were eye to eye with barely enough room for a closed fist between them.

"Michael, listen to me," he said. "I want to talk to you as a friend."

"A friend."

"I mean it. You have a choice here." Harold held his gaze. "You can keep going down this road and end up in a prison cell."

Mike gingerly pressed the blackened nail back onto his thumb. "My father worked at the prison." He grimaced, trying to hang tough.

"Then what about leaving your family destitute after all the lawyers' bills come through?"

Mike felt a bubble of misery form and expand inside his chest. "And what's my other choice?"

"You put an end to this right now and spare us all the charade and expense of a criminal trial, where you'll have to pay for an attorney out of your own pocket." Harold started to pull off his rubber glove. "I'll talk to the Town Board about setting up Marie and the kids with your three-quarters' pension. We'll do it quietly, as if it's survivors' benefits they're entitled to."

"Like I'm already dead to them," said Mike glumly.

"Yeah." Harold nodded, not trying to put a bow on it. "Like you're already dead."

Mike watched each of Harold's fingers pop out one by one with a little puff of resin. "What if I want to take it to trial?"

"Rearranging deck chairs on the *Titanic*." Harold hunched his shoulders. "We've already found bloodstains down here. As soon as we send them to the state crime lab, there won't be a thing I can do for you. Deal will be off the table."

But at that moment, Mike saw the chief's windbreaker ride up, revealing a band of navy Kevlar underneath. And in that small stretch of dark fabric, he saw a tender vulnerability, a piece of history, a place to strike.

"You're lying," he said.

He watched Harold's jaw grind and then loosen. The man was scared. So scared he'd put on a body armor vest today. Right over the place where he'd been stabbed by Brenda Carter.

"Okay," said Harold, feigning nonchalance. "I'm lying."

"You didn't find anything down here," Mike said, realizing he'd been gulled into saying more than he needed to. "You didn't find dick."

He stood up slowly, reclaiming the physical space and forcing them both back a foot. They'd been playing him, trying to make him feel cut off, as if the only way out was through them. He'd done it himself a hundred times at least, only better. He picked up the warrant that had fallen at his feet.

"I don't know what the hell you thought you'd find down here anyway," he said, studying the warrant as if he'd just woken up.

"This is off a three-year-old complaint. It's got nothing to do with Sandi."

"Prior bad acts," Paco said quietly. "We're establishing a pattern."

"You'll get laughed out of court." Mike looked from one to the other, nudging them farther back with his eyes. "Judge would've tossed anything you found here anyway. Fruit of a poisoned tree."

"If you say so." He saw Harold give Paco a worried glance, not ready to be challenged so directly.

"You never were worth a damn as an interrogator, Harold." Mike handed back the warrant and closed a fist around his thumb. "You couldn't even get Saint Augustine to confess. You always needed me to do the heavy lifting."

"Last chance." Harold stooped his shoulders, the vest appearing and then disappearing under his jacket. "This is your only exit."

"My lawyer."

"You sure about that?"

"I want to speak to my lawyer. You don't have a case."

"As we say at my other office: your funeral." Harold reached into his pocket and took out a pair of handcuffs.

"What the fuck's this?" Mike backed up on a step. "You don't have enough to charge me for the murder."

"But I got more than enough to get you on harassing and intimidating Muriel Navarro. Sorry, Mike. We're still within the statute of limitations. You're under arrest, my friend."

53

"OH."

The bright-pink hoop of Molly Pratt's mouth curved into a frozen smile as she realized it was too late to pretend she hadn't seen Lynn standing in line at the post office just before lunch.

"So, what brings *you* here?" Her mushroom-shaped hair bounced as she came over, but her cheeks looked filled with solidifying concrete.

"Just buying stamps," said Lynn, slumped and shy in the confines of her barn jacket.

A red dotted arrow flashed on the wall, moving the line along. Was everyone really looking at her? Testifying in open court had made her feel not merely ashamed but fundamentally unclean. She'd noticed several other moms hurrying past her with their eyes lowered when she'd dropped off Clay this morning.

She told herself that her reputation couldn't already be in ruins. It was mathematically impossible. Each friend who'd been in court would've had to tell ten people, who in turn had told ten others. But somehow she couldn't escape the feeling that wherever she went the person she used to be was strutting visibly and wantonly alongside her, like an image from a double-exposed photo.

"So is anybody talking about getting the book group together again for Tuesday?" she asked, noticing a clerk in a VFW cap, a white man in the gathering dusk of his years, staring at her through the thick glass partition.

"Oh, I don't know about this last one." Molly frowned disapprovingly. "I have such a hard time with not-so-happy endings and characters who do things that I'd never do."

Lynn hesitated, not sure how to take this. Again, she felt the bleak chill of Sandi's absence, of missing the one friend who'd goof on Molly's neo-Victorianism to her face.

"Well, it would just be nice to see everyone at something other than a funeral or a hearing." Lynn moved up a place in line, noticing the Wanted posters taped to the wall.

"I know what you mean." Molly nodded and looked at her watch. "It's gotten a little grim around here."

"Call me, all right?"

"Will do." Molly took two steps and then came back, realizing something else had to be said. "Lynn, I just want you to know that we're all still with you, and no one's judging you for the other day."

Lynn just stared at her as the red arrow flashed again. Judging *her?* As if none of them had ever done anything remotely scandalous. What about Anne Schaffer breaking her leg in three places driving drunk into a tree on Prospect? What about Jeanine stealing her father's prescription pad so she could sell drugs at BU? And what about Molly herself, busted for screwing the circulation manager at work and ruining her marriage?

Did they all think that Lynn was the one who'd been on trial? Hadn't they heard that Michael had been arrested yesterday morning and charged with harassing another woman?

"Hey, lady, next window's open," a man behind her said.

"I'll call you." Molly edged away with a fragile wave.

Feeling tainted afterward, Lynn decided to go on a cleaning purge to set her house in order. As soon as she walked in the door, she stripped off her clothes, put on some sweats, wiped the counters, did the laundry, mopped the floors, changed the linens, then took out the summer clothes and started to fold them to go back in the attic. Why did she wait so long?

She turned her attention to Barry's closet, deciding to be appalled before she even slid open the door. Wasn't some of this his fault as well? He hadn't exactly been a mediating influence, had he? To her disappointment, his suits were all hanging handsomely on evenly spaced wooden hangers. *When did he get to be so anal?* she thought. She slid the door open all the way, seeing his shoes lined up neatly and having the distinct sensation of being unwelcome. The only thing out of place here was an old Nike sneaker box jutting off the top shelf. Where did that come from? She stood on her toes, reaching, wondering if he was stowing a second set of tax receipts that he hadn't told her about. Ever since she'd realized he'd been lying to her about work, she'd found herself snooping around, trying to see what else he'd been concealing.

But the box was too high, and she decided to save it for later. Instead, she went out to the studio to do some work. François was breathing down her neck for a final edit for the show's catalog.

Perspective, he'd said. *I'm not seeing the image that pulls it all together.* Fuck you then, ya faux frog. She opened a file folder and started going over old contact sheets with a magnifying loop, still trying to find the right shot.

Under the glass, her most recent image of William the Revelator's house on Bank Street swelled up. An ancient pearl-colored A-frame with loose roof shingles, a snow-white cupola, and a crumbling chimney. For as long as Lynn could remember, a religious fanatic named William Pickett had lived there, gradually accumulating outdoor religious icons that grew more and more wild and flamboyant over the years. In the earliest picture of the series, taken when Lynn was about fourteen, there was just a modest placard above the door with a quote from Revelation: I AM HE THAT LIVETH, AND WAS DEAD; AND, BEHOLD, I AM ALIVE FOR EVERMORE. By the end of senior year, a three-foot-tall plastic Christ was crucified on the telephone pole on the front lawn. A picture taken on a visit to Mom in the mideighties showed a large plastic bald eagle added to the front porch railing, with a sign saying REPENT! around its neck. By the time she'd moved back a year and a half ago, a small windmill turned slowly beside a barren pear tree, and a pair of mannequins, a male and female in evening clothes, sat in a custard-yellow '63 Ford station wagon parked on the lawn like discarded models for idealized suburban living.

With William the Revelator's broken-toothed blessing (*Record it, child, so that the truth may be known*), she'd taken dozens of pictures of this scene, loving its sheer incongruity in these surroundings, its pure *out-thereness*, its impenetrability, and, most of all, the fact that nobody else in this town seemed to notice it.

But studying the picture in this light, she felt her enthusiasm start to turn on her. *Gawking*, François called it. If your pictures *aren't good enough, you aren't close enough*. She started to argue in her head. This was her hometown. She had a real feeling for this place. Even François

admitted that. But when she asked herself if she'd ever had a substantial conversation with William Pickett, even just to unlock the
true mystery of all this cryptic lawn furniture, all she could conjure
was the image of his fractured beatific grin.

You need to keep looking.

She put the Revelator pictures aside and opened a file marked
"Summer 2000," which was filled with images that she'd been meaning to scan onto the computer for editing. There was another series
of contact sheets inside, but she'd forgotten what was on most of
them. She'd vaguely recalled experimenting with light and the new
Canon, taking pictures of the kids asleep and Barry playing basketball at the Eisenhower Park courts, a man in motion, legs pumping,
arms extended, serving the ball to a hungry hoop. Her eyes moved
along the rows of filmstrips, picking out pictures she'd taken inside
the house and from the backyard, as if she had been documenting
her own life.

On the next sheet, though, the scene changed. A different house,
older and more careworn. A close-up showed tiny cracks on a white
shingle, like blood vessels in the paint. Another displayed a knot-
hole left by a woodpecker just above a window, something a casual
passerby would never notice. A friend's house. Again she remembered the slightly sordid charge she got from taking these shots, as
if each click of the shutter was a small betrayal.

Her eye moved down to the next row, finding Sandi in a two-
piece bathing suit, her ankle not yet marked by the butterfly tattoo.
Behind her was the kidney-shaped pool from the old house on
Sycamore Drive that she'd said was getting too small for the kids.

It was coming back to her. These were pictures she'd taken on a
late-August afternoon, almost a year before Sandi and Jeff's move to
the big new house on Love Lane. In the adjoining frame, the two of
them were dancing cheek-to-cheek at poolside, like Fred and Gin-
ger in swimsuits, the happy couple for all the world to see. But as
Lynn moved the magnifying glass over the shot, she noticed how
Jeff seemed to be looking past his wife a little, as if he'd just realized
they had an unexpected visitor.

It was nothing, she told herself. Maybe one of the children was
crying. Maybe a burger was burning or a phone was ringing in the
house. Things happen. Life doesn't always hold its pose.

She looked at the next shot, wishing this feeling would go away.

Jeff and Sandi on the back deck, Dylan in the foreground, swinging from the old tire hanging from the elm tree. Lynn noticed the mild clench of Jeff's jaw as he looked down at the boards. *Fungus.* She remembered both of them complaining about green algae rotting the deck. Everything about the old house became anathema to them. The kitchen was too small. The walls were too thin. The electrics were old. The neighbors were too close. *We're bursting at the seams!* Sandi had declared. Lynn recognized the familiar litany, the rising diminuendo of tiny tensions coming together.

In the next cel, Sandi was alone on the porch, looking off at the horizon, a woman reviewing her options. Surely it was a testament to their friendship that she'd let Lynn hang around taking pictures while they were having this awkward moment. Or maybe it showed how much a friend with a camera could get away with. A better woman might at least have put the Canon down awhile and pushed Dylan on the swing.

But then she would've missed the next sequence: Jeff coming out through the French doors with that furious clamped-down look. *All right, already. Get off my back.* They'd been fighting when she came over, Lynn remembered. She recalled thinking she should leave, but Sandi asked her to stay to look at pictures of some of the houses they were considering. In the next shot, Jeffrey was in action with a white tank full of bleach and a black sprayer, the Terminator wiping out deck rot. *See? I'm doing it.* In the adjoining cel, though, Sandi was throwing up her hands. *You're killing my roses! Look what you're doing to my ivy! Can't you watch where you're spraying?*

One of those Mr.-and-Mrs. things. She and Barry had probably managed two or three of these fights a week during various stressful periods, when the kids were young. But there was another kind of despair lurking in the margins. Again, she told herself that this was all hindsight, that she was just magnifying elements out of proportion.

But then her eye moved to the next frame.

Jeff was well into the next stage of his clean-up operation. Clear plastic tarp sheets were spread over Sandi's plants. The fungus had been scrubbed off, and the bleach had been put away. Another sprayer tank had been deployed. Jeff had donned thick goggles and a pair of black rubber gloves, showing the women present that this was how a real man took care of his home. Lynn suddenly remembered how surprised and impressed she'd been to see how much of the proper equipment he'd had just sitting in the garage, waiting to be used. Perhaps she'd even remarked that she wished that she could get Barry to be this handy around the house.

And there in the lower right-hand corner, its white label facing the camera so the black letters could be read clearly, was an open gallon of Thompson's Wood Protector.

She moved the magnifying glass aside and got up from her stool, remembering her mother saying how certain things that Diane Arbus saw made her want to kill herself.

54

"NEXT CASE. Call the docket number."

Judge Henry "Highball" Harper, looking something like an old gray pigeon huddled on a window ledge, winced from the sound of his own gavel and turned to his court officer.

"Number 31279984," announced Tony Shlanger. "This is the bail application for the *People versus Michael Fallon.*"

Michael shuffled into the courtroom, wearing the orange jumpsuit he'd been issued at the county jail in Valhalla. He was pale and unshaven, and even though the warden had put him in the protective custody section for his own safety, he hadn't been able to sleep well last night with all the noise and taunts raining down on him from the upper tier. *Hey, sweet thang. . . . Yo, Biggie Smalls, get ready to take my load. . . . Yo, Sergeant, remember me? No justice, no sleep! Yo, Biggie Smalls . . . where's your nightstick, baby? Hey, Officer, you gonna be my honey pot?*

In the middle of the night, he'd sat up with pain shooting up his arm, realizing that his thumbnail had finally fallen off under his pillow. There was so much blood it looked like there'd been a small animal sacrifice on his cot. After all this time, the thumb still hadn't been ready to lose its cover. The new nail had barely grown, and the tissue was mashed and pulpy underneath, like a beaten face. Over the next few hours, his whole hand started to swell, and a fever crept up on him. He called for the guard on the gate, but his father's friend Larry Marshall had gone home and been replaced on the graveyard shift by a black Muslim C.O., who called himself Malik Bin Muhammad and clearly had little regard for pedigree. He waited until six in the morning before he brought Mike a small half-used tube of Neosporin, a little dressing, and two Advil.

But now, as he stood beside Gwen Florio at the defense table, he felt the ibuprofen wearing off and the fever starting to come back. He looked quickly over his shoulder to see if Marie was in the gallery this morning. But there was no sign of her. Only the regular courtroom buffs filling in the first two rows and the old man by himself in the back, his face lean and alert as a falcon's, his self-cut hair a shade of gunmetal gray.

The judge slowly moved his dim filmy eyes from Mike to Brian Bonfiglio at the prosecutor's table.

"Mr. Bonfiglio" — he cleared his throat — "what are you doing here today? This defendant has been in and out of this courthouse so much lately that it's a little hard to keep track of it all."

"Of course, Your Honor." The assistant district attorney smiled ingratiatingly. "We're here to oppose bail for Mr. Fallon on the harassment and intimidation charges. Our office is taking the position that there's a significant risk of flight in this matter."

Perfect that he'd be handling this case, thought Mike. Bonfiglio had been the ADA assigned to cases in this jurisdiction for several years. Most officers in the Riverside Department called him El Exigente the Demanding One because he was always sending them out over and over, insisting they get overwhelming amounts of corroborating evidence so he wouldn't have to put any real effort into prosecuting the drug cases they brought him. But to Mike, he'd always be That Ungrateful Little Bitch.

"Your Honor, with all due respect — or at least all the respect that remark is due — that's absurd." Gwen Florio stood up beside him, huffy and impatient to get on to a client paying her some real money. "This defendant isn't going anywhere. He has deep roots in this community. His family has served this town for generations."

Mike felt his chest cratering as the judge's eyes roamed past him. "Is his wife here today?"

"No, Your Honor." Mike bowed his head, speaking up for himself. "We have three children, and she has a regular job in hospital accounting. She's already missed time at work."

He knew it was over as soon as he saw the teacup with the stain and the caulk gun by the sink. That was the surrender flag. She'd had it. She'd given up the fight. In a way, he couldn't blame her. She'd given him a chance. Said if he could keep it in his pants and let her keep her dignity, she'd try to find a way to carry on with the marriage. But no, he couldn't do it. He just had to keep spreading his seed around town, laying claim to the women one by one.

He thought of throwing himself on the mercy of the court. *Your Honor, I have a sickness. I know I need help. I'm powerless before my addiction. It started with my mother. But you don't know what it's like. Say you're sitting in a Caprice by the side of the road at midnight with your radar gun. You're bored. It's cold. You've got all this pressure building up inside you. And then you see these little lights coming up from the road. It gives you a kind of hope. You see it's a woman. And you know that when you pull out and put on the cherry top, they'll have to slow down. That you already have that much power over them. It creeps up on you, bit by bit. You make them stop, you talk to them, you get a good look in their eyes and see if. . . .* But that was only part of the story. The truth was, all those women had gotten something out of the deal as well. Lynn, Sandi, even that little Salvadoran baby-sitter, who'd been speeding and weaving all over the road. They'd needed him. Hell, he wouldn't have gone after them in the first place if they hadn't been signaling. And if he got a little something in return, well that was his right after everything he'd done for this town.

But oh no, you couldn't say that in open court. *So go ahead. Just make me the bad guy. Blame it all on me. It's okay. I can handle it. Make me the scapegoat for all your little sky-is-falling hysteria. That's what I'm here for.*

"Mr. Bon-fig-glio," the judge said, picking his way cautiously over the rocky terrain of syllables. "I have to tell you that my initial inclination is to deny your motion. This defendant has been in my courtroom many times over the years, testifying as a police officer, and he's always been very punctual and conscientious about his appearances."

"I understand that, but things have changed," said the Demanding One, a chinless wonder preening before the bench. "I'd like to request a sidebar. There are elements pertaining to this matter that can't be discussed in open court."

Mike turned to look at him, the wound under his gauze festering. So this was the thanks he got: lies, rumors, insinuendo. A few words mumbled into the judge's ear about him being the target of an ongoing homicide investigation. Sepsis was setting in. His immunity had been compromised. It wasn't just the nail coming off these last few days. He'd lost all his natural protections. Not a single cop had shown up from the department today. How surprised could he be? These last few weeks he'd felt like his skin was being stripped off a layer at a time. You take a man's job, his reputation, and his family and what does he have left? A wound rubbed raw, oozing blood and pus.

The judge was shaking his head. "I'm sorry, Mr. Bonfiglio," he said. "This is a small-town courtroom, not a secret military tribunal. You either put up or shut up, evidencewise."

"Then I'm asking your honor to set bail at one hundred thousand dollars to insure this defendant's next appearance."

The judge looked wearily over at the defense table. "Can you do twenty-five thousand?"

For a few seconds, Mike didn't react. There was less than seven hundred dollars left in the account. He wouldn't even be able to pay Gwen for today's appearance; already she'd told him he'd have to get a public defender if he was charged for the murder.

He started to steel himself for another night in the county lockup. *Valhalla.* Wasn't that supposed to be where heroes went after they died? He thought about the endless hullabaloo of the cell block and the seething hiss of the shower room, where he knew that someone would eventually be waiting for him.

"I can do it," said a voice behind him.

Mike turned to see the old man with the gunmetal hair slowly getting to his feet and coughing into his fist.

"I can give you ten percent cash bond right now, and I'll put up my trailer as collateral for the rest," the old man said, his voice choked and dry from years of smoking Lucky Strikes and breathing in foul tubercular prison air.

The judge stared at him for a while, only gradually putting the familiar face into context. "Sure about that, Patrick? If he bolts, you lose the roof over your head."

The old man spread his arms, ropey muscles still taut across his chest.

"Ah, for Chrissake, let me take 'im home, Hank." The old man started to maneuver his way up the center aisle. "He's the only son I got left."

55

LYNN STUDIED THE DETECTIVE'S EXPRESSION after she handed him the photo in the police station parking lot. But the shaved head remained smooth, and the black loop of his goatee stayed loose around his mouth. He would've been a hard man to be married to or to play poker with.

"I'm a wreck about this," she said.

"How'd you know we were looking into the wood protector anyway?"

"Jeffrey told me himself when I saw him at the train station. I guess he must've forgotten that I took those pictures." She chewed her lip. "Not that I made a big point of showing them to him later."

Finally she saw a slight back-and-forth movement of Paco's eyes as he scanned the picture of Jeff spraying wood protector on the back deck.

"He did it, didn't he? He actually killed Sandi."

Like most cops she'd met, he acted like almost any question from an ordinary citizen was a potential violation of protocol.

"Have you shown anyone else this photo?" he asked.

"No. I just told my husband about it on the phone and made a print for you."

"I'd like it if you kept quiet about it and asked your husband to do the same. We have an investigation going on."

"Of course." She nodded. "I just feel so terrible about Mike."

"What about him?" A wavy line squiggled across his forehead, as if it were measuring amplitude.

"I don't know. I figured you must've started looking at him as a suspect after I filed that complaint against him. Mr. Davis told me that you arrested him yesterday."

"Yes, we did." The wavy line deepened. "Fact, he's in court right now. But lemme ask *you* something."

"What?"

"Did he do everything you said he did when he came to your house?"

"Yes."

"Did he stop your husband in his car after he complained to the chief?"

"I guess he did."

"And did your husband pay off Muriel Navarro to file a statement against him?"

"No, of course not." She heard the hesitation in her own voice as she realized how much she didn't know about Barry lately. "At least not as far as I'm aware of."

"Then you got nothing to worry about." The wavy line flattened. "Mike made his own problems. Once a man decides to pull the roof down on his own head, ain't a woman alive can stop him."

56

HANGING ON. That rain gutter was still hanging on to the front of the house, Jeff Lanier noticed as he came down the porch steps to get the morning paper. He'd been meaning to get up on the ladder and drill a couple of new holes to screw it back along the eaves, but he had to be careful about looking too handy these days. And the truth was, he'd always had a fear of heights.

Had it ever since he was an eight-year-old going up in the Cessna his father rented outside the base in Frankfurt. Horrible things, those dinky propeller planes. You felt everything inside them. Every little dip and air pocket, every tiny bit of turbulence and wind resistance. To this day, a part of Jeff still felt the tremors whenever his feet left the ground. He'd felt it that afternoon over Labor Day weekend when Sandi made him go up on the ladder to clean the leaves out of the gutter. Lazy cunt. Couldn't do it herself, could she? Had to get him up while he was watching the Mets-Phillies game. She probably liked that part of it best. Making sure he never got too relaxed. Never missing a chance to remind him that he needed to earn his keep around here since they were borrowing so much from her father. Never passing up an opportunity to make him feel like less than a man.

Probably he should have just told her to go take a Valium and lie down. Maybe then she'd still be alive.

But she could never leave anything alone. She was like a little rat terrier once she got her teeth into something. She kept nagging him and nagging him, even though she knew all about his vertigo. So all right. He'd put down the can of Diet Sprite and left the game on. How many leaves could there be in the gutters at the beginning of September anyway?

But, of course, she had to make everything harder. *Don't put the ladder down in my flower bed. Don't lean it against the side of the house, you'll leave a mark on the shingles.* The dizziness started as he put his foot on the second rung. *Don't touch my ivy. Don't leave a handprint.* By the fourth rung, he was starting to get a little nauseated. *Watch out for the trellis* (she had to have the same one her friend Lynn had). *You're crushing my day lilies.* He had to move the ladder again. *Sure you don't want to do this yourself?* he'd asked her as he climbed up again. *Don't hang on to the gutter,* she'd warned him as he reached the top.

The air had seemed thinner up there, the humidity stilling everything but the insects. This one mosquito kept circling his head, drawing close to one ear and then to the other just as he was about to swat it. He took a deep breath, steadying himself, as he reached into the gutter. The leaves had a deep moist primordial odor, as if they'd been trapped there since the Mesozoic era. But then the ladder began to tilt, unbalancing him.

Instinctively, he'd grabbed the side of the gutter, trying to right himself.

Don't do that! she'd shouted from below. *You'll tear it off the house.*

Standing on the top rung, some fifteen feet off the ground, he'd tried to shift his center of gravity, but it was too late. One leg of the ladder was sinking deeper into the soil below.

Help me, he'd said. *Hold it for me.*

But he'd already started to lose his footing. The ladder gave way just as she stepped on the first rung. Then there was nothing holding him up. Blue sky and gray clouds receded as his hands flailed out, catching the edge of the gutter.

Let it go! she'd shrieked as he dangled above her, hanging on for his life.

I can't. I'll fall.

But you're going to break the gutter off. Just let go of it.

And with those words, his marriage probably ended. Because in that moment, he realized she cared more about this damn house and the image of perfection than she did about him. The gutter had wrenched away an inch from the eaves, and he fell then, landing hard on his flank beside the rosebush, leaving a bruise from hip to knee.

She'd actually giggled as she'd helped him up and brushed him off. *Are you all right?* she'd asked. But her concern was an act. Just another role she was playing: the worried little wife. He'd seen the truth when he was up on the ladder, looking down. He was a thing she was arranging in her life, an element to be handled and moved around. It wasn't so much that he'd decided to kill her then. It was that the idea of killing her became just a little bit less of a stark impossibility.

He looked up and saw that the drainage pipe leading from the gutters down to the ground was leaning to the left. He must have kicked it when he fell. An accident, just like the one a few weeks later.

He snap-locked that door mentally. Technically, he was the one who'd been wronged. She'd lied. She'd betrayed him. She'd been talking to a divorce lawyer behind his back. She was going to take everything from him. Her father was going to cut him off and make him sell what was left of the business at garage-sale prices.

And then he found out that she'd been screwing the fence guy. Yeah, okay, she'd finally glommed on to the fact that he'd been getting a little on the side himself these last few years, so she was probably just looking for some payback with this cop, but *come on*. She'd had two kids and a lumpectomy. All that life and death stuff, it wasn't exactly an incentive to keep fucking her, was it? He had to get it from somewhere. But she was doing it in *their house*, as well as the motel up the parkway. She didn't even have the decency to do it in another state, the way he did on the road. She was reckless, that's what she was. Looking for trouble, fooling around with that guy Fallon. What if the kids had come home early one day? Did she even think for a second about what that could do to them? And then after she'd died, he realized she'd left her diary lying around, as if she wanted him to find it. He had to tear out all the pages about himself. You had to admit it: the woman just had no common sense or consideration.

"Hey, slick, I'm glad I caught you. Looks like you're going somewhere."

Paco Ortiz came up the path just as Jeff was rising with the blue-wrapped *Times* in his hand.

"Oh." He buttoned his Armani jacket. "I'm just on my way to a business meeting in the city."

"Yeah? So how's it going?"

"Good." Jeff gave him a mournful smile. "Well, I mean, good as can be reasonably expected. Kids are trying to adjust. We've all been through a lot."

"We sure have." The detective grinned, showing a few more teeth than Jeff would've liked. "That boolshit be so thick sometime I feel like I'm a need a periscope to see above it. You know how I'm saying?"

His Nuyorican accent seemed heavier today, as if he was ladling it on for effect. Jeff found himself looking behind the detective a little, half-expecting to see dirt tracked onto the porch.

"So, what can I do for you today?" He looked at his Raymond Weil watch nervously. "I'm sorry, I'm in a little bit of a hurry."

"Hey, that's all right," the detective said, glancing back at the red Benz in the driveway as if he had all the time in the world himself. "I just had a couple of follow-ups. I guess you heard we locked the lieutenant up."

"I thought that was on a separate matter."

"Yeah, we'll see about that. Town this size, everything eventually connects. Right?"

"I wouldn't know. I'm not from around here originally."

"Riiiiight." The detective snapped his fingers without making a sound. "I'm not a native either. But I'm learning."

"Anyway . . ."

"Yeah, anyway, I'm a want to ask you about something you said the last time."

"Okay."

"Remember how you told me you were no good at fixing things around the house?"

"I don't recall saying that specifically. I might have been feeling a little overtaxed right at that moment."

"I hear you." The detective smiled and reached inside his jacket. "Can I tell you your exact words?"

"Sure."

All right, Jeff thought. *What's he doing here? What does he want?* His eyes went up to the detached gutter beside the roof and then came back, just as the detective pulled out his notebook.

"You said, 'My wife said we were married almost ten years and she never even saw me pick up a screwdriver.'"

"Did I? Well, I guess I *was* feeling helpless."

"Do you remember why that came up?"

"No, not really." Jeff tugged lightly at the end of his tie.

"We were talking about some of the work the lieutenant had done on your backyard fence. Does that refresh your memory?"

"Perhaps a little bit."

His eyes fixed on a rolled-up eight-by-eleven manila envelope that the detective had sticking out of his windbreaker pocket.

"You said, 'I don't get that involved.'"

"I was probably exaggerating slightly."

"Can I show you a couple of pictures?"

"Certainly," Jeff said. "Could I stop you?"

A cold tongue of apprehension flicked the back of his ear. Whatever it is, don't look surprised. Don't react. He's playing with you.

The detective put the notebook away and took the envelope out, slowly unwinding the red twine that fastened it shut. He slid the first picture out and presented it with a kind of half-formal flourish.

The first thing Jeff noticed as he took the black-and-white print by its edges was how much younger he looked in it. Gray had yet to powder his temples. Those two little divots hadn't deepened between his eyebrows. His jawline still had its youthful sleekness. Sandi, on the other hand, looked like she'd been yelling at him all morning. She had those dark circles under her eyes and taut brackets around her mouth. He willed himself not to look at her throat.

"Okay," he said, handing it back to the detective. "Her friend Lynn took this awhile ago, when we were still at the old house. She was trying out a new camera, I think."

"Got quite an eye, that lady."

"Yeah, she's a pro."

The detective handed him the second picture, and immediately Jeff's stomach shriveled to the size of a peanut. The goggles and black gloves made him look a little like an astronaut. The white spray tank glowed brightly against the backdrop of the French doors and drab shingles. The tarp had been carefully spread over Sandi's plants so he wouldn't kill them this time. And, of course, the gallon can of Thompson's Wood Protector was in plain sight in the corner of the frame.

"Well, I never said I was totally useless around the house," he said, coolly handing it back.

Got quite an eye, that lady.

"I'm just a little confused about why you said that originally." The folds in Ortiz's grin sharpened — a smooth operator this one. "You said the wood protector belonged to the lieutenant."

"Obviously I wasn't thinking clearly."

Otherwise I would have remembered that picture. He'd told Sandi he didn't like Lynn hanging around with the camera. He'd said that, hadn't he? *She makes me feel like I'm in a zoo. This is our house. When's she going to leave?* He'd always been suspicious of all her friends, but Lynn especially. She always managed to be just around the corner when you were having an argument with your wife. He remembered how much she'd annoyed him that day with her new camera, to the point where he wanted to rip it from around her neck and throw it in the bushes.

"Looks like you're ready for the cleanup too." Ortiz held the picture up so they could both look at it. "You got the gloves. The goggles. The tarp over the plants."

"My wife asked me to be careful spraying the deck, so I wouldn't hurt her flowers."

"Good for you. Lot of guys wouldn't be that considerate."

All right, don't panic. That was the problem with everything that led up to this. He'd moved too fast. Clear your mind. What does this cop know?

"For real, man." Ortiz shook his head in admiration. "The way I see you clean up after yourself, spreading out that plastic and shit, made me think about the way I do *my* job."

"I don't know that I did any more than anyone else would under the circumstances." Jeffrey shrugged.

"Hey, don't sell yourself short, bro. You're a thorough man."

The Thompson's can. He shouldn't have used the Thompson's to weigh the bag down.

"So now I'm trying to be a little more thorough," said the detective.

Jeff looked at his watch again and smiled haplessly. "You're going to make me miss my train."

"Just bear with me another sec. I-ight?" Ortiz took a small sidestep, blocking the path with his stocky frame. "You rented a car that weekend you were in Boston and Rhode Island, right?"

"Sure. I've been over this with you . . ."

"Okay . . . *no se ocupe.* No sweat. I just wanted to make sure of something." Paco gave him a humble look, as if he expected to be congratulated. "You know, I'd asked a state trooper in Boston to check out the car you'd been driving. And he'd told me everything looked cool. But you know, it's not the same as being there. So I called Avis myself this morning."

"You did?" Jeffrey felt his expression start to buckle and crack.

"And I asked them to check the computer for your mileage, instead of just looking at what you wrote down on the bill, the way the trooper did. And guess what?"

"What?" His mouth felt full of used cotton.

"He missed about two hundred miles you drove that weekend. How do you like that?"

An old childhood fantasy flashed through Jeffrey's head, the one about grabbing a policeman's gun out of his holster and turning it on him.

"Detective, I really have to go." He licked his lips. "People are waiting for me."

"Okay, just hold on another minute." Ortiz put his hands up, as if he was about to grab Jeffrey by the lapels. "This is your wife we're talking about, right?"

"Of course."

"So where'd you go, those two hundred miles?"

"I think I was clear about that." Jeff touched his brow self-consciously. "I went sailing with some friends in New London."

"Well, I'm not much of a sailor, but that ain't no two hundred miles from New London to Providence, my friend. They're not that far apart."

"So, what are you suggesting?" Jeff said evenly, a small cool pearl of sweat forming on the top of his head.

"I'm thinking maybe you went somewhere Sunday night that you forgot to mention to me. Did I ever ask you what *Moulin Rouge* was about?"

"It's a love story."

He'd gleaned that much from the reviews and told himself to see the whole movie sometime so he could describe the plot in detail if a question ever came up.

"A love story." The detective snorted. "Like a love triangle?"

"Something like that." The pearl of sweat began to roll back toward where Jeff's hair was thinning, leaving a damp trail across his scalp. "There's a lot of singing and dancing."

"I see."

Without warning, the detective suddenly reached out and picked at Jeff's breast pocket, as if he'd just noticed a loose thread. It was such an intrusion, such a willful violation, that Jeff actually stiffened. *The temerity.* The nerve. He might as well have just said, "You are my bitch, and I can lay hands on you anytime I like."

"You had a piece of lint." The detective brushed at the fabric with his fingers.

"Thank you."

"It's funny, you talk about a love triangle. I guess you know your wife and the lieutenant had a relationship."

Another sweat pearl formed, following the pioneer across the scalp and down the back of his neck. "That's still not an easy thing for me to hear."

"I'm sure it isn't. But there it is. We've had a chance to look at both of their computers, and it's in the files once you figure out how to get in them. They wrote each other e-mails. Mostly in code, arranging times and places to meet."

"Are you enjoying this?"

"I'm doing my job, Mr. Lanier." Again the fingers brushed Jeff's pocket. "But when I looked at the lieutenant's computer this morning, I noticed something strange."

"And what's that?"

"That his screen name is Topcat one oh five. With a dot between the word and the number. Topcat dot one oh five."

"So what?" Jeff looked down, realizing the fingers were lingering on his chest a little longer this time, almost as if they were monitoring his heartbeat.

"The last e-mail message to your wife, asking her to come to the motel is from Topcat one oh five. Get it? The dot is missing."

"The what?" A third and fourth bead popped on top of his head as he moved back.

"The dot, man. The dot." Fingertips poked him, three hard points digging in. "It's a different address. Somebody else sent that e-mail. It didn't come from the loo."

"Maybe he changed his address."

Jeff felt his heart laboring violently and wondered if the cop could feel it as well.

"No, man. I looked at his computer. He didn't send it. Somebody else did, trying to set your wife up and catch her stepping out at that motel. That's the thing with computers. It's not the telephone or a letter, where you could recognize the handwriting. You could be talking to anybody and not know it. They call that shit *spoofing*."

"Don't touch me," he said, barely resisting the urge to swat the fingers away. "All right?"

"You work a lot with computers in your business. Don't you?" said the cop, not in the least put off. "You trade that old sports crap on-line all day."

"I think I'd like you to leave now."

"Why? Am I upsetting you?"

"No. I just think it would be more appropriate if I spoke to my lawyer before I made any more statements . . ."

"Yeah, and why is that?"

"I . . . just don't feel . . . comfortable . . ."

His scalp was starting to feel like a hot skillet, one bead after another popping up and finding its way through the strands and into the clearing.

"Look, man. I understand. Really I do. If I caught another mule kicking in my stall, I can't say what I'd do. Especially with all her daddy's money on the line. That's what I'd call a mitigating factor, bro. Extreme emotional distress. Any man could understand that."

"This conversation is over." Jeff started to march past him toward the gauntlet of automatic sprinklers. "If you have any other questions, you can call my attorney, Ronald Deutsch. He's in the Manhattan business directory."

Ortiz remained by the front steps, still shaking his head at Lynn's photo.

"You know, she's really got something, this lady."

"To each his own." Jeff palmed the keys to his Benz. "I never cared for her work myself."

57

THE DOG WAS BARKING and scratching at the door as if he were hot-wired with piss.

"Clay, let him out, will you?" Barry turned to his son. "I don't want him going on the rug again."

Nose still swollen and limbs still sore from his karate match, Clay hoisted himself up from the couch in front of the living room TV and the bowl of popcorn he was systematically Hoovering.

"Brian Bonfiglio from the DA's office called," Lynn said, once he was out of earshot. "They let Mike out on twenty-five thousand dollars bail, ten percent down."

"Seems about right." Barry grabbed a fistful of kernels and looked over his shoulder. "Given the circumstances. The judge would be wise to keep his calendar clear."

They were watching the latest news on CNN about a photo editor in Florida mysteriously contracting anthrax.

"I still can't believe Jeffrey had anything to do with this." She hugged a velvet pillow on her lap. "You think he did it himself?"

The picture changed to spores under a microscope.

"I don't know," said Barry. "Killing your wife and cutting her head off? That's a serious job to entrust to somebody else. You'd have to write an awfully big check to cover that."

"You know I saw him at the train station the other day. We had this real heart-to-heart. And there were tears in his eyes almost the whole time."

"They were probably legit. He probably feels like the victim here. I'm sure it was everybody else's fault."

"What are you guys talking about?" Clay came back in, huffing and red-faced, as if just opening the door had winded him.

"Nothing," Barry grumbled. "Either go to bed or go study your Torah portion."

"No, come on. Tell me, please. I really want to know."

Lynn remembered how it used to touch her, this curiosity he had about the way things worked across the Great Divide of Adulthood. *How did you meet Dad? How did you know you wanted to marry him? When did you decide to have kids? What do you think I'll grow up to be?* Lately, though, he'd stopped asking. Instead he'd regressed a little, pulling old board games and toys out of the closet, trying to go back to a less troubled and disturbing time in his life. His older sister, on the other hand, hadn't asked her anything in months. She just stood back, automatically assuming the worst about her parents.

"Things have changed a bit since the last time we talked to you guys." She glanced at Barry, deciding she'd had enough of secrecy for the moment.

"What?" Clay plopped back between them, taking up his position in front of the popcorn bowl again.

"Remember that old friend of Mom's we were telling you about?" Barry said, reluctantly lowering the volume with the remote.

"*The cop.*" Hannah drifted into the room to add a dark footnote. "The one she testified against in court."

"Yeah, what about him?" Clay looked around, as if he was about to be swarmed.

"Well" — Barry weighed the remote in his hand — "it turns out he did some bad things, but maybe not quite as many as we thought."

"They mean he didn't kill Sandi," said Hannah.

Clay's ears moved up and down. "*That's* what you thought he did?"

"Well, he didn't," Barry conceded. "But he did bother somebody else the way he bothered your mother. And that's enough. He shouldn't be on the job."

"He got Mom pregnant when they were in high school." The last word hissed out of Hannah, steam escaping from a radiator.

Popcorn crumbled between Lynn's fingers. "Who told you that?"

"Jennifer Olin again. Did you seriously think no one was going to say anything?"

"I just wanted to find the right time to talk to you about it."

"Yeah, sure. *Hypocrite.*"

Something keen and piercing in her voice made Barry think of tribeswomen gathering in a dusty town square to throw stones.

"Knock it off." He turned around. "I won't have you speak to your mother that way."

"But it's *true.*"

"Get over it."

He heard the dog's bark moving around outside, a coarse annoying yawp that made him think of a stolen car being driven away with its alarm blaring.

"So who did do it?" asked Clay. "Who killed her?"

"We think it might've been somebody else," said Lynn.

"Well, like *duh*," said Hannah.

"Look, I know you did some baby-sitting for the Laniers over the summer," said Barry, "but I'd like you to stay away from there."

"Why?" Hannah's mouth became a tidy little hyphen. "Do you think it was Jeff?"

"We don't know," said Lynn. "No one knows anything."

"So is he mad?" Clay leaned against his mother for support.

"Who?" Barry and Lynn spoke simultaneously.

"The police officer."

"He'll probably get past it," said Barry. "Most of the time I'd rather deal with somebody who's mad than somebody who's scared. When somebody's scared, you don't know how they're going to come out at you. They could do anything. When somebody's mad, they usually just tell you and that's the end of it."

"Unless it's the Old Testament God," said Clay.

"Or the Texas Tower Sniper," added Hannah.

They watched a teaser before the commercial about how the war was probably beginning this weekend.

Barry picked up the popcorn bowl and offered it to Hannah, who'd been standing right behind him, staring holes into the back of his head.

Good work there, Schulman. Helluva world you're bringing the kids up in.

The mobilized yawping of the dog seemed to goad him.

That's right, kids. It's true. Your worst fear doesn't quite go far enough. Daddy blew the college tuition. Mommy once carried another man's baby.

The dog barked louder and closer to the house.

The police can pull you over and fuck with you for absolutely no good reason. And by the way, our neighbor whose kids you once took care of decapitated his wife.

Each little bark was a hacksaw lightly scraping his nerves.

But don't you worry, uh-uh. Because except for the unpredictable and unpreventable acts of terrorism in the future, everything is A-OK.

A part of his mind couldn't accept that all he could do at this point was put on a suit and try to find another job quickly. Shouldn't he be doing something more primal? Sharpening his spear. Building high stone walls around the house. Gathering animal skins for the long winter months. Loading up the catapult. Re-doing his résumé seemed so . . . *reasonable.*

But then Hannah plunged her hand into the communal bowl and slipped him a sideways half-smile. And for a fleeting instant, he felt restored to his place in the family. Okay, we're broke and shit-scared and at one another's throats, but at least we're not apart.

From the yard, he heard Stieglitz give a sharp little seagull yelp and then a low-down mangy growl.

"Think he's ready to come back in?" Barry asked.

"Second time he's been out since dinner." Clay got up again. "He better be."

"Take a flashlight," Lynn called after him. "Don't let him track mud back in the house again."

They all heard the revving of an engine and gravel spewing in the driveway at the same time.

"What the hell was that?" Barry got up and brushed past Clay.

"Is that Dennis's car?" asked Lynn.

Hannah looked mildly offended. "His engine's much noisier."

Forgetting his shoes, Barry yanked open the door and peered out into the darkness. A pair of red taillights flared through the light fog and veinery of branches at the end of the driveway. Closer to the house, where the garage was attached, small pieces of orange light glowed and drifted away, turning blue at the edges before they extinguished in midair.

A strong chemical odor seeped through the familiar smells of autumn and started a faint burning at the back of his throat.

"Oh, shit, the garage is on fire!" He started running. "Lynn, get the fire extinguisher!"

The fire was just starting to graze on a corner of the garage, but he could already hear its hunger panting. The dog was at his heels, chasing and yapping, catching his eye once in the dark, as if to ask, *Are you sure this is what's supposed to happen?* The two of them stopped short in the driveway, watching the flames organize their game plan, gnawing on the trim of the open garage doorway, right next to the stacks of bundled newspapers.

"*Hose!*" he shouted, racing back to the front lawn. "*Where's the fucking hose?*"

He tripped over it in the dark and wasted precious seconds trying to find the spray gun at its head, while the dog kept trying to stick its nose in his crotch.

"HANNAH, TURN THE SPIGOT ON!" he yelled as he ran back toward the driveway, praying the snagged coil would stretch that far.

The fire had matured while he was away. He felt everything on him — clothes, hair, and skin — reversing as he approached it. The flames had turned into an agile tiger, feasting along the inner wall, taking great greedy gulps of breath and searching for flammables. He heard the crackle of boiling paint and saw orange pieces dripping from the trim like food spilling out of a mouth.

He aimed the spray gun at the stack of burning newspapers, but when he pulled the trigger, only a dainty spring mist came out, falling well short of the target.

"ALL THE WAY ON, HANNAH," he shouted, envisioning the whole garage flashing over and setting the main house ablaze.

He heard the dog at his side give a discouraged whimper as a loud pop came from deep within the garage. And in the half-second before he registered it as a small explosion, three things came into his mind. *Dog. Aerosol can. Newark.* An expanding basketball of flame came shooting out at him — the bug spray must've ignited. *I'm going to die.* He turned and pitched himself out of the way, feeling the hot cloud pass, threatening to scorch his face and liquefy his eyeball. He hit the ground and skittered down the gravel driveway, dimly aware of the rest of the family screaming his name from the yard.

The abrasion of gravel on his chest and upper arms told him he was all right, though. Slowly he got up, brushing his hands, sensing someone else was hurt instead. He felt it tangibly as a wrenching, a thing being pulled away from him. Then he turned toward a sound like an old wheel spinning on a rusted axle. By the fire's light, he saw Stieglitz on the ground, writhing and twisting his head, trying to get at the shred of burning newspaper that had wrapped itself around his tail.

"Oh my God!" he heard Hannah shriek from the yard.

"Hannah, don't get near him!" Barry started to back away, realizing he'd lost the spray gun in the fall. "Somebody help me find the hose again!"

Hearing the sound of his master's voice, the dog jumped up, revivified, chasing Barry up the steps and across the lawn, a soft blue-orange glow spreading along his hindquarters. The animal stopped for a second to roll on the dry grass, giving himself momentary surcease but leaving a tiny fire in his wake.

"LYNN, CALL NINE-ONE-ONE!" Barry hollered.

"I DID!" she screamed, standing in the doorway with the phone to her ear. "BUT I CAN'T FIND THE FIRE EXTINGUISHER! IT'S NOT UNDER THE SINK! SOMEBODY MOVED IT!"

The dog started to follow the sound of her voice, thinking he was still welcome in the house.

"NO, STIEGLITZ. BAD BOY! COME BACK HERE!" Barry clapped his hands, realizing the dog would set the living room on fire if he got inside. "Go find the ball! Where is it? *Where is it?*"

The dog came tearing back at him in a blazing blue stink, squealing in pain with his tongue hanging out, ready for the nightly routine of jumping up and humping Barry's leg.

"No baby! No kiss!" He backpedaled again, waving his arms. "Daddy doesn't want a kiss!"

"Over here!" Hannah called from a far corner of the yard, trying to distract Stieglitz.

"No, over here!" Clay cried out from closer to the pool.

The fire had grown into a hairy red mammoth, goring the side of the garage and spewing black smoke at the moon.

"WILL SOMEBODY HELP ME FIND THE GODDAMN HOSE AGAIN?" Barry shouted, feeling around for it in the dark even as the dog kept after him. "THE HOUSE IS GOING TO GO UP!"

A lone siren sounded in the far distance, trying to rouse the local volunteer firemen from their family dinners. He wondered if the response would be just a bit slower once they realized whose place was burning.

"LYNN, GET AWAY FROM THE HOUSE!" he called back toward the front door.

The dog followed the sound of his voice to the apple tree. Now the two of them stood facing each other, with only a few feet between them, no longer master and pet. Blue-orange flakes peeled off the dog, and the stench of burning fur cut through the fog. Stieglitz gazed at Barry with glistening dark eyes, making anguished squeaks deep in his throat. A single fire engine wailed from the bottom of the hill, offering a remote promise of help on the way.

"Easy there, boy." Barry peeled off his bathrobe, as he saw the dog about to rear back on his hind legs. "SIT! SIT!"

The dog just stared at him, baring its teeth, the high whimpering giving way to a vicious growl. Barry edged forward slowly, holding the robe out before him like a matador's cape, not entirely certain his reflexes would be fast enough to smother the flames.

"Just take it easy, baby. No one else is gonna hurt you."

But then the slap of chubby hands and a high boyish whistle cut him off.

"Hey, Stieglitz, come here! Come on, boy. *I'll* play with you."

Somehow Clay had pulled back a third of the pool covering and was standing on the far side of it.

"Come for a swim, buddy. Here we go. The water's fine."

With its remaining instinct, the dog turned and scampered toward the sound of unconditional love. And with one last leap, he dove straight into the pool where Clay had coaxed him to go swimming over Lynn's protests at least twice this past summer. There was a loud splash, a rain of drops, a hoarse despairing cry from Clay, and then a crisp sizzle of scorched hair and chlorine.

58

"IT'S ALL A PACK OF LIES, ya know."

"What is?"

"All of it. Every last goddamn word. The Old Testament. The New Testament. The Code of Hammurabi. The Magna Carta. Book of Mormon. The Geneva Convention. The *Boy Scout Handbook. Das Kapital. Mein Kampf.* The I Ching. Even the so-called Bill of Rights. They're all just meant to keep you in your place."

Mike was spending the night at his father's trailer in the RV park just past the abandoned map factory at the far end of River Road. The place smelled like an old rabbit cage because Dad never threw anything out. Everywhere you looked there were yellowing copies of *Reader's Digest*, rusty door hinges, insecticides made by companies that no longer existed, and jars of peanut butter three years past the expiration date. Just to add to the clutter effect, Dad always left his radio and television on at the same time, a call-in show playing softly in the background while he sat in his easy chair watching *Who Wants to Be a Millionaire?* On his lap were two library books about his latest obsession: debunking all major world religions.

It took Mike awhile to understand that the purpose of all the noise was to fill a gap. After thirty-one years working on a cell block, Dad could no longer handle quiet. It unnerved him, made him snappish and prone to trivial arguments. He needed constant distraction of some kind to stay calm.

"They say Moses wrote the Five Books of Moses, but how can that be?" The old man fidgeted before the old Zenith twelve-inch with one of its antennae wrapped in tinfoil. "Those books say he was the humblest man who ever walked the face of the earth. But how could the humblest man have written *that* about himself? See what I'm getting at?"

"I didn't know you were supposed to take it literally." Mike stretched on the foldout couch, trying to see the set from behind his father's chair.

"And don't go thinking the Christians are any better. Nobody even mentions the Crucifixion until Mark."

"You want a beer?" Mike sighed.

"There was a cross in every church your mother and I ever set foot in. If it's just a symbol then the hell with it." Dad looked over the back of his chair. "Bottles are on the side door in the refrigerator. Get me a glass, will you?"

Mike lurched to his feet, queasy and bloated. The combination of Vicodin and amoxicillin was turning his stomach into a free-fire zone. Full price he had to pay at CVS Pharmacy, now that his Patrolmen's Benevolent Association card wouldn't go through the system anymore. A dollar a pill, and it still felt like he had poison pumping through his bloodstream. The stiffness went all the way from his thumb into his shoulder, and every few hours the fever would start to burn him up and then abruptly fade.

He was riding the rims, ready to come apart at the joints. Especially after this afternoon. Marie home from work early and meeting him at the front door with the address of the new Y in White Plains. Telling him she'd already packed his bags and stuffed them into the truck because it was better for the kids not to see him stomping around with bulging suitcases. Sure, he could've put up a fight and insisted on staying, but what would that prove? That she'd been right all along. That he only took care of himself. He'd show her. At least there was no screaming and yelling. She gave him as much time as he wanted to explain things to the kids. Cheryl and Mike Jr. listened with polite blank expressions, as if there was a TV program they'd rather watch. But Timmy grabbed his good hand and wouldn't let go.

But who's going to take care of us?

What are you talking about? He'd rested his chin on top of the boy's head. *Your mommy's not going anywhere.*

But she's not a police officer.

Of course, neither was he anymore. He was nothing. A disgrace. His heart had been ripped out. His entire life had been a waste. No, worse than a failure. He'd brought shame to a family that had been here since before the Civil War. Every decent thing he'd ever done would be forgotten, and mistakes he didn't make would forever be linked with his name. It didn't matter that Larry Quinn had called last night and said that Harold and Paco were looking seriously at the husband again. Or that Harold himself had left a few messages. He'd still be called a criminal for the rest of his days. His children would deny him; his grandchildren would never hear of him.

But for some crazy reason, what his mind kept going back to was Sandi Lanier. He'd told himself that he'd never really fallen for her; she didn't matter, she was just a substitute, a way to get back at Lynn after all these years. She'd hooked him, though, that fucking Sandi. Especially now that she was gone and he knew what was inside her. He remembered the way she'd looked up at him that day she thought Jeff had come home early. How she'd sat bolt upright and looked around, like a deer hearing a hunter's footsteps in the woods. After a few seconds, realizing it was nothing, she'd sunk down and curled against him again. *You'll watch over me, won't you?* She might as well have taken a pin and stuck it right through his heart, because he'd never be rid of those words. Thinking about them now comforted him a little. At least once he'd made somebody feel safe.

"Would you like a Lifeline?" asked a voice from the television.

He pulled open the refrigerator and stood there, enduring the rotten-egg smell. A milk bottle stamped August 31 quivered under the lightbulb, and something moved inside a cloudy Tupperware container. He grabbed two Buds off the side shelf and shut the door.

"You know why they tell you all those lies?" his father was saying. "To make you think you'll get your just reward in the next life. It's a steaming hot pile of donkey diarrhea. That's all it is."

"I'm gonna look for a clean glass."

He set the bottles down on the counter and peeked into his father's bedroom next to the kitchen, a boxy little compartment noticeably hotter than the rest of the trailer.

"I used to say the prison chaplain helped me put down more riots than my baton," his father gassed on. "Made all those shitbirds think their suffering amounted to something. I tried to tell your mother the same thing, but she never listened. Every Sunday she had you boys dressed like little Kennedys and sitting in the front row of Saint Stephen's, like God himself was looking down."

Mike edged into the bedroom, seeing clothes on the floor, a picture of Mom and Johnny on the night table, and the framed citation from the Owenoke warden on the wall, thanking Dad for his thirty-one years of service at the prison.

"She was a handful, your mother," Dad kept going. "I never met the likes of her before. Always bowing and scraping to the people she worked for up the hill, but Lord she was a tyrant at home. Sometimes I'm sorry I didn't do more to protect you boys from her temper, but you know I was so tired . . ."

"It's all right, Pops. What's done is done."

Mike dropped to his knees to look under the bed, seeing massive dust balls, a squeezed-out Fleet enema bottle, and old bound-up volumes of *Highlights* magazine that Dad tried to peddle off to the grandchildren.

"She always said I'd go to hell for blasphemy. But now look!" Dad snorted. "Five years in the grave she is, and I'm still here."

Mike moved aside a back copy of *Juggs* and reached for the orange-and-white box of ammo he'd noticed under the bed the last time he'd stopped by here.

"I used to tell her that she was kidding herself. The only justice you'll ever get is in this life. And then you better grab it with both hands before somebody else pays for it . . ."

Mike lifted the shells carefully, trying not to rattle them in his shaky hands and draw his father's attention. He set them down on top of the dresser and pulled open the underwear drawer, knowing that old habits die hard. His father's Smith & Wesson combat masterpiece was wrapped up in a pair of Jockey-style BVDs. The Colt .45 automatic was in the sock drawer.

"Hey, who played Alfalfa?" Dad shouted from the next room.

"What?"

"They're asking who played Alfalfa on *The Little Rascals*." Dad raised his voice. "What the hell are you doing in my bedroom anyway?"

"Looking for my socks. I thought they might've got mixed in with yours."

"Shit. You couldn't fit your foot inside one of mine. I never understood how my son wore size thirteen when I've got these skinny little feet. I tell you, I gave the milkman a good look sometimes."

Mike came back into the living room and slipped the guns and bullets into the black gym bag while the old man was looking at the set.

"Where's that beer?" Dad craned his wizened neck and looked over the back of his chair.

"Keep your shirt on. They're not gonna dry up."

With two small steps he was over at the kitchen counter, opening the Budweisers.

"Just come here a minute, will you? Forget about the glasses. I wanna tell you something."

"What?"

He came and stood beside his father's chair, smoke wafting from the necks of both bottles. The chill stung his bad thumb and went right up his arm into the center of his chest.

"Look . . . I know I wasn't always at my best around you guys . . ." The old man's hands pawed the air, trying to conjure a vocabulary he didn't have. "*Shit.*"

His eyes looked out from a sunken face. It was like staring into a barren valley. All the old fury was spent, but nothing had grown in its place. Thirty-one years working in a prison. Forty with a woman who thought she married beneath her station. Three and a half knowing that his favorite son had died before him.

"Look," the old man said, deciding to make it easy on himself, "all I want to tell you is, don't let the bastards get you down."

"That's it?" Mike stared at him. "Those are the great words of wisdom?"

"Just remember, we built this town." Dad took the beer, not daring to meet his eye again. "We can take it apart if we have to."

"Yeah, okay. Whatever you say, Pops."

Mike took a long pull and watched the contestant on the screen, a milk-fed dentist from Des Moines with his eyes fixed on some ever-receding point.

"Jackie Cooper, Robert Blake, George McFarland, or Carl Switzer?" asked the host.

"Carl Switzer," said Mike. "He's the one who played Alfalfa."

"How do you know that?" his father asked.

"Got himself shot to death in a fight over a fifty-dollar dog. Thing like that sticks in your mind."

"Why?"

"Because most of the others just killed themselves. It's a curse on the whole line."

His father touched his arm. "You're not thinking of doing anything stupid yourself, are you?"

Mike felt himself pass through three different temperature zones, thinking how to answer. "Come on, Pops. Gimme a break."

He glanced over at the bag on the couch, wondering if his father had left any rounds in the magazine of the .45.

"I'm just saying it doesn't matter what you do in the next life. There's only this one that counts."

Mike drank half his beer in one gulp, feeling it sluice down into his innards and loosen the stuck gears, the pain ebbing away for just a moment.

"In the end, all you have is your good name."

"Amen to that." He clicked his half-empty bottle against his father's in a toast and drank up.

59

AS HE TURNED on the shower the next morning, Jeffrey thought that he caught an astringent whiff of gasoline on his hands.

It couldn't be, of course. He'd scrubbed with a Brillo pad and Neutrogena soap for about twenty minutes in the shower last night. His arms and legs had pink scaly patches from all the vigorous swabbing he'd been doing lately. Already he was having second thoughts about that number on the Schulman's garage last night. In the clear light of day, it seemed a stupid risk. But for Chrissakes, Lynn was asking for it. How do you like that bitch? First she tells the police about seeing the bloodstain on the wall and helps them get a warrant to search his house. Then he catches her talking to Dylan about the problems Mommy and Daddy were having. Okay, he was willing to send her the Instant Message and leave it at that. But then she had to give them those old pictures with the wood protector. She's lucky he just decided to throw that Corona bottle with a flaming oil rag at her garage. Plenty of other places he could've put it instead.

He looked down at the hot water pelting between his toes and puddling around the drain. *Just nerves*, he told himself. Everything washes away if you scrub long and hard enough. Bloodstains. Bad debts. A bad marriage. Even a bad name. His whole life had been about learning to go with the flow. Dealing with the moment as it comes up. Being who you need to be. Avoiding dead ends. Maximizing potential. Your dad gets shifted to a new army base every three years? You get a new set of friends. Just don't get that close to any of them. Get thrown out of school for cheating? Go to another one and find a girl to write your papers for you. Your software business in California tanks in the eighties, and your first wife turns from a beach babe into a demanding sow? Dump her on her flabby ass, change your name from Lane to Lanier, and start over on the Net in the nineties. With the way money was flying around a few years ago, it wasn't that hard to raise the first five million with a good idea and a cool line of patter. If one venture capital firm didn't like your history, there was always another one that might forgive a stumble or two. Hey, this was America. People started over all the time.

Still, that Detective Ortiz had him looking over his shoulder, scrubbing a little harder. He'd thought things were going to be different with Sandi. The house, the kids, the whole nine yards. It was for keeps this time. Play the Man long enough, you become the Man. Only he hadn't realized how hard it was going to be. The merchandise sitting in the warehouse, refusing to move. The cursor blinking, signaling the world's indifference to Denny McLain's glove and Joe Pepitone's bat. The investors getting pissed off. His father-in-law calling at nine at night, wanting to know when he was going to start to see some decent returns. And worst of all, Sandi grinding away at him every day, with her free-floating anxieties, her constant nagging, her needling dissatisfactions. *You aren't spending enough time with the kids. I can't stand this house. I'm tired.* Nothing was ever good enough for her. Especially compared to her friends' lives. Somebody else always had a bigger house, a more successful husband, a better figure. Their kids were going to get into better schools. They were going to Antigua for Christmas break, not just Fort Lauderdale. *We're not putting enough away for the future.* God, it was almost as if she was trying to make his head explode with all this striving to keep up. He'd awake some mornings and stare at the ceiling for a few minutes before the alarm went off, wondering how he was going to make it through the day. And gradually he'd found himself wishing that he could just chuck the whole deal and start over one more time.

So in a way, she'd forced him to do what he did. It was a matter of pure survival. She was going to cut him off. Divorce him. Take the kids and destroy the business. She hadn't given him any choice. Not that he'd meant to go that far that night. He'd just been trying to catch her stepping out and give himself a little more leverage in negotiating a fair settlement. So he took that diamond stud earring out of her jewelry box and sent her that e-mail with the cop's address on it, saying, *I have a few things of yours that you might want back. You miss that earring?*

The sad irony was that he needn't have gone to all the trouble of driving down from New London. She'd already left the diary out, meaning for him to read it and see what she really thought of him. But of course he didn't know that at the time. So he'd been righteous and furious when he busted her in the Motel 6 parking lot that night.

You bitch. He started in as soon as he got her in the Tempo he'd rented. *I can't believe you did this to me. You ruined my life.*

I ruined your life? I ruined YOUR life? Are you crazy?

Just shut up. He rolled up the windows and looked back across the lot at the red vacancy sign burning over the dimmed entrance light. *Keep your voice down.*

I won't shut up. You call me stupid in front of my friends. You belittle me in front of the kids. You insist on moving into a house we can't afford.

You're the one who wanted that house. I hate that house.

You've got a lot of nerve.

I've got a lot of nerve?

You run up ten thousand dollars a month on our Visa, buying fucking Armani suits . . .

What do you want me to do? Go around in rags?

Spending money on whores when I'm begging my father for money to send the kids to summer camp . . .

Shut the fuck up . . .

Receipts from Club Royale Entertainment in your pants pocket. You think I can't figure out what that is?

Yeah, like you're any better? He pointed to her red Audi sitting across the lot.

At least I don't have to pay somebody to fuck me.

Is this what you want? He'd raised his fist, warning her.

Yeah, go ahead and hit me, Jeffrey.

That what you really want?

Show me what a man you are.

I will!

You make me sick. Go find someone else, you fucking leech. I can't stand the sight of you anymore.

That was when he hit her. Just a quick little jab aimed at her chin. But no, she had to jerk her head back so he hit her in the throat instead. He knew right away something was wrong.

Jeffrey, I can't breathe.

What do you mean?

She'd started gasping and frantically pointing to her windpipe.

Nothing's getting through, she pantomimed, eyes bulging. *I can't —*

In a panic, he turned the key and tore out of the lot. Where was that hospital sign he'd seen a couple of miles up the road?

She can't breathe. She couldn't physically speak anymore. She just pointed at her throat again and kicked the dashboard, her face swelling up and turning bright red.

He put on his high beams. The turn was right here before, wasn't it? His mind was already tripping and stumbling over things he'd say to the nurse in the ER. *We had a fight* . . . No! *She fell* . . . What?

She started hitting him on the shoulder, as if they were playing charades. *Okay. I get it. You can't breathe. You're dying. You're choking like a fish on land.*

The death rattle was starting: a sound he'd never heard any human make. Like an artic blizzard in the throat. Her body arched and stiffened against him, all the muscles and tendons straining to hang on. *We're not going to make it.* Fear swarmed over him. He'd pulled off the Saw Mill into a disused trucker's weigh station and put her on the ground, trying to give her mouth-to-mouth, but the trachea was too badly damaged.

She scratched at his face and pulled on his clothes, the drowner trying to take the lifeguard with her. He remembered seeing one of his father's friends, a retired air force medic, perform an emergency tracheostomy on a beach in Cypress when somebody'd had an allergic reaction to a jellyfish sting. The guy used a knife. Just a regular knife. Jeffrey remembered he still had that little penknife hanging off his keychain that somehow airport security missed at LaGuardia. He opened the blade and tried to steady his hand to make the incision. But she kept writhing and thrashing on the gravel. So instead of making a neat little cut as he'd seen the medic do, he'd opened a tremendous gash, sending blood spurting everywhere, spraying up in his eyes and gurgling down into her lungs. He tried again and felt the blade get stuck in the cartilage, practically lacerating her larynx. She grabbed for his shoulders, begging. He realized he'd never really pitted his strength against hers before, that she'd always been holding back a little, wanting him to think he could win. But now she strained and jerked and gasped until there was absolutely nothing left. Then she'd faded in the passing headlights, staring up doll-eyed in horror.

He looked down at the shower drain gurgling.

Those first few minutes were still murky to him, as if he'd been underwater. He remembered wrapping her up in several layers of plastic from his dry-cleaned shirts and then stuffing her body halfway into his suit bag so she wouldn't bleed all over the trunk. Then he'd started to drive down toward the city, trying to figure out what to do. Cars on the opposite side of the road blinked their high beams. Brake lights flared. Another car stopped short in front of him, and when he swerved he heard a heavy thump in the trunk.

He had a fleeting thought about turning himself in to the nearest police station, but what would he say? Yes, Officer, it was an accident. I lured my wife to a motel, making her think she was going to meet her lover there. And then we had a fight in the parking lot, and I punched her in the throat.

They'd think he meant for this to happen. Instead, he found himself driving back toward the house, almost in a fugue state. He cut the motor and sat before the garage for a few minutes, her blood drying on his face and hands. All at once, he felt stained and contaminated. He had to get rid of it all right away before anybody found out. He remembered the garage had its own washing machine and dryer, in case they ever wanted to rent out the upstairs apartment. There was a can of Carbona carpet cleaner on one of the shelves, so he could at least shampoo the rugs from the car's trunk.

Once inside the garage with the door closed, he opened the trunk, and the stench almost made him vomit. He held his shirttail over his mouth and nose and forced himself to take a good look. He'd dug a deep smile into her throat.

He almost didn't have to make a conscious decision to get rid of the head separately. It just seemed like the natural next step, as if somehow the choice had already been made for him. At least then the police wouldn't be able to identify her so easily.

He struggled to get her out of the trunk and then laid her out on the cement floor, worrying that at any minute the kids or Inez the baby-sitter would come out of the house to see what was making all the noise.

He realized he had to clear his mind and not get stampeded by emotions. *You can do this. Yes, you can. Do it for the children. They're go-*

ing to need you more than ever. He put a drop cloth over her face so he wouldn't have to look at her eyes staring up at him and got to work with the hacksaws he still had from the old house on Sycamore.

He worked right above the drain in the middle of the garage floor. There was a hose hooked up just outside and a bottle of bleach above the washing machine to rinse the blood away afterward. He'd watched enough Court TV and read enough true crime books to know what to do. But after a while, all the cutting and gouging, all the spewing and gaseous bad smells, the sheer physical effort of sawing through bone and containing the quarts of blood spilling across the floor had started to get to him. He decided to forget doing a full-scale dismemberment and just dump the head and body separately into the river, like the drug dealer had done to his girlfriend in the spring. He put the wood protector can in the bag with the head and tied a metal stepladder around the torso to try to weigh it down. The sun would be coming up in a little while, and he figured surely the river would wash them down toward the city before full light.

The drain gave a mighty hollow yawn as he cut the shower off and watched the little whirlpool at his feet. God, who knew the body would backwash on him and end up right next to the train station?

"Daddy?"

A small silhouette appeared through the beveled glass of the shower door.

He shut the water off and wiped his eyes. "Izzy, honey, what is it?"

He opened the door a crack and saw his daughter staring up at him with those big opal eyes, wearing a pink halter top, the quilted denim jacket Sandi bought her last year at The Gap, and a pair of Powerpuff Girls underpants.

"I thought you were getting dressed. I laid the clothes out for you."

"Mommy dresses me."

"But Mommy isn't here anymore." He looked around for a towel. "Did you forget again?"

The Lip came out. It had been weeks since she'd set foot in the bedroom, Jeff realized. Not since the night she'd surprised Daddy in the living room as he tried to sneak upstairs to get a duffle bag and clean clothes to drive back up to Providence in. Everything had been going all right until that moment. In less than two hours, he'd managed to get the garage mostly cleaned, the bleach in the drain, and the body packed away in the trunk, ready to be thrown in the river. He'd even thought of the McDonald's along I-95 just outside Providence, where he'd toss the saws he'd used in a Dumpster. All he needed was something to carry the head in and a fresh shirt and pants to wear to his meetings the next day. But then he'd heard that squeak on the stairs and looked over to see Izzy hanging over the edge of the banister, staring right at him.

I want a glass of milk, she'd said, startling him so badly that he'd actually jumped out of the hallway and tried to hide in the living room.

For the longest three seconds of his life, he'd stood pressed against a wall, footsteps pacing back and forth across his heart, remembering how carefully he'd explained that he'd be away until tomorrow night. Even marking the date on the kitchen calendar so she wouldn't forget.

Daddy? he'd heard her creeping along the corridor, stalking him.

Go back to bed, Iz, he'd called out. *I'm not really here. This is only a dream.*

Dutifully, she'd turned and trudged back up the steps without argument, clutching her stuffed Bullwinkle. This is only a dream. Even now, Jeff wasn't sure what she believed. He only knew that she hadn't mentioned it since. But two days later he found a light-brownish red smear in the living room where Dylan was playing with his Pokémon toys, right where he'd been standing in the chinos with the bloodsoaked cuffs.

"Come on, baby." He turned sideways and tried to cover himself with a washcloth. "Give your daddy a chance to get dressed. I'll come and help you when I'm done."

She stayed where she was, glaring at him accusingly. "But *where is* Mommy?"

"I already told you, hon. She's not coming back."

The bottom lip retracted, and the brown eyes narrowed. And in that instant, a terrible knowledge seemed to pass over the child, like a thunderhead. *She knows.* The water turned freezing cold on his skin. She knows it wasn't a dream. She knows that I was home when I wasn't supposed to be. She knows that she'll never see her mother again. And in just a few years, she'll understand what it all means.

He stood before his daughter, naked, teeth chattering. All this time, he'd been waiting to feel something real for the girl. For all of

Sandi's prattling on, a part of him had always remained unmoved by his own children, perhaps even a little resentful at all the space they took up. But now it dawned on him that this secret would bond him forever to his daughter. One day Iz could just wake up and destroy his life as easily as she could knock over one of her little brother's sand castles. She could ruin him. Send him to prison for the rest of his life, or maybe even Death Row.

And as she stood outside the shower stall, Isadora seemed to sense that something was changing. She opened the shower door farther, to look more plainly upon her father's vulnerability. Jeff reached past her to grab a bigger towel off the side rack.

"Come on, Izzy, what are you doing here?" He wrapped the towel around his middle, finding himself starting to shake uncontrollably.

His whole future rested in a child's unsteady hands. He saw the corners of her mouth pull down and her eyes well up. *She knows.* He started to reach out to touch the child, barely stifling an urge to beg for mercy on credit. *Please. I'm your father.*

But without warning, Isadora suddenly threw her arms around his damp knees, hugged him with the blind fervor of a child who knows this is absolutely all she has left in the world, and then ran skipping out of the room, eager to show her daddy she could finally put her clothes on by herself.

60

DAYBREAK FOUND the side of the Schulmans' garage charred and still smelling from oil smoke. Unable to face it at the moment, Lynn stood by the edge of the swimming pool with a skimming net, watching blackened clumps of dog hair swirl across the aqua-blue surface.

"Don't touch anything." Barry stepped over the yellow crime scene tape with two cups of coffee. "I just got off the phone with Allstate. They're going to send a claims adjuster this afternoon."

"Can't they just take the police report?" She lowered the pole.

Harold and Larry Quinn had shown up a half-hour after the firemen put out the garage fire. They'd hauled Stieglitz's carcass away in a human-size body bag, promising to send someone back today to search for additional evidence on the property.

"Ah, you know you have to argue with these guys about everything," Barry said, giving her one of the cups. "Especially if this turns out to be arson. They don't have much faith in small-town cops."

"I don't think Harold's trying to whitewash this, Barry. He's doing the best he can."

"Maybe, maybe not. But I also called Sean Heffernan this morning."

"Your old supervisor from the DA's office?"

"He said he'd reach out to somebody he knew at the state police, see if they could get more involved. I asked about the FBI, but they're a little busy these days . . ."

She folded her hands around the cup. "Do you think it's smart, going over Harold's head like that?"

"I don't see where we have a hell of a lot of choice, do you? They're not exactly protecting us. And that's supposed to be their job, last time I looked."

Sunlight slowly spread through the surrounding woods, ending just before the fence line and the abrupt slope of the hill that dropped down some one hundred fifty yards to the road below.

"We still can't be sure who did this," she said.

"You gave the detective that picture of Jeff with the wood protector, didn't you?"

"Yes, of course."

"Then I think it's pretty safe to assume that he's not going to nominate you for Friendly Neighbor of the Year or anything."

She buttoned the front of her blue cardigan and shivered in the early chill, noticing how much the dew looked like perspiration on the grass.

"You think I did the wrong thing?"

"I think you did the only thing you could do. You had the picture. She was your friend. You weren't going to sit on it and pretend you didn't see it. This is what you could do for her."

In the sloping distance, he saw the river roll pieces of the sun across its surface like a man studying glass shards in the dark folds of his palm.

"But that doesn't matter anymore," he said. "The thing that we have to get our minds around is that we're on our own."

"What do you mean?"

"I mean, no one else is looking out for us. The police. The FBI. School security. The government. We can't rely on any of them anymore. There's just us."

A lone sparrow sang from a high branch of the apple tree. Wind shivered the sumac just over the edge of the hill and blew pieces of yellow crime scene tape across the lawn.

"You're not making me feel a lot better," said Lynn.

"I got a gun."

"What?"

"You heard me. I bought a .38 from Richie. I've had it for a few days."

From the woods, he heard the muffled *pith* of acorns hitting the ground and braced himself for the inevitable tirade. He deserved the worst. He'd been reckless and irresponsible. He'd brought a gun into the house where their children slept. What if Hannah found it? What if Clay found it? He was an asshole, a moral imbecile, a hypocrite. He'd kept the truth from her even after he'd had the audacity to call her a liar. He'd put them all at even greater risk. Didn't he know how many people got shot with their own guns?

He was prepared to concede all of the above as long as he didn't have to get rid of it.

But instead she gave him that long cool stare.

"So where is it anyway?" she said. "Don't you think I ought to know how to use it?"

61

HE ROSE WITH THE SUN and was out the door before his father awoke.

The day seemed stunned and not quite ready to begin. The river was dark and moving slowly, as if it were still holding a portion of the night under its surface. The other trailers in the waterfront park were silent but for the chirping of the morning talk shows and the disconsolate stacking of breakfast plates. The dressing around his thumb was starting to turn a dim shade of golden brown. Ignoring the fact that he could no longer bend it, he threw the black gym bag onto the front seat of his Tundra and turned the key in the ignition. The engine coughed and raced, and the gas needle refused to rise above the quarter-tank level, but that was fine. He wasn't going far.

He decided to take the long way up into the hills, past the first house he grew up in on Bank Street. He remembered sitting on the wicker sofa with the crushed spokes, trying to comfort his mother after JFK's assassination. Four years old, he must have been. She cried for days afterward. There were newspaper clippings and votive candles everywhere. He'd come running into the bedroom after they said Ruby shot Oswald on the news. *Mom, they killed the bad guy. Everything's going to be all right.*

It took him years to understand why that didn't cheer her up more.

A few blocks up on Haverstraw Road, he passed the entrance to the old aqueduct and remembered the way his father used to explain how water passed through here on its way from a place called Tear in the Clouds, high in the mountains. A tear becomes a trickle, a trickle becomes a leak, a leak becomes a stream, a stream joins other streams in a brook carried along by the force of gravity. And the brook becomes a rushing river. And then nothing can stop it.

Even though he was loaded up on Vicodin, Advil, and Maxwell House, the world had a kind of stark diamond-hard clarity for the first time in weeks. He could remember the names of birds, trees, addresses on his paper route, golfers he'd caddied for, and boys he'd been friends with in fourth grade. He glanced off to the side and recalled pissing with his brother down into the reservoir, hoping it would eventually come out of a tap into some Manhattanite's drinking water. As the sun strobed through the pines, it seemed his whole life had been leading to this. Water seeking its own level.

God knows, he'd tried to be the one person in his family to make it out of this town. Roamed all the way out to Arizona and married an aerobics instructor who couldn't even find Westchester on a map of New York. But part of him dried up in the desert. Too much arid open space and sagebrush, too many Taco Bells and Outback Steakhouses, too many senior developments beside new superhighways. He found himself getting lost all the time, on the job and in the marriage. No, this was where he was supposed to end up.

It doesn't matter what you do in the next life.

He thought of making a detour back to Regan Way, just to see the kids one more time. Marie would have them corralled, washed, and ready for school. But stopping by to try to set things right would only distract from his sense of purpose. He had to keep going. The only solace was that Marie had talked about selling the house and taking the kids to stay with her sister in Florida for a while. At least then somebody in the family would finally get to see the rest of the world.

A half-mile up the hill was the high school, Old Glory just raised. It'd been more than a week since they stopped flying the flags at half-mast. How quickly they forget. He pulled around back and parked in the empty lot by the football field. The blank scoreboard and deserted bleachers reminded him of long sweltering afternoon scrimmages that had left him hurting more than the actual games, and the girls in their kick skirts who jumped and cheered for him when he was playing and passed him by in the hall as if they didn't recognize him without his helmet.

He unzipped the gym bag, took out the .45 and the .38, and carefully started to load the shells in. A mild oily scent made him wonder when the old man last cleaned these things. Didn't it ever occur to him that a weapon could jam? He packed the guns away and set off up the road again, passing the early bird commuters on their way to the train station. He waved going by Sarah Breen's husband in his black '95 Jaguar. Bob, the assistant coach from Saturday morning soccer. He wondered if Bob would recall that little gesture later and make it into something more than it was. Funny thing, memory.

He watched the black car sweep past him and become a speck in his rearview, easily doing forty-five in a thirty-five zone. I will never see that car again, he told himself. I will never see these trees in this light again. I will never drive on this road. I will never pass these enormous white houses with their three-car garages and sprawling lawns. I will never take my sons fishing in the river. I will never listen to my daughter read *Harry Potter* aloud again. I will never write another speeding ticket. I will never have to apologize.

As he stopped to brush his hair and knot his tie in the bedroom mirror, Jeff felt a subtle heightening of his spirits. Maybe the worst was over. Isadora's hug had been a kind of absolution. Even though he was due to spend the first part of the day with Ronald Deutsch and the second part with the estate lawyers, his hair was fully rising to the occasion, fluffing up and cresting above the crown.

He was going to get past this somehow. Up until that moment in the shower, he hadn't quite believed it. But the dark clouds were rolling away. At some point, it would all get taken care of. People forget. They move on with their lives. He'd mourn in dignity a few more months and then quietly announce that he was going to Florida or Texas to look at other opportunities. Saul would probably take the kids in the meantime and give him a cash settlement to go away. He put the brush down and smoothed back the sides of his hair with his palms, hearing the children yelling at each other in the foyer downstairs. Angry as he was, the old bastard didn't have the heart or the energy for a long drawn-out court fight.

Jeff went downstairs and found Izzy wearing a pair of jeans with a huge chocolate stain near one of the pockets and Dylan sitting on the onyx floor weeping piteously over his Scooby-Doo lunchbox.

"What's the matter?" Jeff said. "You guys still aren't ready for school like I asked you?"

"Dylan doesn't want to go. He says his legs don't work."

"What do you mean his legs don't work?"

She hunched her shoulders and gave a small indulgent smile, as if she somehow knew she'd be taking care of her brother for the rest of her life. "He says he needs someone to carry him."

"Mommy would carry me." Dylan sniffled, wiping his nose on his jacket sleeve.

Jeff sighed and looked at his watch. "Tell you what," he said, determined to ride his swell of optimism as far as he could. "I'll pull the car around front from the garage and save you most of the walk. Deal?"

"Deal." The boy hugged the lunchbox to his chest, trying to be brave.

"All right. Look out for me. I'll honk the horn."

He went out, leaving the front door half-open behind him. The day contained multitudes. The air felt charged with possibilities beyond the end of their little cul-de-sac. A warm forgiving sun reflected off the children's jungle gym in the front yard. The chard in Sandi's garden was still a vigorous shade of green with a deep maroon glow in the middle, and pumpkins were growing like small orange muscles on the vine. He felt that quickening of his pulse and heard a crackling sound in the distance like cellophane coming off a new package. Maybe he'd change his name again when he moved. Maybe after a while, he'd send for the kids to come live with him. Or maybe not. They'd probably get pretty comfortable living the good life with Saul and Barbara in Manhattan and going to private schools. By the time he got established enough to send for them, they'd probably be spoiled preteens who'd barely remember him.

He walked along the circular driveway to the garage, reached into his pocket for the remote, and opened the automatic garage door.

The Mercedes ML320 looked as if it had never been driven. *My ride.* The last time he'd brought this baby in for service, the mechanic in White Plains had said, *If you take care of your family the way you take care of this car, they're lucky to have you around.* It almost gave him a little erection of the heart, looking at it sometimes. *Do I deserve this? Yes I do.* He'd worked for it, taken more than his share of brickbats across the skull to earn it. Let everyone else pretend their priorities were the kids and the house; he saw the way they looked over when he pulled alongside of them. They envied him — *that's right!* But they didn't have that durability, that suppleness, that splendid acuity that gave everything he did a little backspin.

He unlocked the door and got in, savoring the smell of the leather seats and the vacuumed carpets that seemed to promise new beginnings were possible even in a two-year-old car. Especially for a man with an eye for detail. He started the engine and backed out slowly, noticing the garage wall looked perhaps a little conspicuously barren since he threw all the saws out.

In the rearview, he saw a red pickup truck sitting at the foot of the driveway, blocking him from coming around the circle back to the front door. His first thought was that someone was lost and looking for directions. Understandable. Some of these roads made about as much sense as varicose veins. Okay, so he'd do his little good deed for the morning and set the man on his way. He turned the Benz around slowly and cruised toward the truck, only slowly realizing where he'd seen it before.

Mike got out of the Tundra and walked around to the front, with the .45 held stiffly down by his pant leg, remembering Sandi looking up at him and asking, *You'll watch over me, won't you?*

He saw Jeff recognize him and then panic. The Mercedes's engine going into overdrive. The foot pressing on the accelerator. The silver grille rushing forward like a set of clenched teeth.

It doesn't matter what you do in the next life.

Steadying his aim with the numb hand, Mike squeezed the trigger. The gun coughed, and Jeff's right ear flew off over his shoulder in a din of shattering glass. He clapped one hand to his spurting temple and tried to steer with the other as his wheels shrieked. With a step to the left, Mike pulled the trigger again, and a hole formed in the middle of Jeff's forehead and started spouting deep-red blood. His eyes rolled back into his head as if he'd just heard something embarrassing, and he slumped forward on the wheel.

The Mercedes swerved off the driveway, fishtailing across the lawn and smashing sideways into a willow tree shading the jungle gym.

Thin yellow tear-shaped leaves rained down on the roof, and the horn sounded, a plaintive German cry breaking the morning.

Mike stuck the gun in his waistband and got back in the pickup, ready for the next stop. *There, the bad guy's dead.* He threw the truck into reverse and started to pull away, ignoring the blaring horn.

But just before he turned off the little dead-end street back onto Prospect, he looked up in the rearview and saw Sandi's two children come bounding out the front door with their lunchboxes, running to find out why their father had parked the car under the crying tree.

62

AT FIRST, Lynn only heard the siren as a subliminal tone, a far-off whine that made her tense up slightly.

She'd finally started to put the garden to bed, finishing the task she started that first day Mike came over to talk to her. Ever since, it'd been one thing after another, jarring the foundations. All she wanted to do was get her hands in the soil one more time this season.

Barry came up from the wooded slope just before the fence line with a wheelbarrow full of mulch, singing "Ol' Man River" in a manly Paul Robeson baritone. The kids had already caught a ride to school, so he was just hanging out and trying to make himself useful as they waited for the state investigator to show up.

"I gets weary an' sick of tryin' . . ." He dumped the wood chips into a mound beside her asparagus plants with their raccoon-devastated leaves.

"Don't just leave them there in a big pile. Help me spread them around."

"*Yes, master,*" he said like a movie zombie.

He took the shovel from her and started gently ladling mulch across the dirt she'd already turned over. She watched the way he carefully distributed the chips, smoothing them out and patting them down with the back of the shovel, his strong shoulder muscles straining and fanning out inside his white T-shirt like an idea taking shape on paper. My man. She'd always thought he'd never cared about her garden, that it was just another way for him to indulge her while keeping her at a distance, like the studio. But seeing him put serious work into it melted the ice jammed around her heart a little. This is us, doing something together. This is us, without the kids. This is us, without money. This is us, getting older.

"I love a man with a good broad back," she said.

"Just trying to build up some sweat equity so you don't let me starve out back this winter."

"Barry . . ."

"What?"

Great feeling welled up in her suddenly, unexpectedly. She thought of all the things she'd wanted to say to him over the years that always seemed to get lost in the maelstrom of days. Little bits of neighborhood gossip, unfiltered observations, funny things the children said, startling juxtapositions and connections that only he would appreciate. She realized she'd been missing that part of him, that private world they used to have, those lazy Sunday mornings before they had kids when they could spontaneously roll over and fuck on top of the Real Estate section.

"What?" he repeated, staring at her.

"Never mind," she said. "Can you get me a little more mulch?"

"Yes, milady."

He bowed and pushed the empty wheelbarrow past the side of the house and down the slope to where the chips were. As he disappeared among the barren trees and rotting stumps, she looked toward the horizon, hearing the distant wing beats of geese and glimpsing the gray train moving against the backdrop of the gray river.

The siren sound was becoming louder and more distinct. A high screech that split the morning like an acetylene torch. Later she would tell herself that she remembered everything before and afterward as two distinct entities. She wiped her hands on the front of her sweatshirt and walked down into the front yard, thinking it might be headed their way. Maybe Harold had heard about Barry calling the state police in and wanted to make a grand reentrance to show who was really in charge.

But then the wailing kept going right past them and on up into the hills, toward Jeff and Sandi's house on Love Lane. Something else had happened. She could feel it, like a sudden drop in the temperature. A different siren swept up the hill, chasing the first one. A psychotic *walloo walloo* that scraped the sheathing right off her nerves. An ambulance. A tug in her gut made her want to call and make sure Dylan and Izzy were all right. But then what if Jeff answered?

A squirrel scurried across the lawn. Two crows stood together on a rock, beak to beak, as if they were conspiring. The wind in the dogwoods made a hissing sound like the needle landing in the groove of an old scratched record. A stretch of yellow crime scene tape came tumbling across the lawn.

From the bottom of the driveway on the right, she heard an engine revving and the squeak of a chassis humping up their hill. A chrome fender gleamed among the trees, giving fair warning. Then a red pickup truck roared into view, bouncing over a pothole and accelerating, as if it was about to come right up on the lawn. It stopped short, and Mike Fallon glared at her through the tinted windshield.

He opened the door of the cab and slowly climbed out, looking like he'd been in an explosion. His eyes were glassy, his face was puffed out, and his hair had grayed in places, as if it had been sprinkled with plaster dust. The gauze around his thumb was a sodden dingy mustard color that seemed to signal that he no longer belonged to the segment of the human race that worried about consequences.

"Michael," she said, "I don't think you should be here."

He kicked the door shut behind him, not caring about the dent he'd made, and then stood there staring at her, letting his silence spread across the lawn until it reached her.

"Somebody got shot, Lynn," he said finally.

"What are you talking about?"

Even the crows fell silent now.

"Jeff Lanier got shot in the head. He's not going to make it."

"How do you know?" A band tightened around her chest.

"I was the one who shot him."

He opened the front gate and started walking toward her, the butt of a handgun riding casually in the front of his waistband. Just a friend stopping by to say hello.

A third siren screamed past Grace Hill Road, entering and then leaving their zone of quiet. An acorn hit the ground behind his pickup like a spent shell casing.

"Okay," she said, stepping back, "let's take it easy."

She cast a quick look toward the wooded area down the slope, wondering where Barry had gone. The red wheelbarrow stood alone in the shade of the elms and dogwoods.

He'd been in the house, getting a glass of water, when Fallon's truck pulled up. The gun was back in the Nike box on the bed, where he'd left it not ten minutes ago after showing it to Lynn. He went upstairs and got it and made a quick call to 911, knowing that most of the squad cars were busy up the hill and probably a good five minutes away. *We're on our own.* He went to the window and saw Fallon cross the yard toward Lynn with a gun plainly visible in his waistband. He thought of throwing open the window and taking aim, but the Tree Guy had never come to trim the maple, and its branches were in the way.

"Know what your problem is, Lynn?" Mike was close enough to put his arms around her neck. "You're blind. You've got all these expensive lenses and foreign cameras, and you're still blind as fucking Stevie Wonder. You don't see what's right in front of your face."

From the corner of her eye, she finally spotted Barry about sixty feet to the left of them, crouched down and creeping slowly along the fence behind the column of trees. He must have come out of the back door of the house and taken the long way around, to try to sneak up on them. She registered the black gun in his hand against the background of his white T-shirt. Mike needed only to turn his head a quarter-inch to see the same.

"I know how hard these last few weeks have been," she said.

"You don't *know* anything. Okay? Not a single thing. Because you don't see anything. You don't see things that go on every day. I mean, you think you're up on top of this great big hill, but you're just another ant in the fucking ant farm. You don't see the ants who built the tunnels you're living on top of. You don't even know there *are* tunnels."

"Michael, what is it that you want from me?"

"I want you to open your eyes. Is that asking too much? I want you to see the people that give a shit about this town and gave their whole lives to it. I want you to see *me*. I want you to take that great eye you're supposed to have and see what's right in front of you. I want you to take a picture of me and keep it in your head the rest of your life."

Another breeze blew the yellow tape around the lawn, snagging weeds and blades of grass on its way.

"I'm not the bad guy here," he said quietly.

"Michael, I want you to slow down a little. Why did you shoot Jeffrey?"

"Because he comes into *my* town, marries a girl I know, and then kills her and dumps her in *my river*. On *my watch*. While she's carrying *my baby*."

His face seemed to blur and then come back into focus as she tried to make sense of this.

"I may not have been a lot of things," he said. "I wasn't the world's greatest husband. I wasn't the world's greatest father. And I had more than my share of trouble with women. But I was always a servant of this community."

The word *was* buzzed and sizzled in the back of her brain. She realized she had no idea whether he was about to kill himself, kill her, or both.

"Michael, I think we need to call Harold," she said calmly. "Where's your wife? Where are your children?"

"They're gone. It's all gone. It wasn't meant to last. You do your job for a little while and you're either good or bad and then they throw the dirt over you and somebody else builds another anthill on top of that. That's what it's all about, isn't it?"

"I think you need to talk to somebody."

"I thought I was talking to YOU, Lynn."

Barry kept ducking and crawling among the tree stumps and sumac, trying to get a clear shot at Fallon from about fifteen yards. All these branches and shadows kept getting in the way. And the two of them were standing so close together, there was a chance he'd hit Lynn.

"It's all your fault," he heard Fallon say. "Because you made me feel like there was more to it."

"I'm sorry," Lynn answered.

Sorry? About what? He knelt down behind an elm trunk, trying to get a better angle.

"Hey, you remember that one time we went swimming in the river?" Fallon was saying, his voice resonating down the slope. "Senior year. Right after they started to clean it up a little so it didn't turn red every time they painted cars at the auto plant upstream?"

Barry peeked out from behind the tree and saw Lynn listening with her shoulders tilted and her head hanging to the side, somehow looking smaller and more tentative than he was used to seeing her.

"You remember how we got drunk and left our clothes on the rocks? Must've been October. Last good day of the year."

He watched his wife nod and touch the ends of her hair self-consciously. It was like seeing an old picture of her come to life.

"You remember how cold the water was that day?" Fallon said. "Man, my nuts were up around my hips. It's a miracle they still worked afterward. I couldn't believe the current was so strong. You were like this little chick about half my size, but you were always twelve lengths ahead of me. I could never figure that out."

"I guess maybe I was just showing off."

There was a dip, a kind of concession in her voice. He saw them move a little closer together, and for a moment they looked like they were the real couple that belonged here, enjoying a sunny morning in front of their house, while he'd been turned into a trespasser. Everything seemed to get sucked down toward a draining funnel in the pit of Barry's stomach. He started to stand up behind the tree. A shadow moved, giving him perhaps a foot or two of cover in the clearing.

"I kept calling for you to come back, but you weren't listening," Fallon was saying. "You just kept going and going until I could hardly see you. But you know what I never told you?"

"What?"

Barry took a step out into the open and then crouched down against a rock, getting ready to fire.

"That there was one second when I looked back over my shoulder and I saw the town. We must've been like two hundred yards out. And I realized I'd never seen it that way before, from that distance. And you know what? I didn't like it. I don't even know why, but I couldn't stand to get that far away. I had to turn around and start swimming back right away. But you just kept going."

"I know," said Lynn.

"Lemme ask you something, Lynn." Fallon started to reach for her arm. "Did you ever once think of looking back? Did you ever think of coming back for me?"

As Barry stood up with the gun, Lynn forced herself not to look over at him, but something in the movement of her eyes alerted Mike. He whirled around, as if he'd been aware of Barry being there the whole time. He pulled the gun from his waistband and fired.

Barry's left side exploded in an angry red pop-spray. Lynn cried out as she saw him collapse against a sagging part of the fence. She heard mesh ripping, and then he was falling away from her, tumbling down the side of the hill and out of view.

He felt stinging and air seeping through a hole in his chest. And then he was rolling down the side of the embankment, picking up speed, spinning in the wrong direction from the rest of the world, on his way to becoming just a body in the woods. He saw sky and then ground and then sky and then ground, as little pebbles and twigs stuck to his skin and tore at his clothes.

He lost the gun and crashed sideways into a rotting tree stump some twenty yards down the incline, and found himself surrounded by discolored old fence posts and pickets with huge rusty nails sticking out of them. That idiot Anthony who'd replaced their old fence a few months ago must have just tossed the wood down over the side instead of tying it all up and taking it over to the town transfer station as he promised he would.

Barry's body took a pause and then screamed in agony. He wondered how long he'd be here before anyone found him. His thigh was ripped by rose thorns, the cap of his bad knee felt like it was on backward. His ankle was twisted at an impossible angle, and a warm ooze of blood had soaked the front of his shirt. *So this is what it's like.* This is what it's like to die within shouting distance of your home. He tried to pull himself up on the stump and call out to Lynn, but the rising wail of a siren coming down Prospect Road below drowned him out. Forty-eight years. That's it. That's all you get. He smelled pine and saw little white shreds of milkweed floating past his face, like pieces of a dream coming apart, and then he heard more sirens and the scampering of hooves somewhere high above him.

As the police cars came tearing up the driveway, Mike grabbed Lynn by the throat, moved behind her, and jammed the barrel of the gun into her ear. Whatever fragile connection they'd made a few minutes ago was gone. He'd shot her husband. He smelled like emergency rooms and bad coffee, like stale sweat and the air after fireworks.

A navy Buick pulled up in the shade of a great oak. Harold got out on the driver's side, and Paco Ortiz climbed from the passenger seat.

Two more Riverside Police patrol cars screeched to a noisy halt behind them, and a pair of officers jumped out of each one, assuming amateurish-looking shooter stances behind the open car doors, as if they'd never actually done this in real life. But to Lynn, it all seemed to be happening on a television playing in another room. She was dazed, seeing her husband falling off the edge of the world over and over again.

"Hey, big man." Harold put his hands up as he stepped out from under the oak branches. "What's the story?"

"I was about to ask you the same thing."

She could feel Mike's heart beating against the top of her spine. The stench of infection from his thumb turned her stomach. *Where's Barry?* The shock was just starting to set in. *Did I really just see the father of my children get shot?*

"I guess you didn't get any of my messages," said Harold, taking a cautious step forward.

"I guess you didn't get any of *mine*," said Mike. "Otherwise, we wouldn't be here, would we?"

"You have me there, don't you?" Harold gave a quiet chuckle, the undertaker trying to impose grace on squalid confusion.

"Keep it where you got it, Chief." The muzzle forced its way deeper into Lynn's ear. "This is turning out to be one shitty day so far."

"I know that."

What if he is dead? What am I going to do? Her thoughts were tumbling wildly.

"He had it coming, Harold. He dumped her in the river like she was trash. And you were going to try and put it all on me."

"I know that too."

"So now what do we do?"

"I don't know, Mr. Mike. I'm looking in for the signal."

A drop of greasy sweat on the back of her neck caused her to turn her head slightly and see some of Barry's blood drying on the fence post. *People get shot all the time and live. Sure, they do.*

"I'm not going to lie to you, man." Harold shook his head. "It's still a murder. Even with extenuating circumstances, we're talking mandatory state time."

A few feet behind him, Paco Ortiz had his gun drawn and his arms extended in the shade of the oak.

"That's all right," Mike said. "You don't have to tell me what's on the books."

"I'm just saying there's time and there's *time*. All right? I was thinking you'd maybe like to see the kids again before they get to be our age."

"You're a little late on that one too, Chief. I got thrown out at home. Game's over."

Baseball. *My husband may be lying there bleeding to death, and they're talking about baseball.* Lynn tried to keep looking at the place where Barry had fallen, praying somehow he'd reappear, but Mike wrenched her face forward again, the mouth of the gun grinding a deep metal circle into the side of her head.

"Let it go," she said, her legs starting to tremble with cold marble knowledge that she could die here as well.

"What?"

The trembling started to work its way up her body. *Where is Barry? Why isn't he calling for me? Why don't I hear his voice?* Her nervous system was beginning to break down. *You're not outside the frame anymore. You're the picture.* Her eye began twitching. The sky became unnaturally bright. *Stop it*, she told herself. His forearm choked her, trying to get her to keep still.

"You can't keep holding on," she said.

She saw Harold give a tiny imperceptible nod, as if to say, *Listen to the lady.* Standing next to him, Paco closed one eye and looked down the sight of his Glock, focusing on Mike's head just over her shoulder.

"Just let it go," she said. "I heard what you were telling me."

With that, she felt Mike's lungs expand and compress against her back. The grip on her throat began to slip. The unibrowed sergeant who'd been ducking behind one of the patrol car doors started to rise with his gun. The slant of light Harold had been standing in widened, as if a door had opened in front of the sun.

But then an acorn from the overhanging oak hit the hood of his Buick. Lynn saw it happen. A little breeze stirring the branches. A tiny nub falling and ricocheting off metal. Just a sign of the changing season. But the men, already on edge, panicked, thinking they'd been shot at. The sergeant with the monobrow ducked halfway into his car and fired wildly over the door, a bullet sizzling over Lynn's head and splintering tree bark behind her.

Muscles seizing, one arm crooked tight around Lynn's neck, Mike shot back, fire jumping from his hand.

The report echoed down the driveway and faded among the elms and oaks.

Looking strangely befuddled, Harold slowly opened his navy jacket, as if he was checking the designer's label.

A red dot thickened like a wax seal over his breast pocket and then dripped down the front of his white shirt.

"Oh my God!" Mike shouted. "Where's your vest? Where's your fucking vest?"

Harold staggered back against the hood of his car and clapped his hand over the wound, blood pouring out between his fingers.

"Are you insane?" Mike screamed at him. "I told you never to take it off. Didn't I? *Didn't I?*"

Mike reeled back, still keeping Lynn in a half nelson, gasping and wheezing, "What'd I do? What'd I do?" under his breath. The other cops scrambled around Harold as he collapsed, trying to bear him up like the fallen king.

"What happened?" Mike dragged Lynn back to the wooded edge of the slope. "What the fuck just happened?"

"Okay. You have to give up now." She gagged, hearing stirring in the brush behind her. "It's over . . ."

"But is he all right? Is Harold going to be all right?"

The shock had loosened his grip on her neck again. She bolted, trying to pull away from him. He lunged after her off-balance, grabbing her by the collar. But then a sudden fierce grunt made them both turn at the same time.

Barry smashed Michael in the side of the head with a fence post.

Michael staggered back with the wood sticking to his temple and blood running down his cheek. Barry yanked it away, and Lynn saw there was a long crooked rusty nail on the end of it.

Michael gave a long primal scream of anguish, as he cupped a hand over the wound. He spun around, and his other hand went up, firing the gun.

Lynn hit the ground, covering her head as the bay window exploded behind her. When she looked up, Barry was hobbling frantically toward her, thinking she'd been shot. She started to wave and tell him she was all right.

But then Mike lurched up right behind him, about to shoot him in the back of the head.

"BARRY LOOK OUT!" She pointed behind him.

He whirled around and hit Mike with the fence post again, flat in the face, right above the eye socket.

Mike fell howling to his knees. The gun in his hand came up again, the hole a blind eye at the end of the barrel. Barry raised the wood above his head and brought it down on top of Mike's skull, the wood splintering and making a sickening hollow *thock* as Mike fell face forward. Barry brought the post down a second time, and Mike's whole body shuddered.

"All right, that's enough." Lynn started running over.

But Barry was in a tribal frenzy, clubbing him again and again, blood spattering with each blow.

"Stop it!" She grabbed him and pinned his arms to his sides, trying to pull him back to his senses. "It's done."

He pushed her aside and brought the wood down one more time across Mike's back before he tossed it in disgust, finally exhausted and satisfied that the other man wasn't getting up.

Lynn reached up and took his face in her hands, forcing him to meet her eyes, dimly aware of Paco coming up into the yard and a phone ringing in the house.

Gradually Barry's breathing slowed, and after a few seconds, a crackling of twigs made both of them turn.

Two gray-brown deer were bedded down at the edge of the property. Realizing they were being looked at, they both stood up at once and stared back at the humans, wondering what these strangers were doing on their trail. Then they turned and leaped away, supple-spined and indifferent, over the part of the fence that was still standing.

63

THE SNOW NEVER REALLY CAME this year. Just a light wedge of frost before the holidays, not even enough to merit getting the driveway plowed. It was as if someone knew they already had enough cleaning up on their hands.

All around town, slightly chewed-looking Christmas trees were lying on lawns and sidewalks, waiting to be picked up. The giant wreaths and snowflake decorations were coming down at the mall, and the post-holiday sale signs were going up. There were long lines to see the new movie about wizards and old demons in dark caves. On the radio, Afghan women were going to the hairdresser and painting their nails again, but a tall man had been caught trying to blow up a flight from Paris with explosives in his sneakers. Lynn heard the news and found herself wondering if it was the same flight they would've taken if they hadn't ended up selling their tickets on eBay.

"You got the check?" she asked as they left the closing at the lawyer's office, across the street from the train station.

"I got the check." Barry patted the inside pocket under his bad shoulder.

"You've still got fast hands." She slid in on the driver's side of the Saab in the parking lot and unlocked the passenger's door for him.

"I can catch two flies at a time. I used to be able to catch three, but the flies found out about me."

They sat there quietly for a moment, not quite ready to go. The trunk was sagging with things they'd collected in their final walk-through of the house, before the sale was finalized. They were loaded up with boxes of old linens, stray socks, second-best china, books that had been hiding under the bed for a year, pots that no one wanted at the final tag sale.

"I didn't see Emmie come in the conference room," she said. "Did you?"

"No. I just looked up from signing the papers, and there she was. She just materialized on the other side of the table while we were talking about when the oil company made deliveries."

"She looked good, I thought. Considering."

"Yeah. Considering."

This had been the season of funerals without the funeral director.

Jeffrey's was first. Saul quietly arranged for one of the national chains to spirit the body out of town and perform a service somewhere out near North Babylon on the island. According to Jeanine, no one from Riverside went. Michael's funeral was a more complicated arrangement. Because he'd been suspended pending dismissal at the time of his death, there was no way to justify a full dress-blue, bagpipes, and war-drums ceremony. Instead there'd been an Irish wake that lasted for a few days, with Michael's father propping himself up by the casket, warily accepting condolences from various cops, retired C.O.s, and half-forgotten friends who'd long since fled the Hollow. Again, there was no way Lynn would have attended, but Jeanine said that as acting chief, Paco Ortiz arranged for the family to receive three-quarter benefits.

Harold's was the last of the services. There were too many mourners for the old AME church in the Hollow to accommodate, so instead Saint Stephen's was filled to the rafters with cops, town trustees, schoolteachers, Chamber of Commerce types, soccer moms, slacker dads, go-for-the-throat Wall Streeters, and, surprisingly, even a few local pot dealers who apparently held no grudge. It took a funeral to show the man knew everybody. Reverend Ezekiel P. Philips thundered from the pulpit about how Harold paid the price for being a pioneer, and sitting near the back, Lynn understood the larger point he was trying to make. But Emmie seemed far closer to the spirit of the man when she got up afterward and talked about Harold sitting in the living room late at night with the children asleep upstairs, paying his bills and watching a big polar bear on the Nature Channel, swimming back and forth across his little pond.

"You think she blames us for what happened?" asked Lynn.

"I don't know how she could. Most of those balls were in play before we even got here, but . . ." He hesitated, not quite ready to exonerate himself so easily. "It's hard to say. Maybe we could've done some things differently."

She looked out the window, watching a white gull walk along the empty platform, as if wondering where all the commuters had gone. Behind it, the river churned implacably, turning the color of melted green toy soldiers.

"She said we would be happy here," said Lynn. "Remember that?"

"But she didn't say for how long."

"You think that's what she meant by that other thing?" She adjusted the side mirror.

"What other thing?"

"What she said today. That some houses are like states of mind. You're not supposed to stay in them. They're just stages you go through."

"Hippie bullshit," he grunted as he tried to pull his seat belt strap over a shoulder joint held together by titanium screws.

"Works for her."

"I guess."

He grimaced, trying to find a comfortable position for the full cast on his leg and his cane.

"So, what's going to work for us?"

"Getting on the road." He adjusted his seat back.

"You seriously don't want to go up the hill and take one last look?"

"I do, but what's the point? I don't think the Davises need us poking around anymore."

"You think they'll be happy there?"

"Why not?" He shrugged.

She thought of the young couple who'd just signed the contract across the table from them. He, a medical supplies salesman, beginning to bulk up a little from road food. She, a hugely pregnant former kindergarten teacher, ready to nest and have her own garden. Lynn had watched them stand before the oak tree in the backyard, gesturing grandly, outlining plans in the air, murmuring quietly about the baby's room, the tree fort, rocking chairs, and how things were going to be different once they moved in. And in some melancholy way she'd been touched by them, as if these were the people who'd come along to complete the dream she couldn't finish for herself.

"And how about us?" asked Lynn.

"I think we're gonna be all right," said Barry. "I think we're going to rent for a while in Hawthorne and Hannah's going to go off to school and Clay's eventually going to find a group of friends who don't beat the crap out of him. I think you're going to do your gallery show in the spring and eventually, if miracles come to pass, we'll get the money from the insurance company and I might even get another job."

"Did you talk to Lisa yesterday?"

"Yeah, you're not going to believe it. She wants to apply for a new patent for a drug she's working on and start another company with me."

"What does it do?"

"It blocks the neurotransmitters that help you store and retrieve memories."

"Oh my God. You're kidding me. You mean it's the opposite of an Alzheimer's drug? Why would anybody want that?"

He shrugged as she started the car. "I don't know. Seems to me like they got a few million potential customers these days. What's the point of remembering something if all it does is make you miserable?"

"Because you need to," she said. "It's evolution. What about remembering you got burned the last time you stuck your hand in a fire?"

"Well, we have pictures to tell us that, don't we?"

She stepped on the gas, throwing him back against his seat.

Because of the holiday week, it wasn't just day laborers out on the street for once. People stood in clusters outside stores, upholstered in heavy down coats, breathing out little white puffs of condensed air, shaking their heads in wonder and talking about . . .

The dead. They were everywhere. You couldn't get around them. They lowered real estate values. They distracted the kids at school. They discouraged shoppers. They made you lock your doors and check your windows at night. They practically stood on corners and dared you not to look back at them.

A line of cars was moving slowly ahead of them on River Road. Each had a Christmas tree tied to its roof like a silent movie damsel lashed to the railroad tracks. These were the people who didn't want to wait around for their trees to be picked up from the end of their driveways. As she drove on, Lynn heard the ferocious grinding of a wood mulcher and saw the cars making a right turn into the Department of Public Works yard just past the train station, where the gates were usually closed to the public.

Without really thinking, she made the turn and followed them.

"What are you doing?" said Barry. "We're supposed to meet the kids at Jeanine's by four-thirty."

She put the car in park behind an idling Navigator and got out with the loaded Canon she had beside her seat. The smell of fresh pine was everywhere. People stood around the mulcher, watching one tree after another get fed in. They entered tip first, smallest branches disappearing, the machine jolting, threatening to choke on the size, and then somehow fitting it all in and spewing out the wood chips. On almost any other day, it would be a picture worth taking, but this time she walked straight past it, starting to see another image take shape.

Black bags were piled up along the edge of the water, full of mulch to be spread around the trees in Eisenhower Park — just enough to stay under the circumference of the branches at high noon. But today, they didn't interest her either. She turned left at the great unused salt pyramid with its attendant spreader truck and then walked out onto the gritty beige spit of beach, a few yards beyond the lot.

"Hey, lady, you're not supposed to be there," a garbageman called from behind her.

But his voice was drowned by the smashing of the tide against the long jagged jetty that stretched out into the river like a beckoning arm. She ignored him and stepped out onto the rocks, trying not to slip on the algae-encrusted surfaces and rags of seaweed caught in the crevasses. Gulls dipped and pivoted in the sky before her. The smell of ground wood gave way to mud and brine. The vicious cold wind ripped at her clothes and her hair. But she kept walking to the end of the rocks, even as Barry hobbled after her on his cane and joined the garbageman on the shore, yelling for her to come back.

The river swelled and slapped on either side of her, a freezing rain spraying her every few seconds. The wind made ridges on its surface, making it look like a long corrugated gate. Then she turned around and saw it: almost the view Michael had been talking about, but closer. Half her life she'd been here without ever realizing this angle existed: far enough back to frame the town from top to bottom, but near enough to see all its knobby distinct features and patches of greenery. It was like glimpsing her memories carved into the side of a mountain. The rock face rising from the riverbank; the train platform; the prison guard tower; the little winding streets leading up into the hills; the riot of trees; the steeple of Saint Stephen's; the farmhouses on Grace Hill, where she'd once thought she'd spend her sunset years with Barry; and, of course, the rows of tiny white tombstones in Green Hill Cemetery, where her mother was buried a stone's throw from Sandi, and Harold rested a couple of football fields away from his old friend Michael.

The dead — the one neighborhood that would always take you in, no matter what you'd done.

In the late afternoon, it had a subdued amber shading, as if it were already a fading photograph. If she waited too long, she'd lose the light. A grip on her heart told her to shoot quickly. She took a meter reading, adjusted the lens, raised the Canon, and pressed the little button. The shutter in her head clicked at the same time as the camera's, closing and then slowly opening up again.

Water cascaded over the rocks on either side of her. But she held her angle, wiped the drops off the lens with her shirttail, and clicked the shutter two more times. Then she turned and carefully picked her way over the rocks back to the shore.

"You get what you need?" Barry was waiting with his good arm outstretched.

"Yes," she said, putting the lens cap back on and nestling against the undamaged part of him. "As a matter of fact, I did."

They turned their backs to the boiling river and staggered away together.

ACKNOWLEDGMENTS

I would like to give special thanks to Peter Bloom and Michael McElroy for their patience, wit, and good company in helping me research this book.

I would also like to thank William Kress, Tom Reddy, Randy Jefferson, Lisa Kovitz, David Crowley, Sarah Jane Crowley, Elizabeth Keyishian, Sarah Siegle, Jason Cohen, Milton Hoffman, Michael Cherkasky, Nancy Pine, Ray Stevens, Jeff Parthemore, Arney Rosenblatt, Matthew Nimetz, Joe Reed, Jane Hammerslough, Samuel G. Freedman, Constance Hall, Tim Tully, Donna Dietrich, Lori Grinker, Ellen Binder, Joyce Slevin, Bob Slevin, Julie Betts Testuwide, Lori Andiman, Art Levitt, Gene Heller, Joseph Mitchell, Fred Starler, Jordan Fields, Jimmy Wall, Eva Merk, Jesse James Lewis, Bob Merk, Alexander Morales, Richard Ligi, Stephen Brown, Audrey Winer, Richard Sokolow, Lynn Saville, George Johansen, Shannon Langone, and, of course, Richard Pine.

ABOUT THE AUTHOR

Peter Blauner is the author of four other novels, including *Slow Motion Riot*, which won an Edgar Allan Poe Award for best first novel of the year, and *The Intruder*, a *New York Times* and international bestseller. His books have been translated into sixteen languages. He lives in New York with his wife, Peg Tyre, and their two children.

For more information, visit www.peterblauner.com.